Yogev Ben-Ari has been sent to St Petersburg by the Mossad –
ostensibly to set up business links. His life is solitary, ordered
and lonely, until he meets Anna. Neither is quite what they seem
to be, but there is no doubt about the love they feel for each
other.

This encounter is definitely not part of the Mossad plan and
they hatch a dark scheme to drive the two apart. Ben-Ari has no
time to discover the truth about Anna's real identity before the
Mossad resolves the issue for him. But still Ben-Ari doesn't give
up, determined to learn the truth about their love.

Amid the shadowy manipulations of the secret services, Mishka
Ben-David depicts the world of a Mossad agent who chooses,
against all odds, to fight for his right to be with the woman he
loves.

Mishka Ben-David served in the Mossad for twelve years,
becoming a high-ranking officer. He is now a full-time novelist
living outside Jerusalem. *Duet in Beirut* was his first novel to be
translated into English, and received great media attention.

D1490585

Duet in Beirut

Duet in Beirut is a spy thriller that will raise your blood pressure and set your heart to pounding as Mr Ben-David ratchets up the pace and suspense of his narrative. The sense of utter realism is so overwhelming that the book should carry the iconic warning of 'don't try this at home.' ... *Duet in Beirut* is on a literary par with *The Spy Who Came In from the Cold*, and highly recommended.   *NY Journal of Books*

... an original, well-written thriller that examines the ethical complexities of covert operations ...The irony of the setup is rendered fully plausible in the service of a suspenseful story line that doesn't follow predictable lines. Le Carré fans will enjoy Ben-David's look behind the scenes of government-sanctioned hits and the tension between loyalty to the chain of command and dissent.   *Publishers Weekly*

Ronen and Gadi may have the best bromance going since Butch Cassidy and the Sundance Kid. Let's hope Ben-David returns stateside for repeat performances.   *Library Journal*

In the meticulous layering of detail about a dangerous Mossad initiative in Lebanon, Ben-David almost — but not quite — provides a handbook to the inside track of Israeli intelligence.

There is certainly the whiff of authenticity and the aura of ' clear and present danger. But more than that, this is a book with proper adult themes of love, patriotism, regret and shame.

Jewish Chronicle

Duet in Beirut gives us a fascinating look into a 'dark, deceptive, treacherous world in which you never really know what is good and what is evil, in which the permissible is forbidden and the forbidden permitted.'   *Times of Israel*

Brilliantly translated from the original Hebrew by Evan Fallenberg ... the book's amazing insider detail is matched by beautifully (re)created characters, families and locations, plus an utterly convincing portrayal of the inner wranglings of a secret service, and the political context in which it operates.

There are odd plot echoes of *The Bourne Identity* movie and you can pick up resonances from other films too, especially *Syriana* and of course *Munich*, but the book's building of tension and pace until the almost unbearable finale is exemplary, cool and very accomplished ... in the end, this is among the very best and most revealing spy novels I've read. And it works because a gifted author has harnessed his experience to tell a great tale very well indeed.

Tom Morton, Thrillfilter

FORBIDDEN LOVE IN ST PETERSBURG

MISHKA BEN-DAVID

Translated by
Dan Gillon

HALBAN
LONDON

First published in Great Britain by
Halban Publishers Ltd
22 Golden Square
London W1F 9JW
2015
www.halbanpublishers.com

A CIP catalogue record for this book is available from the British Library.

ISBN 978 1 905559 77 0

Originally published in Hebrew under the title *Ahava Asura Be-Peterburg*
by Keter Publishing House Ltd, Jerusalem, 2008

Published by arrangement with
The Institute for the Translation of Hebrew Literature

Mishka Ben-David has asserted his right under the Copyright,
Design and Patents Act, 1988 to be identified
as the author of this work.

Typeset by Spectra Titles, Cambridgeshire
Printed in Great Britain by
Berforts Information Press, Stevenage

FORBIDDEN LOVE IN ST PETERSBURG

Prologue

1

THOSE WHO LOVE the city as much as I do, simply call it Peter, said Anna. We were standing on a narrow bridge straddling one of the canals that flow into the River Neva and on into the Gulf of Finland. It was a clear, chilly evening. A thin layer of snow covered the streets. We leant on a steel railing, feeling its patterned engravings, admiring the old mansions on both banks of the canal, so rich in colour, so elegant with their porticos and carved cornices.

The cobble-stones beneath our feet may once have allowed for the easy passage of horse-drawn carriages, but now created a difficult surface for cars to negotiate. But there were no vehicles crossing now, and the few pedestrians to be seen were scurrying to get to their homes in the small lanes on either side of the waterway. On the bridge itself there was nobody but us.

Anna covered her mouth and slender, straight nose in a white woollen scarf. I gazed at her. Between the fur-topped hat, also white, and the scarf, all that could be seen were her high cheek bones and almond shaped brownish-green eyes. As she caught my stare a few creases appeared in the corners of her eyes, giving her that special look – something between laughter and astonishment.

And you do love it, your *Peter*.

Yes, I do, very much, she laughed ruefully, her eyes glowing, their greenness sparkling. We both knew that her love of the city was weighing down one side of the scales on which our own love was balanced so precariously. I couldn't, after all, stay here for long. As if to postpone the obvious next question about where we would live, if indeed we were to be together, she told me about the long line of the city's names.

What is it? she wanted to know, as I continued to gaze at her. The creases of laughter and astonishment assumed a tinge of anxiety.

A wisp of black hair escaped from her hat and settled on the bridge of her nose, forming an arc over her eyes. Anna blew at it lightly, making it flutter. She smiled, her eyes once more changing expression, turning childlike and mischievous. My heart missed a beat. Just a pair of eyes and yet such beauty.

There was a slight movement under the scarf and I imagined her moistening her lips in the way I had found so alluring months earlier when I first saw her sitting a few tables away from me in that tiny neighbourhood restaurant.

I brought my face closer, gently lowered the scarf, my lips lightly brushing hers.

They're dry, she said, moving away slightly and passing her tongue over her lips. Again I drew my face closer, my tongue adding its wetness to hers.

That's better, she said, and placed her mouth over mine, lightly at first, then as if searching for the right angle, and finally with desire.

The pale light of the ancient lamp-posts at both ends of the bridge, the silvery streaks across the water, and the blanket of snow around us, somehow coloured her eyes a shade of purple just before she closed them and pressed her body into me. I was giddy with the delicacy of her perfume and intoxicated by the taste of her tongue against mine.

Anna, my Annushka, I whispered, as we drew apart for a moment to catch our breath.

And you are mine, she said, her eyes filled with laughter. We'd come a long way since I told her, with uncharacteristic daring, that her eyes reminded me of Sophia Loren's.

She shook her head slightly from side to side as her nose, rubbed mine in an Eskimo kiss. If only I could swallow you whole and not just your tongue, she murmured, and once again sucked at my lips.

I hadn't felt like this since I was sixteen. Not since I used to pinch myself, finding it hard to believe that Orit was really kissing me back with such passion and allowing me to caress her tiny but very desirable breasts. I didn't think that I would ever feel that way again. Nor could I believe that this beautiful solitary woman was so completely mine and I so totally hers. These things simply

3

did not happen twice in a lifetime, I warned myself – at least not with such intensity.

Then I felt the full force of the blow to my back.

The punch landed on my shoulder blade and sent a paralyzing current of pain through my neck, head, and every part of my back. My knees buckled and I lurched forwards head first into Anna. She screamed. I saw her terrified face and from the corner of my eye spotted something moving. I quickly pulled myself up, turned round, and raised my arms defensively.

But the large ungainly figure had fled, clutching Anna's handbag.

Are you OK? I asked, holding both her cheeks. Anna couldn't utter a word but nodded a yes, her eyes deadly serious.

I didn't stop to think as I pulled away from her and chased the retreating figure. Running on the snow-covered paving stones slowed me down. But the assailant, perhaps not suspecting that he was being followed, was even slower than me. He apparently didn't hear my footsteps until reaching the junction of the bridge and the street where he could have upped the pace but didn't. Instead, he stumbled on, only once looking over his shoulder in my direction.

The handful of people on the street, were all heavily wrapped up against the cold, and were all in a hurry. I knew that they couldn't have seen the attack and didn't expect that any of them would help. Nor did I want them to interfere.

Even though the blow to my back had been powerful, it was not particularly professional. Had the mugger aimed his strike ten centimetres higher and to the left, and hit me in the neck with that kind of force, I would have been knocked out. His sluggish pace suggested that he wasn't in very good shape. All the same, I was taking nothing for granted so, when I caught up with him, instead of grabbing him by the throat I leapt up and kicked him in the back.

He staggered forwards and stopped, but didn't fall. He quickly spun round to face me. His grey eyes stared straight at me in a way I found surprising. This was certainly not the glazed look of a drunk, nor the defeated look of the homeless. Apparently he was still feeling the pain of the kick and the exertion of the run – yet he was focused and purposeful. For a moment I even thought that I detected a flicker of irony as he offered to hand over the handbag.

I could have just taken it and with that the incident may well have ended. But it might have been a trap and I was far too hyped up by then to simply let it go. I extended both hands, but instead of going for the bag I grabbed his wrist firmly, gave it a mighty backward twist, and ducked beneath our locked hands. I swiftly bent his arm to an impossible angle. The faint but sickening sound of a bone cracking could be heard, then a cry of pain from his clenched lips, and the man was hurled to the ground, dropping the bag. When I knelt to pick it up, he suddenly kicked my thigh with surprising force. As I stumbled, I saw him trying to get up. But I was able to straighten up more quickly than he was, and prevented him from standing by kicking him hard in the ribs.

He rolled over, then tried once more to get up. Beneath the heavy coat there was obviously a strong physique. It was clear to me that the man had no intention of giving up easily but, now that I was holding the bag, my moves were limited and the will to continue fighting had deserted me. I wanted to get back to Anna but the mugger was now upright and facing me. His large head and bulging neck tilted forwards as he lunged at me like a raging bull.

Had his head rammed into my stomach the blow would surely have sent us both reeling to the ground and I wasn't sure I would have the advantage in an ensuing scuffle. But hundreds of hours practising evasive tactics was time well spent. A split second before impact I moved aside and kicked him in the face with all the force I could muster.

Because of the short distance between us, and the speed at which it all happened, it was my shin bone and not my foot that struck him. I felt his nose squash and shift sideways. His head wobbled as he fell to the ground clutching his face in an attempt to staunch the blood streaming from his nose.

I stood about a metre away ready for a kick should he try to get up. Instead, he looked at me through his fingers, then freed one hand and raised it slightly. Perhaps in Russia this was a sign of surrender or cease fire. In any event, I had no interest in hitting him again. I moved away, but kept a watchful eye on him. He struggled to sit up, still staring at me, holding his bleeding nose with one hand

and leaning on the other. Clearly he was not defeated, and I knew that in a moment or two he could get up and, enraged, go for us.

At the corner of the bridge Anna was waiting for me, her eyes full of tears.

Let's get away from here, she whispered quickly, looking back at the assailant who was now kneeling and still looking towards us. From where we were standing it was obvious to me that Anna had seen the entire incident. I thrust the bag into her hands, saying nothing. She grabbed it somewhat impatiently as if angered by the misfortune that the bag or I had brought us. She took me by the arm and pulled me back towards the bridge.

Annushka, he's not coming back, I said trying to calm her.

Anna quickened her steps, anxiously glancing back from time to time.

They are never alone, she said, and then I too looked back and saw two men approaching the assailant and helping him to his feet. I didn't think there was a real possibility of passers-by getting involved and trying to block our way but even from where we were standing in the middle of the bridge – quite a distance from the three men – I could tell that they were looking at us menacingly.

I hugged Anna and as I held her more tightly I could feel her trembling.

Annushka? My darling?

Tears continued to stream from her beautiful eyes. I didn't really understand what was stirring her feelings to such an extent. That her bag had been snatched? My gallantry? The danger posed to me? Anna said nothing, again covered her mouth and nose with her scarf, and continued walking quickly.

We walked towards the first wide street after the bridge where Anna flagged down a cab. Chernyshevskaya, she said to the driver, naming a metro station not far away.

Before we got there she pulled out a note larger than necessary, handed it to the driver and, as soon as he stopped, made a beeline for the station's entrance. Sheer panic prevented her from standing with everyone else on the right hand side of the escalator as it descended into the bowels of the earth. Instead, she scurried down the left with all the other hurrying passengers. I followed in her wake.

It was only when we were safely on board and the train began moving that I hugged her again, trying to help her relax. But the look of fear in her eyes remained. Even when we changed trains at the Technological Institute to line 2, our line, she still seemed anxious. We passed Victory Park station, my usual stop, and got off at the next one. Anna looked left and right and only then walked quickly towards her street and home.

The huge brick apartment block had many entrances and was devoid of any sort of character. Her hands trembled as she fitted a circular magnet into a matching socket, thus opening the door to the building. Her hands shook again as she inserted a long serrated key into the lock of her own front door. As soon as we were inside she threw herself at me, flushed and excited, first with a hug and then with a series of eager kisses that left my mouth hurting

I wasn't in the mood but her body clearly ached for me. She pulled me onto the bed and pounced. The delicate, deliberate touches of the previous few times we had slept together now turned into a wild sexual dance. Before I could give myself over to her I needed a few moments to dampen down the violent feelings that still coursed through my veins. For the first time I discovered the power of her heavy buttocks and firm thighs, clutching them and her soft white breasts if only to temper her lascivious movements. Once again I was surprised to discover how white and soft her skin really was – almost like a baby's.

After our dash home, her body was steeped with the exciting smell of sweat mingled with her perfume. It filled my nostrils, intoxicating me and sweeping me along with her into a frenzy of passion.

My crazy, crazy man. This is Russia, you know? She said a little bit later, lying on her back, panting.

All the muggers belong to the Mafia. The cab driver has already long since told them where he dropped us off. If we hadn't hurried, they would have been waiting for us at the entrances to all the metro stations to get even with you. You're not to do this again, understood? she said, turning towards me with a frown. Here all the heroes are dead heroes. And I want you alive, alive the way you are right now, the way you were a moment ago. I'm not prepared to lose you, understand? I'm not prepared yet again to lose the one I love.

Without thinking about it, I turned to glance at the photo of her mustachioed, smiling, dead husband looking down at us from the bedroom wall. Anna noticed my gaze, sighed, got up – still naked – and took down the picture. My eyes followed her generous, slightly rounded buttocks, and noted the hint of a tyre round her waistline. The light was faint, but I could see the folds of skin under her arms as she raised her hand towards the picture. I was filled with love. Here was this sweet woman turning over a new leaf in her life. She propped up the photo with its face to the wall, turned to me, and with an embarrassed movement of the hand covered her breasts. Again she sighed. The bitter cold brought her back to bed, slipping in between the sheets and into my arms. My Annushka! Now I too was unwilling to contemplate the possibility of loss.

She wrapped herself round my body. Once her tension had gone she was as soft as lamb's wool. I felt the wetness of her tears on my shoulder, raised her head slightly and looked at her.

Enough, Annushka, that's enough.

My little hero. You've no idea what you did. You don't understand who you're dealing with. This isn't Canada, OK? Here, to be a thief you've got to be either an addict or ex–KGB with friends. Promise me you won't be doing anything like that again, OK?

Stop it, Annushka, just stop it.

I want you to move in with me. I want you like this every night and every morning I want you to be part of my life, she said.

Just as I was about to respond I felt a sharp bolt of pain shooting through my temples.

Headquarters. HQ's instructions.

I should have told them about Anna after our first time together. I'd put that off. I didn't think this relationship would last very long, not with such a beautiful woman. But if I'm going to live with her I will definitely need their approval.

I tried to imagine living with Anna. Sleeping every night beside her. At times her body would be soft and loving, at others ardent and lustful. I would no longer be alone in my apartment in the big Stalinist building on Moskovsky Prospekt just ten minutes walk from Anna's home. The idea was irresistible. I felt like someone who'd crossed a desert, seen a green papyrus plant on the horizon and knows that water lies hidden below. I felt like the desert itself in whose distant skies welcome rain clouds were gathering.

Anna fell asleep in my arms while I spent half the night mulling over what I would tell HQ in the morning. They'd want a precise account of the chain of events. Step by step. To what extent had our meeting been accidental and at the same time plausible? Who approached whom, and what was said? How had the liaison developed?

And it's only now, they'd be bound to ask, that you've remembered to report it? Did you really consider it so trivial that it didn't warrant even a mention in your weekly briefings?

Being reprimanded didn't bother me. But what if they say no?

2

THIS WAS MY first experience of waking up in Anna's apartment and I was surprised by the sense of tranquillity that enveloped me. It seemed as if I'd always been there, as if this was my natural habitat. This was also the first time I'd seen her bedroom in daylight. On the few occasions we'd been there together at night, Anna had turned off the lights and asked me to leave before dawn.

Like the kitchen, the modest living room, and the cramped toilet and shower areas, Anna's bedroom was typical of such small apartments in an old high-rise residential block. There was no trace in these buildings erected during the 1950s and 60s, of the city's beauty, the magnificence of its bridges, palaces and squares, or even of the imposing neo-classical residential structures of Stalin's era. Khrushchevist buildings, Anna called them, making me acutely aware of the differences between my apartment and hers. In the pale light filtering through the heavy curtains, I could see plaster peeling off the corners of the ceiling and blackening wallpaper beneath the window sill, evidence of seeping rain. The beautiful woman at my side and the wretched apartment she lived in were no match for each other.

Our clothes were strewn across the well-worn, wooden floor in the narrow area between the bed, the wardrobe, and the front door. A few landscapes, the figure of Jesus on the cross, and the empty space where the picture of her husband had been hanging, all looked down on me from the wall. Though I hadn't stirred, Anna opened her eyes just moments after I had woken. I let the feelings of closeness and domesticity gently caress my temples. Anna turned towards me, her black hair with its sprinkling of grey slid over her brow, almost masking her face.

For a moment I held my breath. I knew that the first response to seeing me, a stranger in the bed she had shared for years with her husband, would be the most genuine reaction I could hope for. Anna brushed aside the strands of hair over her eyes. For a moment they were still bleary but then from deep inside her came a new light that made them sparkle once again.

My love, she said, using a phrase that could only sound so alluring in the Russian she spoke. *Lyubimy moi*, my love, the words resonated as if from an old song. Her eyes filled with tears as she quickly snuggled up and hugged me.

There were tears in my eyes too. I hadn't cried when saying goodbye to my parents on the morning I enlisted as a paratrooper, or when I lost friends in battle and later when I lost men serving under me. Nor were there tears after my first 'kill' serving in the ranks of the Mossad, nor after those that followed. I'd hardly cried at all during the last few difficult years that Orit and I lived through. Instead of each tear that should have been shed, another droplet of calcified rock was added to the stalagmite growing inside me.

Now I could feel the rock crumbling and giving way to something else, an upsurge of quiet love, reassuring and yet at the same time new and exciting.

Instead of 'my Annushka' what came out of my mouth was a sigh. Despite not knowing or being able to know anything about it, Anna appeared to understand exactly what the sigh was meant to express and perhaps even the pain that preceded it. For her, at least I thought so at the time, I was Paul, a Canadian businessman of Indian extraction who was separated from his wife and had chosen a new life in a place where the prospect of making money seemed promising.

You're going to stay with me, right? she asked, lifting her head from my shoulder and fixing her almond eyes on me – eyes that in the soft morning light and through a film of tears shone like emeralds. And you'll never ever, ever, leave, right?

I kept silent. What could I say? That my life didn't belong to me but to an intelligence service that she'd probably never heard of? That I was tied to a far away, hot country that was the complete opposite of everything here in this cold, magnificent city? That the man she was falling in love with wasn't, in fact, a quiet, amiable Canadian businessman of average height who had even managed to develop a smallish paunch since he'd stopped working out? That instead, her lover was a retired Mossad hitman, who along the way had also wiped out his own life? That beneath the already noticeable pot belly there is – was – a six-pack of abs, and that his seemingly gentle fingers had pulled the trigger more than once? And that the brown eyes she said were so kind became unmerciful at the sight of the terrified faces of the enemy?

What could I tell her? That everything I'd said till now

was a lie? A legend, as we euphemistically called it at the Agency, but which for her was nothing but a lie?

Then an even more painful thought flashed through my mind. I was the one living a lie. For Annushka it's the truth and it's me who's having to live with a constantly churning gut. It's me who's been forced – for the second time in my life – to lie to the woman I love. And if Orit – a down-to-earth woman from the Arava desert in southern Israel – hadn't been able to take it, what chance had I with Anna?

She looked into my eyes with a mixture of curiosity, suspicion and apprehension. I still hadn't answered her. It seemed to me that she was closely reading every movement of my pupils and through them looking into the very depths of my soul. Her gaze hardened and suddenly seemed remote.

At a loss for words, I hugged her and once more rested her face on my shoulder. I couldn't bear her stare, that questioning look in her expectant eyes. Nor could I bring myself to lie – not to the first woman who'd restored the hope, long since abandoned, of love returning to my life.

But Anna broke free from my embrace and looked at me with that piercing glare of hers. She had meant every word. Perhaps, like me, she'd finally met someone who could fill her days and nights and be the love of the rest of her life.

Suddenly I heard myself saying, I am here to stay, Annushka.

But the look in her eyes gave no sign of re-kindled hope.

I am staying with you, and no, I will never leave, never, ever, I said.

From beyond the mists of time, a distant memory from another life flashed through my mind. I remembered a similar promise made to Orit and not kept. And now, even more than then, powerful forces that I wasn't sure I could handle, stood between me and the keeping of that promise. But this time I was prepared at least to face up to them.

Anna showered me with kisses. We made love again and again. At first it was as if each of us was implanting our oath of allegiance deeply inside the other. Again I was surprised that this lovely face belonged to such a wild body whose softness and whiteness turned out to be so misleading; astonished once more by the full buttocks, the firm thighs, the ample, pendulous breasts, and the nipples which hardened and produced such waves of inexhaustible energy in me. She rose above me, moving up and down, forwards and backwards, asking, demanding more and more, her face a mixture of effort, desire, pain, and, at the same time, sublime pleasure. Again and again, together with her rapid breathing, came fragmented words and groans. And when it seemed that it was over, she rested for a moment and then began once more until suddenly she stopped. Enough, the spasms are going all the way to my head, I can't anymore, she said, embracing me with a joyful smile.

Having let go of the reserve we had maintained till then, we now made love again, gently and pleasurably, reminiscent, in a way, of the caution of our first encounters. But this time it wasn't bashfulness and uncertainty that was controlling us, but rather a sense of serenity, confidence and love, a love that was destined to endure. What a long way we'd come since that first, hesitant, and unsuccessful time, after which I was sure that Anna wouldn't ever want to see me again.

But I was in turmoil. I had given two contradictory commitments, one to my employers and one to my lover. I could live with only one of them. And I knew which one that would be.

Anna got up to take a shower, leant towards me again, and kissed my forehead.

Don't be so serious, you look almost gloomy, she smiled somewhat sadly and disappeared into the small cubicle.

It was as clear to me as was the daylight streaming through the window, that I'd be unable to admit to her that I'd lied. Acknowledging the truth was something I couldn't bring myself to do. She wouldn't be able to cope with it, our relationship wouldn't be able to cope with it. If I chose her, the only way open to me was to make my cover story the real story of my life. To make the lie a truth. The only truth Annushka was aware of.

My body was already shivering from the cold. Then a blast of freezing air blew in from a duct above the double windows Anna had flung open, and an even more powerful shudder rose from deep inside me.

3

IN MEASURED STEPS I made my way from the metro station to my office on Liteyny Prospekt, leaving behind me heavy footprints on the soft sheet of snow. As I walked, I drafted in my mind a number of possible letters to HQ. So preoccupied was I with this task that I even forgot to take my usual precautions along the route to ensure that I wasn't being tailed.

Dear friends, my moment of truth has arrived, I wrote in my head. What I thought would never happen to me after the experience with Orit which you know about, has happened: I have fallen in love again. This is a love between two forty-year-old adults, a profound love. I don't think I will have another such chance and I don't intend to give this one up. I understand the implications and I understand that I have to choose. It's a difficult choice but, in the end, not an impossible one, and I'm making it.

And I began another letter by saying – intending to soften them up – you have been my home for a decade and a half; you gave me direction and purpose, trust and training, help and support. Just as your ad promised, you were not merely a workplace but a home and a way of life. For this way of life I paid, as you well know, a high price and living alone, as I am, in this inhospitable, distant land, it is a price I am still paying. And what can happen in such situations of extreme loneliness, and has probably

18

happened to many others, has also happened to me. I have met a woman.

As these thoughts raced through my mind, I began to realize how genuine they were. I became conscious of how much I loved – and still love – this organization that turned me into a professional almost against my will; that enabled me to make a unique contribution to my country, the like of which only a few can make; that demonstrated concern for me from my first day of training as an operative; was at my side, supportive and considerate, throughout my difficult times with Orit, and lifted me off the floor after the separation. So was my choice really so clear-cut?

I tossed these thoughts around in my head as I walked down the street. I paid no attention to the old houses renovated in a variety of pleasing colours, or to the Lutheran church and its green domes, or the Japanese garden in the middle of the street. I didn't even glance at the menacing building that was once the district court – marked as such in the map that I'd had when I rented the office – and which I only later discovered was home to the Federal Security Bureau, the FSB, the successor to the KGB…

I'd set up the offices of my trading company in an old building at the quieter end of Liteyny Prospekt, close to the river. An unpretentious building that didn't attract any particular attention and that housed about a dozen other offices. The only traces of its grand past were large columns at the front, the marble slabs covering its outer walls, and the smell of old wood that lingered inside. I climbed the old staircase to the third floor and entered my office. Although the building's old and constant heating system worked, the little heat that came from it was lost to its high ceilings. I was burning inside so I didn't feel the cold and didn't turn on the electric heater.

Once a week I sent a message to a certain electronic address. The message was disguised as a business email and the receiver was invited to participate in a forthcoming tender. In reality, the message was to inform the Mossad's Tel Aviv HQ that at my end everything was OK. On only a few occasions since settling into my office had I used the special software program that scrambled the text and enabled me to send secret communications. The first time I'd used it was to send a detailed report on how my re-location was proceeding, my address, a description of the apartment I had rented on Moskovsky Prospekt, and of the office on Liteyny Prospekt. Later on I'd received special instructions via this channel and also used it to send reports at the end of my various missions. Now I set up the program again, perhaps for the last time.

The program signalled that I could begin writing. First I had to write the cover letter that would appear if someone tried to retrieve what I had written. Then I keyed in my password and started typing the letter to HQ – which even I wouldn't see as the cover letter remained on the screen. Given my mood, this included a squabble with a firm whose tender I had once failed to win. Each character I now keyed in appeared in a bold font in the cover letter so that I was able to see the exact point up to which I could write.

Sitting facing the computer, the words I composed as I was walking disappeared from my mind.

Re: An Acquaintance, I wrote finally. The restaurant where I usually eat in the evening is also frequented by a single woman. We got to talk. She is a widow and owns a bookshop. The relationship became closer and last night I slept in her apartment. We are both interested in continuing the relationship and it's my intention to do so. I shall, of course, maintain my cover. For your information.

And that was it. Not for 'your approval' but also not 'this is the last communication between us'. The remainder of the words in the cover letter remained un-bolded. And in my heart I could also feel a big void. I was shivering again. I touched my brow. I was burning up with a fever. How on earth had I allowed such a dilemma into my life?

Part One: Orit, Arava, East

4

I SET UP the ambush on a rocky stretch of terraced scrubland about thirty metres above a winding road along which a Hezbollah convoy was expected to travel on its way from Tyre to villages further south.

On the second day of our reserve duty we were briefed by an intelligence officer while still in the assembly zone. Every night small convoys, sometimes no more than two vehicles loaded with weapons and explosives, manage to sneak in and resupply Hezbollah fighters in the south. Our objective, added the battalion commander, is to stop them feeling secure and able to move at night. Currently the situation is the opposite of what we want it to be: we are holed up in our outposts, and the night belongs to them. So, during this stint of reserve duty you'll barely be seeing the inside of an outpost. You'll spend three nights in ambush, then to Metulla to rest a bit and regroup, and back again for another three-night spell of lying in wait. That much I'm sure you can cope with.

My men looked at me, clearly astonished. Someone must have lost his mind. Three whole days in ambush? Who on earth do they think we are, an elite reconnaissance unit? Even as young paratroop conscripts we didn't have to do anything like that and certainly not now when we are in the reserves for only a month every year. But in reading their expressions I knew they were also thinking something else; that I was new to being a company commander and wouldn't be going to war with my superiors over this issue.

I'd led some of these men as a platoon commander when they were first drafted. By now most of them had already done two stints of reserve duty with me as their deputy company commander. But being number two is a world away from being at the top, in charge.

My idea is, I told the battalion CO, that we take our time on this. After all it's been a year since these guys' last spell in the reserves. People aren't fit, some of them even have potbellies. Let's just start with a one-night ambush, run through the drills, sort out what needs to be sorted out, and then move things up a notch.

The soldiers listened attentively. I discovered – not for the first time – that the kind of courage needed to face up to your superiors is different, but no less demanding, than the sort you need to confront the enemy.

The CO made the decision. Start with a two-night ambush.

I was given a sector overlooking three arterial roads and it was my job to decide where the ambushes should be set. I was no longer the impulsive young paratrooper immortalized in my battalion for storming my way barefoot up a thorn-infested precipice and firing an FN MAG machine-gun simply because the alarm had been sounded and it seemed a pity to me to waste time putting on my boots. Now I was a student in the Department of East Asian Studies, about to graduate and with the prospect of marriage.

I don't have the strength for this anymore, Orit said tearfully after I'd finished packing my kit-bag. It's OK for you, you know exactly what's happening to you when you're there, and as usual you're in control. But I can't sleep at night and bite my nails all day long. I can't take the uncertainty any longer.

That uncertainty had also spilled over into our relationship, and the conversation ended with an understanding that when I came back from this spell in the reserves, we'd set a date for the wedding.

For the first time, I felt a burden of an altogether different kind tempering my natural instincts. Many people tended to think of me as an adventurer. The reverse was nearer the truth. For me being adventurous in the army meant not doing my best, in effect leaving my survival in the hands of the enemy or fate. I wanted to be master of my own destiny and never leave it to others. That had been an ingrained principle of mine ever since the Holocaust Memorial Day ceremonies at our elementary school. My determination had been reinforced while listening from behind the living room or kitchen door to the few stories my grandparents were willing to tell. These were mostly about what they'd been through during the years my dad, as a child, was hidden away in the monastery where he'd been left when his parents had to flee for their lives.

So that is why I had to practise at the firing range three times every day, run until I felt I was about to faint, go the extra mile the next time round, always charge up a hill, vomiting from the sheer stress of it. And then, having done all of that, at the end of the day I would return to the firing range to practise shooting at night because my previous results hadn't been good enough. I also had to learn to lie in ambush in the most advantageous spot and for the longest time possible. As a result my frustration knew no bounds when the Lebanon War broke out while I was still a raw recruit barred from taking part in the fighting. There I was, aimlessly walking around in a paratrooper's uniform, while others were risking their lives to protect our homeland. Later on, that sense of frustration almost had me court-martialled when I refused to accept the campaign ribbon. The messages of the pacifist 'No to the Ribbon' movement had spread among the soldiers in the field, and it took me quite some time to convince my superiors that I simply didn't think I deserved the award. After all, I told them, I wasn't a combatant in this war. At the time, I didn't yet know how much of the horror of Lebanon I would have to stomach during my years as a conscript and then as a reservist. Each additional stint in Lebanon and Gaza moderated my views. I came to understand the awfulness of these two treacherous quagmires into which we were sinking. At the same time my studies and forthcoming marriage diminished the importance of the army in my life.

My men – especially those who'd known me since our time together in regular service – were happy about my slightly more moderate approach. I even compromised on the ambush sites. I still insisted, of course, on choosing spots with the best firing line and the easiest position from which to mount an assault, even if that happened to be a rocky, thorn-covered ledge. But I balanced these considerations against the value of an area where we could spend two consecutive days and nights in relative comfort.

I also didn't take any chances with the size of the force. I split my scaled-down company into two: one platoon led by my second-in-command and the other by me. I didn't have enough men for a third combat unit. Every night we covered two of the three routes in my sector and every night Hezbollah travelled along the third road. Conceivably, Hezbollah's intelligence officers had probed the area and marked possible ambush sites. Perhaps their spotters had seen us coming and going. Whatever the reason, not a single vehicle passed the ambushes we'd laid. Yet on the roads we'd vacated their convoys travelled freely.

When the time came for the last ambush, I decided to try and outsmart them. We went up to the pre-planned spot immediately after dusk, and settled in. On the second night, when the sector was completely quiet, I quickly moved my men to an alternative location on the third road, coordinating the move with my deputy and battalion HQ.

From an operational point of view, Lebanon is quite unlike anywhere else. Not even Gaza. And not only because of the difficult terrain. At night in Lebanon you move like an ant fearful of being trapped in the mouth of the devil. You know he'll spot you, then overpower you with his tongue, pulverize you with his fangs, or swallow you whole. Lebanese mountains are blacker and steeper than in Israel, the whistle of the wind shriller, the shrubs thornier, and the dark shadows cast by trees and bushes could well be mistaken for the enemy.

My men didn't like the order to pack up and move to the alternate position. And that's putting it mildly. But after almost three weeks under my command, with everything working so smoothly, no one could really object. After all, despite our strenuous efforts, we had achieved nothing. Of course we'd functioned well – set out punctually and silently, taken up our positions properly, were constantly on the lookout, and returned safely. But that wasn't what we'd been sent here for. True, that in the atmosphere of those blood-soaked days, even getting back to base in one piece was an achievement but for me that simply wasn't good enough.

Navigating our way there was easy. I led my men to the road below us, then along it until we reached the junction. We moved in combat formation ready to engage the enemy in case a Hezbollah convoy suddenly appeared. Finally, we reached the foot of the mountain, making our way along the second road to an area just below the ambush site. In single file we climbed to the spot I'd chosen and settled into our positions.

The rocky, weed-ridden ledge overlooked a bend in the road that would force any passing vehicle to slow down. I checked it on aerial photos and through binoculars. Although it was clear to me that this would not be an easy place in which to remain, I decided that we'd stay there till dawn, something like five or six hours. That was manageable.

There was a bit too much of a commotion as the men dug themselves in, some of them uprooting or flattening several large and very prickly bushes. But apart from a rather aggressive whisper of 'quiet' from me, we managed to keep our mutual hostility under control.

Everyone was alert and keyed up when we heard the sound of traffic close by. Tomer, our point man, put on his night-vision goggles and reported sighting one Mercedes and two Land-Rovers.

Get ready to fire, I ordered, and assigned a team of gunners to cover each of the vehicles.

Guns were cocked in silence, eyes lowered to the night-vision viewfinders. At my command, the soldiers armed with rifle-launched grenades rose to a crouching position.

The vehicles were now rounding the bend and coming into view. Even if they were to see us, I thought, it would be too late for them to escape the ambush. There was little if any chance of them accelerating at this spot in the road.

Fire!

The guns were all discharged simultaneously. Even so, only one jeep was hit. The vehicle, its passengers and ammunition, rose to the sky in a ball of fire. Though we peppered the lead Mercedes with bullets, it wasn't enough to halt it. Apparently the driver was unhurt for the vehicle continued moving. The jeep at the rear of the convoy swerved sharply off the road. But the machine-gunner sitting in the middle, with his weapon traversing our site, managed to fire one salvo at us before being taken out. I saw tracer bullets heading towards us, the flares forming a spectacular arc. Instinctively, I ducked. My men then released a second volley at the jeep. The crackle of gun fire merged with a scream coming from somewhere to my left.

A third volley ensured that no one remained alive in the two vehicles below.

I ran to the wounded man – our medic – who only six months earlier had completed his service as a conscript and was joining us for the first time in the reserves. He was in the second line of the formation but had apparently stood up to take part in or watch the shootout, and been hit in the shoulder.

I saw it coming, he whispered. The tracer. It's not that bad, just please stop the bleeding.

I contacted the battalion commander via the field communications system. Against his advice, I decided not to send a team down to pick up documents and perhaps even bring back corpses. My fear was that the passengers from the Mercedes would return to the scene and engage us in combat. I also wanted to get our one casualty out of there fast, and carrying the dead would slow us down considerably.

Reluctantly, the CO agreed to let me leave these potential 'bargaining chips' in the field. We regrouped and began our long trek back. We walked along a ridge, with the stretcher swaying to and fro as the men carrying it stumbled over shrubs and stones, to a place where a helicopter could land. Once the road had disappeared from sight, we didn't expect any further fire. I handed over the lead to one of my platoon commanders and took over the front handles of the stretcher. Unlike some of my guys, I'm no sprinter, but I was stronger than most of them and wanted to share the burden of the immediate consequences of my decisions.

When we reached a wide flat area, I checked the wounded medic. His condition seemed stable and I decided not to put a helicopter in harm's way in the black of night.

At first light the chopper rose from the wadi, its blades almost scraping the hilltop, kicking up an awful lot of dust in the process. I managed to get the wounded medic and half of my men into the helicopter. I took the rest of them and linked up with my deputy and the soldiers who were with him. In the bracing chill of a Lebanese dawn which quickened our pace, I led my company swiftly and in silence to the southern entrance of the nearby outpost.

Even though the battalion CO, brigade CO, and division commander, all complimented me on my decision to swap the location of the ambush, the debriefings were exhausting. That's what I expect from an officer in the paratroops, said the division commander, himself a former paratrooper. Seeking contact with the enemy, initiative, determination, all the things we've let slide here sitting in the outposts. My men also felt they had done something. No one was happy about having apparently missed the Mercedes, but that's life. The battalion commander raised the issue of not bringing back bodies and documents.

The enemy of the good is the very good, I said. Returning to the scene could have cost us lives. And in my heart I already knew what was and would remain, my guiding philosophy. I want to do well, but not better than anyone else. To be among the good, but not necessarily the best.

The brigade CO had no problem with my response. Maybe now those SOBs will creep back into their shells for a while, he said, summing it all up. We were all dead tired and wanted to go home. The only 'seeking contact' we could think of was with our wives and girl friends. I was so wiped that I forgot to call home, even though the six o'clock morning news which both Orit and my parents listened to when I was in Lebanon had already reported the battle. It ended, said the newscaster, with 'about eight Hezbollah men killed and one of our soldiers lightly wounded'. It sounded good, except that they'd be sure to think that the lightly wounded soldier was me.

I know you, Orit wept on my shoulder. You always pick the spot where you're most likely to engage the enemy, don't you? And aren't you always the first to fire and storm ahead?

Orit, a dance and movement teacher, and quite an acrobat, had been waiting for me for three whole weeks. And I, never much of an athlete, was on my last legs. However much testosterone I may have stored up during the ambush and firefight, there was no sign of it that night. I fell asleep on my back, soon after I thought I'd heard Orit – still on top of me – climaxing. I was so exhausted that I didn't even know if I had also come.

By the time I woke up, Orit had already showered and seemed relaxed. She told me about a letter that had arrived for me from The Bureau of International Relations, asking to meet me.

But first we're going to fix a date for the wedding. I beckoned. She came towards me. I pulled her back into bed to celebrate, once more, the future that awaited us.

5

OUR MARRIAGE WAS a surprise to no one. The story had its beginnings in the ninth grade at a youth movement rally for all the moshavim – the collective villages – and the kibbutzim in the central Arava desert. As I climbed onto the towbar of a brightly-decorated trailer, a pair of legs came into view. And what legs! Long, slender, smooth, and shapely. These were not the legs of the local girls I usually met at such events. We sat facing each other on the festively bedecked benches along both sides of the trailer. My eyes travelled from the legs and up, fixing on an embroidered floral blouse. This too marked her out from the rest of the girls who were all wearing the standard blue shirts of the youth movement. Through the blouse I could just about see the outline of soft but still tiny breasts. I then stared at her long neck, her finely drawn, beautiful face and deep blue eyes that looked straight back at me with an expression of rebuke that told me – could you perhaps stop ogling me like that? But beyond the petulant gaze, her delicate lips revealed a smile of resignation as if to say –

ok, these games aren't new to me. As I was still trying to filter these mixed messages, which would one day become a pivotal part of my life, she suddenly offered her hand. I'm Orit, she said. We moved from Givatayyim to the Sapir Centre this summer. My parents teach at the high school.

While I regained my composure, her hand remained extended for what seemed like ages. Here in the desert we don't shake hands, we just go ahead and talk. Yogev, I said, shaking her hand almost formally, her delicate fingers squeezed in my grip. My hands aren't big, but as early as ninth grade there were already signs of my strong physique; well-developed biceps, wide shoulders, and a powerful chest. In what appeared to me a blend of amity and awe, my friends used to joke that since my bar-mitzvah I'd gained plenty in width but little in height. Something about the fragility of her hand, and the delicateness of her slender body, made my heart skip a beat and from that very moment I took on the role of her protector.

Tractors towed the trailer and its passengers to the place where the event was to take place. The area was festooned with bales of hay and the flags of the regional council, the movement, and the nation. Making a home in the desert was still in its early stages and the inhabitants eagerly looked forward to every communal event.

When we got off the trailer, Orit stood at my side. She was a few centimetres taller than me, but I consoled myself with the thought that she was fully grown and I still had some way to go, an assumption which turned out to be not entirely correct. Come and sit with our group, I suggested, trying to be gracious, and ignoring the fact that the group's instructors had been the ones to place her in our trailer. Her smile was friendly, though perhaps somewhat ironic, as she walked with me to our seating area.

In honour of the fourth graders joining the youth movement, the pupils from my year had arranged a set of original songs about the Israeli southern desert. I was the soloist in 'On a Clear Day I Travelled South'.

It wasn't easy to persuade me to sing solo in front of a crowd. I'm naturally quite shy, and in those days I was even more so. But now, as I climbed onto the stage and saw that Orit was all by herself in my year's allocated seats I was happy to do it.

I travelled south, to work in the Arava, I continued with the opening words in my deep bass voice. I ploughed, I sowed and reaped, but managed to find love. My friends joined me in the verse: She was like the sun in the sky, and in her eyes a spark of gaiety and joy.

Once they had joined in the singing I was able to shed my shyness and look straight into Orit's eyes. She responded with a smile, a sparkle of gaiety and delight in her blue eyes staring right back at me.

From that day on we were a couple. Afterwards I sometimes thought that I hadn't left her much of a choice. We became a couple before she met Yoni, who was a lot more amusing than me, or the tall Gidi, or Yonatan, the first to appear in Israel's southern desert with a punk haircut playing hard rock music, or Dori, the class genius, or Yariv, the regional school's champion at both the high and long jump. But Orit lovingly accepted the protection I offered. Before long it was clear to the whole school that we were a couple for good.

Not for a moment did Orit let me feel that she was with me because I'd 'chosen' her. The mystique that went with her being a stranger in town occasionally gave the impression of a young girl who knew exactly what she wanted and how to get it quickly and in the most effective way.

There's not much to do in the desert, certainly not in our small moshav. There were only five boys in our year. Ninth grade was when my friends discovered cigarettes, then the nargileh, then grass, and spent their time smoking behind the clubhouse. None of that was for me. I helped my parents on the farm. After school, I worked in the tomato, pepper, and watermelon fields, and helped with sorting in the packing shed we'd set up in the big yard. My evenings were spent reading.

When the regional high school opened we got closer to classmates from the five other villages in the area. But the distances we had to travel took their toll and at the end of the school day we all had to go our separate ways.

Then Orit came into my life, filling it with a new harmony and a different tempo. After school I'd stay at her house in a residential neighbourhood close to the school and soon became one of the family. The small neighbourhood community set against the vastness of an arid desert landscape was home to a few teachers, two doctors, and some council and water company workers. They lived in cramped, asbestos-roofed houses, their brown coloured exterior walls blending beautifully with the yellowish-grey sand all around. I swapped working on my parent's farm for helping to nurture Orit's family's small garden, happy to be at their disposal and offer them my newly acquired horticultural skills. I raked the loose crumbly soil, planted vegetable seedlings from my parent's fields, together with a few ornamental plants that Orit's mother brought.

Orit's little brother enjoyed throwing a basketball through an improvised hoop attached to the wall of the house and her parents were impressed by my seriousness. Her father expressed his surprise at the books I read, sometimes even engaging me in detailed conversation about various fictional characters and indifferent interpretations of the novels. Occasionally, he would recall his own passionate enjoyment of the same books.

I loved watching Orit paint. Her murals added stunning patches of colour to the walls of the school, a building that had been designed, with its greyish plaster and reddish clay walls, to merge with the desert all around it. I also liked accompanying her to her gymnastics and dance lessons in the hall adjoining the school, and was amazed by her supple, cat-like, movements.

She welcomed my love – and the poems I wrote to her. At least I think she did. Being with Orit brought out the romantic in me, a sentiment I didn't know I was capable of. I wrote her a poem almost every week, and every now and again I'd set the poem to music and sing her the lyrics to the accompaniment of my guitar. We went for long walks along the ancient Spice Route through a wadi that led to our school. From there this biblical path wound its way to the slopes of the low hills in the distance. I always had my guitar slung over my shoulder and I'd play it as we occasionally took a break in the shade of an acacia tree. Orit would sit facing me, hugging her long bare legs, exposed by her ever so brief shorts, and listen to my music attentively, her blue eyes reflecting a happy smile. When I finished playing she'd put her arms around me and kiss me.

One evening, when we were all alone, she really surprised me. Do you masturbate? she asked. I did, but that particular word wasn't yet common in our part of the world. The liberated girl from a more cosmopolitan part of the country wasted no time waiting for my answer and decided instead to tutor me. First by caressing the bulge in my jeans, and then by sliding her hands inside them.

My poems thus far had described her blue eyes (which if you believe the poems were bluer than the sea and sky), the blonde fringe across her forehead, and her long plait. Now there were poems about her ripening breasts that already filled the palm of my hand. I searched for new words to describe the mystery hidden between her thighs, by then rounder and more like those of a grown woman.

On my seventeenth birthday Orit announced that she wanted to give me a present. She'd been holding this gift back, she explained, for almost a year and now the time had come for her to give it to me. After school we took the bus to my parents' home. Once the heat of the day had subsided, we rode our bikes out beyond the residential area, through the east gate and continued past the hothouses and vegetable fields that bordered the patrol path along the Jordanian border. The last rays of the setting sun coloured the peaks of Edom with the redness that gave them their name in Hebrew, and which made them seem higher, closer, and more menacing than ever. The farmers had already left the fields. The army patrol that would check the dirt road for the footprints of intruders was not due till nightfall.

Orit guided us to an area in the lower reaches of a date palm plantation where there was more shade. To my surprise she had planned it all to the nth degree. From the wicker basket attached to the front of her bike she took out a light woven blanket, a bottle of wine, two glasses, and even a corkscrew.

I'd already got to know every feature of Orit's face and slender body. I was more familiar than she was with the almost imperceptible slant of her mouth, formed by her asymmetrical cheekbones. This was a feature I spotted – apparently the only one to do so – when we were doing our homework together one day and a pencil held in her mouth was slanted instead of being horizontal. My discovery led to prolonged orthodontic treatment, during which I had to get used to the braces and wires in her mouth. You've only yourself to blame, she would say, chortling. A moment before she laughed or got angry, I could tell what was about to happen from the tiny creases that appeared in the corners of her eyes, or the slight shadow that darted across her face. When she became an outstanding gymnast, captaining the girls' regional artistic gymnastics team, her magnificent legs turned slightly more muscly, sinew that was barely visible to the naked eye. Yet I immediately knew she was about to move because I could see a thin muscle tense up like the string of an archer's bow. But now, here in the plantation, was a different Orit. Serious, keyed-up, excited, practical and dreamy, all at the same time.

She spread out the blanket, handed me the bottle to open and sat at my feet as I took my time to figure out how the corkscrew worked. The cork broke, and I had to push half of it back into the bottle. We drank wine with fragments of cork in it, bits that I swallowed in silence and Orit spat out in disgust. And then, without saying a word she took off her shorts and pulled me on top of her.

Had she not insisted on us doing it again soon after our first, not very successful attempt at love making, we would have returned home bitterly disappointed. After months of passionately exciting foreplay, gradually doing everything but, penetrating her was unexpectedly difficult, hurried, unsatisfying. And I was left wondering why she hadn't bled.

Maybe it's because of the bike, Orit said, and then she let me into the secret that was to make our sex life so wonderful: the tip of her bike saddle presses on a spot that drives her totally crazy. It's not inside her, inside isn't so important, she told me. Then she took my hand and placed my finger on that exquisite point between her legs. Rub your finger gently around it, pressing it just like the saddle does, she explained.

We called the spot 'Magic' on account of the magical sensation Orit felt whenever it was touched.

With her help, I discovered exciting places in my own body, areas it would never have occurred to me to explore. Who would have thought that a gentle caress just beneath my scrotum could be the source of such intense pleasure? Or licking the inside of a thigh?

From the moment she decided to do it, Orit transformed us from a couple of enthusiastic kids into a pair of passionate adults. Within a few days I felt I was living in a different world. I couldn't see the point of spending time with my friends smoking in our village or, for that matter, with Orit's gymnastic team mates at school. The two of us wanted to be together twenty-four hours a day. We simply couldn't wait to be alone.

Orit's parents were more broad-minded than mine and I often slept there with her, in her bedroom. When she stayed at our house my mum and dad made up a bed for her in the living room and I'd sneak down there during the night. On rare occasions my parents went to Tel Aviv, leaving me alone in the house. The moment I knew they were going, I'd pass Orit a note in class and she'd return it with a giant blue smiley face and just one word: Yes!

A dazzling light that constantly shone from Orit's eyes permeated our love and was even there when she smiled, still on top of me, after our passion was utterly spent.

Orit's love was so natural that I accepted my worthiness of the love of such a wonderful girl as a given. It was during that period that I realized I wouldn't be growing any taller and regretted it. But my adoring Orit, ignoring the fact that she was slightly taller, embraced and kissed me saying: you don't know how good it is to hug and kiss someone of the same height. But then she noticed the look of surprise on my face and was quick to reassure me: not that I've had any other experience, but it looks so clumsy in the movies when he's so tall and she's so tiny. We're so good together, face to face, chest to chest. That was all she said, and just let the blue of her eyes envelop me in pleasure.

We fantasized about dropping everything and running away to live together. We talked about a farm in the desert, the summit of a mountain, even the Yarkon estuary, like Gi and Go in Orpaz's *Daniel's Voyage* which we read together, in her bed and mine, falling in love with the love of the two protagonists. When we finished the book we decided that, just like them, we would go to the Yarkon estuary and pitch our tents there. It was the start of the Passover vacation, matriculation exams were looming, and extra lessons were being offered at school. Instead, we took a tent just big enough for two, got on the first Eilat–Tel Aviv bus, excited, holding hands, planning how we were going to spend the next few weeks on the white sand where the river flows into the sea. From the central bus station we went straight to the spot we had fantasized about, only to discover that the estuary was no more, just lawns and a sea port complex.

We slept on a narrow strip of sand until wardens woke us up and told us that sleeping there was prohibited.

On the way home we called ourselves Or and Ar, Or of course for Orit, and Ar for my surname, Ari, a small homage to Gi and Go and the vanished estuary.

A short while after the metric exams, an interval that was far far too brief for both of us, I joined the army.

Yogev Ben-Ari! The platoon commander bellowed, clutching a blue envelope in his hand. Sir! I yelled back excitedly. Do fifty! He ordered. Orit's letters, sometimes two a day, had me doing more push-ups than any other cadet in the paratroops, and I did them at speed so that I could get my hands on the blue envelope and what it held. Orit knew how to describe her sexual longing for me so openly and palpably that it literally hurt me physically, far more than my shoulders hurt from carrying a heavily loaded stretcher. I got such a hard erection just thinking about her – which I did almost all the time – that route marches and runs became a nightmare, with my erect penis trapped in my pants.

Orit was serving in the air force in Tel Aviv, where she shared a small apartment with three other girls. From time to time we were stationed at our brigade's home base just a few dozen miles away from where Orit was living. On such occasions, I would scale the camp's perimeter fence after lights out, hitchhike to Tel Aviv, and sneak into her apartment. As I was showering, cleansing my body of its army sweat, Orit came in wanting me to make love to her standing in the shower, reminding me once more of the advantages of being the same height.

Orit had this sultry moan that sounded like 'Oi'. At first, when I thought it was a signal of pain, I was alarmed. But when I realized my mistake, alarm turned to amusement and the moan got louder and louder and

'Magic' swelled to my touch. As Orit wriggled with excitement, imploring me to enter her, the 'Oi' was already heavy, and though its pitch remained a very low alto it was loud enough to wake not only her three friends in the adjoining rooms, but also the landlord in the next apartment. After I'd put my hand over her mouth and been fiercely bitten for doing so, I never tried that again. I just waited for the ripple of spasms that suddenly made her whole body quiver, then for the silence, and then for that hint of a smile, as she continued moving with obvious pleasure. Open your eyes just a little, please, I would say. But that particular request went unanswered. It was just her smile that became wider and which she tried to suppress by pressing her face into my neck. A little blue, I insisted. She raised her head, glanced at me, and the now visible blue melted me with love.

I got back to base, sometimes having to run for miles through deserted streets, smuggled my way into the camp before dawn, and started a new day without even a moment's sleep. In my mind's eye I could see her smile and the blue slit of her eyes, while my ears continued to ring with the sound of her moans of desire.

Whenever we had time to talk, we planned our future together. Orit didn't know whether she wanted to be a dancer or a painter. Perhaps, so that she'd also be able to make a living, she'd study at the Wingate Institute and become a sports instructor.

I said I wanted to be a Buddhist monk – but with a wife, I quickly added, seeing her look of bewilderment.

Random encounters with books about religions of the East drew me, as if by magic, to a place that was as far away as I could possibly imagine from the grim military reality that I had to endure in Lebanon and Gaza.

Orit eventually enrolled as an architectural student at the Bezalel Academy of Arts and Design, just as her parents had suggested. I completed the period of army service I'd committed to when I took up an officer's course and then, having decided to take a course in East Asian studies, joined her as a student. We lived happily, enjoying the little things of life, a life of blithe banality that is the destiny of every young couple. We studied together, we bought matching kitchen utensils, bed linen in 'our' colours of orange and mauve. Orit developed a taste for acquiring pieces of art that began to fill our small apartment and I framed and hung her paintings, a gift that made her weep with joy.

Not once did I question our love. It was as natural to me as was any part of my body. And not for a moment did I cease to be excited by her scent, her taste, her look, the feel of her smooth skin, her smile, and more than anything else, the alluring 'Oi', and the grins of happiness that followed it were mine and mine alone.

6

I CALLED THE Bureau of International Relations to fix an appointment. Orit and I were sure that the letter I'd received from them had something to do with my studies

– I was already in my third year. But whereas Orit was convinced that the Bureau was part of the foreign ministry, I had a hunch that it was a branch of the security services.

I was a good student, and because of my keen interest in East-Asian cultures I took many more courses than required. I also learned Chinese. The language's use of ideograms which are, in fact, words, interested me and I enjoyed uncovering the logic behind them. The word for 'small' for example, is drawn like a parent's hands pointing at a little child; 'big' resembles a man with his hands outstretched to the sides; and the ideogram for 'huge' looks like the word for 'big', but with an additional upper line, and can also mean 'sky'. Concepts, made up of a number of symbols, both amused me and were indicative of great worldly wisdom about life. 'Struggle' for example, is depicted by two women living under one roof.

In the lectures on Buddhism, a convenient substitute for my one time wish to become a Buddhist monk, I learned how the Buddha gave up a prince's life of ease and freed himself from all of Hinduism's commandments and gods. Instead, he focused on trying to understand suffering and its causes, attempting to discover how to rid mankind of these ills. Did you know that in order to avoid suffering I have to stop holding onto you? I asked Orit after one of the lectures. But I'm prepared to suffer and go on suffering and not give you up.

I found it difficult fully to understand the idea that it was impossible to hold onto anything because whatever it is you may be holding onto inevitably changes and so do you. At the time I had no idea how much Orit and I would change in the years ahead and how much we would suffer by holding onto one another.

I realized that I had a long way to go before I really understood the Buddha and thought that the forthcoming meeting at the Bureau, which might end up with me being sent to the East, could, perhaps, be a shortcut.

The meeting was to take place at *Beit Hadar*, near Tel Aviv's old central bus station.

The letter instructed me to go to a room on one of the lower basement floors and I took some time to find it. A balding middle-aged man greeted me and gave me various forms to fill out. Together we pored over my responses. He picked up on a note I'd written about wanting to finish my studies before starting work. If you want to work for us, he told me, you'll have to undergo a prolonged series of tests that will last until the end of the academic year. But you must understand that if you're accepted we won't be offering you a run-of-the-mill position or a nine-to-five job. Working for us is about a way of life and a lifelong commitment.

Are you from the Mossad? I asked, my heart atremble.

It says here The Bureau of International Relations, doesn't it? he replied without even the hint of a smile. I never raised the subject again.

The man proceeded to talk to me about the geo-political situation in Southeast Asia, displaying considerable knowledge about the politics of the area, its colonial history, and the respective influence of China and the Soviet Union. To my shame, I understood very little about any of this, and all the information I'd accumulated about the area's history, its ethnic makeup, and its religions, suddenly seemed virtually worthless.

It's unbelievable, said the man from the Bureau. In China, only a hundred and fifty years ago, the British and French did whatever they wanted: they stole, pillaged, appropriated territory, burned down temples, forced the Chinese to produce opium and then sell it to them. The emperors were terrified of them. He skipped stating the obvious – that nowadays the pendulum is swinging the other way. If you want to do well, he told me, take as many courses on China as you can, and focus on the language. There our conversation ended. We parted without him seeing me out, shaking my hand, or divulging his name. He merely said that I'd probably be invited for some more tests in the future.

The invitations duly arrived. Every few weeks I found myself devoting a day to language, psycho-technical, technical, and psychological tests – convinced I'd failed the latter by saying that all the Rorschach ink blots reminded me of a woman's hips. But I passed. I also got through the three days of arduous and unconventional field exercises involving several violations of common law and a breach of at least five of the Ten Commandments. Most of the remaining five were breached on the job itself. My examiners apparently concluded that I was sufficiently daring but not overly zealous and always kept my head. These were the qualities that got me accepted to the course. The word 'Mossad' had still not been mentioned.

*

Before the course began I managed to complete the final requirements for my degree. Orit also finished her course in architecture and joined a small successful firm of architects based in Jerusalem. At the same time, the two of us were busy with last minute preparations for our fast-approaching wedding.

We were married at the end of summer. The scent of autumn was already in the air and in the last few days before we were to be wed clouds covered the sky and in the evenings a chill northerly wind swept across the desert plains. We worried that the first rains could ruin our big day. So, just in case, two groups of friends, one from the paratroops and the other from the village, set up a huge canvas awning and a spacious Indian tent. As it happened there was no need for either.

The sight of Orit in her wedding dress was stunning. The baring of her beautiful shoulders and the elongated slit that both revealed and concealed one of her long legs, was a brilliantly conceived idea. So was the way in which the fabric that crisscrossed her breasts exaggerated their fullness. A string of sparking white pearls adorned her swanlike neck. Orit's face, makeup highlighting that beguiling twinkle in her eyes, glowed with happiness. She looked so ravishingly beautiful that it came as no surprise to me to see many of those present burst into applause when she appeared.

The nameplate on the front door of our rented apartment now read: Orit and Yogev Ben-Ari. At first she found it odd that her name had changed overnight. But when I suggested that she keep her maiden name she refused, naturally accepting married life and its consequences. My brother will be the guardian of our family's name, she said. Evening after evening when I got home she'd be there to hold me tight and kiss me, her face beaming, her eyes closed. And I would ask her to open her eyes until she finally relented, revealing that intense blue. I didn't think it possible to still be so in love after being together for so long. But I was.

A handful of us were instructed to meet at a certain café. A transit van with tinted windows picked up the small group and took it to a training facility in the middle of what looked like an abandoned army base. At long last we heard the words we had been waiting for: Welcome to the Mossad. Immediately after this greeting we were told: that's the first and the last time you'll hear that word in this place. Then it was straight down to business as we were each handed a pair of blue overalls and marched to a pistol shooting range. Before the weapon itself was handed out there was a brief explanation of how pistols are handled and some safety instructions. I was a good marksman with various types of assault rifles, but had hardly ever fired a pistol. At first my results were nothing short of mediocre. An hour or so later there were some signs of improvement but when we began practising instinctive shooting and fast draws I was back to square one. Towards the end of the session I got slightly better results in these areas as well and left the shooting range with a feeling of cautious optimism tinged with a some hesitance about my real abilities – a mixture of feelings that stayed with me throughout the year's training.

After the shooting practice, we were given tracksuits, taken to a hangar that turned out to be a gym, and had our first session on the martial art of face-to-face combat. Each of us in turn had to charge at a human wall formed by our fellow trainees and dive into it. The others were all taller than me, perhaps an advantage to them during the more advanced stages of close combat training. But they were also slimmer than I was, a definite plus for me during this early phase of the exercises.

I got home just before midnight, tired and in pain. Orit listened to my account of the day impassively, restricting herself to one comment only: just so long as they don't turn you into a killer. I was surprised. She knew I'd taken out quite a few terrorists in Lebanon and the Territories, and she'd never said a word about it.

Inexorably, the course removed me from the routine of domestic life. We studied until late in the evening and by the time I got back to Orit I was dead to the world. Then, when our field training began, the exercises lasted well into the night. There were also surveillance and round-the-clock intelligence-gathering drills when I didn't get home at all. The studying, the training, and the action fascinated me, and I was a bit saddened by the fact that Orit didn't share my view of it all. She didn't think that uncovering a surveillance team tailing you was at all exciting, or that to follow and observe someone without them suspecting a thing could be in any way thrilling. As was common among people who joined the military at the same time, she had readily listened to the tales of my exploits in the army. But she described my training to become an Israeli James Bond as amounting to nothing more than 'playing at being cowboys'.

My commanding officers apparently assumed that I was going to complete the course successfully. So, before exposing me to even more important and highly confidential information, they invited Orit to a meeting at which a psychologist was also present. I didn't join them but from what Orit told me afterwards I got the gist of what had been said.

I know he's a patriot, Orit had told them, and that making a contribution to the state is very important to him. But he's neither right-wing nor an ultra-nationalist. As for me, well, I'm even a bit of a lefty. I know he killed in the army, but the army's the army and one thing is certain – he's no murderer. I want a man at my side whose hands and conscience are both clean.

My commanders assured Orit that the Mossad isn't engaged in liquidations, and that I wouldn't be involved in any such actions. True, my role would be operational, including some tasks she knew I'd been training for; intelligence gathering, covert photography, and occasionally breaking into places to gather valuable intelligence. But the training I'd received in close combat and gunfire was mainly for the purposes of self-defence.

Perhaps once in a decade, they told her, the Mossad does kill someone. But that wouldn't be part of my work and the chances that I would be involved in anything like that were remote.

Orit came home clearly perturbed. I'm no psychologist, she said, but I could tell from the way they fidgeted, wriggled in their seats, exchanged looks, that they were lying. I expect that you will never dare lie to me, never. I can cope with all the rest.

Her candour and courage made me love her all the more, and she had every reason to believe that I wouldn't ever lie to her. I was as straight as they come, lying wasn't my way.

The next stage of the course hadn't yet begun. Indeed, I was not even aware of its existence or of the fact that it dealt with such matters as recruitment and handling human sources, inventing cover stories, deception and lying to trap targeted people, frame them, and then recruit them.

I enjoyed the operational side of the first part of the course and even became good at it. But the second part turned my stomach. More than once I very nearly failed to carry out the assignment and faced being kicked out. Towards the end, my superiors found a compromise; I would do as little Humint – human intelligence – work as possible, and be more involved in the operational side of things. Inventing cover stories and lying was something I was clearly no good at. It runs counter to your inner being and basic values, wrote my commanders in their final evaluation of my performance. So instead of doing that which did not come naturally to me, they decided I should gain experience in intelligence gathering in an area of the world close to my heart: I was sent to the Far East.

7

My superiors thought it would be easy for me to pass myself off as the son of an Indo-Canadian marriage who had lived most of his life in Canada. My appearance – average height and dark skinned – fitted such origins, as did my English accent which, though not Canadian, was not Israeli either. The spoken English of someone who had grown up in Canada with an Indian parent was bound to sound slightly different. But such an impersonation required me to get to know India, find the place where I had supposedly been born and had lived during the first few years of my life. I would have to invent parents – preferably a Canadian father and Indian mother – find out where and how they'd met and what they had done with their lives, and be able then to continue the storyline in Canada.

I asked to take Orit with me to India, arguing that this needn't interfere with my mission. Hatching a cover story was itself in many ways a kind of journey and after the long and exhausting course I had been through we needed time to be together. But my request was met with a hostile look from my controllers who sent me off to the Mossad's library to prepare for the trip.

Nothing could have prepared me for my head-on encounter with the reality of a place I had only read and heard about. Bombay greeted me with a stifling airlessness and an unfamiliar odour. The first thing I saw in the dim light of pre-dawn as the cab drew away from the terminal and headed for the main road, was a row of bare bottoms squatting over a roadside gutter. I rubbed my eyes to confirm the sight but by then we were already passing the hovels of cardboard and plastic sheeting that lined the sides of the road where three million of the city's homeless lived.

My next reality check was Bombay's beggars. Getting out of the cab I was immediately surrounded by girls – who couldn't have been more than twelve years old – clutching their babies, pointing to their mouths to let me know they were hungry. I didn't yet have any local money, just large dollar bills. After this experience I made sure that my pockets were lined with rupees which I lavished on the many needy people who continually approached me. Until, that is, I discovered that such generosity was turning me into an all too recognizable a person in the neighbourhoods I frequented while evolving my legend. Even in the Temples I re-visited to understand the liturgy better, people began to look at me suspiciously.

I marked out a middle-class district on the crest of a road leading to a wealthy neighbourhood atop a large wooded hill in the very heart of the city. There, I came across a street of dilapidated colonial-era houses that managed to retain the charm of bygone days, and picked a particular two-storey building doomed for demolition. This, I decided, would be my parents' house, the house in which I was born. I photographed the street and the building, and even went inside and noted the names that were still fixed to the doors and mailboxes. Neighbours looked at me inquisitively and I concluded that asking about a 'Mr Thomas Calvin' who had lived here about twenty years ago with Indira, a local woman, would help the credibility of my cover. I was directed to an elderly resident who assured me that no Canadian had lived there since 1947. I updated my story, deciding that my father would be the Indian who'd come from here and met my mother in Canada where I was born. I'd concoct the rest of the legend in Canada. I also decided that the time had come for me get to know India as a normal tourist.

I quickly visited the sites of Bombay and then embarked on a long journey through Rajasthan. I was fascinated by the way the women's colourful saris blended in with the desert landscape, and by the smooth fusion of fruit and vegetable markets and roadside eating places, where pigs foraging for food in the garbage mingled with the diners. At this stage of being a novice operative, my risks were limited. The two biggest dangers I faced were driving amid the charred remains of vehicles that had crashed during the night, and overtaking trucks with stickers in English at the back asking passers to 'horn please'. Apart from having no lights they had no wing mirrors either.

Obeying the orders of my controllers I passed up on visiting the Taj Mahal and northern India – they preferred that there be 'gaps' in my knowledge of India and that I not sound like a run-of-the-mill tourist. But I didn't let go of the chance of visiting Benares – or Varanasi – on the banks of the Ganges.

For hours that turned into days, I sat on the ghats,

watching women washing saris and spreading them out to dry, a fascinating display of colour and sound; I gazed at the people coming to bathe in the sacred waters, at the monks praying and meditating, seemingly oblivious to the interminable buzz of life all around them, and at the street vendors pedalling their wares. I was astonished by the otherworldly calm that appeared to envelope the entire scene. This air of tranquillity also hung over the narrow side streets and alleyways covered in cow dung, where I had to move aside whenever a cow lumbered towards me. The alleyways were far too narrow for both of us to pass, and the animal certainly had no intention of making room for me. While in Benares I even took some lessons in yoga and meditation, surprised by how good that made me feel. I don't know how many Mossad operatives practise these arts, but I decided I'd continue even when I started my real job. Like so many other plans I had at the beginning, this was another that never materialized.

My surprising inner response to yoga and meditation told me that the main elements of my cover story were in place, I'd succeeded in feeling Indian; after a delay of several years I'd got closer to my old and somewhat whimsical desire to become a Buddhist monk and, if not for real, then at least to feel that some bits of my soul were truly Indian. Before the deadline was up, I'd finished establishing the Indian part of my legend.

Back home I found that Orit had been missing me, wanting me, but was also angry and worried. So this is how it's going to be? I'm going to be a grass widow for weeks at a time whenever you go away? Just so you know, I can't take it. I don't know what you do to satisfy yourself, but I'm climbing the walls.

I didn't have an answer, and didn't have the guts to say, 'ride your bike'. Luckily the trip to Canada was shorter – my controllers were able to point me directly to places that would become part of my legend. The subsequent trips were also shorter – to Tokyo, Seoul, Hong Kong and Singapore – and were designed to establish my identity as a businessman specializing in East Asia. I called them business-card-collecting journeys.

Then came the operational trips. Representatives of a North Korean firm had arrived in Hong Kong to close a deal with a Syrian company, and HQ wanted samples of the documents they'd signed there. A shadowy Chinese businessman was putting together inexplicable deals with Persian Gulf Emirs, and HQ wanted to know who the Chinaman really was. A suspicious cargo was being loaded onto a ship in Shanghai and HQ also wanted to know what the cargo looked like and the name of the vessel carrying it.

Before every such trip there was a briefing, a presentation of intelligence, a preparatory drill, and a discussion of what might happen and the possible responses. There was also a pep-talk at which the head of the division would explain the importance of the information I'd be bringing back. I almost always delivered the goods, making use of everything I'd learned, of my personal and business cover, my creativity, and more than anything else, of my audacity.

In the hotel where the North Koreans were staying, I managed to have my room upgraded so that I was moved to their floor. With the help of a smile and a modest tip to the chambermaid I got copies of the documents HQ had asked for. I ensconced myself in the lobby where the shadowy Chinaman met the sheikhs and secretly photographed him. Afterwards, as I demonstrated my knowledge of Chinese ideograms to the receptionist, she helpfully translated the characters of the man's name from the hotel register. In Shanghai, I toured the city's port with a local exporter, claiming that I was about to purchase some very expensive equipment and needed to see exactly how the goods would be loaded. He also photographed me against the background of the ship and its unknown cargo, which experts at air force HQ later identified as medium-range missile launchers.

I didn't always deliver a comprehensive report of what I had done to accomplish the mission – my controllers certainly wouldn't have been happy to know about the mistakes I'd made as an enthusiastic novice, such as climbing the port fence to get a better shot of that vessel.

My routine was, in fact, entirely practicable. I was usually away for no more than a week every month. I acquired skills, a good knowledge of the field, experience, and confidence. Orit too learned to more or less put up with my short trips, and 'Magic' longed for my return, as I yearned for her.

This was the pattern of my work for almost two years. On only two or three occasions did anyone suspect me, forcing me to produce my papers or use my cover story which always sounded credible.

Once HQ was confident of my abilities, they began sending specialists with me – surveillance personnel, men with experience of breaking into properties, lookouts, photographers, recruiters. With their assistance I was assigned to deal with more complex missions. Within about another year I had a highly trained team around me, able to provide far better intelligence than I'd been able to on my own.

I no longer had to sit for hours on end in hotel lobbies waiting for meetings between Asian manufacturers and Middle Eastern buyers – the lookouts did that and alerted me when the target subjects turned up. I didn't have to plant hidden cameras – the professional photographers took care of that, arriving whenever I needed them and then departing without leaving a trace. And I no longer had to entrust my fate into the hands of kindly chambermaids. Instead, I would call the break-in team who skillfully, swiftly, and quietly let themselves into any room, expertly opened any case, enabling the photographers to take their shots. Within minutes they were gone. The recruiters, past masters in interpersonal relations, made contact on my behalf with guards, drivers, anyone, in fact, who had to be distracted, so that my team and I could gain entry to virtually any place we needed to and do our job.

At HQ it was decided that we would be the team for special missions in East Asia. Who commanded the team depended on the nature of the mission: sometimes it was the chief recruiter; on other occasions the break-in team's leader; from time to time it was me – the businessman who knew the region – or the leader of the surveillance team when the case involved more complex monitoring than usual. After dozens of operations led by me, I was relieved to hand over the baton to someone else every now and then. Wherever we happened to be, we picked out the restaurants we most fancied, taking care to wear suits and ties, like young businessmen. In hotels, we preferred to be in groups of two or three to relieve the loneliness. The results were good and we felt we could accomplish any mission.

But there was one mission in which I failed.

I stopped taking the pill this week, Orit announced to my surprise. I wanted us to decide this together, she said, noticing my look of displeasure, but your return was delayed again and again. I had my period and I didn't want to postpone it for another month. I had to decide on my own.

But my love, we spoke on the phone almost every evening.

Yes, that's true, she replied, looking straight at me, and for the first time I noticed how penetrating her eyes could be. 'Everything all right? Here too. Going to bed? Me too.' That's how our conversations usually went. Do you really think I can talk to you on the phone about it being time we had a baby together?

So just now, this week, is the right time? My pique refused to be tamed and I began to conjure up various accusations about the impulsive decisions that Orit makes on her own. But then I remembered that I'd been the main beneficiary of those decisions, from the date plantation on my birthday, to the garden where we'd been married.

This has been eating me up for quite a while, she said. Even when you're in the country you get home dead tired and your thoughts are miles away. But then I thought that you might not want to have a baby. In any case we can use something other than the pill which in any case is a health risk if you keep on using it for too long.

And you – do you want a baby?

Two, she replied, and after a moment of silence, with an impish look in her eyes, she burst into that rolling laughter of hers that at once dissolved my anger. I mean it, two, she said, trying to be serious, but only one at a time.

My frequent trips abroad, and all the preparations that preceded them, had pushed Orit to the margins of my life. Now my love for this woman of mine, so mischievous yet so adult, so girlish but at the same time so feminine, once again consumed the whole of my being. Suddenly, more than anything else in the world, I wanted to please her.

I wasn't yet ready for a baby. Operational activities took up all of my days and the desire for Orit filled my nights. In my mind I was still the same young paratroop officer and even, as Orit used to say, a kid playing cowboys. Not a father. But someone who spends their evenings and nights alone at home has different thoughts and other wants. I realized, as I had done way back then on the date plantation, that Orit was maturing faster than I was, and didn't want her to have to wait for me to 'grow up' –

especially since I didn't even know when that would be. That very night I tried to make her wish come true and did so with great love.

She caressed me and kissed my skin. What a smooth, soft baby we'll have, she said, reminding me of how skillfully she'd banished my regret that I wasn't hairy like some of my friends.

You'll have to be home more with Ar junior, she said, taking me back to our days of Gi and Go, Ar and Or. But that was a commitment I couldn't make. Across her face I saw that familiar shadow appear and stay. I haven't the strength to raise a child on my own, she said, and certainly not two.

Feeling pressured, I promised that before the birth I'd ask for a job at HQ for a few years.

That's the way it works anyway isn't it? said Orit, somewhat tetchily. After something like four years in the field you do a stint at HQ, no?

That was true of operatives who'd been abroad full-time, not of home-based people like me. But there was no point telling her this because Orit didn't listen to such explanations.

We tried and tried, but without success. The pregnancy, it seems, had a mind of its own.

Every second ovulation you're overseas, Orit said bitterly, and the fact that we fuck all night when there's no available egg achieves nothing.

8

MY NOW PROVEN ability to accomplish any mission ultimately led to a most unwanted outcome.

I was summoned to the office of the head of the operations division, a man by the name of Hezi. Also in attendance were the division's intelligence officer and the head of its planning department. Hezi, a thin, grey-haired man with a five o'clock shadow, came straight to the point: a meeting is expected to take place in Hong Kong in three days' time between Muhammad Zaif, the head of the institute developing chemical weapons in Syria, and a senior official from the North Korean ministry of defence. We've been following their contacts for a number of years and at a certain stage you were also involved in that surveillance. They've signed multiple deals during this period but on the table now is a contract for the delivery of a chemical weapons production line. That is something we simply can't allow the Syrians to have. Both sides are so nervous that news of the deal will leak, they've even decided to halt the planned arrival of a high-level Syrian delegation to North Korea. Instead, the deal is to be closed in Hong Kong in such secrecy that the parties will arrive there under cover. As far as we are concerned, there's no way this contract can be signed and it's important for us that they know that we know what they're up to and that we are determined to stop it.

So the mission is to scare them? I asked.

It's more than that, was the immediate reply.

Burn their documents? I joked.

Utter silence in the room.

Hezi looked me straight in the eye: we've spent hours talking about possible plans of action. We've looked at a large number of options and the likely consequences of each one of them. We've decided that the head of the institute simply won't get to the meeting.

A kidnapping? I asked.

We've checked that out as well said Udi, head of the planning department, a big balding man with a combover. It's almost impossible to organize in three days, and we were only informed yesterday morning of the meeting in Hong Kong.

A red briefing document has been compiled on this man, the intelligence officer added. I knew that 'red' meant a recommendation to liquidate. Zaif is behind most of the non-conventional weapons development programs in Syria, the intelligence officer continued. There was a meeting yesterday of the heads of the intelligence agencies. They decided to recommend to the prime minister that Zaif be taken out.

Why are you telling me this? I asked, impulsively. I had spent four years gathering intelligence in the Far East, filling a role tailor-made for my humble skills in that field and covering a part of the globe for HQ which, though not central, was also not insignificant. As a result, I had become almost completely detached from the Mossad's other areas of activity. I found the prospect of my being involved in an assassination difficult to digest and distressing. What about the Kidon unit? I asked trying to break the silence in the room. They have people who deal with this kind of thing, don't they?

No one responded. That's according to foreign reports, of course, I added, trying to inject a little humour to lighten the mood in the room and relieve my own feelings of anxiety. The existence of Kidon has never been acknowledged by Israeli authorities.

You're our man in the Far East, the head of the division told me in all seriousness. You know the area, you've been there on numerous missions. We simply don't have the time to send Kidon to explore the area, formulate possible plans of action, and map out potential escape routes. You more than anyone else know how to blend in with the local population, how and exactly where to do the job, and how best to get out of there in one piece. We haven't yet understood the full significance of the recent return of Hong Kong to China; what it means in terms of border crossings, the police, keeping track of foreigners, and so on. For you it's a different story, you're at home there.

They're already waiting for you at the Kidon facility to start your training, said Udi . The course you took with us gave you a good foundation. Add a bit of polish to that and you'll be as skilled as any other Kidon operative. Anyway, you won't be on your own over there. I'll be flying out with you to approve the plan you decide to go with. The others in your regular team will be around, so you'll be well supported.

Everyone sensed how downcast I'd become from the moment this assignment was dumped on me.

We've looked at who'd be the most suitable person for this mission, Hezi said. We've considered every member of your team. You've all had the same basic training and each one of you is specialized in some field or other. None of you are professional assassins, but you seemed to us to be the most suitable and capable candidate. Take that as a big compliment.

I felt slightly less weighed down, but not much.

You know that the Mossad doesn't force its people to do anything they don't want to do. You want a few minutes to think it over?

Through the window of the division head's office, I looked out towards the sea for a moment. Hezi was sitting in his comfortable chair at the top of the long boardroom table with Udi and I facing each other to his right and left. They both had their eyes fixed on me. The Mossad doesn't force you to do anything. That much was true. But a refusal would be the end of my career. You won't be alone over there, I'd heard Udi saying. I'll be going with you. That offered me a degree of comfort. The powerfully built Udi had an attractive face and a gentle expression. He'd been seconded from a naval commando unit to help plan sea-based operations but had fitted so well into the division's command structure that he stayed on. Though he'd been involved in numerous operations that he both planned and took a part in, he was not an authorized operative. He didn't have a foreign passport and so was always on the fringes of an action. If he'd ever killed anyone it had been in his marine commando days. I didn't feel that his presence in the field would provide me with the right kind of support. At the moment of truth I'd be on my own.

I very nearly said 'no'. My career was not the issue here. On the other hand, if this was really the right solution, then why should someone else have to do it? I tried another way out: are you sure that threats, beatings, a fire, intimidation, not just of the Syrian but the North Koreans as well, won't produce the same result? Especially if we make it all public and engage in some psychological warfare afterwards.

I've told you we considered that, said Hezi quietly. Maybe the prime minister will go for such a plan rather than the one we are recommending. We haven't yet presented him with all the options, so it's possible that in the end that's what will happen. Even then, the intention is for you to be the leader. Before the decision is reached you'll have to be in the field and what we ultimately do will also be influenced by your and Udi's reports from there, he said nodding at Udi. The various weapons you'll need will already be in place when you arrive. In fact, they'll be on the move tonight.

OK, I said, still clinging to that one ray of hope – the influence my reports might have on the final decision.

Since my childhood and the books I read then, Hong Kong had been for me a place of adventure, daring buccaneers, voyages of discovery, and whores. Like the Cape of Good Hope and Gibraltar. I went there for the first time before Britain had come to terms with the new balance of power in the world and honoured the treaty it had signed with China a hundred years earlier. I was also there subsequently but hadn't noticed any real changes.

Coming in from the sea, Hong Kong Island appears as a steep green mountain, sloping all the way down to the water's edge. High rise residential blocs dot the mount's upper and middle levels, its base and shore crowded by row after row of modern skyscrapers – Hong Kong's very own Manhattan. The scene is particularly spectacular at night when the buildings are bathed in the light of dozens of colourful billboards promoting the world's major communication and high-tech companies. But the magic vanishes once you reach dry land. The way from the ferry to the harbour led me directly into the lower town's alleyways. Despite the height of the buildings, many of which are banks whose architecture I found disturbingly modern, the streets lining the length of the harbour area are extremely narrow and packed with shops selling every imaginable commodity. Pedestrians mostly make their way through this district on elevated walkways the like of which I haven't seen anywhere else in the world.

After the initial excitement of that first encounter, I came to think of Hong Kong during those visits as a mixture of Haifa, Manhattan with its own Chinatown and Tel Aviv's Carmel market.

This time, however, I landed at the new international airport and within minutes I was on the express train to the centre of Hong Kong. Udi, who was keeping an eye on my every movement, hurried along some paces behind me. We'd both arrived on a flight from Paris, while the three other members of the team flew in via Vienna and

Istanbul. Alighting at the station closest to the harbour we walked to a taxi stand controlled by a very bossy uniformed supervisor, and travelled separately to our respective hotels.

According to the latest intelligence reports, the North Korean delegation was due to stay at the Kowloon Sheraton, located on a beach on the mainland side of the narrow waterway: Kowloon had become a densely populated city of old high-rise apartment blocks resembling a huge bazaar. Udi went to check out the hotel. The Syrians had booked into the Garden View Park on the slope of the mountain near the botanical gardens. As soon as I had checked in to my own hotel, I went to have a look at theirs, a twenty-storey building with only a tiny lobby which made it impossible to sneak in without being spotted by the reception clerks.

Udi and I arranged to get together with the rest of the team in Lan Kwai Fong, a cluster of alleyways jammed with bars and small restaurants which attracted large numbers of young visitors to the city. I'd marked it out as a place where we could meet and, when the time came, as a possible initial exit point for me and the team.

We met up in a small quiet bar I knew where we could talk in a corner without shouting. I reported on my findings and the conclusion I had reached that we shouldn't attempt to deal with the Syrian in his hotel. Udi told us about the Sheraton. We knew that the meeting with the North Koreans could take place in any one of the city's hotels or restaurants, of which there were hundreds. Udi also informed us that a yacht hired to carry the weapons and explosives for the operation had already left Taiwan and was just one day away.

We'll have to work hard, Udi said, and tail them until our plan is firmed up. We would be far more effective, he suggested, if I were to move into the Garden View.

You realize that means I'll be burned after the operation, finished. But Udi stuck to his guns. I'll report the implications to HQ, he said. His expression was one of understanding, even affection, but it was clear to me that his concern was the operation's success, not my professional future.

I couldn't argue with the operational logic of Udi's proposal, and moved in to the Garden View the following day. A moment after being given my room's magnetic key, a transit van carrying the Syrian delegation drew up outside.

I went up to my floor and hung around for a few minutes, checking the landings on which the elevators were stopping. I was on the tenth floor, and the Syrians on the eighteenth and twentieth. My window faced the mountain and another apartment hotel, and I assumed that their rooms overlooked the harbour.

I arranged to rendezvous with my colleagues for our evening meeting at The Peak, a well-known tourist trap at the top of Mt Victoria, a place swamped by a mass of shops and restaurants from which the only diversion is the stunning sight of the lit up city at the foot of the mountain. After updating each other, Udi suggested that I ask to change rooms in the hope that I'd be able to be nearer to the Syrians.

On my return from The Peak, feigning excitement, I asked the receptionist for a room 'with a view like the one from The Peak'. She promised that such a room would become available the next day and that I could have it.

In the morning, while breakfasting in the hotel dining room, I was easily able to identify our man; a distinguished-looking individual, his hair streaked with grey and surrounded by young, brawny security men. As soon as they appeared, and before we'd made eye contact, I left the dining room by a side door.

The Syrians later left the hotel in their people carrier – closely followed by two of our men, Motti and Levanon – for what turned out to be a tour of the city's sites. Meanwhile, Micha, another team member, Udi and I, got together for a planning session.

A little research by us revealed that the Syrians had booked a block of rooms, and we needed to know which of them was Zaif's. As bait to get this information I used my fake Breitling watch that I'd bought for just a few dollars on one of my previous trips to Hong Kong.

We got a message from the surveillance team that the Syrians had ended their tour and were on their way back to the hotel. Meanwhile I'd been given my new room on the sixteenth floor, and there I waited. I was notified that the Syrian security men had gone to the hotel bar and Mr Zaif had entered the elevator. I watched it go up, and when I saw it stop on the twentieth floor, I called it down and took it to the lobby.

I found this watch in the elevator, I told the receptionist.

It probably belongs to the gentleman who went up a few minutes ago, she replied. Let me call the floor manager and ask. As I leaned forwards, placing my elbows on the reception desk, I overheard the floor manager confirming that the guest in 2012 had just entered his room.

I thanked the young woman for her help and left the hotel. On my return a few hours later, she calmly told me, 'Mr Zaif says it's not his watch.'

Bingo! The target's name and room number had been confirmed.

In the evening we analyzed the situation. As night fell, Udi, Levanon, and I were sitting at a table on the veranda of a restaurant on the Kowloon promenade, watching the lights come on across the straits in Hong Kong Island. Motti and Micha were keeping an eye on the entrances to the Garden View and the Sheraton hotels, with instructions to alert us if any member of either delegation was seen leaving.

Levanon, fascinated by the sun descending over the western approach to the bay and disappearing behind clouds of mist, drew our attention every now and then to the grand spectacle of Hong Kong's brightly illuminated signboards. The view itself was by then of little interest to me. But I did find myself looking at Levanon's handsome profile silhouetted against the background of the setting sun, and thinking how odd it was that because of the rules of our game I really knew nothing about my partner in this operation. Did he too have a wife back home? Perhaps even children? I could only guess his age, late twenties, the same as mine.

This is how I see our options, said Udi. Correct me if you think I'm wrong. And if you have any other ideas let me know. Option One: Attach a bomb to their vehicle in the hotel car park. Option two: Take the target out in his room, using a silencer. Three: Do it inside the hotel as he goes into or out of his room. Four: Aim to hit him when they are all inside the transit van or, five, shoot as they get out of the vehicle. Udi then proceeded to list the pros and cons of each option.

Any other suggestions?

Much to my regret I had to agree that getting it done in his room was the best plan. The downside was the locked door. On the other hand there would be no witnesses and no one else would get hurt. Break-ins were Levanon's specialty. He was sure to be able to deal with the security chain on the inside of the door provided I gave him a photo and the measurements of the chain on my own door. Levanon's evident composure had a calming effect on me. He was a quiet, easy-going operative who had quietly accumulated a great deal of operational experience and, with it, an impressive air of confidence that wasn't at odds with his modesty. And yet that voice inside me saying 'no' to liquidations refused to be silenced.

I told Udi that we now had to inform HQ that we had a good plan.

I'll send a message, he replied matter-of-factly. They're six hours behind us, so it's now 2 p.m. in Israel. The head of the Mossad and the division head are meeting with the PM at three, and I assume we'll get their OK for one or other plan in the course of the next few hours.

Hearing these words sent a shudder through me, a blend of excitement and alarm resembling the mix of expectation and fear that grips you before an exam. I was nervous about getting up from my chair in case I released the gasses that had suddenly accumulated in my stomach. Instead, I made do with a hiccup.

The equipment's arrived, Udi informed me as he read a message he'd received on his cell phone. Let's go to the marina. We should meet the people and have a look at what they've brought.

The skipper who'd hired the yacht, a bearded, tanned, well-built man with blue eyes, shook our hands firmly, a broad smile across his face. At long last we're going to do it then? he said, surprising me with his heavily French-accented Hebrew.

Udi had requested that I not ask the man any questions about his identity, and so I tamed my curiosity.

A short time later, as we sat below deck, Udi's phone rang.

The meeting with the PM has finished. We've been authorized to shoot the target in his room. The PM's insistent that nobody else be harmed. It's a go for tonight.

I could feel my stomach churning. Deep down inside me I had known all along that my 'ok' back then, in the division head's office, was really a 'maybe' and based on the hope that a different plan would be adopted. But there was no room now for 'maybes'. All hope of another plan had vanished. On the other hand, I consoled myself, planting a bomb in a vehicle was a far worse option. Shooting him in the van or in the street might also harm others and, in truth, beating him up was something I simply couldn't do. He was my father's age, and even looked a little like him.

So kill him?

Yes. If all those clever guys at HQ think that taking him out will prevent the Syrians from manufacturing lethal chemical weapons under North Korean auspices, then, yes, kill him.

Out came the pistol from its hiding place; a Glock 17 like the one I'd trained with for hours only a few days before.

Get going, Yogev, Udi said affectionately.

I picked up the oiled weapon, disassembled it, wiped the excess oil, cleaned the barrel with a pull-through brush, and reassembled it. I cocked and released the hammer a few times. The piston moved smoothly. I then cleaned the magazines, wiped the silencer, and attached it to the barrel.

I'll take just one magazine, I said. Should be enough bullets.

When it comes to shooting, you're the boss, Udi said, giving me a feeling I would rather not have had. I had no desire to be proud of what I was about to do or of my status.

The skipper offered me a number of options for concealing the weapon. I chose a simple, soft, black-leather shoulder bag with a zipped front pocket. That way I'd be able to put the pistol inside, sling it over my shoulder, and just slip my hand in and shoot through the leather. Udi and Levanon each took a small Beretta.

Once we'd finished dealing with the weapons, our host invited us up on deck for light refreshments. We sat on plastic armchairs and put the finishing touches to the plan: Udi and Motti would be in the car close to the hotel's entrance in case I ran into trouble and required rapid armed assistance to deal with the possible intervention of the Syrian's security personnel. Micah would be in the second car at the top of MacDonnell Road – the one-way street on which the hotel was located – ready to seal it off if a police car happened to come by. Of all of us, this likeable, portly, Humint expert, was best suited to keeping a bunch of cops distracted with his array of adventure stories. Levanon would come into the hotel with me pretending to be a friend who was booked onto a late flight and was spending time with me before he had to leave for the airport. I'd also tell the hotel people that my flight had been brought forward and I'd be checking out in the middle of the night.

Levanon was to be my number two in the operation, making sure the target's door was professionally unlocked and covering me from the doorway in case someone unexpectedly appeared on the scene.

The plan was to fire three bullets at Zaif's head. If everything went according to plan, we'd also search the room for documents. The hit was set for 2 a.m.

Now let's work on the getaway, Udi said, and we started planning our withdrawal. After arranging the details of the drive from the hotel and the return of the weapons, we all booked flights leaving Hong Kong between 4 and 7 a.m. If everything went smoothly, by the time Zaif's body was discovered we'd be in the air on our way home.

At this stage of the plan I suddenly felt icy calm and focused. There wasn't a trace of my earlier tense excitement. I was entirely ready for action. I recalled that I'd felt exactly the same before every big operation in the army. Anxiety, even fear, during the preparations, and the moment that everything was ready and we were about to set off – absolute peace of mind, alertness, and focus.

The team dispersed to check out of their hotels. I entered mine with Levanon who had a small suitcase with him. In the event, the explanation we had prepared wasn't needed. The reception clerk looked up from her computer, welcomed me with a nod, and resumed her work. Half an hour later when I called to say I'd be checking out that night, she asked no questions.

At about midnight Levanon and I finished cleaning my room: we assembled anything I might have touched, washed the glasses clean of possible fingerprints, scrubbed the sink and bath tub so that not even a strand of hair was left, wiped the taps, and stuffed the towels I'd used earlier in the day along with the pillowcase – which certainly bore traces of my DNA – into my bag.

And we're surprised when they say that Israelis steal towels, Levanon smiled. I wasn't in the mood for jokes, but was glad that this amiable, cool-headed, and pleasant looking guy, was at my side. We practised on my door chain with the device he'd brought – a seemingly humble pair of scissors, that were, in fact, a highly effective pair of forged steel wire cutters.

The two hours now left to us until 2 a.m. were probably the longest of my life, longer than any two hours lying in ambush in Lebanon or being on night watch in some Far Eastern country.

Just before 2 a.m., Levanon and I again went over our every planned move from the moment we left my room until we were back in it, had picked up our stuff and were on our way downstairs where Udi was due to take back command of the operation. We again tested our communications system – Udi, Levanon, and I had our cell phones open in conference call mode – once more inspected our weapons, and left the room.

To avoid the elevators suddenly moving up and down in the middle of the night, especially from my floor to the target's, I decided we'd use the internal emergency staircase. By the time we'd climbed the four floors, I was breathless. It took a moment or so for me to recover, then I signalled to Levanon, and the two of us moved silently towards room 2012.

As we trod cautiously along the carpeted hallway, the floorboards creaked a bit, making me think that the noise might wake up the sleeping security men. I decided to stay put for thirty seconds or so outside the target's door. But all was quiet in the hallway and Levanon urged me on.

While he was busy picking the lock, I kept a watchful eye on both ends of the corridor and had my hand firmly gripping the butt of the pistol concealed in the shoulder bag. A few seconds later the door opened with just the slightest press of the handle. There was a light on in the bathroom and the security chain was clearly visible. A faint click could be heard as Levanon applied the wire cutters to snap the chain. Then, with a gracious gesture of the hand, he ushered me in. If our activity had woken Zaif, now was the time for him to spray us with bullets, call his security people, or try to escape. But there was complete silence.

I edged further in. Levanon, one hand on the Beretta in his jacket pocket, lingered by the door keeping watch on the hallway. I tiptoed past the bathroom, illuminated briefly by the light, and then into the room itself. There was a slight movement from the bed that momentarily immobilized me. Zaif rolled over. The light from the bathroom made it easy to identify him. And there was no need to fire from the shoulder bag. I took out the pistol, stood by the side of the bed, placed the muzzle close to the nape of his neck and turned my head away as I fired.

Even though the silencer was particularly big, the shot sounded like a handclap, startling me. Almost without aiming, I immediately fired the second shot and left quickly with the gun in my hand, convinced that Zaif's security men were about to rush in.

Levanon looked surprised when I appeared with the gun still in my hand, but didn't say a word. He signalled me to wait, went into the room, from where the dull sound of another shot was heard. He emerged a moment later with Zaif's file of documents. We pressed the interior lock button, closed the door, and walked quickly towards the stairwell, our guns still drawn in case any security people appeared. I was punch drunk, operating like an automaton, not thinking, not feeling. The almost total darkness of Zaif's room had also saved me from seeing things better not seen. It was Levanon who'd kept to the original plan; three shots to the head and the documents file which turned out to be a very big catch indeed.

When we reached the sixteenth floor I put the pistol back into the bag. The hallway was empty. We went into my room, I washed my face and Levanon told me to pack the hand towel as well, an instruction that produced a little smile. Then he asked me gently if I had purposely not fired the third bullet. He was still alive when I went in, he told me.

The job would have been accomplished even with just one bullet seriously wounding him, I countered. I put on my jacket and we went down to reception. My bill was ready and moments later we were in the waiting car.

I flinched slightly when Udi patted me on the shoulder. His hand was warm, big, and heavy, and its touch pleasant. But Udi knew how I felt and didn't say a word. I was disoriented, filled with raw emotions. There was no longer a sense of suspense or fear; no feeling either of release or relief; no satisfaction from a mission accomplished nor remorse for having blasted the man's head open. For the most part the drop in adrenalin simply left me feeling very tired and I allowed myself to close my eyes. Fortunately, command was now back in Udi's trustworthy hands.

Udi drove, and Motti collected the pistols from Levanon and me. He was to return the weapons to the skipper. We dropped Levanon off at a taxi stand, from where he was to make his own way to the airport. I watched this tall man, who'd just saved the mission, walk calmly away into the distance wheeling his suitcase.

I got out of the car at the station in order to catch the express train to the airport. The doors of the silver train were wide open. This early in the morning there were only a few passengers and I was worried that the train's departure might be delayed. But right on time the doors closed and the train slid out of the station.

Once on the plane I counted the minutes. Only when I'd seen Levanon enter the cabin, exchanging smiles with an attractive stewardess, did I accept we were out of danger.

Lots of things could have gone wrong with the operation, but in the end nothing had. The hotel receptionists hadn't suspected anything, none of the security people had woken up, no hotel guest had surprised us by returning late from a party, and the target had behaved impeccably. My shortcomings in execution were put right by Levanon. The yacht sailed at dawn, and at 7 a.m. Udi, the last of us to leave the island, said goodbye to Hong Kong.

9

I HADN'T THOUGHT about Orit before the mission, during it, or while we made our getaway. But I did think about her throughout the long journey home. I certainly had plenty of time; ten hours from Hong Kong to Istanbul; there I had a brief meeting with people from HQ, an initial debriefing, and swapped equipment; finally I had another two hours or so for reflection before landing in Israel. After coming to terms with my doubts about the mission and its results, and successfully convincing myself that what I'd just done was no different to killing a terrorist in Lebanon or Gaza, I now had to deal with Orit's obstinacy. I remembered only too well her unequivocal opposition to assassinations and her crystal clear warning that I must never lie to her.

The pretence, the cover stories, and the lies about my identity and actions, became an inseparable part of my daily life abroad. But these stratagems continued to make me uncomfortable and even remorseful towards anyone who accepted my story at face value. In this sense, I differed from my colleagues who were proud of their ability to deceive, trick and frame either the target himself or simply anyone who might possibly get in their way or could assist in accomplishing the mission.

What really preoccupied me was the same rather naïve question I had grappled with in my days in the youth movement, a decade and a half earlier; is not telling the same as lying? I didn't think I could lie if Orit asked a direct question. But not saying anything was a little different... Despite the previous sleepless night, the fatigue that had overwhelmed me right after the operation, my numbed feelings and my usual ability to doze off on planes, this time I simply couldn't sleep.

Eventually, I made a decision that was perhaps reasonable but also fairly cowardly. If Orit asked I would tell her. If not, I wouldn't say anything. It was a decision that, years later, would blow up in my face.

When I finally got home Orit was in the midst of calculating the exact date of her next ovulation. Because, by sheer good fortune, I'd retuned this time at the right moment, she was much too busy planning our mating schedule to ask what I'd been up to abroad. I wasn't surprised. How many times can any normal woman ask about another break-in, another photograph, another surveillance in which her husband and his companions had played a part in the Far East? During the long hours we spent in bed before and during her ovulation, I had difficulty suppressing my thoughts about the operation and felt constantly very uneasy. When we made love at night, I preferred to fall asleep immediately afterwards. But after having sex in the morning I couldn't sleep. That was when Orit started to question me.

Tell me, she said a few minutes after we'd finished, her head on my shoulder and my fingers lightly stroking her back. Where did you say you were on this trip?

I tensed up. Here it comes, dammit.

Bangkok, Hong Kong, and Istanbul, I replied, giving

equal importance to the scene of the operation and the two airports where I'd changed planes. I waited anxiously for her next query. Had she seen something in the paper? Was she going to ask me a direct question that would throw us both into an uncontrollable tailspin?

So let's say it was Bangkok or Hong Kong. There are probably a lot of bars there, and massage parlours, and escort girls and all that, no?

I almost breathed a sigh of relief. But relief was soon replaced by a strong urge to tell Orit what I'd been through. To share with her the difficulties I'd faced, my inner moral struggle – and yes, to tell her also about the operation's success.

Haven't you got anything to tell me about it? A hint of concern stole into Orit's voice, and I suddenly realized how close I was to jumping into the whirlpool that was only one sentence away.

There are, if you're looking for that kind of thing, I said, and assured her that I wouldn't even think of going to a whore.

What an absurd situation, I thought, when such a highly-charged subject could seem so marginal to me. What a twisted relationship had developed between us. And what a shame that such an important event in my life had to remain beyond the boundaries of our marriage. By its very absence that event had become a void, a discord between us.

I consoled myself with the fact that it was a one-off, that with time the memory would fade. I tried to be content with the thought that I didn't have to explain my actions to Orit and get into a confrontation with her. As the days went by and she didn't ask any more about what I'd done on that trip, the pain of concealment dulled and eventually turned into shadowy fragments, buried remnants of a feeling that only a mighty storm could raise to the surface.

My reception at HQ, somewhat different to the greeting I got in bed, was spontaneous, warm, and noisy. In the Mossad they don't drink a toast to celebrate a successful liquidation but the debriefing began with a sort of sociable ceremony. Hezi and Udi both made speeches praising me. For my part, I paid tribute to Udi and, in the days that followed, practically everyone in the division, including those I barely knew, shook my hand in appreciation. Other divisions of the Mossad were not supposed to know the identity of the hit man, but I did clearly see people looking at me in the corridors and in the canteen and heard their whispers of approval. Though I didn't openly respond to these snippets of praise, deep inside me there was a wide smile. In the debriefings I gave full credit to Levanon for having got hold of the documents. But as the 'number one' the operation had my name stamped on it.

Once Muhammad Zaif's body was found, the Syrian delegation fled the hotel. Their hurried departure had the local authorities assuming that they were responsible for the killing. Two of them were arrested for possessing unlawful weapons – an incident that cast a dark shadow over relations between China and Syria. When the North Korean delegation was informed that its senior Syrian partner had been murdered, they swiftly left Hong Kong and North Korea suspended any further contact pending a thorough investigation of the affair.

Even though Zaif was a well-known figure, the Syrians managed to conceal his identity from the media as well as from the Island's authorities for two whole days. However, the arrested security men didn't remain silent for long. This, plus our carefully measured and planned leaks, gradually revealed more and more details that helped both the local administration and the media to complete the picture. In the week after the liquidation there were a number of unsensational headlines suggesting that the hit was linked to a deal for the supply of North Korean non-conventional weaponry to Syria.

The delay in publishing the identity of the deceased or the nature of the spiked deal, and the belated responses accusing the Mossad of the murder, meant that Orit – if, in fact, she paid any attention at all to these stories – didn't in any way link them to my trip abroad.

Later on, I was invited to a meeting at which an officer from military intelligence's technical department talked about the operation's outcome. The Syrian institute for weapons development had been practically crippled since, as he put it, the 'the top guy had died of unnatural causes'. All the employees of the institute were undergoing checks in an attempt to identify the leaker; all trips abroad had been suspended and, because Zaif headed a number of the institute's key projects, activity there was at a standstill and the transfer of the production line from North Korea had also been halted.

The man from military intelligence added that the file of documents we had brought back was priceless and that we now had a clear understanding of the Syrian chemical weapons program. That would make it much easier for us to monitor future developments. I asked that a note be made expressing special thanks to Levanon who was not present at the meeting.

Hezi went on to say that it had been a very long time since such a fast and clean attack with no traceable leads had been carried out, and delivered such significant results. His comments settled the remaining doubts I harboured deep inside me about the operation itself. As we left, Hezi put his arm around me and said, you see, when we decide to use force like this we are not always fools or maniacs. A lot of thought went into this, a complex analysis of possible outcomes, gains versus risks. The operative may assume that those above him did their work properly. Ideally, everyone should focus on doing their very best with the task they are given.

I understood that this was his way of summarizing his discontent with the reservations I had had. Anyway, I noticed that my standing within the division had changed. My silence – merely an outcome of my numbed feelings – was interpreted by Udi and the other members of the team as evidence of my self control. As for my superiors, their conclusion was that in me they had found a natural 'operator', the man who pulls the trigger. They rarely sent me to the East on non-essential missions and I began specializing in the areas of expertise required of an 'assassin'; firing a pistol, fast draw and instinctive shooting, firing a sniper's rifle, shooting while on the move. I learned to ride a motorbike, and operational driving. I had training in the use of explosives and in break-in techniques. Though I still went abroad quite often, anything that kept me in the country was seen by both Orit and me as a plus. It turned out that even 'essential' missions were almost a monthly event.

There were those in the division who thought I wasn't suited to this new role. The head of training, who was at my side throughout the course, said that I didn't have the 'killer instinct'; that I operated through understanding and recognition, rather than from a gut feeling. Hezi, on the other hand, thought I was OK; he wasn't looking for 'natural born killers'. My senior trainer had his own analogy: If you were picking a football team, you wouldn't pick him as a striker, he said. You'd make him a defender or a midfielder; that's his natural position.

The division's psychologist was asked for his opinion on my suitability for the role. Ilan, a pleasant man, was apologetic. It's not that there's something wrong with you, he said. It's just that an 'operator' is exposed to things that are likely to make him a bit of a schizophrenic. So I need to get to know you better and understand more about what happened to you in Hong Kong and afterwards.

Weren't all the interviews and exams before the course – sentence completion, arithmetic progressions, psychometric exams, and Rorschach tests – enough? I asked, fatigued more than resentful. No, not for this kind of role, he answered, and went on to ask me a series of pointed, though gently formulated, questions.

It's true that I did what I did without being totally committed and only because I understood how damaging it could be to the country if I didn't act, was my response to the most difficult of the queries. On the other hand my doubts didn't prevent me from carrying out the mission to the best of my ability.

Was not the fact that you recoiled at firing the third shot somehow linked to your general reservations about the action? he asked.

I gave it some thought. I don't think so, I finally said. The third shot seemed superfluous to me because there was a big bang and the security men could have come in at any moment. I wanted to get out of there quickly before success turned to failure. That's why I also forgot to get the file of documents.

That only goes to show that you are normal, Ilan said. Do you have flashbacks of the incident or dream about it, he asked. Perhaps of the victim's cracked skull after he was shot, or of a muzzle flash in the darkness of the room? No, I told him, I don't have dreams about the operation, or any trouble sleeping. So what visions do you have, he asked. I told him that mostly I saw images of Orit and me having sex.

Ilan laughed, and said that my priorities were really OK. I explained my difficulties in not telling Orit, told him about the feelings of deception that were disturbing me in my relationship with her.

Does this feeling bother you more that the fact that you killed somebody? Ilan asked, giving me the impression that his curiosity was more personal than professional.

Yes, I replied. He was an enemy. An enemy whose ultimate purpose was to kill. She is my wife. But don't get me wrong. Don't think, not even for a moment, that I don't understand that from an ethical point of view what I did was immoral, bad, inhuman, call it what you want. I know that at least as much as anybody else does. But I don't relate to this act as being moral or immoral but as an act of survival, and such an act is not judged according to its morality. The little lie to Orit, however, is.

Ilan listened intently, with even the hint of a smile. Then he asked if I was capable of saying out loud that I was a Mossad assassin and stand by what I'd said. My answer was negative. I maintain the right to decide whether or not to carry out an operation depending on how critical it happens to be, I replied after thinking it over. And that prevents me from defining myself that way. But I can say out loud that I have killed while in the service of the Mossad or state.

Our unproductive attempts at conceiving led to a series of tests. My sperm was pronounced OK, Orit's ovulation was found to be regular and all her other tests also proved OK. There was no apparent reason for our lack of success.

Orit pinned the reason on our way of life – which was another way of saying, my trips abroad. Given that for a few years already I had been away from home at least once a month, it could very well be that we were apart on the days when conception was a possibility. The tension that she felt while I was travelling also didn't help.

I believed that things would happen when they were

meant to happen. But Orit didn't want to wait for the natural outcome. In addition to ultrasound tests, she also had a hyperoscopy of her womb, which turned out to be especially painful, and again nothing untoward was found. There was no blockage of the fallopian tubes nor was there any problem with the thickness of the lining of the womb.

We have to pay more attention to finding out when I am fertile, Orit said, and began using ovulation test kits. A positive meant that we had twenty-four hours to fertilize the egg before it died. I would get a phone call in the office and, to the extent possible, cancel scheduled meetings or training sessions for the rest of the day. I would then hurry home for sex that was purposeful, at times even fiery, depending on what it was that I had cancelled. If I happened to be abroad on such days I would get angry with the work I'd chosen, with the geographical area I'd picked – too far to dash back home for a day – and angry with HQ for defining practically every mission as 'vital'.

And sometimes, when the mission really was imperative and linked to preventing Iran, Lebanon, or Syria from being armed with non–conventional weapons, or preventing a terrorist attack – I would get angry with her frustration, then with her, then with myself and finally angry again with the work I was doing.

I explained the situation to my CO and got permission to fly home when the chances of her becoming pregnant were high. But from the Far East it took me at least twenty-four hours to book a flight, get to the nearest international airport and fly home, by which time it was already too late.

In order to give me adequate notice, Orit had extra

ultrasound tests every month that projected the development of her ovarian cells so we knew the timing of the next ovulation. This way, I managed on a number of occasions over the next year to arrive in Israel on time. But still there was no pregnancy.

Come in, I'm ready and waiting, was Orit's standard greeting at the entrance to our house. The loving glint of blue was not visible in her eyes, nor could I see that guarded smile on her lips. We didn't kiss or play with each other's tongues. Orit undressed and expected me to undress myself. Then she lay on her back in a provocative position but dispensed with pleasuring 'Magic' or me.

She groaned, yet that deep 'Oi' of hers was no longer really audible and I suspected that her moans were intended only to speed up my coming into her. When I rose slightly and left her the space to pleasure 'Magic' by herself, she dispensed with that too, wrapped her long legs around me and after I'd come wouldn't let me move as she fought for every drop of sperm that might otherwise seep out. The quivering and contractions that could have helped take it all in, simply didn't happen.

Only then, when she was sure that her 'work' was done, did she let go and allow her body to unwind. And only then, as long as she wasn't too angry or too tensed up, did she agree to stay in my arms, and let me stroke her back as she nestled her head between my shoulders. I no longer asked her to open her eyes just a little to see that extraordinary blue, nor did I expect her to show an interest in the place I'd been to. I knew she was busy planning the next act of procreation. That's what it was all about, love wasn't really any longer part of the picture.

There was one occasion when I couldn't get back and that was to be my second kill, this time in Seoul. The target was a Hezbollah activist planning a suicide bombing against the Israeli embassy in South Korea. I was angry with myself and the situation. According to Levanon the target was also the object of my fury. At my request, Levanon was, once more, my number two.

This time I had fewer personal qualms about the target. The man, Rashid Nuri, had already planned a series of terror attacks against the IDF in Lebanon and against Jewish institutions all over the world. Some of them materialized and resulted in quite a few victims. In Thailand, the truck bomb he'd organized didn't reach the embassy only because, miraculously, it got involved in a traffic accident.

Through an agent in the West Bank, intelligence was able to identify Nuri's phone number but we needed Micha's skills to locate it. The Koreans are a friendly people and wanted to help. The baby-faced Micha went into the first post office he saw and was told that all numbers beginning with 925 were in one area in the southern part of the city. At the second post office he entered in that area of town, he told them he had arranged to meet a friend on the corner of the street he lived in but had forgotten its name and that the friend had already left the house. The post office gave him the name of the street matching the phone number.

Immediately afterwards when 'the friend was obviously already on his way home', Micha also got the house number 'even though strictly speaking we are not allowed to pass on such information'.

It was an old, dilapidated neighbourhood, very different from Seoul's glitteringly modern downtown area. Nuri wasn't the only Arab at the address. From a parked car, we photographed everyone leaving the building and sent the photos to Israel; our agents who had infiltrated Hezbollah were then activated and we got a positive identification on one of the individuals, a bearded balding man in his forties. After twenty-four hours of trailing him, it transpired that Nuri spent all his days in a Mosque except for lunch. To eat, he left the Mosque accompanied by a group of friends who looked very much like him. In the evening, as darkness fell, he slipped out of the Mosque and, alone, made his way to the red light district of Seoul, an area of dingy alleyways in the old part of the city where the only illumination came from the lanterns above the entrances to the brothels. Getting away from there was easy; within just a few minutes you could disappear into the town's centre or get onto the highway leading to the airport.

At this stage, the plan of action was clear. It so happened that this was also the day on which Orit got in touch to tell me that she would apparently be ovulating within a day or two. Even without getting in touch with HQ it was obvious to me that I couldn't possibly leave before the mission was completed. According to the intelligence we'd received, the job of getting the truck bomb ready was almost done and it could be on its way any day now.

I knew that if I was to consult Udi, the calm and fatherly head of the planning division was likely to release me. Levanon could carry out the mission without me and in a place as isolated as this, any member of the team could be the number two. In fact, this option, which I rejected, filled me with a huge sense of frustration. You don't leave an operation at this stage, that's clear. But neither do you leave your wife at a time like this. More than feeling like Nuri's executioner, I felt I was my own judge and jury.

Cursing, I booked a flight for the following morning in the hope that by then we would have completed the mission. But Nuri didn't leave the Mosque that evening.

I postponed the flight for a day. Orit told me she was ovulating and that as far as she was concerned if I didn't get there in the next twenty-four hours I could stay where I was for another month. I swore at whoever I could, mainly at myself, and, of course, stayed put. In my eyes, this decision was no different from the decision to shift the ambush on that last night of reserve duty in Lebanon. And there was as much pain attached to it as there was lying for forty-eight hours on top of thorny shrubs on a rocky ledge. There are pains that you have to grin and bear.

The following night, Nuri made it easy for us. He set off for the red light district with two friends but parted from them on the way and went to the prostitute we'd seen him with on the first evening. We positioned ourselves around her small den of iniquity and planned our precise exit route as well as our responses to potential incidents.

We had two vehicles at our disposal to be used to block any car chase after us, and a motorbike to make our getaway. Levanon and I sat in Motti's car about ten metres from the entrance to the apartment of Nuri's favourite whore. Yoni, a skilled biker who had joined the team recently, waited for me in a nearby alleyway.

As soon as Nuri was spotted leaving, I got out of the car and walked towards him. Levanon was a few steps behind me. From his car, parked on the street corner, Udi could see the entire area of the operation. He signalled to us that we could go ahead and added an unplanned movement of the hand that told us, calmly, guys, there's time.

Nuri, it seems, heard our footsteps, glanced back once in our direction, turned round and continued walking away. In line with the night drill, I fired three shots into his back. He fell to the ground like a doll whose strings had been detached. I went close up to fire the two additional bullets at his nape, but, as I looked down at the crumpled figure at my feet and wondered whether it wasn't enough for him to be immobilized and dying, I heard two shots being fired from right next to me. Once again Levanon had completed the job.

In the open air, the sound of the shots was fuzzier than it had been in the hotel room. I got onto the bike and Yoni sped away. Levanon returned to the car in measured steps, Motti turned on the engine and they were off. Udi brought up the rear of the convoy, driving slowly and preventing any possibility of us being chased as we drove through the narrow, dark alleys.

During the flight to Zurich I went to sit with Levanon who, once more, looked as if he had just signed a million-dollar contract; animated, smiling, lightheartedly flirting with the stewardess. Afterwards he told me that when I'd fired the first round I looked at the fallen man and blurted 'stinking Arab'. He'd assumed that this closed my account with the target and intervened.

I was surprised. I didn't remember saying such a thing and indeed have nothing against Arabs. Against an Arab terrorist – yes, of course. But the same goes for a terrorist of any other nationality. I realized that my frustration at not having been able to get home in time was greater than I had thought.

For his part, Levanon began to believe that I was not capable of killing somebody in cold blood. Not when the dying man is lying helplessly in front of me. I didn't think he was right, at least not yet.

The telephone call made by the people from the psychological warfare department the moment that Udi reported back to HQ on the mission, had the local police scurrying to the scene with information that 'the Arabs who shot their friend' are hiding in the apartment of some other whores in the area. The efficient Seoul police immediately closed off the district, and two of Nuri's partners were arrested together with some other innocent Arabs looking for sexual relief among the city's less pious women.

Further phone calls that linked the murder to struggles within the terror group sent the police to the Mosque, where the truck bomb was found in a small garage in the basement. With the truck's seizure almost everybody involved in the terrorist attack was arrested.

When I got home again I found Orit angry. Once more she didn't ask me anything about my activities abroad. She didn't even ask where I'd been, and I didn't volunteer the information. The first reports of a Lebanese who'd been found dead at the entrance to a brothel in Seoul didn't attract any attention despite the assessment of informed journalists that the man was a Hezbollah activist. Very surprisingly, reports of the discovery of a car bomb in a Mosque didn't make the headlines. The Korean authorities had their own reasons for playing down the matter and in Israel nobody wanted to be 'too well informed' so as to avoid divulging our involvement.

Nonetheless, I wondered whether Orit didn't know or simply didn't want to know. Didn't want to know anything about my activities, or didn't want to know that I'd been in a place where, as she saw it, we had committed a murder. I knew that my silence was costing us dearly. I could feel the distance I was creating between us because of my fear that intimacy might lure me into saying something. But this transparent and malleable 'glass' barrier I had erected between us, turned into a hermetically sealed double glazed booth when Orit also shut herself off, avoiding all intimacy in case it uncovered the things she didn't want to know about.

10

WE BOTH TURNED thirty. For me the round number was nothing more than a clichéd excuse for soul searching. All in all I was content with where I was in my life albeit not so at ease about the direction in which I was heading. I knew that I was doing important work, but I was well aware of the price I was paying and there was no sign of things improving. I'd never been a careerist and my operational successes didn't seem to me to be a launching pad for promotion to head of a department.

But for Orit the date was a moment of crisis. She was an introverted woman who controlled her emotions in the same way as she controlled her still supple and youthful body. Only her womb refused to be controlled and her worries kept on multiplying.

One evening, after celebrating her birthday in a restaurant on the way to Eilat with both sets of worried parents, we were again sitting in our Jerusalem apartment. On the big computer screen in the sitting room were drawings of a new house that she had planned. Orit used to bring work home to fill her evenings of solitude and went on doing this even when I was there.

It cannot go on like this. We'll have to do something more drastic about it, Orit said.

We hardly ever quarrelled. Even our most sensitive conversations were held without raised voices, without drama, without tears. But lately, an element of estrangement and pain had crept in. This time we were snuggled up on the sofa about to watch a movie. Some kind of unconscious suicidal urge had driven me to bring home a library copy of the movie *Crying Freeman* about an assassin who sheds tears of regret each time he kills.

Thirty is not a critical age, she agreed with me. But if this goes on, we'll have a problem when it comes to our second child. We know it's not clear where the problem lies. The tests on both of us were fine, but time won't be on my side for long, one day there will be the question of my age. We can give it more time, even as much as a year or two, but if I still haven't become pregnant by then, we'll have to think about artificial insemination.

I turned off the TV and hugged her. My Orit. We'd been together since we were fifteen, half our lives. I knew this woman inside out, as she knew me. We wanted each other, we wanted to live together for the rest of our lives and now a maddening and mysterious stumbling block was denying us from getting what virtually every couple in the world takes for granted.

The words 'it's not clear where the problem lies' suddenly hit home. Is it conceivable that in addition to my absences and Orit's anxiety, the lie I harboured was preventing me from surrendering myself to our love? Could it be that the body has some concealed mechanism that says, from this mating, under these circumstances, nothing good will come?

I pushed the thought out of my mind. It didn't suit a rational man like me.

And if I was always to be here, with you, before,

during, and after the ovulation? I asked. Always, always, here when you need me?

Orit's blue eyes peered at me in the dim light.

Your good intentions are sweet, she said, but you are a prisoner of the work you do. Of the state, of the Mossad. Not of mine.

How much better than I was this wise but woeful woman who was able to read me and the world.

She turned her head away and curled herself around me, covering her body more fully with the quilt that wrapped us both. When I stroked her cheeks they were wet and my eyes misted up. What was I doing to this woman who I so loved? It was I who took control over her life when she first came to the Arava, and now, instead of being her protector, I've become the one who is stifling her happiness. She doesn't ask for much. Not even of me. All she wants is what practically every woman wants.

I was no longer willing to risk our love on account of a job that in any case I was doing as if in a trance.

That's how it will be Or, I said. They'll agree to this. And if not, I'll take a job at HQ. I've already been globetrotting for five years. They can't go on insisting I do this work against my will. They've already met some of my demands, now they'll go that extra mile.

Orit's moist eyes expressed a mix of disbelief and hope. I owe her this, owe it to both of us, and owe it to myself. You can't save the homeland at the expense of your home.

*

As soon as I asked his bureau chief for a personal meeting, Hezi agreed to see me. He listened intently to things he already knew and then said: I'm one hundred per cent behind you. We have to find a way for you to be with Orit whenever she needs you. I can't imagine what you are going through and all I can do is refer you to the contacts we have in the hospitals. They will do everything for you. To ensure that you are with Orit whenever necessary, there are two options. One is for you to be posted abroad. I don't want to transfer you to the Tevel Division, which co-operates with foreign intelligence services, and expose you to them. But I can visualize a situation in which you settle in a particular part of the world, with Orit of course, and use this base as a springboard for activity in the area. From my point of view, and for many reasons, the preferred place would be Beijing. China is beginning to open up for us and you, as a Chinese speaker, are naturally the most suitable person for the job.

I took a deep breath. That wasn't what I was after. And, of course, to say that I could speak Chinese was an exaggeration. My division head understood what the deep intake of air meant, and carried on: the second option is for you to become Kidon's permanent number one. For all sorts of reasons you were the one who carried out the two latest Mossad liquidations. The squad's mythological number one has retired and not one of the up and coming youngsters seems to us to be good enough to replace him. As I'm sure you know, there are things that you too need to improve on, but we think that you possess the requisite qualities.

It was clear that Levanon had said nothing.

I didn't see myself as Kidon's 'operator' and didn't want to take on the role. The two liquidations I had participated in accounted for only a tiny fraction of all the operations in which I had taken part, dozens every year. I couldn't deny their importance or their efficacy, but I felt that this simply wasn't me. Even to lie and frame wasn't me. So to kill? And to do that as my avowed and principal pursuit? Certainly not. I wasn't blind to the 'changed priorities' in the work I did and the time devoted to firearms training and other drills connected to liquidations. But this was only for the purpose of an emergency in my territory, the Far East. That was entirely different from being 'Kidon's number one'.

Up till now Orit had no real reason to think that I had been involved in activities that were quite unlike the dozens of operations I did tell her about; breaking into an Arab diplomat's vehicle in Bangkok and stealing a file of documents; puncturing the tyres of a car from which a Malaysian intelligence agent had been observing us and so preventing him from tailing us as we went after an Al-Qaida cell; or slipping a sleeping pill into the beer of a Chinese scientist in a hotel bar, allowing us to work quietly in his room. These were nice and fairly innocent stories. She was less happy to hear the tale about fitting up cameras in the hotel room of a target, filming him as he undressed and got into bed, and then filming a female agent of ours in an identical room, enabling us to make a composite of the pictures, present the target with the photomontage and quickly get him to cooperate. She wasn't happy but accepted it. And I could tell that this was more or less as far as she was willing to go. She wouldn't listen to an explanation of a necessary one-off killing that saved the homeland and certainly wouldn't stomach two such operations. As for it being my 'vocation' there was simply no point in talking to her about that.

What about a job in Israel? I asked.

A desk job? That would be a shame both for you and for us, Hezi answered. You are not built for it and you have qualities that we are not prepared to lose.

What about training? Recruitment? There are, after all, other jobs at HQ.

A shame for you and for us, Hezi repeated.

So I have to accept this as a 'no'?

Things are not always black and white. But as you know every decision has its price, Hezi replied. From his gesturing I understood the meeting was over. The ball was in my court.

Orit surprised me: I don't mind giving Beijing a try. I didn't tell you but I'm also trying acupuncture and medicinal herbs and perhaps that's better done in their country of origin.

And you didn't tell me? I blurted out and then shut my mouth. Who was I to complain about her concealing things from me? Orit noticed that something had been left unsaid. I didn't think that you would believe in or support such things, she said. Did you know that according to Western research traditional Chinese medicine has a high success rate? And besides, a change of place, a change of luck.

The sparkle that I hadn't seen for a very long time stole into the blue rims of her eyes. And when she hugged and kissed me while we were still standing at the entrance to the house, images and feelings flooded into my mind taking me back a good few years to her soldier's lodgings and our student apartment and to the love that had been so charged with undefined but tangible and absolute optimism.

Her optimism overwhelmed me. Who knows, she could be right.

11

OUR STAY IN Beijing began well but ended badly and earlier than planned. This is not what I expected, Orit said as we left the airport north east of the city and drove to our hotel in its centre. We travelled on a wide and straight highway, four lanes in each direction, which cut diagonally across the urban expanse to the first of the ring roads that circled the city's mid-town area. To our right and left, box-shaped multi-storeyed residential structures soared above us, a gilded or red ideogram at the top of each the only sign that we were in China. The huge cluster of skyscrapers was matched by the number of giant tower cranes raising the skeletal frames of new constructions ever higher on every possible vacant plot. I'd already got to know the place from previous visits but for Orit the sight was perplexing, even a disappointment.

When we got off the highway and on to the ring road

that took us closer to the centre, the two- to four-storey buildings of the China Orit had imagined came into view. Restaurants identified by red paper lanterns, small grocery stores, and food stalls, were on the ground floor. Above them all a display of Chinese ideograms.

We decided to stay at the Hotel Beijing which was less modern and also less expensive than the St Regis and other centrally located hotels. I suggested going up to the top of the building to see the layered roofs of the Forbidden City and, to the west of the hotel, the giant Tiananmen Square and the magnificent structures around it. But Orit was eager to explore the narrow streets and alleyways, known locally as hutongs, described in the novels about China she read so voraciously in the months after we decided to come here. At the rate of a few thousand a year, these alleyways were disappearing and being replaced by huge modern buildings.

Not far from the hotel we found a neighbourhood of hutongs bordered on each side by high stone walls with an assortment of oddly angled gates every few dozen metres or so. In the past, these gates were the entrance to a single family home built around an inner courtyard. But the Communist regime confiscated these houses and squeezed in more and more people. Every such gate now had the names of five or six families attached to it, each one occupying a different side of the courtyard while others lived in makeshift buildings in the middle of the yard.

We strolled through the hutongs, each of us registering a somewhat different impression. Orit enjoyed the exotic sights whereas I complained about their gloomy drabness:

she was amazed by how content the residents seemed to be despite having so little, while I drew attention to the poverty the regime had forced on them. The houses didn't even have a drainage system and every few hundred metres we came across public toilets for the use of the hutong residents.

Years of lookout duties, including those on icy cold nights, trained me to hold in the urge to pee. But when my bladder could take it no more I rushed into one of these public buildings and then fled as quickly as I could, breathless from the overwhelming stench, embarrassed by the sight of bare bottoms in the open cubicles around me. Fortunately for Orit, as was true of most women I knew, she was more skillful at controlling this particular impulse and managed to keep going till we returned to the hotel.

She wanted to eat at a local restaurant and so, much to my regret, I had to give up on the promising-looking hotel eatery and stroll back with her in the direction of the hutongs. I found the smells coming out of the kitchens of some of the tiny restaurants – apparently the odour of various insects being fried – nauseating. But Orit thought them intriguing, even appetizing. We compromised on a bigger restaurant at the juncture of the hutong and the main street.

The English-Mandarin phrase book, used very skillfully by Orit from the moment we arrived, proved, on this occasion, to be of little use. One expression, *bou-yaou-la*, not spicy, was understood, and the second, do you have a fork? was answered in the negative. Not one of the suggested dishes appeared in the phrase book and none of the meals written up – other than rice and noodles – was available. Three years of learning Mandarin at the university turned out to be of no use; not only were the five thousand ideogram-words dependent on a context, but every slight variation of pronunciation or intonation utterly changed their meaning. I became tongue-tied when I discovered that, for example, 'ma' meant mother in one intonation, a lewd curse in a higher tone, a different sort of curse if the pitch was lowered, and a horse if the lilt went down and up.

After a tiring negotiation, the restaurateur invited Orit into the kitchen. She entered it with a huge smile which caught the fancy of the cooks, and chose our dishes. It's good you didn't go in there, she told me after we'd left, you wouldn't have eaten a thing.

The following morning we visited the Temple of Heaven, located slightly to the south of our hotel.

In the vast gardens that surround the glorious complex of ancient buildings, we were surprised to find several couples dancing, somewhat theatrically, to the sound of a Strauss waltz. Further in were groups of people training in Tai chi or practising swordsmanship. In each corner of the square, close to the Temple gates, four elderly men were playing on what appeared to be improvised or ancient stringed instruments and below the arches of the gate itself, a man and a woman, each holding a loudspeaker, stood singing.

We paused, hugging each other, gazing at the magical scenes. Amazing, isn't it? said Orit, her eyes gleaming with happiness. Did you know that it was going to be this lively?

Our belongings, shipped after we had left, were delivered directly to the apartment we had picked in a new multi-storey building in the diplomatic quarter of Beijing. Immediately after settling in, we continued with our tours of the city and the surrounding area. We felt like a couple on an extended honeymoon, a rite of passage we hadn't celebrated at all after our wedding.

Once more I heard Orit say the words 'I love you' as we made love. She was in love again – with me, with the city, with the Chinese, with hope. I'd never stopped loving her and now, in Beijing, that love was being reciprocated once more.

The period of settling in was over and I had to go back to work. I needed to get to know different cities and prepare field files of various neighbourhoods in these urban areas. As the only agent in China, these tasks took me far away from home. Though the timing was up to me, the enormity of the country and the astronomical cost of airline tickets compelled me to complete my work in every region in one go – never less than a week. At first Orit joined me on trips to the more beautiful areas. But in due course she ceased to do so. While I prowled the city streets to complete my field-files, Orit roamed through the parts of Beijing that she loved – the silk market, food emporiums, the artists' quarter with its numerous galleries and coffee shops, and the restaurants and cafés along the lakes in the city centre. She much preferred that, even if it meant being without me.

I knew that Orit's love affair with Beijing was tied up

with the hope that Chinese medicine would help her become pregnant. By simply taking her pulse, the Chinese doctor who treated her while we were still in Israel diagnosed the extreme tension Orit was under, especially when I was away. Later on, she also identified weaknesses in both Orit's kidney and liver energies. I didn't understand the connections, so the doctor patiently explained that kidney energy is linked to hormones and the quality of a woman's ova, and that liver energy plays a role in regularizing her periods. She suggested that I also have acupuncture but I was not free at the time and found it difficult to accept the idea of energy channels in the body – meridians as the doctor called them – in which blockages are released by acupuncture. Unless a billion Chinese are mistaken it seems that I was wrong.

In China, they deal with internal problems, including fertility issues, mainly with the aid of 'medicinal herbs' defined to include a host of ingredients from crushed snakes to cooked beetles. Fortunately for Orit, the only non-vegetarian content in the gynecological medicinal herbs that she had to drink twice a day was the innards of a sea turtle's shell.

At the clinic, Orit watched as one woman after another became pregnant. When her hopes led to nothing but disappointment, she decided that artificial insemination was our only alternative. And that is something I don't intend doing in one of the hospitals here, she said.

In her dejected mood, Orit now seldom left the apartment as she had been doing whenever I was not in town. My trips became more and more difficult for her to bear, and she felt increasingly homesick for her parents.

I informed HQ that we wanted to come back so that Orit could undergo fertility treatment in Israel. The pressure on me to postpone this was unexpectedly light and the authorization for us to leave came surprisingly quickly.

There was one good outcome from our time in China: when word of the attempted assassination of the Hamas leader Khaled Mashal broke, Orit and I were on a week's trip to Guilin. We biked from one village to another through the terraced rice fields spread across hilltops like a multi-layered wedding cake, and sailed in a bamboo raft down the Li river amid the exceptionally beautiful steep and narrow wooded mountain peaks of the area. While watching the only English television channel in China in our hotel in Yangshuo, a vibrant village packed with tourists, we heard about the failure of the operation and the arrest of the Israeli agents.

At least now I know that it's not you who is responsible for these outrageous acts, said Orit, and my heart sank. Are they crazy or what? she asked, angrily. I'm not talking about the fiasco – Orit interrupted me as I tried to explain that this was usually a matter of luck. All it took for the two Mossad operatives who were trying to eliminate Mashal to be caught, was for a passer-by to draw the crowd's attention to the incident. Forget the details, she said, her temper rising even further – I'm talking about the very idea of killing!

Sixteen killed and two hundred wounded by Hamas

in Jerusalem's Mahane Yehuda market, Orit, just a few months ago; and more killed and wounded on nearby Ben Yehuda street – have you forgotten? Are we supposed to just let them continue?

So they murder us, then we murder them? Is that how it is – tit-for-tat? Why can't we be the ones do the right thing and stop retaliating? I didn't marry someone who might one day become a murderer. Nor do I want my country to legitimise murder!

But Orit, that's not how it is, I said in despair. We are not trying to kill as many as we can, only those who are killing us.

Open your eyes, Yogev. You're still talking like a newly-recruited member of a youth movement from a village in the Arava desert. Five million Palestinians in the West Bank and Gaza are trying to kill us, and another five million in Jordan and the refugee camps in Syria and Lebanon. What difference does it make that someone sent the killers. If not him then somebody else will do the sending. This is everybody's war, don't you understand that? Do you really not see that guns are not the solution?

I kept quiet, trying not to intensify the emotional storm that was engulfing Orit. But she wouldn't let up. You should know that I'm finding it harder and harder to live with the organization you belong to, with the way our government uses it, and with the direction in which this whole country is going. The government is the real villain, isn't that clear to you? Isn't that clear to the leaders in Jerusalem? Force won't work against two hundred million Arabs and that's before we scratch the wound of the

Temple Mount at which point we'll be facing a billion Muslims across the globe.

There was no point in my saying that in my view, given our bleak situation, yes, the government had no choice. There was no point in going into this when the ground beneath me, as a representative of one of the institutions which, in my wife's eyes, symbolized the power of the state, was on fire.

12

ORIT'S WORDS WERE still ringing in my ears when I met up with Rafi, the new division head, immediately after our return to Israel. At the meeting I also came to understand why no pressure had been put on me to stay in China.

Rafi, a slender man, his hair cropped and his appearance and tone of voice shaped by many years of commanding special units, saw me in his office. Since Hezi's days it had been redecorated in military style, with certificates of merit, shields, and photos of him with the last few chiefs of staff hanging on the walls.

Since the Mashal affair, Kidon has been neutralized, said Rafi, and it will be a long time before it gets back on its feet. But we – in fact the state of Israel – cannot be left without the protection of a 'long arm'. In your file I saw that Hezi had already once suggested that you join Kidon as its number one and you declined. I am repeating the request, in a slightly different form. Kidon will in time, and in its own way, recover. You, when required, will be our operative, and around you an ad hoc squad will be set up to help you. As it was in Hong Kong and Seoul, locations Kidon was not familiar with. I've gone over all the debriefings. You did well, and now that you are a few years older you probably won't be 'in shock' or lose your cool.

Apparently both my kidneys and heart were all over my personal file and analyzed to the umpteenth degree.

I said nothing. Orit's words continued to echo in my mind. She'd been more vehement than ever on this issue. It was only a matter of time till she asked me directly where I'd been and what I'd been doing, or, worse still, whether I'd been involved in a killing while abroad.

It was as clear to me as daylight that I wasn't going to lie to Orit. Our relationship was facing a doubly difficult test and wouldn't be able to withstand a long term lie.

I rejected the offer.

For a while, Rafi said nothing.

Here's a revised proposal, he said finally, and this is not open to negotiation. I want the best for you. I want you and Orit to have children, and I understand that you need to be available. The treatment Orit is undergoing is a tremendous burden and you will need to be on call for her. On the other hand, I, the Division, the Mossad, need you. And you personally, as I understand it, don't have such a big problem with the role.

I didn't respond. Where did he get this 'understanding' from? Rafi watched me closely and continued:

Go and learn. Become a student for two years like they do in the army service program. Do a second degree, on full pay. After that you'll be committed to us for four years.

I hope that by the time you complete your studies you'll already have a child, and perhaps another one on the way. That's how it is when a load is lifted. We'll try and do without you. But if there's no alternative, we'll call on you. And if we do, that, of course, will reduce your period of obligation to us.

You remember the ad about this being a home and a way of life and not a place of work? I asked. That's what they said when I was accepted. Now it sounds like an offer of work. A give and take contract.

Our original intent hasn't changed. But we're not used to people saying 'no'. That's what turns us into a workplace.

Again I said nothing.

In our last few conversations, before we'd finally re-arranged our belongings shipped from China, in our Jerusalem apartment, Orit had said that she wanted to be near her parents while she was being treated. The separation was difficult for them as well as for her and she now felt she needed her mother at her side. Your parents too are no longer young and it won't do any harm for you to be with them a little, she'd said. Altogether it would be good for us to think a bit about the future. How much longer are you going to carry on running around the world and how much longer is your father going to be able to work in the fields? And what's he going to do with the farm when he can no longer cope?

And indeed when we got back to Israel I was alarmed to see how my parents had aged. My father had lost a lot of weight, and though he'd never been a tall man, he now seemed to have shrunk. They delicately reminded me that a number of additional plots of land had been cleared for building in our village. It would make them happy if Orit and I bought one of them and built a house for ourselves. They could even help. You've already helped us with the apartment in Jerusalem and we're financially OK, I smiled at them lovingly. But the idea didn't go away without making an impression on me. Perhaps I could combine Orit's wishes and the pleas of both sets of parents, with Rafi's proposals, and settle down in the Arava? Two years of studying would be ideal for making such a move and building a home. What then? Wait and see. That's what a deal with the devil is all about, isn't it?

I think that's OK, I said to Rafi, and we shook hands on it.

Orit was over the moon when I told her about the new option.

I'm not interested in what happens after these two years, and I don't want to even think about it now, she said. But I'm dying, absolutely dying, to design a little house for us in the Arava, and to be with you every day. I'll open up a small office for desert architecture, she continued excitedly, and we'll bring up a little bare-footed Yossi close to our parents. So let's start right now, she said, pulling me onto the bed. A smile spread across her face, her eyes closed, and from deep inside came that melodious purr of contentment. Till then I hadn't experienced such a blend of passion and serenity and thought that only the tortuous path that our lives had followed could have brought about such a fusion. Little did I know then about the ups and down that this voyage still had in store for us.

The plots extending the area of our village came at the expense of a few vegetable fields on its eastern side facing the Jordanian border and the mountains of Edom. The parcels of land closest to the village had already been sold and in the more peripheral areas only a few tracts were still for sale. Orit and I toured the area on a smoothed but as yet unpaved gravel path between two rows of houses. We stopped at the entrance to the very last plot, holding hands, our fingers tightly interlocked: the land overlooked a date plantation, the very same one in which I made love to her for the first time. Both of us looked towards the grove at the far end of the plantation, the spot to which Orit had led me way back then. In our mind's eye we could see the two bicycles left leaning on an inner line of trees so as not to attract attention. I could see the young, slim girl, unloading the wicker basket attached to the front of the bicycle, taking a pinkish-blue woven blanket with which, until that day, she had probably been covering her youthful body, and spreading it on the ground. I was even able to visualize the look of surprise on my face, its almost clownish expression, when she also removed the bottle of wine from the basket.

'Here', we agreed with a broad smile and hugged each other. I embraced her tightly, she buried her face in my shoulder and I felt a slight wetness where her eyelids brushed against me. Here we'll try going back fifteen years, to that moment when everything seemed so full of promise, when it seemed self evident to both of us that our lives would forever revolve around the desert and the Arava, facing the mountains of Edom; a point in our lives when we couldn't imagine the iniquities of Hong Kong and Seoul or the disappointments of Beijing.

I love you, Orit suddenly said, so quietly that it sounded as if I had only imagined it.

And I love you, so so much, I responded as a much younger man would, and felt rejuvenated. Again everything was ahead of us, again everything was possible.

The village secretary told me it was good that I was coming back because my father was 'no longer the man he used to be'. He sees him coming to the secretariat at lunch time, bent and clutching his back after several hours on the tractor or picking vegetables. He's perhaps not yet a pensioner, said the secretary, and the Thai workers do help him, but somebody else has to take control. Among his peers the sons are already in charge.

Our imminent return gave my parents a new lease of life. My father who very much wanted me to carry on with his lifetime's work, was revitalized, as was my mother who was exhausted from years of working on the farm and was now employed by the regional council entering data into the computer from home. The move also breathed new life into Orit's parents. They had been thinking of retiring from teaching and going back to their home in the centre of the country after her younger brother had come of age and moved to Tel Aviv. They now decided to extend the tenancy on their home in the Arava. Nobody said a word, but the shared hope and longing for a grandchild and son strongly united us all.

Orit plunged into the work of designing our home, investing the project with all her love and passion. In front of my very eyes, on the computer screen in our Jerusalem apartment, a small house in the Arava sprung to life.

We never talked about the way our lives would be when we had children but designing the house forced us to think about it. When the children finally come, we will extend the second floor, Orit said. In the first year I, in any case, want our baby to be really close to us, so that when he opens his eyes at night he will see us. And even afterwards, until we have more children and until he is at least seven or eight, he can be on his own upstairs, Orit decided, and I, of course, agreed.

I felt how I too was being sucked into this heightened sense of expectation. The understandable theoretical wish for a child had suddenly become an animated desire. A yearning. The hope that had returned to our lives made us believe that the power of our love would make conception possible.

Orit drew a three dimensional computer sketch to which she was able to attach the separate annexes on the second floor, printed it out and showed it to both sets of parents with a running commentary about their future grandchildren's rooms. My mother couldn't restrain herself, burst into tears, and fled to her room, overwhelmed by it all. Orit's parents, though unable to hide their tears, nodded in appreciation, highly impressed by their daughter's enchanting design.

Orit's plans incorporated bits of the Edom mountains, the date plantation, the Arava plains and its soil. Then, the real structure began to sprout on our plot.

I started my course for a second degree in the International Relations Department at the Hebrew University in Jerusalem. I had no intention of specializing in the Far East – that pursuit had already taken me to places that were much too dark. By the time the house is finished, and we can move in, I thought to myself, this academic year will be over and I can complete the rest with a weekly trip to Jerusalem. While we waited for our new home Orit returned to the architect's office that she had left.

As the pattern of our life changed so did our passion for each other. The smell of the other's body is no longer intoxicating, the need to be close to it, to touch it, and breathe it at every possible moment, fades. But the lost desires of youth are replaced by something else, no less beautiful. The love of a body so known, whose every curve is familiar, sensing how Orit will respond to each touch, how she will move, what sounds she will make, has a magic all of its own. There is beauty in our simply sitting together, even at two computers that are close to each other; me with my course material she with her drawings; our legs touching every now and then. Or stretching out a hand and my touching her gently, our eyes meeting, delivering a smile that needs no words and doesn't even divert our attention.

The only thing that came between us was the tension

of the elusive pregnancy when once a month it became clear that yet again it had failed to materialize. We had sex, loved, hoped – then days later Orit would go to the bathroom and almost immediately come out, her eyes full of tears. I've got my period she would say, her lips trembling.

After months of unproductive attempts, Orit decided that we could no longer postpone artificial insemination.

Only once during the first year of my studies did Rafi call on me.

I have no alternative and I don't want to tell the head of the Mossad or the prime minister that I can't do this one, he said to me. And it's important, he added, completing his list of justifications before explaining the operation itself to me. I wasn't asked if I was prepared to take on the task. There's a Pakistani scientist, one of the pioneers of the nuclear program in his country, who is selling himself to radical Islamists. Until now the US has been able to verify that Pakistan had kept its nuclear secrets to itself. But this guy is a loose cannon. To cover his tracks and conceal what he's up to even from his own government, he has his meetings in neutral countries. This time it's going to be in the Gulf. We want to delete him from our list of targets.

But I'm not qualified to operate in hard-core enemy territory, in 'target states', I tried my luck with him.

As far as we are concerned the Gulf states are not hard-core enemy territory, so you can't really call them 'target states'. They are not Syria or Iran. They are open to Westerners, even to Israelis. Anyway it's worth your while to start familiarizing yourself with the Gulf, Morocco, Tunisia, countries that are defined at most as 'soft targets' – you'll have lots of work there in the future.

Can that be after the two years are over?

Maybe. But this operation is urgent. Your men are waiting for you.

I had no basis for hoping that intimidation of the target would have the desired effect. There was also no point in suggesting that we simply leave him badly wounded, something which, unconsciously, I had striven for in previous operations. I set off with a heavy heart, yet also in the knowledge that there was no alternative.

And so one more virtual notch was added to the handle of the pistol I never wore or wanted to wear.

The architectural monstrosities of glass and steel that sprouted out of the white sands appeared to be a futuristic mirage as did the green golf courses in the heart of the desert. These attracted western businessmen along with millionaires who wanted to buy a piece of land on one of the artificial islands built along the shoreline. All of this made it easier for us to blend into the local scene.

Rooms were booked in the hotel in which our target was staying. In temperatures as high as 40 degrees in the shade we didn't even want to think of carrying out the task outdoors. We'll do it in real style, said Levanon, who I was happy to be working with again. A liquidation in the air-conditioned presidential suite in a bath with golden taps.

That's also style, said Udi, pointing to two whores, wrapped from head to toe, including a veil, sitting on a sofa in the lobby. One of them joined me in the elevator, two smiling blue eyes peering at me from the blackness enveloping them. I wondered what she really looked like, but had to suppress my curiosity.

At night, with Udi's help, I removed the naked and still wet body of Mustafa Quader – the mercenary scientist – and put it in his hotel's garbage bin which was also a trash compactor.

On the flights to Europe and then home, I felt as if I was dreaming. The whole episode didn't seem real to me.

News of the Pakistani nuclear scientist's disappearance in the Arab Emirates didn't make the headlines. With my stomach churning, I told Orit that I had been in a new area. I had only very partially come to terms with what I was doing, and was far from being able to say that I had truly accepted such operations, however much I might have thought them unavoidable.

13

BEFORE THE FINAL touches were made, we moved into our new little house on the fringes of the Arava village overlooking the date plantation and the mountains of Edom which straddled the Jordanian border. While our house was being built, the village secretariat had managed to tarmac the road between the two rows of houses, construct a pavement, and install street lighting. Some of our neighbours had long since finished building their homes; others were at various advanced stages of completion so that the tranquillity of the desert was only rarely disturbed by the noise of ongoing construction.

In a burst of enthusiasm Orit began to set up her desert architectural office and promoted her skills in the villages of the Arava as well as in the Negev's various kibbutzim which were in the process of expanding and absorbing young families. Our home became a show house for the few who were interested.

Once a week I made the trip to the university in Jerusalem and for the rest of the time I was free to help my father. It was as if he had been looking forward to this moment for many years. He simply dropped everything and handed over the reins to me. Mounting the tractor I felt that no time at all had elapsed since I last drove it through the open fields. I was back to being a born farmer.

My happiness was almost complete. That's the only way I can describe the feeling that washed over me every morning as I went out to the fields driving the tractor. The sun had not yet risen over the mountains of Edom, so the chill of sunrise had not yet given way to the heat of its desert rays and the fields remained covered in dew. In the bright light of early dawn and its cool breeze, I drove the tractor and its trailer to where the farm's Thai workers lived. Despite the balaclava hats covering their faces, I'd learned to recognize them all. In silence, they sat themselves down in the wagon and we headed for the open fields.

The Thai workers spread themselves out among the rows of vegetable plants while I attached a plough to the tractor and worked the bare land. During those hours I thought of almost nothing else. I threw myself into physical work and occuppied myself with what the fields and the season of year demanded of me, sowing, tilling or reaping. However, so far as my happiness was concerned, 'almost' remained the right word to describe my state of being. This was because at any moment, just as Orit and I were moving from the insemination phase, which produced no results, to trying out the painful and frustrating procedures of IVF treatment, Rafi could call.

For two weeks every month Orit endured the misery of hormone injections. Given her experience of Chinese acupuncture these didn't at first phase her. But as it became clear that we were only at the beginning of a painfully long process, her resistance to the pain of the jabs diminished. Her fear both of the needle and the pain made self-injection impossible so it was left to me to do it for her every day.

In the dim light of our bedroom after a day's work in the fields, I prepared the syringe and its contents, gently uncovered her firm buttocks, bending over and looking for a spot that hadn't yet been pierced. I kissed the chosen area trying to loosen the tension that had gripped her entire body and with an aching heart inserted the needle.

Orit sighed, pursing her lips. I felt the needle penetrating, feeling her pain. Tears welled up in my eyes as I wiped the tear spilling from hers. I put the syringe on the chest of drawers and slid between the sheets, hugging

Orit and she, limply, embracing me. From time to time this closeness even led us to making love.

Orit wanted to continue the treatment at Hadassah Hospital where she'd been treated while we were living in Jerusalem. Given what lay ahead, the journeys there were spent in a tense silence.

The hospital was expected to notify us within a few days if there were any suitable embryos that could be transferred to the womb. These were days when we were afraid to hope but couldn't avoid doing just that.

On the morning of the expected news from the hospital I left the Thai workers in the field and came home early, ready to take the call before Orit managed to get to the phone. Deep inside me I knew what the answer would be: I'm sorry to tell you Mr Ben-Ari, but there are no suitable embryos. I went up to Orit's studio and found her sitting on the sofa, her face ashen, her eyes closed.

You don't have to tell me. I know, she said. Your silence and your heavy footsteps on the stairs said it all.

She burst into tears. I knelt, taking her precious head into my arms. Perhaps next month, my dearest Orit, let's believe. But all she could do was to weep silently. In the months that followed the outcome was the same.

The injections, which at first led to fleeting moments of intimacy between us, now turned into occasions of anger. When Orit's strength had waned and she could no longer tolerate the extraction procedures, she asked that they be administered under a general anaesthetic from which she found it difficult to come around. She remained fuzzy headed all the way home. Somehow we got through the nerve-wracking wait for the results of the fertilization. Orit tried to ease her anxiety by smoking. All I could do was comfort myself with the thought that at least she wasn't drinking. Then the disheartening news would come, hurtling us both into an oppressive silence and Orit into a state of utter despair.

When there are suitable embryos, they will be implanted, the gynaecologist reassured Orit. But I see that you've started smoking and that's a great pity because the surrounding membrane is thicker among women who smoke which makes it more difficult for the sperm to penetrate.

When he stops travelling, I'll stop smoking, was Orit's immediate response. I hadn't gone anywhere, but in Orit's mind I was always on the move. And the pregnancy continued in its refusal to materialize. We lived from month to month around the schedule of treatments, unable to plan anything, re-experiencing every time the rollercoaster of expectation and disappointment. And all the while the periods of silence between us grew longer, each of us withdrawing into our own private world. We could well understand why couples split up during treatment and prayed that we would get through it in one piece.

To our joy, a kibbutz chose Orit to design an entire neighbourhood. This was followed by enquiries from a number of other kibbutzim and private clients, keeping her busy all hours of the day and night. She engaged a draughtswoman who also helped to ease her solitude. My own feelings of loneliness were overcome by immersing myself in the work I loved in the fields. With each of us doing what we had to do, but separately, we were able to deal with the anguish we were both experiencing and, from time to time, also managed to get through the evenings when we were alone at home. Fortunately, the frequent visits of my parents and hers didn't leave us with too many such hours.

Orit also began to join me on my weekly trip to the university in Jerusalem. There is a support group there for women undergoing fertility treatment and I've been told it would do me good to join, she said. Who recommended, when and why, she didn't volunteer and I didn't ask. I knew that I was no longer her confidant when it came to sharing her fears. Perhaps her parents were, perhaps a neighbour from the village.

On our long journey home after her first meeting with the group I dared to question her.

Orit uttered a string of sentences that sounded to me like a repetition of what the counsellor had told her. Giving birth is the be-all and end-all of womanhood, she said. And when a woman fails to conceive, it's difficult, very difficult.

And you feel that way too, that giving birth is what your life is all about? I asked carefully.

What do you think, to be an architect? To design other people's houses?

I remember that you wavered between being a painter, a dancer, or a sportswoman, I said.

Yes. I think I had skills in those areas, she said after a long silence. But that isn't what I'm all about.

And what am I all about? I wondered. Unlike Orit, I had no remarkable skills. I also didn't feel that my manhood revolved around having children. But are my 'hunting' pursuits in various parts of the world some sort of a realization of such manliness? Perhaps they are even an alternative to having children? I thought to myself.

Would having a child free me from my almost compulsive need to defend my People and my Land? And are not all these activities of mine actually pointless if they don't in the end protect my very own offspring?

Orit continued to talk, further disrupting my already disjointed thoughts. Do you realize what a woman whose femininity remains unrealized feels? Sometimes I feel as barren as this desert around us. And sometimes like the tomboy I was at fifteen, doing my exercises on the equipment in the gym. But now I'm an ageing tomboy and my biological clock is ticking.

You're my woman Or, I said, and nothing can change that. She rested her head on my shoulder for the remainder of the long journey home in the dark. We were left with our own thoughts.

The meeting with the other women improved Orit's mood and perhaps, in a roundabout way, kept us together as a couple. I already understand, she told me, that my energies are attuned to coping with just one thing, our child, and not with you as well. This, despite all the sadness it entails for you and also for me. I bit my lip, accepted what she said, and attempted to keep my love for her intact.

A little while later she said: we'll try once more and if that doesn't work we'll look for an egg donor.

We both knew that that option, which would have to be carried out abroad, was expensive, a significant addition to the already high cost of the private fertility treatments we were now having. But that wasn't what bothered me.

The child...I stammered

Won't be mine? Orit completed the sentence and, with a softness in her voice that I hadn't heard for a long time, added: but it will be your child, and when we bring him up he will be our child. And that is what I want. Your child in our home.

This expression of Orit's love overwhelmed me and I agreed. At some point in time, when a sweet little boy or girl is running around our living room among parents, grandfathers and grandmothers, we'll forget the torment we endured. I found myself looking at little children playing in the village and felt a pang in my heart. I saw young parents running with their children and my own lack of a child pained me physically, as if my body was short of a limb. I could easily visualize myself with my children on a tricycle on the way to the playground or kicking a ball in our garden – an area I also took care of after my work in the fields was done. My desire for a child no longer stemmed only from identifying with Orit but now arose from my own new-found capacity to feel the need.

Orit's biological clock was not the only one ticking. My father, who had handed over the management of the farm to me, was going downhill at an alarming rate. Within a short space of time he stopped taking an interest in what was happening in his fields, and not long after that ceased going out of the house altogether. The many years of hard work on the land had left their mark both on his body and his mind. Back pains that he attributed to his parachuting days in the 1960s, kept him in bed and when he got up he felt acute pains in his knees. Very soon we discovered that he no longer had the strength to walk unaided. At first he refused to use a walking stick and when he finally gave in and agreed, it turned out that the stick would not support his weight and that he already needed a walking frame.

After the Six Day War of 1967, my father had joined an encampment in the arid lands of the desert and then, with his friends from the army unit, he moved to the permanent village. The place became his entire world. He did nothing but work the land and now was left without any other interests to occupy him. My mother's attempts to get him to meet up with the village secretariat, go to events at the club, or be with friends, fell on deaf ears. He simply refused to allow others to see him in such a state. My mother sat for hours on end at the bedside of her youthful idol watching him fall apart in front of her very eyes. In turn she too began failing at work, was unable to meet deadlines, made numerous mistakes with numbers, and was finally fired. That triggered her own downward slide.

Whichever way one chose to calculate it, the decline came too early, far too early, and pained me greatly. In my childhood and youth, my father was a source of pride. His story of being handed over as a baby by his parents to a nearby nunnery at the beginning of the German occupation, their own extraordinary tale of survival and his rescue from the nunnery after the war in the face of objections from the nuns and his own opposition, was a story I knew by heart. So was the account of their 'illegal' immigration to Palestine in the dying days of the British Mandate, their clash with a British patrol vessel, their swim to shore, and their time spent in a makeshift transit camp in their new-found homeland. My father's recruitment into the paratroop unit and his participation in the liberation of the Western Wall in the Six Day War as a reservist – and already a young father – was as familiar to me as were the stories of the difficulties my parents and their friends experienced when they first came to live in the isolated and blisteringly hot desert village.

My father was the last to employ Thai workers in his fields and he only agreed to do it when my mother – a country girl with no illusions – proved to him with the aid of dry numbers that without their help there was no chance of us keeping the farm. By then the caravans that were home to the Thai workers outnumbered the residences of the villagers themselves. During daylight hours the Thais were the only people to be seen in the village streets and in its fields.

In my mind I could link my father's physical decline to his childhood experiences. But I couldn't explain my mother's sudden deterioration. She was the daughter of Galilee farmers who gave up the green of her childhood landscape when she too joined the army group in the Arava where she met my father. To me she was a deeply-rooted tree whose leaves never withered. I associated her with this verse from Jeremiah as soon as I first read it, recalling the great love with which she nurtured the fruit trees in our garden which she planted immediately after we moved from the encampment to the village proper. In family albums of that period I appear first as a child of about three helping her to water the trees and then, when I was a bit older, helping to prune and pick their fruit. The trees still yielded their sweet crops at a time when, as if contrary to nature itself, she herself began to wither away before my very eyes.

In the midst of all this I received the second phone call from Rafi. A group linked to Al-Qaida which had already been organizing itself for a year in a region where the borders of China, Laos and Vietnam converge, was planning a terror attack on Israeli tourists. Approaches by the Americans had failed to spur the local governments to act and I was given the task of making that happen.

We toured the various villages we'd been directed to go to by our intelligence services, getting looks of surprise from farmers up to their knees in their rice fields. As we passed by, female farmers dressed in colourful traditional costumes abandoned the potato fields and hurriedly took their children indoors. In the narrow pathways of the village, vegetable vendors stood up after hours of squatting and offered us their produce, while farmers on their way to market lowered the long pole on which two heavily laden baskets were suspended to make room for us to get through.

While travelling through the region inhabited by various minorities in northern Vietnam, we made an overnight stop in Sapa – a major centre for backpackers. At the entrance to the village, in a stone-built two-storey hotel, we located a vehicle with a number plate that had come up during a briefing from our intelligence people about the group linked to Al-Qaida. In the middle of the night we placed a small quantity of explosives in a suitcase in the boot of the car, and connected the fuse mechanism to the ignition with an electrical wire that would burn itself up. By morning we were in Hanoi where we mingled with the thousands of sweating tourists in the city's old quarter around the lake.

The explosion triggered when the car's engine was turned on injured the vehicle's occupants and brought out the police. From their initial check, they believed that devices in the suitcase had accidentally exploded. The group's members were arrested, and at long last the desired investigation got underway.

Perhaps you'll leave the service and that will be that? Orit said when I returned. After such a long period at home I had to tell her the details of this trip and hoped that she would appreciate the fact that in line with my decision, the members of the cell had only been lightly injured. But she didn't think that was OK and wasn't at all interested in 'such games of cops and robbers that could end badly'.

I have an agreement with them Or, I said. I don't violate agreements. I can't leave.

Buy back what they've paid you, tuition fees and salary

over the past two years. Enough's enough. You have a farm to run, I have an office, we are both busy from morning till night and in between we have the child project.

I won't do it, Or, I said again. We have another four years to go before the contract ends. Let's try and get through that time as best we can.

But Orit refused to yield and barricaded herself behind a wall of silence.

14

MY PERIOD OF study had ended and with a heavy heart I returned to the service. Rafi understood my need to be with Orit for a certain number of days every month and even agreed to the office funding the cost of a nurse to replace me and administer her daily dose of injections. So far as your father's farm is concerned, that's a problem you'll have to solve yourself, Rafi told me; we can't help you with that.

This I did with the assistance of Yehiel, a farmer from the centre of the country who'd gone bust. Yehiel ran the farm well. We also got the go-ahead to employ a foreign carer for my father whose condition continued to deteriorate.

Our home was less well maintained. Orit invested all her energy in her successful architectural office, greeted me with indifference whenever I got back from Tel-Aviv – a journey of almost three hours – and with a frown whenever I returned from abroad.

These trips became increasingly frequent. As time went by I was put in command of more and more complex missions and an ever larger number of men. This growing burden of responsibility provided me with a good excuse to escape from what was happening at home. The passion and love that we had once known had given way to momentary expressions of kindness. What little sex was purely mechanical, engaged in merely to avoid reaching ovulation with stale sperm.

I won't be able to go on like this for four more years, Orit said to me once when the topic came up. And if you don't care about me, at least think about your parents. They're reaching the end of their days and when they are gone you'll be full of remorse.

On three occasions during the year after my return to the service I was about to raise the issue of my job with Rafi and each time missions important enough to postpone the discussion cropped up. The first involved an operation to prevent an anti-aircraft missile being fired at a plane belonging to the Israel charter company Sun D'Or which had started to operate a weekly flight from Tel Aviv to the Seychelles. The combination of virgin forests, sandy white beaches, and the clear turquoise waters of the Indian Ocean, attracted a mass of Israeli tourists – deep-sea divers, lovers of nature, or simply people who enjoyed idling their time away. The islands had also become a highly suitable location for terrorist activity. We had no intelligence infrastructure set up there, and no clue as to how and when the terrorist group was planning to attack, or the identity of its members. All we knew was that it existed.

To me this appeared to be mission impossible. The international airport was located on the big island of Mahé. The lengthy landing strip was just off the shore at the foot of a high wooded mountainside. In the crystal clear waters on the other side of the airport were a number of smaller islands with hotels right on the beach. How could one possibly prevent a group of determined terrorists firing a missile from the woods on the mountainside or from one of the cabins on the water-front?

In the recent past, the Seychelles had been a British colony. The current administration, however, was unstable and could be of no help to us. A yacht, hired in Zanzibar, sailed the thousand nautical miles eastwards and smuggled in the weaponry we needed. The local language, Seychellois Creole, sounded like broken French to us, a remnant of an earlier period when the islands were ruled by France, but even the French speakers among us realized that it was more effective to talk to the locals in English.

Micha set up a tour company for us and hired four jeeps and three speedboats. This immediately attracted a large number of tourists to the office which he opened by the shore. We also rented two rooms in hotels overlooking the airport which at least partially covered the target area. We hoped that this would close most of the opportunities for firing anti aircraft missiles at the plane but I knew that that too was to a large extent a matter of luck.

On the day the Sun D'Or flight was due to arrive our jeeps patrolled the upper reaches of the mountain overlooking the airport while the speedboats criss-crossed the narrow sea lane parallel to the fields and the shorelines of the islands closest to its runway. The jeeps and speedboats were equipped with mini-Uzi sub-machine guns. In each of the hotel rooms were two sniper rifles to be taken out of their hiding place only moments before the landing. Our beefed-up team worked nonstop for hours on end prior to the landing, during the time the plane was on the ground, and continued their labours until it had taken off and disappeared over the horizon. Though we had covered the possible launch sites, the terrorists were nowhere to be seen.

I pressed for permission to return to Israel before the next Sun D'Or flight was due, but HQ insisted that we stay for at least another week. For me this meant losing one ovulation but since the office had been so accommodating over the previous few years I couldn't really object. I called Orit. She said nothing and it seemed to me that I could hear the sound of sobbing. I was left with no option but to curse myself. At the same time I couldn't avoid being angry with her: did she not realize that the fate of three hundred passengers travelling on an Israeli plane hung in the balance?

I deployed my people to the two other bigger islands, Praslin and La Digue as well as to the smaller ones within firing range of the airfield. There they looked for possible suspects and between searches relaxed beneath date palms and coconut trees, stroked sea turtles and sunbathed on the white sands with their granite rock formations. The diving aficionados reported that the coral reefs were superb.

I stayed with Micha and Levanon on the island of Mahé. We went north to Victoria, the small capital city, and set ourselves up there. I used the many hours of tropical rain repeatedly to go over the various scenarios with my colleagues and spent the rest of the time looking for suspects in town. We went to bars, toured the colourful markets, combed the wooded mountains overlooking the airport and strolled through the artists' town in the southern part of the island, close to the airport but saw no suspects. I wondered how reliable the intelligence that had brought us to this place really was, and who among the seemingly apathetic Creole natives – a people formed from European, Chinese, Indian and African migrants, a majority of them Catholics – could possibly have a hand in helping to organize a terrorist attack of this kind.

Towards the time of the next flight's arrival we again went over the drill. Previously I had chosen to be in the jeep because of a feeling, which turned out to be wrong, that we would find the terrorists hiding in foxholes overlooking the airfield, perhaps somewhere on the fringes of the woods. This time my instinct told me to be in the Raff Hotel to the north of the airfield.

I closed the shutters in my room save for one thin panel, placed the bipods of the sniper rifle on the table which I pushed up against the window, secured the room's door, and waited. Pierre, a professional sniper who'd joined my team, did the same in the second hotel overlooking the airport.

Moments before the plane approached, Micha called

on the transceiver to say that he had spotted a suspicious-looking group at the northern entrance to the airport. He drove up to them in the jeep, asked for a cigarette, and was able to confirm beyond doubt that this was a group of four Arabs. The jeep drew away, but Micha kept them within sight. I dispatched Levanon's jeep to the spot as a reinforcement.

Now it was my turn. A quick check revealed that the group was on the slope of the mountain, sitting in the shade of the large bushes about 100 metres from the airfield's perimeter fence. I pointed the gun's scope at them. They were about five hundred metres away from me and could be seen very clearly through the telescopic lens.

Sun D'Or's security officer, on the line with us, announced that the plane was entering a circling mode and would land in approximately two minutes. I instructed Micha and Levanon not to approach the area. I mounted the silencer, cocked the rifle, opened the safety-catch and locked in on the group. I myself didn't see the plane but the four Arabs apparently did. I noticed movement among them as they dragged an elongated sack from either under the ground or a hiding place in the bushes. A moment later the long launcher of the small but deadly Strela SA-7 missile could be seen being shouldered by one of the Arabs. I spotted another member of the group picking up the missile which he was about to slot into the launcher.

Though I had accumulated dozens of hours of experience in training as a sniper since returning to my role in the service, I wasn't sure of a direct hit with the first bullet. I knew that if I aimed at his body and not his head I would certainly strike him and that he would merely be wounded, not killed. That was enough for me. I aimed at the torso of the man standing with the launcher on his shoulder, went over to automatic and fired a short burst. The noise deafened me, my eyes filled with smoke and, after a moment that felt like an eternity, he fell to the ground.

His friends, who hadn't heard the sound of gunfire, couldn't understand what had happened and tried to pull the man up. At any moment one of them could get hold of the launcher and still manage to hit the plane. I aimed at the one still holding the missile and fired another short burst. Again, a terrible noise, searing smoke, and a man falling after a brief eternity.

The other two in the group, seeing the blood on their friends' clothing ran for their lives. I had no time to deal with them. The chances of hitting them were slim and in any case I didn't want to do that. But because I had forgotten to radio instructions to the others to withdraw, Levanon took it upon himself to close in on the remaining duo. His jeep made a short detour and blocked the path of the two escapees. Before they had time to realize the extent of the danger they were in, both were shot dead by short bursts of fire from Levanon's mini-Uzi.

Someone was knocking on the door of my room. Despite the silencer the shots had, of course, been heard, and one of the hotel staff had apparently been sent to find out what had happened. The disassembled rifle, already in its travelling case, was back in my bag which had been packed and readied prior to the shooting. I thought about how to overpower the hotel worker at the door – or deal with two of them if that is what I had to do. I breathed deeply and opened the door.

God damn it, it was a woman. A tall, buxom, black woman. I invited her in and very reluctantly struck the nape of her neck, gagged her, tied her hands and feet and placed her, unconscious, in the bathtub. I yanked out the inside door handle and locked the bathroom door.

Over the communication system I announced that I was leaving. Micha's jeep picked me up at the entrance to the hotel and shot off to the speed boat. We were then ferried to the yacht which, in keeping with our getaway plan, was anchored about a mile from the shore. Our two other speed boats picked up the rest of the operatives who'd pulled back in haste leaving behind them three jeeps perfectly parked at the entrance to the company's now closed down beachside offices.

In the first debriefing back in Israel we were severely reprimanded for having shot the two members of the group who were on the run.

I can sort of understand the rationale for shooting the man carrying the launcher and the other guy handling the missile. So long as the group was there, the others could step in and replace those who'd been hit. But to shoot after they'd fled? Why? Rafi asked angrily. For the first time I understood that he too was capable of pitying the enemy.

This was my chance to repay Levanon for his help in the Hong Kong and Seoul operations. Those were my instructions, I said. I was never told that they should be allowed to run away. Firing from the jeep was one of the authorized operational options. Levanon thanked me with a slight nod of the head.

Rafi said we'd discuss the matter further some other time. Meanwhile he complimented us on our performance and clean getaway, and told us we were free to go home.

There I found Orit with dark rings under her eyes. Four Arabs killed in the Seychelles did not perhaps make for big headlines but the Strela missile found next to their bodies certainly did. So too did the chambermaid in the hotel who, wearing a plastic neck brace, was endlessly interviewed by CNN and the BBC giving a fairly accurate description of me. On the Israeli television channels the foiling of the terrorist attack was widely praised by professionals and commentators alike, though there were those who questioned why we hadn't tried to get the Seychelles authorities to intervene. The arrest of the airline's security officers on suspicion of being complicit in helping us definitely didn't help. But since there was no real proof against them and everybody had a strong alibi, they were released after a short while.

Listen carefully, Orit said to me, her expression serious, her body thinner than ever, rejecting all my attempts to hug her. I'm not asking whether you were there or were involved in this. That way you won't have to lie to me. Your tan speaks for itself. According to the descriptions there was a whole bunch of you over there. Jeeps, speed boats, hotels. I'm not interested in what precisely your role was or if you were simply the communications centre for these guys. I'm also not prepared to get into a discussion about the vital necessity of what you did or did not do, and whether it saved lives or not. It certainly destroyed life. As far as I'm concerned it's unacceptable, understand?

Unacceptable? I was bewildered.

Don't get clever with me. You understand perfectly well what I'm saying. And that's before discussing the missed opportunity of me conceiving. That's certainly something I am not going to forgive.

The waste is also mine, Or, I said. The loss is also mine.

The sin is yours, and for that we're both being punished. Don't you see that? You took life and lost a life you could have given.

Or, really!

But Orit, utterly tense and glowering with pent up anger, fled to her studio. I was left speechless with conflicting desires raging inside me. Let the storm pass, said one voice, while another said: I can't accept statements like the ones you've made; not from a moral perspective, nor from the plain, rational point of view; and certainly not if there is a religious or metaphysical aspect to it. Other strident voices shrieked inside me; yes it was me who did it. Thanks to me our plane landed safely. And yes, I'm proud of that. And no, I don't want to hide this from you. And no, I am not prepared to be ashamed of it any more. And I want you to want to know, and to be involved in my feelings of satisfaction.

These screaming voices almost overwhelmed me and only a huge effort enabled me to stay silent though I did manage to give vent to a small, strangulated cry. I went to wipe off the sweat pouring down my face.

How do we move on from here? I wondered afterwards.

Work had also become routine – gathering intelligence, surveillance, break-ins – and towards every ovulation I was at home. It was obvious that we couldn't go on like this for the full term of my contract. But again, just as I was planning a conversation with Rafi, another call to action came and again I was unable to say no. Following the breakup of the Soviet Union, a few dozen missiles with nuclear war heads together with their launchers had been left behind in the newly independent state of Kazakhstan. Through local Islamic groups Iran succeeded in bribing a number of sufficiently high-level officials in the country's defence ministry, army, and missile command, enabling it to buy a number of mobile missiles and their launchers. A supposedly well-guarded convoy of such weapons was about to make its way to the port of Atyrau on the northern coast of the Caspian sea at the mouth of the Ural River. From there the cargo was to be shipped on board an Iranian vessel to its final destination.

Because of the great importance of this particular preventative action HQ decided to send two teams to the area. One, a slimmed down team under my command, would cover the roads from the missile base inside Kazakhstan to the port. Our mission was to try and attack the convoy on its way there. The second team, reinforced by a sea commando unit, was to fly to Astrakhan, the biggest Russian port on the Caspian Sea, on the border with Kazakhstan. There they were to hire a vessel and sail in the direction of the nearby port of Atyrau. If I failed in my attack on the convoy, the second team's mission was to sink the Iranian vessel. Udi, a former naval commando officer, took charge of this expanded squad.

By the following morning, together with Levanon and two additional operatives, I was already on the roads of western Kazakhstan heading for the port of Atyrau.

Fortunately we were not far from the convoy when we received news of its exact location, information that was obtained from satellite images. According to the intelligence we were given the three huge vehicles carrying the missiles were not guarded at all: it seemed that only a small number of people were in on the secret and they wanted to keep it that way.

As darkness fell we by-passed the convoy and put down some not very large stones on a deserted stretch of the road just moments before it got there. My three colleagues and I spread ourselves out opposite the spot where we thought the vehicles would be forced to stop. When they came to a halt we discovered that in fact in every one of the missile transporters there was an armed guard. Nonetheless, we had the advantage of surprise. The shooting lasted only a few seconds. We also managed to hit the front wheels of the three vehicles before hurrying back to our own cars that we had left on the other side of the stone barrier.

HQ's assumption that the Kazakhstanis would try to keep the incident under wraps proved to be right. Not a word on the affair appeared in any of the media. From Orit's point of view this had been another routine trip. From my point of view it was less so. Those killed on this occasion could well have been relatively innocent drivers. I comforted myself with the thought that had I not succeeded, Udi's group would have had to sink the ship with its entire crew or gain control of it by force of arms and in doing so spark an international sea lane conflict.

At home we'd grown used to the dreariness of our routine; grown accustomed to the silences; to Orit's seclusion in her studio; to the continued and depressing deterioration in my parents' health; to the pain that went with Orit's treatment; to the nerve-wracking periods waiting for a result, followed by the disappointing call from the hospital. We'd also grown used to the infrequency of our sexual relations and the almost total absence of any expression of love.

And yet we were together. Neither of us thought of dissolving our marriage. Behind us were twenty years during which our love had never been in doubt. We were bound together by the prolonged and distressing effort of bringing our child into the world and knew that, one day, I would once again become a farmer and that our little child, even if he were to be born through a donor egg, would be running around our home.

On the rare occasions when we did sleep together all the despair and hope, love and hate, passion and rejection, erupted. These were times when we made love at length, our bodies refusing to part from each other, refusing to be satiated. We imagined ourselves growing old together in the place we knew so well, where we'd taken our first joint steps in learning, with each other's help, the magic of love.

Even in the frustrating moments of masturbation in the shower, in those periods when Orit didn't want me, it was her I visualized. I didn't imagine myself with another woman. I didn't *want* to imagine another woman.

On the Island of Mahé, I'd seen the plumpish Micha going into his room with a Naomi Campbell look-alike and Levanon with a Halle Berry clone – hugely sexy local prostitutes. When I indicated that I was not comfortable with this behaviour, Levanon said to me, Loosen up man. We're married too. We've already been here a week and it will be another three days before the next flight. Let us unwind.

In practically every hotel in the big cities, beautiful prostitutes approached me. When my stored-up sperm began to do my head in, I almost said 'yes' but somehow held back, and came in my hotel shower. If nothing else, I wanted the purity of the love Orit and I shared to remain intact.

When for a third time there was yet another call to arms, I insisted on talking to Rafi before the trip.

He heard me out and it seemed that this time I had succeeded in making clear to him the extent of our distress. Orit's and mine.

If you decide to break the contract and resign I won't stand in your way, he said. And if you want a job at HQ I'll take care of that as well. But now we have an urgent operation on our hands. If you end up deciding to quit this will be your last.

My last, I said.

15

HIS NAME WAS Wolfgang Schultz. The intelligence officer showed us a picture of a tall, heavyset man of about fifty, with reddish cheeks and slickly combed back thinning, blond hair. This picture is ten years old, he said, and presented a number of computer-generated images showing how Schultz's appearance might have altered in the intervening decade. He was seen getting fatter, getting thinner, shedding more hair, wearing a wig and glasses. We all remember how, despite his wig and glasses, Shkaki, the leader of Islamic Jihad was identified, and have to be prepared for every possible disguise that Schultz may have opted for.

The man is Austrian, but over the past ten years he has rarely set foot outside of Syria. He organizes most of the sensitive purchases made by the Syrian Institute for the Development of Weapons and the Syrian arms industry. Of late he has also begun to arrange the shipment of advanced equipment to Hezbollah. Practically their entire surveillance system, which includes long-range field-glasses for day time use and night-vision goggles, and all their eavesdropping equipment, was purchased through him.

The intelligence officer spread out a map with red circles around the places where Schultz had companies, and a diagram explaining the structure of the firms and his subsidiary companies. This is virtually the only channel through which banned components continue to reach Syria, and this is its gateway to the next generation of weaponry. Most of the companies are legitimate. We have made numerous attempts to stir the EU and the Americans into action to block his activities but without success. In the meantime the head of this pyramid lives like a king in a villa on the coast near Latakia and has a luxury apartment in Damascus.

Then Rafi took to the floor. A year ago his grandson was born in Vienna and Schultz has decided to go and see him. He also has a connection with a woman in Salzburg whom he intends to meet first. He is leaving tomorrow for Austria and plans to return in a week's time. We don't want him to come back.

I rehashed the same old questions. What about frightening him, exposing him to the authorities, even beating him up?

We've already threatened him and twice sent him small parcels of explosives, Rafi replied. The man is a born anti-Semite, the son of an SS officer, an Austrian of the worst kind. That sort of thing won't deter him in the slightest.

Udi, now the division's deputy, and about to succeed Rafi as its head, turned towards me. Speaking gently, he said: I have known about your reservations, Yogev, from as far back as the operation in Hong Kong. They are reasonable and we respect them. But as you'll remember, and as has been your experience in the more than ten years that you have been in our division, a great deal of thought goes into the various operational options. We are not trigger happy and the long line of authority goes all the way up to the prime minister.

This may perhaps sound racist, I said, but up till now we have only killed Arabs with whom we have a clear-cut account to settle. Now we're talking about an Austrian.

What's the difference between Schultz and that man, the head of the Syrian Institute, what's his name? Rafi wondered out loud. Muhammad Zaif, now I remember, he said as he continued. They cause the same kind of damage, both are addicted in the same way to waging war against us. The only real difference between them is their nationality.

And if we're already talking about it, Udi added, I'm not at all sure which of them is worse.

So let's get on with it, I said.

We arrived in Vienna carrying Israeli passports and continued our journey on a domestic flight to Salzburg where we landed only moments before Wolfgang Schultz's incoming flight from Damascus. Our team, hurriedly brought in from various nearby locations in Europe, took up positions at all the exit points and approaches to the small airfield just in time.

At passport control Ayala, a young, European-looking woman who was new to my team, stood in the line for Austrian and EU citizens where she was able clearly to identify Schultz. From a distance it was easy to slip up; he had shed at least ten kilos, coloured the little hair he had left black, and grown a goatee beard giving his large, rounded head a slightly elongated look. He was wearing a pair of thick-rimmed glasses and looked altogether different from the photo we had.

From that moment until he departed this earth, Schultz was never out of our sight. From a distance we kept tabs on him on his way to the baggage carousel, to customs, and from there to the exit.

Schultz scanned the welcoming crowd. A woman waved to him, left the barrier where people were waiting, and rushed towards him. They then walked together to the car park.

I switched on my mini communications device and told the team they'd be tailing a private vehicle. Those keeping watch on trains, bus stations, and taxis withdrew. The two cars in the car park that were to follow him and his companion had their engines turned on, and my team and I got into a third vehicle. We all set off in the direction of the city centre.

Despite the tension of the operation, I could not but enjoy the wooded mountains overlooking the city, and the squares and their fountains which we crawled past in the noisy traffic.

The woman dropped Schultz off at the Palace Hotel in the centre of town. Ayala, carrying a small suitcase, entered the lobby immediately after him. One lookout was left at the entrance to the building and I instructed the two pursuing cars to continue tailing the woman. Her home would undoubtedly be a kind of trap – either because he might go there and we would get him, or because from there his friend might lead us to him. Levanon and I substituted our travel documents with foreign ones and booked in at a nearby hotel.

From our room's window we had a view of Salzburg's ancient citadel and, across the street, could see the gently flowing river that divides the old city from the new. I breathed deeply. In a short while the mission would be pumping adrenalin into my system, bringing the target into sharp focus, not allowing me to see anything else. Meanwhile, I still hoped that we would manage a visit to the seventeenth-century cathedral in Mozart Square, and perhaps get to one of the stunning vantage points overlooking the city from a height of one thousand metres. But that wasn't to be.

Ayala made contact. She had been standing next to Schultz as he checked in to the hotel and was now able to give us his room number. A short while later the team tailing the woman messaged her address to us and there I went in order to check out the area. The quiet neighbourhood of two-storey homes with small, well-kept gardens was a place where the neighbours probably knew each other and where strangers didn't visit. We'll work here only at night, if at all, I decided.

The woman picked Schultz up from his hotel at seven that evening. To our utter astonishment the couple seemed to be taking the road back to the airport. Along the short route I tried to figure out where we'd gone wrong. What was it that had so alarmed him? Frenzied plans for mounting an operation before the target managed to slip away from us raced through my mind. I turned to consult Levanon who was sitting in the back of the car behind the driver. Neither of us could come up with an idea that wouldn't expose us to more risk than we could afford.

Then, to our great relief, we noticed that they were heading to a highly regarded restaurant by the name of Ikarus which was located in one of the hangars in Salzburg's luxurious airport. We waited.

After the meal the pair drove back to her house, and we followed closely behind. The woman drew up in front of her garden gate, opened it, drove her car into a small parking bay and returned to close the gate. This left Schultz alone in the vehicle for about thirty seconds. That should be enough, I whispered to Levanon.

We parked two houses along, all the while waiting for a suspicious neighbour to approach us or even call the police. But only a very few cars went by, and in the bitter cold sweeping down from the Dolomites, not a single pedestrian was to be seen.

It was nearly eleven by the time the pair came out of the house and the woman re-opened the gate. I instructed our driver to turn on the ignition. Schultz's friend reversed her car out of the parking bay and braked at the very edge of the pavement almost parallel to the road. Then she stepped out of the car to close the gate. Schultz, sitting in the front passenger seat, was now alone.

Get going and open the window, I told my driver. The woman was standing with her back to us, shutting the gate, as we came to a halt alongside her car. Because the driver's door had been left open, the vehicle's interior light was on and I could see Schultz looking towards us as I fired. His window shattered, his head drooped to one side. I fired again. Once more his massive head shook. Drive on, I said, and heard Levanon winding up his window behind me. This time he didn't have to shoot. I reckoned that we had disappeared round the first turning by the time the woman had turned to her car and found her friend's body slumped across the seat.

I'd been away from Israel for about a day and a night. Just hours after the shooting I was already across the Austrian border in Bratislava. Levanon crossed into the Czech Republic and made his way to Prague while Ayala travelled on the night train to Munich. We'd got rid of our weapons and the communications system which the European team took back with them. In the morning I flew from Budapest to Israel, Levanon left from Prague, and Ayala continued on to Frankfurt and flew home from there in the evening.

On the morning of my arrival it turned out that Orit's ovulation was imminent. Because the ad-hoc squad recently attached to me was under my command, I was given the rank of 'Station Head Abroad' which afforded me the right to a service car. The driver came to the airport where I gave him my equipment and documents in return for my genuine ID and set off for home. Later that afternoon, Orit and I were to present ourselves at the hospital. This time I feel confident in a way I haven't before, she said on the way. I remembered harbouring such hopes in the past but this time I too felt particularly optimistic. As a result of our virtually nonexistent sex-life my body was less needy and produced less sperm. But on this occasion, despite my concerns about the mission and with adrenalin still coursing through my veins, I felt like a boxer forced into abstinence until after the fight and now I could barely wait. Orit told the doctor that this was the last time.

As if to etch this last throw of the dice in her memory, Orit asked for only a local anaesthetic, and felt no pain during the procedure. Her bleariness turned into a deep sleep while we were on our way home. I carried her from the car into our bed, saddened by the sight of how thin and frail she had become. The next day I returned to HQ to be debriefed.

The Austrians were sure that this was murder, but fortunately for us Schultz was travelling with forged documents and for two whole days the police thought that there was a romantic background to the killing. The woman strenuously guarded her lover's real identity and insisted that this was a 'politically motivated murder'. Only when Schultz's son called from Vienna and complained that his father was not answering the phone at his hotel and that there had been no contact with him for several days, did the police make the crucial connections. Then the whole story broke in the media.

How journalists got to know every detail about our target was beyond me. It was as if they had access to our intelligence files. I suspected that despite the Mossad's objection to any publicity, they had unofficial channels to the media that carefully leaked details to the press when it suited them. And this time, too, they knew exactly how to publicize the story of who the man was, of the damage he had wrought, and of previous attempts made to warn him. Also published were fairly accurate details of the assassination. It turned out that neighbours had, in fact, noticed a waiting car with three men in it and that at the sound of gunfire Schultz's friend had turned round and seen us making our getaway. It also transpired that the police followed the footsteps of a mysterious Israeli woman who had booked into Schultz's hotel 'at the very same time as he did' and disappeared immediately after he was killed.

On the morning of the fourth day after my return home, the story was all over page one of the paper delivered to our house with a banner headline above a large photo of Schultz, a picture of the shattered car window, and detailed descriptions, including an identikit picture of Ayala and three silhouettes of the 'killers'.

We sat around the kitchen table drinking our morning coffee. The phone call from the hospital was due at any moment. Orit was smoking, tensed up. Then she saw the headline. She turned the newspaper towards her and went over the main points of the story.

On Monday evening, which is to say when you weren't here, she muttered without lifting her eyes from the newspaper. Were you there?

I always knew that if Orit asked me directly, I wouldn't lie to her. And I said, 'yes'.

Her expression became threatening and frightened at one and the same time.

You took part in the shooting?

Yes, I answered, lowering my eyes.

Orit stubbed out her cigarette and stood up.

Son of a bitch, she said quietly, you promised me.

Orit, look at who he was.

I see who he was. An arms dealer. And who are you, God? God's executioner? Who do you people think you are?

Orit...

None of that Orit stuff! now raising her voice. I don't want to hear any excuses. I was suspicious of you when the story about the Arabs on those islands and the plane broke. I didn't want to know because I understand that when somebody's pointing a missile at an aircraft and is about to fire it, there is no option but to shoot them. But an arms dealer? Are you crazy? Don't you realize that is murder? Not self defence, not foiling terror, not nothing. It's simply murder!

Her eyes pierced me to the core as if I'd been hit by a salvo of bullets. It seemed to me that any answer I gave would only make matters worse. I kept quiet, stunned and bewildered. I always understood her opposition to my participation in liquidations. I understood her hurt at my lying to her. But only now did I understand the extent to which our points of reference were so utterly different. Mine was intended to enable the state to exist. In such a system you kill the enemy. When you have to. Orit's world was one of purity, based on a system of values that are certainly right, so long as they don't come up against reality. In a utopian world I could easily believe in such a system, but in the real world, it made survival impossible.

She clutched her head between her hands. What happened to the boy who wrote me poems, she asked, lifting her tear-filled eyes, peering at me quizzically, where did he disappear to?

I shifted to the chair beside her and placed my hand on her shoulder. She flinched in alarm and pushed my hand away.

Is that the hand you fired with? she asked turning towards me as she stood up. That's the hand that held the pistol?

In truth, no, I began to say and stopped after the first word. I saw a look of sheer contempt in her eyes.

That truth changes nothing. This wasn't your first time, correct? I hesitated for a moment. Was it right to try and calm her down now and then tell the truth when she was in a different mood? That surely would only make the situation even worse. She'll never be able to believe me if I lie to her now.

That's right, I said.

Orit's scream frightened me. It rose from the depths of her being, gobbling up all the air in her lungs and scaling her entire vocal range on its way. That's the cry of a bereaved mother, was the thought that flashed through my mind.

So we are living a lie! So you've been deceiving me all these years! I'm living with a murderer, oh God!

She was hysterical. I felt I had to do something; embrace her, slap her face, pour a glass of cold water over her – something, just not to let this irrational storm take hold. I moved up close, wanting to hug her.

Don't touch me! she snapped in an icy tone. Don't you dare touch me. Not now, not ever! You've killed off twenty years of my life and for that I won't forgive you. Never. I can't bear being near you any longer. I don't want to see you again.

Or, that's enough, I pleaded.

Please, get out of here. I don't want you here.

Or. Please calm down. I understand your disappointment. I understand the anger, but I had no option…

No option but to murder? No option but to lie to me? Can you hear what you are saying? Have you no soul, Yogev? And as you have lied to me for all those years, then what we had between us was also a lie! It's all erased! Gone!

The phone rang and Orit lifted the receiver. She listened, expressionless. Then I heard her saying in a quiet but determined tone.

I'm not coming. I don't want it. As far as I'm concerned you can destroy it.

I quickly picked up the second receiver and asked the woman at the other end of the line to repeat what she had said to Orit.

There was a good division of the cells, we have a suitable embryo, and your wife needs to get here for it to be transferred.

With alarming precision Orit repeated her earlier instruction.

You're not going to destroy a thing! I screamed down the line. We'll get there, if not immediately, then a bit later.

I'm sorry about the situation, Sir, madam. But we need to know.

You can freeze it? I asked, realizing that Orit was not about to recover any time soon.

When there are a number of good embryos we freeze what is not transferred sir, but of course it's preferable that the transfer be done now.

I won't come, I don't want it inside me, so there's no point in freezing either. I'm not prepared to allow you to do that. Orit put the phone down.

I'll get back to you, I told the clearly bewildered woman on the other end of the line. Keep it as is for as long as possible, and then freeze. Don't destroy it under any circumstances!

I too put down the phone. Again, Orit sat at the table lighting yet another cigarette. The signs of the storm were no longer visible on her face, but her expression reflected a new, unfamiliar decisiveness.

Or, we've been trying to conceive for more than ten years and now, just because you are angry with me, and I understand your anger, you're going to throw it all away?

I'm not going to give birth to your child, she said quietly, without looking at me, her forehead supported by her hand, her elbow resting on the table.

Or, there's something I haven't told you. That was my last trip. I agreed that with Rafi. That's it. Finished. He promised to make it possible for me to retire or arrange a job for me at HQ.

Can you really just push 'rewind' and go back in time? Can you erase everything you have already done? Does the fact that you're not going to murder again absolve you of all the murders you have already committed? Does promising that you will never lie again purge you of all the lies you've told me?

I could no longer restrain myself, nor was there any point. The line behind which Orit had barricaded herself was leading to an absolute breach between us. I had never been drawn into a quarrel with her and had almost never responded to her accusations by blaming her. But now it seemed to me the last resort, the one thing that might make her come to her senses.

I never lied to you, Orit. You knew exactly when to ask and when not. It was you who decided when to know and when not to know, I said quietly.

When I saw that the look of anger and contempt was still there, I continued.

You too are selective. You decided that it was OK to kill terrorists firing a missile at a plane but that it's not OK to kill an arms dealer who supplies them with such missiles. I don't make decisions, Or. I carry them out, I put plans into practice. I don't play God, so don't you play Him either. That's what you're doing with the embryo.

Not a muscle moved in her face.

Think of me as a soldier Or, I said almost begging in light of her silence. Think about Lebanon, about Gaza. In those situations you said nothing, and there I killed a lot more. We're in a war, Or.

I won't bring up the son of a murderer, she said quietly, her words fired one by one at my chest.

Or, I jumped from my chair.

Murder is murder is murder. Once upon a time you

163

also believed that. When we went together with the whole village to Rabin's memorial ceremonies after his assassination. Remember? And don't call me Or. Or and Ar are also dead.

I left the house.

16

I mounted my four-wheeler and headed for the fields. The workers recognized me from a distance, raising their hands in greeting, but I didn't want to stop for anyone just then. I drove on to the patrol road, changed gear, and pushed down the accelerater as hard as I could. Dust blew into my eyes triggering a trickle of tears which helped to relieve a little of the anguish I felt. But only a little. I refused to believe that the twenty years Orit and I had spent together could end this way. I refused to accept that our hopes for a child of our own could evaporate just like that.

I was angry. With myself. With the Mossad. But most of all it was the anger that I felt towards Orit that took hold of me. What she was doing was simply crazy. Her lie was at least as big as mine. You don't kill a child, the hope for a child, for the sake of some sort of adopted belief.

I drove on until my versatile vehicle ran out of fuel. That left me standing, covered in dust from head to toe, by the edge of the patrol path, a few dozen kilometres from our village. I started walking back across the open fields and along the way I was picked up by a military car. The driver was good enough to return with me to my vehicle and pour some of his reserve fuel into my tank. By the time I reached home I knew what I had to say to Orit.

She'd heard me arrive and was coming down from her studio as I walked in.

Even before I had a chance to open my mouth she began. This is no fleeting moment of madness. The murder clinched it for me but we haven't been a couple for a very long time. Because of or not because of the child we don't have, because of or not because of your work. The way things are, I do not want to carry on. I can't live with you any longer. Even if there is a chance of us having this child, you've killed off any possibility of that actually happening. You won't understand. You may even think that it's crazy. But I am absolutely not prepared to have your child, nor do I want you or any part of you in my life. I can't be clearer than that.

I tried to approach her but with a wave of the hand she signalled me to stay away.

And if you don't mind, please take your clothes off outside.

I spent the following week at my parents' house.

Their situation was such that I didn't need to give any explanations. My father hardly ever got out of bed and had no idea what was going on in the rest of the house. Recently, my mother's memory had declined to the point where she didn't even remember that I had moved out long ago.

Orit's parents were more affected by the news of our

separation. What made it particularly difficult for them was a lack of information – Orit hadn't told them a thing and they couldn't understand what had led to the breakup. They – as well as I – believed that in the end everything would be OK.

Not feeling able to go back to work in the state I was in, I asked HQ for a short leave of absence. Every day during that week I went out to the fields and the small adjustments I made in the way the farm was running helped to improve my mood a little. Twice during that week I went to the house I had shared with Orit to fetch clothes or documents and found her matter of fact and cold.

After a week of convalescence which brought no real relief but was a good pointer of things to come, I returned to the office.

Udi – who had recently been appointed head of the division – suggested that I become head of his planning department. It's a job tailor-made for you, he said. We don't have anyone with even half your operational experience.

But I wanted to get away from operational activity. Not only did I not want to pull the trigger, I also didn't want to be around when somebody else was pulling it – I didn't want to be in any way involved with that side of things. I also had no desire to plan an operation for others to execute. Perhaps Orit is right and I have no soul. Maybe, if I cut off all my links with such operations, my soul can be rehabilitated.

What I'm interested in is an assignment at HQ that has nothing to do with operations, I explained to Udi, and suggested that Levanon take the job he had offered me. I've watched him in the field. He's much better than me, I said.

No, said Udi, with a paternal smile. He's much more determined than you are. For all his smiles, when it comes right down to it he's an Amstaff. In the field, as well as at HQ, we need someone who goes on using his head until the very last moment, and beyond, into that last critical moment when the shooting has begun. Not someone who 'fires and forgets'. There is no shortage of courageous and determined people. And those who follow orders are also in plentiful supply. If you check all the mishaps we have suffered you'll discover a surfeit of determination, of courage and obedience. You are among the few who operate without ceasing to think and question. That's why, from our point of view, you were the classic number one and Levanon the archetypal number two. It's not that we didn't notice your hesitancy, in discussions as well as in the field. But your collaboration with Levanon produced the ideal duo.

As for the rest, he continued, I completely understand what you are saying. But if that's what you really want then our division is not the place for you. What can I possibly offer – training? Head of the training department? That won't answer your desire to disengage completely. There you would also be involved in training operatives, shooting, preparing explosive devices. It's OK with me if you want to check out the options in other divisions. Look how well Motti and Micha have integrated into and moved up the ladder in Tevel and Tzomet. Contact with other intelligence services and even agent recruitment are areas that might also suit you.

My round of visits produced similar if not pre-arranged responses. Tevel – foreign relations – didn't want someone who couldn't be made known to other services because of the numerous violent operations he'd been involved in. Tzomet – recruitment – could only suggest my continued activity around targets. Not liquidation as such, but recruitment by all the various means that I didn't want to employ and didn't think I was good at.

If you managed to conceal what you were doing from your wife for so many years, then believe me you're good at it, Tzomet's head of manpower told me as I left his office, more astonished than angry. Other divisions had nothing to offer me. It's not personal, they said, it happens a lot with people who return from the field and want to fit into HQ. There simply are no jobs for them. And apart from that, those who are skilled in the field often don't have the qualifications needed at HQ, sitting at a desk for eight hours a day, getting stuck into the detail, and filing things away.

I also assume that I radiated an air of fatigue and frailty that didn't exactly make me attractive to a would-be employer. I'm not one of those who think they've achieved much and are therefore 'deserving'. Nonetheless, I felt somewhat humiliated when I got back to Udi empty-handed.

I don't mind simply being a clerk, idling away the time left until my contract is up. Alternatively just let me go. At the moment I don't have the money to repay what I received during my studies as our spare cash has gone on the treatments. On top of that, if I have to leave the house and start all over again from scratch I shall get into debt. And anyway I haven't the energy for the role you offered.

Give it a try and see how it goes, Udi suggested in a spirit of friendship. Be head of planning. I've known you for long enough. The energy will come with the missions. I also have a little bonus for you, he added. We'll cover your rent if you decide to take an apartment somewhere near here. For a head of a department to have a three-hour journey to and from work, even if it's not every day, is sheer madness.

The temptation was great. I also knew that I would be comfortable working with Udi. But I couldn't give up on the hope of rebuilding my life with Orit. I turned the offer down. We'd reached an impasse.

It had been a week since I had last seen Orit and I didn't want to set foot in our home unannounced. On the other hand it felt odd to have to make an appointment to visit my own home and talk to my wife.

I have something important to tell you, I said on the phone.

So say it, she replied drily.

It has to be said face to face.

Fine, she said in that same frigid voice.

Orit was thin, ashen-faced and sloppily dressed. From above came the sound of music, and over it the voice of her assistant. I went into the kitchen, the most intimate and secluded place I could allow myself to enter at that moment, and sat down. Orit remained standing.

I've had time to think, to see what went wrong, I said.

I've also had a conversation with Udi. He's now head of my division, by the way, and he's offered me the job of heading the planning department.

The expression on her face remained frozen.

I refused his offer. I decided to quit the office for good and come back here. I will take over my parents' farm and pay the office whatever is necessary, just as you wanted me to do a long time ago. You were right.

You can do whatever you like, she said. That's what you've always done. It has nothing to do with me anymore.

Or, I'm not only talking about returning to the village. I'm talking about coming back to you. About giving us another chance.

You're too late, she said. I wondered whether in her voice I was detecting a note of sadness, of disappointment, or was it simply the same impassivity that I'd heard in our brief phone conversation. You can't turn the clock back. I don't want to know what they're offering you or what you do there. I pity you and pity them if you are thinking of cementing this twisted union of yours. If what I am saying isn't clear enough, I'll put it another way, and then you'll finally realize that I really mean it. I want a divorce.

My heart fell, and I could only repeat, Or, I told him no, that I wasn't going to continue with them. You forced me to choose, and I made the choice. All I can do is regret that it didn't happen years ago.

You don't have a choice here, Orit answered, her eyes closed, her face tightly drawn. Then she opened her eyes and stared at me. I too had a week without you, and with no expectation of you returning. And I'm sorry to tell you it only did me good.

There was no sadness there, no malevolence, and no note of victory. Perhaps just a huge sense of weariness.

I'm no longer an option that is open to you, she continued. Now I want to go back to work.

She turned and climbed the stairs to her studio, closing the door after her and, with it, two decades of life.

Bewildered, I went to our bedroom to collect the rest of my things. To my surprise I found dumped in the corridor two suitcases and several boxes full of my possessions.

Almost without thinking, my legs weighed down with fatigue, I loaded up the car. When I reached my parents' house I went straight to my room and to sleep. The suitcases and boxes remained in the car, and for days I didn't bother to unpack them.

I considered returning to the village to run my parents' farm, living with them and enriching their remaining days. I knew that I would enjoy working in the fields.

Equally, I knew that my nights would be full of pain and that every time I went anywhere near our/her home, and at every chance or arranged meeting between us, I would hurt. There would also be the constant temptation of going into the house and testing the waters. And so I informed Udi that I was accepting his proposal and rented a small apartment not far from the line of beach hotels in Tel Aviv. Glimpses of the sea could be caught through the narrow spaces between the houses opposite. In the

171

evenings I'll watch the sunset. At night I'll walk along the corniche, drink beer in one of the restaurants with their chairs and gaily coloured lights spread out across the sand all the way down to the lapping waves. And in the mornings, if I have the energy, I'll run the length of the shoreline.

In the event, never getting back to the apartment before nightfall, I saw no sunsets. After making my way down to the corniche a few times to sip coffee, nurse a beer, or drink a milkshake among constantly changing groups of young revellers with whom I had nothing in common, I stopped doing it. I felt closer to the homeless, with their matted hair, lying along the promenade or roaming aimlessly along it, than to the youths passing by as if shadows in the night.

Tel Aviv is a sad city for single people, especially if they are already in their late thirties. Once or twice I thought of taking an escort girl, less for the sex for which I hardly felt the need, more for the company. But I was too tired for it. I would linger on in the office and once back in my apartment, went to bed early. When I had difficulty falling asleep, I read. And because I wanted to fall asleep quickly I reached for the 'big bores', those classics that seemed to me to have been written exclusively for the literary elite. Proust, Joyce, Yizhar. To my surprise, I managed to really get into them and stretch my reading time until my eyes finally closed. And only on odd occasions when I got up very early and didn't want to go to the office and appear to be one of those workaholics, did I go down to the beach and walk along the shore. The running never materialized. It was more than my body could cope with.

I embarked on the role of head of the planning department with indifference, and again my low-key approach was misunderstood. Once more a few considered words from me were interpreted as the result of measured thinking and composure. And somehow my suggestions were always accepted. Experience allowed me to fly on autopilot. I wasn't in a hurry to be somewhere, and sat late into the night poring over charts of men, missions and stages of a mission. In the morning everything I proposed was approved.

I was giving the impression of being very industrious, so no one guessed at the turmoil that had taken over my mind or the tiredness that overwhelmed every limb of my body.

I put one mission after another on the road. All of them went according to plan and produced good results.

The success was always that of the operatives, not of operational planning. Only the agent in the field can read the situation and decide whether, when, and how to act, or whether to postpone, or perhaps withdraw. In this sense the concealment of a listening device in the basement of a Hezbollah man living in Switzerland doesn't differ from the liquidation of an arms dealer in Salzburg. The young operatives were easy going, alert, and good at what they did, and none of them guessed how worn out I was.

I couldn't avoid it forever and nor could Udi postpone the inevitable. There are missions that require the head of planning to be with the men in the field. This happens when the territory is unfamiliar or when the squad's commander needs to get authorization in the field for the chosen method of operation.

I found myself travelling to operations all over the world, including places that were categorized as 'soft target countries'. Though I was a good advisor, I don't think I was a good commander. The adrenalin in my body didn't reach a level sufficient to banish the tiredness or restore my focus. In such cases experience made up for the lack of enthusiasm and talk of my 'indifference' did not yet point to a problem.

Each Saturday I drove to the village. My father now needed round-the-clock nursing and a carer had been assigned to him. He was a mere shadow of the man I remembered from my childhood. He spoke only with difficulty but when I sat at his side, holding his emaciated hand, straining to capture his whispered words, I knew that he was aware of my being there, but the little spark left in him could no longer bring him back to life and, in fact, filled me with sorrow.

Various tests were arranged for him. How can it be, I asked the doctors, that a person of his age can become nothing but skin and bone, barely alive, just like that. There must be a hidden cancer or something else you haven't found and are not treating.

You're right, old age is not an illness, one of the doctors caring for him admitted. Perhaps there is something else. But whatever it is we haven't found it. The tests have revealed nothing more than the inevitable physical failings of advancing years which, I agree, doesn't explain the state he's in.

My mother wandered around the house, gaunt and restless, as if looking for something. When she came across me she would ask if I knew where the boy who used to sleep in this bed was – pointing to my room – and whether perhaps I could remember his name. This was no belated sense of humour, but a real decline in her condition. I was filled with sadness and tried to hug her, but she pushed me away as if I was a stranger. I thought that my weekends with her would renew the connection between us but even when I'd taught her to call me by my name and to repeat as a baby the words 'you are my son' she continued looking for the little child from that room, and didn't understand at all who I was and what I was doing there.

I felt heavy hearted. About her and about myself. That little child was no more. Not there, not anywhere. He barely remained in her memory or in mine. And the youth who slept there after the child was also no more. Neither was the young man, or his hopes, dreams, and passions. And the vitality of the man who arrives every weekend resembled more the fading old man and the demented old lady. Like them he couldn't understand where his youth had vanished to or who he was and what he was doing there. There, or anywhere else for that matter.

When I left the house on Saturday nights, my father's carer would lock the doors because from time to time my mother tried to walk out and 'go home'.

I didn't see the other woman who had spurned me as if I was a stranger. We talked once on the phone when Orit asked me to sign a document waiving any claim to the frozen embryo. I thought that holding on to this group of cells as a way of getting Orit back would not be an honourable thing to do. I also didn't want to exploit this issue in order to meet up with her. I saw no point in telling her yet again that destroying an embryo was also murder. Nor did I really believe that.

I suggested she leave the form at my parents' house, and told her I would think about it. I knew she went there every few days to see how they were getting on and offer her help.

At the weekend I picked up the form several times, read it, but couldn't bring myself to sign. It was a waiver written by the Department of Health's legal advisor necessitated by the problem we had created – one of us wanting to destroy the frozen embryo, the other wanting it to be kept. Various ideas flashed through my mind. To keep the embryo frozen until times were different – Orit would perhaps change her mind; perhaps keep it until I wanted a child of my own, whether or not Orit was involved? If ever such a time would come. Somewhere in the recesses of my brain a realization began to dawn which I tried to push away; that if till now I had failed to bring a child into the world my prospects of future success were much diminished. And, slowly, one thing did become clear. Orit was never going to allow a child of ours to be born.

Signing the form would consign me to an eternity of childlessness and loneliness. But I could think of no rational, sober, honourable, or sound reason for turning down Orit's explicit request.

A moment before going out to the car that Saturday evening, I signed and then fled the house. I could barely breathe as I heard my father's carer lock the house door. The sound of the double lock triggered two locks within me, one closing off the past, the other shutting off the future. All that was left of my present reality was a thin, hollow layer of brittle veneer.

There are other things Orit will have to do, I thought in despair; take the form, add her signature, and hand it to the hospital. Perhaps something will intervene and stop her.

A week later I was informed that the embryo had been destroyed. And with it the remaining hope I had of a different future.

17

ALMOST HALF A year had passed since our separation when Orit phoned and asked me to come and see her. It's not a conversation you're going to like, she said, sparing me any false hope.

But she didn't save me from shock and heartache.

Again we sat in our kitchen. It looked different though I couldn't put my finger on what it was that had changed. Orit also looked different. Ending the treatment had apparently done her good. She'd filled out a bit, was a little tanned, a spark of life in her eyes. But her demeanour remained serious, very serious. I want us to divorce formally now, she said, cutting to the chase. I've met

177

someone. I think it has a chance. And I can't afford the luxury of wasting any more time.

I'm thankful for your trust, I told her. She could, after all, have withheld the news about this 'someone' till after the divorce.

I've known you since our childhood. You won't make it a problem, she replied.

I'm perhaps a murderer and a liar but I'm neither petty nor vengeful, I said trying, unsuccessfully, to smile.

You said it, she responded.

The calm I felt surprised even me. As the months passed I hadn't pinned my hopes on Orit changing her mind. In fact, I'd almost stopped thinking about her.

I'm ready to go with you to the Rabbinate whenever you want, I said. Orit burst into tears. I couldn't decide whether this was a cry of relief at my having agreed or of sadness that our fate was now sealed. And then I too felt a gut-wrenching sadness.

A week later we attended the regional Rabbinical court in Beersheba. I thought it more than a little ironic that it was in a street named 'hope'. Orit was wearing a particularly dark pair of sunglasses, looked very stressed, and said almost nothing. When the Rabbinical judge suggested reconciliation and I told him we were skipping that stage, I feared for a moment that my tone of voice would sound insincere. In the event my sorrow turned out to be more under control than I thought. The die was cast and I was deeply aware that things could hardly have been otherwise. Not in the face of the punishment inflicted by the lifestyle I'd imposed on both of us. Like Orit, that was the only way I could understand the barenness of two healthy people.

What awaited us next were the religious proceedings. These reignited all the misgivings I had towards every religious ritual and any intrusion of the state in my private life.

We asked the same two classmates, Guy and Dori, who'd been witnesses at our wedding, to confirm our divorce. They were clearly upset and Guy said: your divorce has destroyed what faith I still had in married life. And I felt utterly dazed when the Rabbinical Judge checked whether I understood that Orit would from now on be permitted to any man and again when I saw her, as if through a fog, taking off the ring and displaying her thin now ring-less finger to him.

This is your divorce certificate, I repeated the words of the Rabbinical Judge, and with it you are now divorced from me and are permitted to any man.

Actually it's Orit who divorced me, I thought to myself, when the word 'divorced' spilled from my dry mouth. How come that everything has been turned upside down?

She picked up the document, tears streaming from beneath her sunglasses which she had not removed even in the bleak light of the court room. She then took a few steps back and returned to where she'd been standing. A sudden surge of hope overwhelmed me when I saw her returning and placing the certificate on the table. But that wish immediately faded when I realized that this was merely part of the ceremony. Only then did I understand how much, despite everything, I wanted to turn the clock back.

When we stepped out into the brightness of the desert sun lighting up the paved concourse and stone-walled buildings, we were close to one another and I thought of kissing her on the cheek. Apparently that was a somewhat quixotic and uncalled for gesture judging from the way Orit remained standing still, as if at attention. Offering to shake her hand would also be theatrical, I thought. So all the best, I said, trying to smile, and she replied, to you too, and hurried to her car. Guy accompanied her and I walked with Dori to a nearby kiosk in an attempt to relieve the lump in my throat. Both Orit and I, it seems, hoped that once the procedure was over the distress would ease. That's not how it went for me.

As I turned back from the kiosk I caught sight of Orit, sitting in her car. The engine was running, her head was leaning on the driving wheel. Alarmed I hurried towards her. But at that moment she sat bolt upright, turned her head, and at speed reversed out of the car park.

Orit wanted to stay on in the house and offered to buy my half. Her new boyfriend, who was going to move in with her, was well off. I thought of using the money to buy out the remaining period of my contract with the Mossad but then realised I had nowhere to go back to. My father had to be moved to a geriatric ward in a hospital in Beersheba, and I was advised that my mother should also be hospitalized there. The geriatric psychiatrists examining her there could not agree on whether she was suffering from dementia, senility or Alzheimer's. At her stage in life there wasn't much difference between the three and there was no cure. I placed her in the department which treated people suffering from severe dementia and where the nurses seemed to me to be especially humane.

Every time I went past the house I'd shared with Orit, I saw her boyfriend's brand new Toyota jeep parked outside, its very presence an assault on my eyes. Clearly, if I were to move to my parents' empty home I would have to cope not only with this disturbing sight but also with watching Orit's new man embracing her as they walked along the village footpaths. To stay in the Mossad and in Tel Aviv was the least worst option.

In the following two months I travelled a great deal and didn't ask to be released from journeys that fell over a weekend or during a holiday period. Yehiel ran the farm successfully and I suggested that he move into my parents' house with his wife and children whom he'd left behind in the centre of the country when he first came to us. That would enable him to keep an eye on the farm also at weekends instead of me doing so.

With that I had almost severed my last link with the village. On my free weekends I visited my father in the geriatric ward and my mother in the hospital's dementia department. Only occasionally did I return to the village to check the situation on the farm and go over the accounts with Yehiel.

Slowly, I became accustomed to my new lifestyle. I got to know two other guys from the office who lived not far from me and went out with them from time to time for a drink. Put together, I saw more films in the cinema and on television in the course of that year than I had ever seen before, particularly after treating myself to a big, flat-screen TV. Once I called an escort agency's number from a newspaper advertisement. The woman was a brunette of about thirty, good looking and pleasant but the sex was terrible and I asked her to leave almost immediately after we'd finished. In due course, when my urges and loneliness got the better of me, I invited another call girl to the flat and again it proved to be a waste of time and money. I couldn't feel anything for the purposeful blonde and the sex was mechanical, even squalid. Again I asked her to leave as soon as we'd completed our business. I had no desire to talk to her or even sleep with her again although the terms of the deal allowed me to do so. Friends from the office attempted to introduce me to various women but I wasn't interested. My reserves of emotion were utterly drained.

I was in no real state to fly around the world, but couldn't allow myself to stay at home not doing anything and shirking missions. On one such assignment I very nearly led the team into difficulties. I don't understand, said young Josh during the debriefing. Yoni informed you that two policemen on horseback were moving along the street in our direction. From the window of your command post in the hotel you should have seen them. How come you didn't notify us?

You had enough time to finish up and get away before the policemen arrived, Levanon, who'd begun to serve as my deputy, explained on my behalf. There was no point in putting unnecessary pressure on you.

Even in my heart of hearts I couldn't thank him. HQ should know that I was losing concentration. It hadn't occurred to Levanon that I'd heard the report about the mounted policemen and a moment later forgot all about it.

In retrospect, the decision not to alarm you was reasonable, Udi concluded. And the main thing is that you carried out the mission and it all ended up well.

I continued flying.

I set up a meeting with Yehiel at the village secretariat to go over a number of charges that we wanted to query. While we were sitting with the accountant in one room I heard Orit's voice in the corridor. Without thinking about it, I excused myself from the meeting and went outside to say hello. Orit was visibly pregnant.

The blow I felt to my stomach could only have been delivered by a well-trained boxer. It took my breath away, and I felt an intense weakness in my whole body. I leant against the wall.

Are you OK? she asked, in a tone of genuine concern. I quickly pulled myself together.

Yes, I replied, in a voice that wasn't mine. Congratulations. I didn't know.

It's a girl. I'm six months pregnant, said Orit, not trying to hide her happiness. I realized her response was intended to make it clear that the pregnancy only came about after we'd divorced.

You're not around anymore, she added as I remained silent. Would you like to call by for a coffee?

I'm on my way north, someone answered for me. I wish you an easy birth if we don't see each other before then.

Orit looked at me worriedly. I turned away and staggered back into the accountant's room.

I can see that you're in no state to continue with the figures, the accountant said as he went on checking the computer data, assuming my mind was elsewhere. Perhaps you want a glass of water? A coffee?

Yehiel, who realized what had happened, put his hand on my shoulder and said: it doesn't have to be now, we can meet another time. He suggested I go to the house for a nap before returning to Tel Aviv. But fuzzy headed as I was, I wanted to get out of this accursed place immediately, even if my destination was the very source of the curse.

18

UDI CALLED MY mobile while I was sitting by the pool in what is perhaps the most luxurious hotel in the Gulf. I was taking a break from the squad's attempts to get into the room of a Saudi Sheikh suspected of having financial ties with Al-Qaida. The Sheikh used to hop to neighbouring states to transfer funds and spend time with local prostitutes, something he couldn't do in his own country. Because most of the transfers to Afghanistan and Sudan were made during such rushed trips, HQ hoped that photographing the documents in his room would lead us to the organization's set up in these countries. The hotel, with its golden chandeliers, ivory ornaments on the walls, and deep pile carpets, had a huge staff which made it difficult for us to find a single moment when there wasn't a chambermaid in the corridor. Whenever a member of our team managed to distract one of them, another would emerge from the housekeeper's room and the break-in kept on being postponed. Because of the sensitivity of this particular region, the squad's commander was ordered to consult me, HQ's senior representative in the field, after any run in with the hotel's staff and such instances were indeed becoming increasingly frequent.

The Sheikh was now resting in his room. For a while, I and other members of the team staying at the hotel spent our time playing tourists. When I heard Udi's voice on my mobile I joked with him a bit, but to my surprise he quickly switched to Hebrew and said, listen, I have some bad news for you.

I'm listening I said, letting a number of possibilities race through my mind, barely managing to wipe away the remnants of a smile or get up from the sun-bed. Your father is dead. The news confirmed one of the possibilities I'd considered.

I see, I found myself saying.

They're waiting for you for the funeral, so you need to get there as quickly as possible. We've booked you on a flight to Athens leaving in three hours from now and you have a seat on the flight from Athens to Israel at eight in the evening. The funeral will take place in the village at eleven tomorrow morning. Let me know if you can make the outgoing flight so that I can tell Orit.

Why her?

Because she's the one who informed me. No one else knew how to find you.

Will do, I agreed.

I was left sitting on the sun-bed, drained, a dull, indefinable pain in my chest. I felt as if the remnants of the light lunch I ate by the pool were turning over inside me. I got up, rubbing my chest to relieve the pressure, and went up to my room to get ready to leave.

His death was expected. But why now? And why without me being able to sit at his bedside in his final hours; once again to hold his emaciated hand and listen to his whispered words? On my last visit a week earlier, he was, at times, still lucid, although nothing but skin and bone, barely able to utter two consecutive words, refusing to eat and spitting out the food his carer spooned into his mouth. He declined signing an authorization to feed him intravenously or through a gastric tube. The doctors said that this couldn't be done against his will and remained in the dark about the disease that was ravaging his body and sapping every ounce of his strength.

I continued to think that after turning over the management of the farm to me he simply lost the will to live. And when my mother could no longer recognize him, complained that this was not her home, and asked who the old man lying in her bed and interfering with her sleep was, he decided to stop living. But his body hung on for a few more agonizing years.

The driver who picked me up at Ben Gurion Airport was prepared to drive me south but I said that there was nothing for me to do in the village that night and that I would make my own way there in the morning.

At eight the following morning, when I was already at the Beit Kama junction in the northern Negev, I phoned the village secretariat but all I got was the answering machine. When I reached Beersheba I tried again but still no one picked up. Perhaps no one is there until nine, I thought, and though I didn't feel comfortable about it, phoned Orit. She was sympathetic and businesslike. Everything is ready. All you have to do is get here. There are even notices in the morning papers.

I'm bringing my mother, I said. There was a long silence at the other end.

Do you think that's necessary?

I think I owe it to her.

I don't know if the nurses in the dementia department had given my mother a tranquillizer but she was certainly calm and wrapped in her own thoughts. The agitation had gone, as had her suspiciousness and obstinacy. She was dressed in black, in clothes that were now far too big for her shrunken body. She let me lead her by the arm to my car and was silent all the way from Beersheba to the Arava. Who could possibly tell what was going on in that much loved and mysterious head of hers? At one of the junctions I leant over and kissed her but she merely smiled a faraway smile, her eyes still clouded over.

I hoped that images of our life together would come

to mind, but all I could conjure up was my last time with my father, his emaciated, lifeless hand in mine, his withered jowls trembling, in his eyes a look that was decidedly not human.

Forcing myself to recall pleasanter images of the three of us, all I could manage to evoke were some photos from the family album. My father in uniform, wearing a paratrooper's beret with a lock of ruffled hair escaping from the front; my mother, in her flowery dress, her hair tousled; the two of them walking down Dizengoff Street in the 1960s, two young people with wide grins on their faces. My father, with his powerful arms, holding me up, still a baby, at the entrance to their small Jewish Agency-built home, with nothing but the sand of the Arava desert around us and my mother looking on tenderly. Me with a hose, watering newly planted seedlings in our fields. My parents on either side holding my hand on the beach in Eilat. I'm a chubby child, my father a well-built man, my mother a bit on the plump side, beautiful, smiling.

I also remembered trips in the car when my mother would enrich my mind with sums and rhyme games. 'There isn't without' was our favourite. 'There isn't a house without a door' she would begin. Then it was my turn, 'There isn't a room without a floor' and father from the driver's seat would chime in 'There isn't a sea without a shore' and so on.

These childhood recollections gave way to images of the dying old man and the elderly woman at my side with that dreamy, distant look in her eyes. Sadness overwhelmed me. I could feel it in the mounting pressure in my chest, the sense of suffocation in my throat, and the tears welling up in my eyes. I breathed in deeply to release the feeling of strangulation and prevent the tears from flowing.

A few dozen people stood waiting at the village cemetery, my parents' peers and mine. Also standing by was the private ambulance with my father's body on board.

Orit and her parents came up to us. She looked youthful again, and I saw that she must have given birth. Kindly, Orit had saved me from that particular piece of news. Her parents, whom I'd not seen for a very long time, were clearly ageing. They leant on my mother and gently embraced her. She responded to the love surrounding her, letting the three of them kiss her and then took the time to hug and kiss the circle of her old friends – members of the core group who, together with her and my father, had built the village. Orit turned to me, kissed me and burst into tears as she clutched my neck.

A lament for my father, or was it for my mother as well? Was she perhaps crying about me, about her, about the two of us? Were these the tears of sadness for the baby we could have had together or an expression of unease about the child she now had? I didn't know, yet her tears triggered my own.

Some of my classmates and pupils from other years as well gathered around me placing firm, sun-tanned hands on my shoulders as we walked behind the stretcher on which my dead father lay. Out of the corner of my eye I saw Orit and her partner, a tall, thin, pale man, walking behind her parents who were supporting my mother. Around the grave were the villagers who took it upon themselves to dig out the soil and then use it to cover the body. One of them, the only one wearing a skull cap, read the burial prayers and then invited those who wished to say their farewells to come forward. I didn't. I was choked up as it was. I'm no wordsmith, nor did I know what to say. Some of my father's old army friends, men in their mid-sixties, robust, sun tanned, dressed in their work-clothes and boots, one in shorts, said words of praise about 'Ben-Ari', the way they always called my father. One spoke of the difficult conditions in the early days of the village when my father told them to 'go and do battle with the bureaucrats at the Jewish Agency's offices while I grow tomatoes so that there'll be something to show them when they come'. Another friend spoke of my father's vacillations when changing his name from Aaronson to Ben-Ari and referred to me by saying that my father had a son in his own image who had gone far across the seas and oceans of the world. I couldn't tell whether this was intended as a veiled criticism for my having left the village or an implied praise for my Mossad service.

I recited Kaddish for my father. Within me I felt an aversion to the incomprehensible words of the Jewish prayer of mourning which glorifies a Being in whose existence I didn't believe, and made mistakes pronouncing the ancient Aramaic phrases. Only when my friends came up to shake my hand in parting and asked where the Shiva would be held, did it occur to me that we would need to sit the traditional seven days of mourning and that the most logical place for it was my parents' house.

Yehiel quickly vacated the living room, the room I used, as well as my parents' bedroom to which I brought my mother. He housed himself and his wife in the fourth room which was built for the brother or sister that I never had and dispatched his children to the family home in the centre of the country.

My decision to let my mother stay for the Shiva raised eyebrows, but I felt that there was something in what was going on that was kindling her confused consciousness and I wanted her at my side. This was a one-off opportunity to be with her for a whole week.

My mother hardly spoke throughout those seven days but listened dreamily to what friends said, let them hold her hand and kiss her. She sat next to me and I sensed that she was seeking out the warmth of my body or at least a point of contact with it, which I always gladly provided. Madeleine, my father's carer who'd been at his bedside in the hospital, joined us and devotedly took care of my mother, accompanied her to the toilet which she could never find on her own, and got up with her at night when my mother announced that she wanted to go 'home'.

Orit visited twice. Once on the day after the funeral, when she arrived with her partner. She planned the visit for a time of day when the house would be full of people from the village. That way I didn't have to talk to the man at all. Our contact was limited to a handshake. With Orit, there was just a mutual embrace and kisses on both cheeks. I felt nothing, neither towards her nor him. She spent the rest of her time at my mother's side.

Her second visit was relatively late on the last evening of the Shiva. The baby was in her arms.

I'm really, really, sorry, she said, but my husband – my husband is what she called him – told me he was running late. I knew this was the last day, and I had no one to leave her with.

My mother, who was sitting far into the room, suddenly understood who'd arrived and the shock of that realization could be read on her face. A light that had vanished years before was rekindled in her eyes. Small and nimble, she stood up and rushed towards Orit. My little cutey, she said, offering her hand to the baby and, without asking permission, snatching her from the bewildered Orit. She gently hugged the child to her breast and peppered her head with kisses. My little sweetheart, my little sweetheart, she murmured.

Orit stood there confused and at a loss. The little girl was in no danger but no one could know what was going through my mother's mind. I gestured to Orit to take the baby from my mother. She gently stretched out her hands but my mother clasped the child to her bosom even more tightly. Then suddenly she turned to me and without saying a word handed the infant into my arms.

Instinctively I took her. I couldn't remember if or when I'd held a baby in my arms. Certainly not a little doll like her, only a few months old. I handled her tenderly, peering at the round, tranquil face, the tiny nose and the perfect, pinkish, slightly parted, lips. Her enormous round dark eyes opened, looked at me for a long moment, then her face crumpled and a heart-rending bellow erupted from the depths of her throat.

I immediately passed her back to Orit. She held her tightly, rocked her a bit, until the child settled down.

I don't think bringing her with me was such a good idea, Orit said. I'm sorry. Tearfully, she left.

I couldn't stay in the room and cope with the pitying looks of the others so I took my mother to the bedroom. I understood that I should go back to the mourners who had, after all, come to see my mother and me. But the pressure I had felt in my chest had returned and I had no reserves of strength left in me. They will excuse me, I thought. I lay next to my mother, on my father's side of the bed, and closed my eyes.

Intermezzo

19

I was willing to let you go, said Udi when I returned to the office, but you can't imagine the chaos here in the week you've been away. Actually, come to think of it, in the nearly two weeks since you went to the Gulf.

This was a matter on which I was unable to express a clear cut view. I knew that I didn't have the strength for more trips abroad. I wasn't sufficiently alert nor did I have the energy that such operations required, and I also wasn't focused enough to sit down at HQ and draw up operational plans. On the other hand, I also didn't have anywhere else to go.

In short, Udi continued, as far as I'm concerned, you are staying. I also don't hear you objecting. So let's get on with it. On your desk are the initial drafts of three operational orders. All I have done is to indicate HQ's objectives. The rest of the planning is up to you.

I began mapping out three different operations, two

in Europe and a third in another 'soft target area'. Before I'd finished considering these three, more 'outline' plans of HQ's objectives in operations in South America and Africa landed on my desk. But the thoughts of the head of the department responsible for the planning of these missions were roaming between the houses of a small desert village.

Udi called me into his office twice to ask why the preparation of the operational orders was so delayed and whether I was all right. The task was finally completed with the assistance of Levanon, my deputy. Members of the teams had numerous comments to make on the details and the chosen methods of operation and I incorporated most of the changes they asked for.

Udi himself, Levanon and I, were to lead the three operations and our departures were to be staggered.

I was sent to Paris. The government in Jerusalem took a dim view of the contacts the French intelligence services had begun to establish with Hamas. Their protests achieved nothing. According to information we received, Abu Ali Fayyad, one of the leaders of the Ezzedeen al Qassam Brigades, the military wing of Hamas, was due to arrive in Paris from Gaza for talks with the heads of French intelligence. When this became known, the decision was taken to put a violent end to the talks. Although Fayyad had a great deal of blood on his hands, I again had reservations. These were referred to the head of the Mossad for his consideration, and once more rejected. Now, without Orit's moral compass, I felt that these qualms were nothing but lip service, a procedural pretence that was obvious to everyone; I protest, my objection is dismissed, and I carry out the operation. I also knew that my hesitations did not absolve me from responsibility.

A quick reconnaissance of Orly airport revealed that Fayyad had been received by just one person – apparently an employee of the local intelligence service – who took him in one of the service's official cars to his hotel.

Our team was small. Splitting the operatives between three different operations meant that the manpower available to me was stretched to the limit. This made it impossible for me to keep Arnon, my number one, unexposed until the operation itself and also forced me to involve him in tailing the target.

The keen-eyed Fayyad noticed that the person walking into the hotel after him was the same individual who had stood by his side while they were both waiting to be picked up at the entrance to the airport. He pointed this out to his host. The Frenchman lost no time, went up to Arnon, presented some sort of official ID, and asked him to identify himself. At first, Arnon expressed his astonishment and indignation, but when the man insisted and threatened to arrest him, he took out an Australian passport, answered a number of questions, and was allowed to go. He just managed to hear the escort saying to his guest 'At seven then.'

I sent the disappointed Arnon back to Israel and took on his role myself, cursing and vowing that this was the last time I would go abroad. That's it. I have no patience for such stupidities and no stamina for this kind of mishap. I have no energy, period.

Towards seven in the evening we deployed ourselves around the hotel. At exactly seven Abu Ali Fayyad was waiting outside the entrance. I had a choice; either hope that his host would be delayed for a couple of minutes in the heavy Parisian traffic or embark on a long, drawn-out pursuit until I managed to find another opportunity.

The street was dark with very few passers-by. Around Fayyad himself there was no one to be seen. I decided to gamble. My car was parked on the other side of the road, opposite the hotel.

I'm going for it, I said to Josh, my driver on this occasion. Turn on the ignition and prepare for a rapid getaway. I notified the team over the communications system, got out of the car, crossed the road in the direction of the hotel, and from a distance of two metres drew my pistol and fired three shots at his chest. The bullets sent him flying as if he'd taken a powerful blow and he fell flat on his back.

According to the intelligence we had, Fayyad was likely to be wearing a flak jacket and I was to complete the task by firing at his head. But I heard a crack as his skull hit the ground and a pool of blood began to spread around his head as well as trickling from the sides of his mouth.

Apparently I lingered there aimlessly for a few seconds. Then, from the waiting car, its engine running, the horn blasted, waking me up to reality. I turned and re-crossed the road as a number of passers-by rushed towards the slain man. A cacophony of voices could be heard behind me followed by the sound of running and shouting. I saw Josh getting out of the car, drawing a pistol, and taking aim.

The footsteps halted. As I reached Josh, still unhurried, he pushed me in the direction of the car, returning to it by walking backwards while continuing to point his gun at those following me. Only when he heard my door closing did he get into the car, press down hard on the accelerator, and close his door as the vehicle sped away.

You gone crazy or what? he fumed. You fell asleep there? They nearly caught you! But I didn't respond. Some time after we merged with the Paris traffic, I asked Josh to stop the car. I opened the door and spewed out my very soul.

I think we've reached the end of the road, Udi told me, sounding dejected, as we sat together in his office after the debriefings. When I add up all that has happened during the last few operations, it's pretty clear that you can't go abroad anymore. You're not focused, you are slow, you don't finish the job – something that's been part of your behaviour since the first missions – and worst of all, you put yourself and whoever's around you at risk. Josh is sure that you were in a state of total shock and that even the possibility of being caught didn't bother you.

The truth was actually worse. When I re-crossed the road, walking slowly, and heard the voices, I knew that one of them might belong to the French intelligence officer who'd come to pick up his guest. I could feel the bullets hitting my spine, my heart and my neck. I continued crossing slowly, heard the footsteps and voices getting nearer and nearer, and expected a volley of bullets, or at least a pair of hands to grab me by the shoulder. Slumped shoulders; powerless to resist.

When I didn't react, Udi, still speaking softly said: and as far as the operational orders are concerned, you know they weren't good. You heard what the guys had to say. Various details were omitted and the plan was far too conventional. The vision, creativity, brilliance and meticulousness that were once your hallmark have vanished. You weren't concentrating and didn't visualize the possible scenarios. You wrote the orders like an automaton. I doubt that it would be right for you to continue as head of the planning department.

He seemed to be expecting an acrimonious response from me. But he didn't get one. Wasn't that what I'd been saying for a year or more?

Perhaps you returned to active service too quickly and you need more time to recover, Udi said finally. The head of the Mossad wants to speak to you but he's on a trip to South America and won't be back till next week.

He's with the guys? I asked.

Yes. A new arena. Netzach wants to be there in person to give the final go-ahead. It's not like it was when you and I opened up places left, right and centre and they simply trusted us, he added amiably.

I looked at him. Since we first met, Udi had become completely bald. If there was any hair left on his head he'd made sure to shave it off. The little paunch he'd developed since he ceased being in the field and began spending his time in conferences, the black rings around his eyes – perhaps the outcome of a chronic lack of sleep – and the reading glasses dangling on his chest, made him look like a bureaucrat. How, I wondered, had his family coped with the decades of active service, beginning with his years as a naval commando and then in the Mossad? What kind of a home does he return to each night? To what kind of woman does he return? An unwritten hierarchical social code makes anyone in the Mossad who wishes to socialize after work do so with others of the same rank. I never wanted any part of that, and in any case Udi was always a rank above me so that I knew nothing about his 'other' life, if he even had one.

That's absolutely OK with me, I said. And until he's back?

I'm not dismissing you. Until then carry on as usual unless you want a vacation.

If I were able to sleep for a week, I would have opted for a vacation. But in my solitary state I wouldn't know how to be idle in Tel Aviv, and returning to the village for a break wasn't an option.

For the time being I'll carry on as usual. And after I've gone I hope you'll appoint Levanon. You don't have many people who are as highly professional as he is and at the same time courageous, modest and sensitive. Determined is not a bad word, certainly not after my lack of tenacity.

Udi smiled. He'd already expressed to me his opinion of Levanon, but in the present constellation Levanon's chances were good.

I had no particular expectations of my meeting with the head of the Mossad. I didn't know if I wanted to be released, I also had no wish to be assigned to any particular role I knew of. The Chief pointed to a comfortable sitting area in a corner at the far end of his office, rose from his desk, and joined me there. He greeted me with a two-handed handshake, a simple gesture that warmed my heart. We had met many times, mainly when he came to final briefings before an operation. Since becoming head of the planning department I'd also gone to his office on a number of occasions when we presented plans for his approval. Netzach looked a bit like an exaggerated impersonation of me, though shorter and broader. I thought that the similarity in our physical appearances also created some sort of an affinity between us.

I've spoken about you a great deal and thought a lot about you, he said. And we've also known each other for a number of years. You are one of the best people we've ever had and you still have a great deal to contribute. But I think I know where you stand and what you're experiencing just now.

So explain it to me I said and he burst out laughing. I wasn't really joking.

I have an idea, he continued. At one time you opened up the Far East for us. It was pretty violent because a great deal of terrorist activity had found its way into that area and a vast number of arms deals were signed there. Now there is another area that we want to open up in an orderly way because the signs are that it will be active in the coming years. The area I have in mind is Russia and the former Republics of the Soviet Union.

He looked at me for a moment and saw no reaction because I didn't feel anything.

The direction in which Russia is moving is not helpful to us. The Russian government is beginning to position itself as the polar opposite of the US and in a fairly consistent way supports whoever the US opposes and vice versa. This can be seen in Russia's backing of Iran's nuclear reactor in Bushehr and the building of small nuclear plants in other Muslim states. This trend is likely to continue. In some of the Republics of the former Soviet Union there is an evidence of strong Iranian influence, so much so that they have become its satellites and can serve as terror bases. I'm not talking about the ones that already have nuclear missiles. You know about those from personal experience – a reference to my operation in Kazakhstan.

Again, he looked at me and I was still waiting for the bottom line. He certainly wasn't intending that I respond to his strategic analysis, particularly given that his forecasts on Syria and Lebanon had materialized in the past few years and had been widely praised.

In your previous work you went on numerous brief trips. The attempt to station you in China also proved to be short lived. Now we want you to go to Russia for a number of years. Settle in, establish a trading company, begin to make import and export deals and in that way move around and get to know the country and its satellite states.

The FSB. – the KGB's successor – inherited its pre-decessor's suspicion of foreigners. So the plan is that for the first year or two you'll busy yourself with entirely innocent commercial activities. We won't bounce you to any other country, and you won't be given any operational missions. We would also want you to leave the place as little as possible.

That, from my point of view, won't be a problem, I said.

After the week of mourning for my father, my mother rapidly went totally downhill and stopped communicating with those around her. She didn't respond to me at all. Apart from her, there was no one else in the world I cared about. I also didn't have a home I wanted to be in or could be in. Yehiel suggested buying my parents' farm and when I agreed to sell, my last tie to the village was severed.

Russia – for me a complete mystery, but a country whose poetry I loved – suddenly seemed to be a possible refuge. I remembered Orit's saying 'a change of place a change of luck'.

You'll also be able to rest there, the head of the Mossad said. You won't have to earn a living from your dealings, of course. And it seems to me that you really are in need of a long rest.

So perhaps a set up in Barbados or Jamaica?

Again, he laughed, though once more I wasn't joking. Then he stood up signalling that the meeting was over. As he accompanied me to the door, his hand tapping me on the shoulder in encouragement, he asked, so am I to understand that we've agreed?

Agreed, I heard myself saying.

Part Two: Annushka, St Petersburg

20

A THIN DAWN coloured the clouds beneath the aircraft's wings during the long flight from Montreal to Saint Petersburg – the way the city's name was assiduously pronounced by the employees of the Canadian airline company. From my window seat I gazed as if hypnotized at the narrow strip of colour that began to emerge out of the blackness. The evening meal had already been served, the cabin lights switched off, and the passengers, their flat bed seats fully extended, covered themselves up and got into their sleeping positions for the flight. Here and there the light of a laptop computer flickered in the dark.

As befits a Canadian businessman, I travelled business class with its luxurious seat-cum-bed making the tedium of the long journey so much more bearable. The break of day was also helpful. At first I didn't realize that what I was seeing was the dawn. Across the width of my window a dark blue streak emerged from the dusk, a ribbon visible enough against the blackness above it but too dark to colour the layer of clouds below – a mass I only noticed when the blue streak turned to purple and an hour later to orange. Then it widened a little. Above it the skies remained pitch black, while beneath, a layer of clouds resembling flocks of sheep that stretched from the plane's underbelly to the horizon, was being dragged slowly backwards.

I could feel a slight quiver of excitement in my stomach. Perhaps excitement isn't exactly the right word. I felt a sense of expectancy, an anticipation of something that remained undefined but carried with it the certainty that what lay ahead would be different from the past I had left behind.

I once read that live multi-cellular organisms were discovered in the depths of icebergs; right there, in the kingdom of ice, the conditions enabling these organisms to form and develop were found to exist. So it may also be that at the bottom of the iceberg that was my soul the conditions existed for a creature of expectation, even of hope, to be spawned. It too was undefined, but powerful, twisting and turning in my stomach.

The sea of cotton-like clouds below was being painted in shades of orange, pink, and yellow. Threads of blue also sneaked their way into the dark azure of the sky which became increasingly bright as the moment of the sun's appearance drew nearer and nearer. Like a dreamer, I gazed at this celestial beauty, a beauty not visible to earth dwellers below the layer of clouds.

My mind was a blank. For the first time I was on a mission with operational orders limited to just one page, no mention of forces, tasks or stages. Land in Petersburg, settle in to a hotel, locate an apartment, find an office. Your budget for settling in is such and such. Start making business contacts in Russia and beyond, with a focus on the former Republics of the Soviet Union. Within that area concentrate on the Muslim countries. As to your security: Don't form close social or intimate relationships…

I was alone, no one was waiting for me at the airport and no one expected a briefing from me in the coming days.

Ariel, HQ's man who from now on was to be my controller, had arrived at my hotel in Montreal to bid me farewell. I gave an explanation of the company I'd opened and of the service office from which a secretary would answer the phone in the firm's name and take messages which she would forward to my email address. As per our standard procedure I'd added Ariel as a signatory to the company bank account, for any set of circumstances that might arise.

He asked how I was feeling ahead of the new mission and I asked, what mission? It took a moment or so for him to let out a quick and forced laugh.

Well, after Zaif, Rashid Nuri, Mustafa Quader, Schultz, and Fayyad, for you, perhaps, this is not a real mission. And there were also, of course, the Kazakhstani drivers and the cell in the Seychelles, he added.

Ariel wasn't an historian of the Mossad and the organization's agents don't, as a rule, memorize the legacy of its liquidations. His reminiscences about all the operations in which I had killed someone – a handful out of hundreds of missions, mostly intelligence related, in which I had taken part during my fifteen years in the organization – was not unplanned. It was clear to me that he'd been armed with this information in case I showed signs of trying to dodge the mission. With the steely subtlety by which the office holds on to its personnel – something I would have much experience of in the future – he suggested that we were blood brothers, that we were linked by the sort of powerful bonds that must not be broken.

At that time I had no intention of severing these ties or of settling down in Canada. Having sold my parents' farm and received my half of the value of the house in which Orit remained, I already had sufficient funds to buy myself out of my contract if that's what I'd wanted to do. The beautiful cities of Montreal and Toronto were, indeed, part of my past. In those distant times of innocence and happiness these were the places in which I set up my cover story as an Indo-Canadian. But now these cities belonged to bygone days I so wanted to forget.

The truth was that Russia, faraway, cold, huge, with its inspiring poetry, its novels, its soul, and St Petersburg, built to be the most beautiful of cities, were for me the fount of a veiled, indefinable, attraction. I'd been sent to forge commercial contacts in the former Soviet Union without even having to make a profit from these connections. I didn't at all feel like someone embarking on a mission.

In fact, I didn't feel anything. That was also how I responded to Ariel who didn't know what to say and so simply wished me well. For the first time I didn't have a yardstick by which to measure success.

An hour before I left for the airport he had shaken my hand warmly. His presence there had proved to be so unnecessary that I thought he'd been sent from Israel simply to verify that I hadn't changed my mind at the last minute and decided to settle in Canada.

On the plane, with the expansive dawn still visible through the window, the first hesitant buds of understanding surfaced within me. They were not the kind of feelings that could melt a block of ice. The sadness over my mother was no longer a running sore. She was living in a world of her own that only Madeleine, who I'd arranged would look after her, could understand – a world in which I had no part to play. I no longer felt sad about my father, Yehiel had promised to care for his grave and say Kaddish in my place on the first anniversary of his death. Nor was I grieving over Orit and the love we had which died an agonizing death, certainly more agonizing than that of the cluster of cells that were destroyed on her orders and which could have been our child. Now, deep in the block of ice within me which the combination of all these events and circumstances had created, the first signs of life appeared.

When the blue of the sky spread across the whole window, the colours of the dawn disappeared, giving way to the bright light of day. The ocean sparkled below us. At that moment I fell fast asleep. When I woke, the mountainous and wooded landscape of Scandinavia was visible from high up. The pilot announced that preparations for landing were underway and informed the passengers of the local time, nine o'clock in the evening.

We crossed the Gulf of Finland and decended through clouds that became denser and denser the closer we got to the city. The plane shook, passengers put on their seat belts and the long-legged, flat-chested stewardesses hurried to their seats.

When we dropped out of the clouds, light suffused the cabin. This was the middle of summer and the northern sun was late in sinking below the horizon. From the window I could see forests, vast fields, creeks, as well as clusters of rural houses and dachas in the coves of the meandering rivers.

Along the length of the runways of Pulkovo 2, St Petersburg's international airport, stretched a line of modern luxury jets, obviously belonging to the new class of oligarchs, as well as a number of old and dismantled helicopters.

A bus took us to the antiquated terminal building where we were greeted by two signboards, one with the city's name Sankt Peterburg in Russian and the other in English. Despite the Russian language course I'd taken I had difficulty in deciphering the Latin 'c' as an 's' and the letter 'p' as an 'r'. For me this served as a short introduction to the many names of the city which in the operations order was referred to simply as 'Peterburg', as it is called in Israel.

Inside the small building, workers were in the process of erecting a skeleton of metal and glass which in a few years time would become the new arrivals and departures terminal.

A secret agent is supposed to be somewhat anxious as he enters the bastion of the KGB but my emotions were rather different. I had the feeling one gets before a blind date with a woman who, it's been promised, would be beautiful. Perhaps it was the smile on my face that made it possible for me to get through passport control so quickly. The one baggage carousel and my suitcases also played a helpful hand and within minutes I was in a taxi.

The city boundary stretched almost to the airport and all along the route into the centre were newly constructed car supermarkets stocking the products of the best European automobile manufacturers. A monument commemorating the Nazi Siege of Leningrad, a tall column surrounded by statues of the fighters and the besieged population marked the official entry point into the city.

Stalin's buildings, said the driver as we came into Moskovsky Prospekt, the boulevard that leads to the centre of town, and pointed to massive structures on either side of the street adorned with pillars and crescents. Stalin knew how to give the street the appearance of dignity and power that was not diminished by the grey and beige colour of the buildings themselves.

When we reached the city's majestic centre, I was surrounded by glorious buildings in a riot of colours – red and green, blue, beige and yellow, which produced an inexplicable sense of joy in me. The magnificent mansions, once the palaces of the nobility who Peter the Great brought with him to the city, had been converted into offices, restaurants, and shops, including well-known international clothing and food chains. We drove past big bridges spanning the web of canals that interlace the city, making our way through a brisk traffic of both vehicles and pedestrians. It was by then after ten and still daylight.

The Grand Hotel Europe excited me from the moment I got out of the taxi and the doorman in a red jacket hurried towards me with a trolley on which he loaded my two suitcases. I'd stayed in more sumptuous hotels than this, in line with the needs of any given trip. But this hotel was housed within a number of elegant old buildings, with architectural and decorative features that I remembered being described in Russian period novels, and lined with cafés and prestigious shops.

The registration process reminded me of where I was. The receptionist asked for my passport and immigration form, scanned the documents and sent them to the immigration authority or ministry of the interior. I could only hope that the Mossad had done its work properly and that no problems would arise from the passport and the details recorded in it.

I took a suite on the top floor. I knew that I would be spending a few weeks there until I found an apartment and wanted to start my new life surrounded by ancient beauty. I was pleased when the doorman, who'd glued himself to me, opened the door with a big key rather than a magnetic card; to be welcomed by the smell of old wood; happy to see the suite's pleasant sitting-room with a working corner, a lounge area, and thick carpeting throughout; and pleased when the young man took my suitcases into the bedroom with its huge canopied bed standing in the middle, a bed in which, given my modest dimensions, I could sleep either lengthwise or crosswise.

When I drew back the heavy curtains and then the more flimsy lace curtains, the view from my room was of a garden in bloom and at its centre a big statue. It took me a minute or so to register what I was looking at. The statue was of Pushkin with his arm raised, pictures of which I'd seen in albums when getting ready for the journey. Behind the statue I could see the yellow palaces of the Russian Museum and of the Mikhailovsky Theatre with their porticoes of white pillars. What particularly caught my eye however, were the amazing onion-shaped domes on top of the Church of the Spilled Blood, visible beyond the palaces. Some of the domes were gilded and some, painted with diagonal and square patterns of blue, white, yellow and gold, looked as if they were the work of kindergarten children. A slight cough reminded me that at the door to my room stood the lad in a red jacket waiting for his tip.

Although it was by now late evening and an obstinate darkness was creeping over the city, I decided to go out and wander the streets. The warnings I'd been given to beware of night-time drunks came to mind, but I saw only people ambling along, filling the cafés, their beaming faces also lit up by the lavish lighting that illuminated the grand buildings. In the recesses above the elongated windows one could see decorations and statues, the cheerful colours of the surrounding houses and palaces turning gold. Even the nearby two-storeyed shopping centre, Gustinyi Dvor,

suddenly took on the appearance of a dream-like dolls'
house bathed in dazzling light.

It was long after midnight when I slid into my
luxurious bed. I hadn't closed the curtains and, later, when
the light came flooding in I was amazed to discover that it
was only 4 a.m. It seems that white nights also have their
white mornings. Happy as a lark, I got dressed and once
again went out onto the street.

I spent my first morning walking the length and
breadth of Nevsky Prospekt, the city's main tourist
thoroughfare where my hotel was located. As if
intoxicated, I walked up and down this beautiful street,
thronging with pedestrians all day long, revelling in the
cacophony of sounds and colours. I took my time to study
the buildings that reflected the best of European
architecture with their meticulously maintained facades,
immaculately cleaned in honour of the city's three
hundredth anniversary.

I was seeing St Petersburg in the period that followed
the Festival of White Nights. The northern lights no longer
illuminated the city round the clock and the celebrations
that attracted tourists from all over the world had ended.
But the days were still very long and allowed me to tour
the palaces, churches, theatres, gardens, bridges and canals
for hours on end. Only the cold, which at night, even in
July, sneaked in from the Gulf of Finland, limited my
hours of wandering around – though it did nothing to
dampen my increasingly cheerful mood.

In the days that followed I ambled aimlessly, propelled
by an inner drive that I didn't even know I possessed,

enveloped by sounds and colours, sights and smells, trying to understand the magic. And the magic, it has to be said, was confusing. The large buildings jammed together overwhelmed the street with such force that I was reminded of the streets of totalitarian capitals. But the shops and restaurants, the pedestrians, street musicians and souvenir sellers, combined to create an atmosphere of freedom and gaiety.

The wide bridges across the grand River Neva, linking the islands that together form the city, impressed me by their mightiness. On the other hand, the much smaller bridges spanning the canals that connect the river to the Gulf of Finland were redolent of the romance of Venice and Amsterdam, a magical hideaway for lovers. The mixture of might and tenderness, romance and rapture, happiness and simplicity, was as intoxicating as it was impossible. Something didn't add up, something was wrong and yet it undeniably was all there and imbued me with its magic.

I set aside one whole day to tour the Hermitage which occupies most of the space of what once was the Czar's winter palace. Uncharacteristically for me I stood patiently in line at the entrance gazing in wonder at the green façade with its white columns capped in gold. At the entry level I found myself walking serenely between Egyptian sarcophagi and Greek statues, my composure a far cry from the hurried visits I used to make to Egyptian or Greek museums in the course of my work.

With difficulty I navigated my way in the direction of the European classics. My route took me up a magnificent staircase to halls walled with tapestries and filled with gilded wooden furniture. I walked through long passageways in which were hung hundreds of paintings of generals, followed by rooms crammed with Chinese ceramics, coins and jewellery, until finally I reached the top floor housing the art of the 20th century.

Out of the wealth of art around me – entire galleries filled with the works of Picasso, Cézanne, Matisse and their contemporaries – I found myself lingering in particular in front of portraits of strong, solitary men. Cézanne's 'smoker', a moustached man wearing a jacket and hat with a pipe in his mouth, his head supported by a fist; and at his *Self-portrait in a casquette*, a tangled beard, wild hair, the body wrapped in a heavy winter coat. A glimpse, perhaps, into my own future. If I'm not like this already, I thought, I certainly will be in a few years' time.

The portrait of a man whose nose and mouth appeared to be bleeding and warped, at first made me flinch and then, inexplicably, drew me to it. Something in this painting reminded me of myself in the most intimate way. I went up close and discovered that it was a self-portrait by Chaim Soutine. The name, known to me not from the history of art but from the streets of Tel Aviv, immediately brought to mind images of the old northern neighbourhoods of the city and the countless objects I had tailed in Soutine Street and the roads bordering it during my training course.

With difficulty I dragged myself away from the portrait and wandered off to another wing, on the same floor but on the other side of the palace, which was built around a large internal courtyard. There I stumbled on Renato Guttuso's *Portrait of Rocco and his Son*; a large painting of a father with a fierce expression, the face dark, harsh, and angular, with huge black eyes looking out defensively, his immense arms clutching a little boy sleeping peacefully, resting on his shoulder.

Whereas Cézanne and Soutine's paintings offered me a possible reality, I was now forced to accept that the reality I was looking at was no longer an option open to me. I couldn't take my eyes off the powerful blue painting, away from the hands that were so enormous they seemed deformed; nor could I stop staring at his look of determination and the expression of tranquillity that enveloped his child's face. I knew nothing about the painter and certainly nothing about Rocco and his son. And yet I was ready to change places with the anonymous Rocco in an instant.

Spellbound, I continued to stand in front of the painting – unknowingly ignoring a public announcement in Russian – until, over my shoulder, I heard an attendant saying to me: Sir, the Museum is about to close in five minutes.

I didn't feel it necessary to begin my business activities in any sort of rush. The plausible tourist would certainly want to spend his time sightseeing and a genuine businessman would want to get to know the place in which he was about to live before renting an apartment and an office. For the first time in years, the city's beauty gave me the feeling of being a real tourist.

I hadn't had such a feeling in any of the cities I'd previously worked in.

I clearly remembered how I'd run up the steps of the Acropolis in a short break between tailing and surveillance, solely in order to be able to explain to the police what I was doing in Athens if the need arose. I bought an entry ticket that I tucked safely into my wallet, covered the site at speed and left at a run to take over from my friend as a look out, promising myself that I would return someday for a proper visit – which never happened. I did the same thing in Athens' amazing history museum, hurrying between hundreds of striking statues managing only to ask myself the meaning of all the men having such well developed shoulders and arms and such small genitals. I recalled my dash to the antiquities in the ancient city of Jerash, and to Madaba with its mosaic floor depicting an age-old map of the region. I had also stood on the peak of Mount Nebo in Jordan, looking out at the Dead Sea and imagining the way down to my house in the Arava. Filled with emotion, at first I refused to leave the place but finally made do with a few touristy snapshots. And so I passed through but didn't really see dozens of other sites and museums across the globe.

And now not only didn't I have to hurry, it was as if the city had control over me, or my new situation had taken control. I actually became that tourist, that Canadian businessman my documents said I was.

This struck home when I realized that the many policemen stationed in groups on every street corner, instead of making me apprehensive, gave me a feeling of

218

security. That applied to the men in black uniforms as well as to those in grey with their big, officers' hats. I felt the same about the men who turned up towards evening in spotted battle uniforms and prison vans. They were on my side.

I understood this even more clearly when I started looking at Russian women. I don't remember looking at girls in Israel after Orit left and I'd done very little of that before I knew her. Whereas Russian men were dressed in ways I was used to seeing in Tel Aviv, women of my age in St Petersburg wore lace party clothes to work, with stiletto-heeled shoes. The younger ones, those whom nature had endowed with long legs, wore very short shorts and tights, while those not blessed with such sylphlike figures walked around with highly exposed necklines, ignoring the danger of catching pneumonia from the frequent gusts of cold wind blowing in from the Gulf of Finland.

In the course of touring the city I came across Pushkin's home on the embankment of the Moika River. There I saw inscribed the words he once wrote to St Petersburg: 'I remember the wonderful moment when my eyes first saw you.' I felt that for me too, without yet knowing why, these were wonderful moments that I would one day pine for. And that this future still held in store for me some magical moments.

After days of sightseeing I went to a local property agent who showed me a number of office buildings. He took me initially to Nevsky Prospekt, a street in which banks, airline companies, and foreign restaurants had branches.

The buildings were well maintained and it was a place where one could merge into the crowd. But my fear of it being in a place where I could bump into tourists and acquaintances from Israel was also real, so I didn't take it.

In the end, I decided to open the office on Liteyny Prospekt which runs from the centre to the River Neva. This elegant street with its imposing buildings on either side and a fair number of restaurants, shops and companies, appeared to be well suited to my purposes. It was within walking distance of the American and British consulates and other important hubs. At the quiet end of the thoroughfare, close to the river, there was far less business activity and the movement of pedestrians was more limited.

The building I was shown had kept the splendour of its early days and that attracted me. Most importantly, there was no concierge to report to the authorities on my comings and goings or the complete absence of visitors to my office. An old staircase led from the street into the building and on every landing there was a nameless door to yet another office. I decided that my trading company would be set up behind one of these doors on the third and last floor with its windows facing the street.

A few days after the furniture had arrived, and the computer and a copy machine had been installed in the office, I sent the Mossad a message informing them that I had set things up. I also sent an email to a number of companies whose addresses my controller, Ariel, had given me before I left Canada. Some we were interested in developing contacts with were in the former Soviet Union, some were unsuspecting European companies, and one was like mine: a front for the Mossad. The email, which had been composed in advance in Israel, announced that my Canadian trading company was opening a branch in St Petersburg with the objective of acting as a broker between firms in the former Republics of the Soviet Union and Canadian, American and European companies, with respect to a variety of products we specialized in.

Few firms bothered to respond and the other front company wrote in polite terms that in light of an earlier advice of my intention to open an office in Russia, they were surprised that it was only now that the announcement of its launch had arrived.

The Mossad's dissatisfaction perplexed me a little; the state of Israel sent me on a mission – dormant but important. For a moment I even thought of activating the secret communications system by typing a complex password into the computer and explaining that I was OK. But the moment passed and with it the slight confusion I had felt.

The estate agent began showing me apartments in areas of new construction some distance from the centre of town. But I wanted a place that maintained the flavour of authentic old St Petersburg. The tours with the agent were a better way of getting to know the city than those I had made on my own in dozens of towns in which I'd operated. In none of them did I have the chance of going into houses and apartments and getting an impression of the local way of life but now I had the opportunity of discovering the 'other face' of a city. Beyond the sparkling and well-preserved façades there was poverty, neglect, and decay. Standing in the street, I could have been in Paris or Vienna at their best. The entrances were also relatively well kept. But a climb up the stairs revealed rusted railings and mildew on the walls. The apartments themselves exuded smells of mould and on the balconies overlooking the back, stores of crumbling wood, scrap metal and junk were visible.

In the end I chose an apartment in a large Stalinist building on Moskovsky Prospekt where the first floor was covered in big slabs of granite and the rest in square blocks of grey stone, though the window bays were decorated with pleasant inlays. I was happy to discover that there was a café on the ground floor that also served pastries and light meals. It was a branch of the Coffee-Khouze chain, an amusing transcription of Coffee House, with the Russian 'X' which transcribes as 'KH' but cannot be pronounced in English. It never failed to make me smile every time I saw it.

This building had another advantage: once again there was no concierge to check on my movements. The magnetic mechanism for the entrance to the building together with an elongated key to the door of my apartment, beyond which there was another internal door, only added to my feelings of security and domesticity. Opposite the building was Victory Park and the metro station that took me to the centre of town in minutes.

The apartment itself was more than a bachelor could possibly want or need. The living room was big, the bedroom spacious, and there was also a small study. The ceilings were high, the windows large and what mainly attracted me was that it was furnished with everything I required; from a sitting area and a large television – unfortunately for me, broadcasting in Russian only – in the living room, all the way to reading lamps. A renovation carried out on the apartment shortly before I moved in, gave me hope that the heating would work properly and that the taps would also be in order. I felt I could be comfortable in this place. The little creature inside me stopped chiselling a home for itself in the iceberg and even began to dig a tunnel to the outside world.

Somewhat to my surprise I discovered that, with the arrival of the cold of early autumn, I was drawing my new life into me and a distance I found difficult to measure was growing between me and my life there, in my warm homeland. I was merging into the mist rising from the canals and streaming in from the frozen sea, beginning to feel comfortable in my new environment. At the same time an ever thickening fog was settling between me and the land of the eternal sun where I was born and bred. I took advantage of the early mornings and late evenings to stroll in the park opposite. I meandered around a variety of trees, circled the lovely lake in the middle, and even introduced myself to some of the neighbours who rose early and ended the day exercising by running along the park's footpaths.

A month has passed since I landed here, I said to myself, and it's time that I get in touch with my mother's carer. When I was in Montreal I called every few days and always got the same answer. There had been no change in her condition. A phone call to Israel from St Petersburg required me to follow a route along which I could spot anybody following me; an anonymous conversation from a phone booth nowhere near where I lived or worked; and a quick exit route I could use before a team of snoops from counter-espionage were summoned by their eavesdroppers who'd have traced a suspicious conversation. I assumed that calls to Israel would be regarded as suspicious. I didn't call.

The thought that Orit would have loved this beautiful city much more than she at first loved Beijing crossed my mind just once. Crossed, and never returned. Orit too began to be a distant and ethereal memory.

21

I PREPARED BREAKFASTS in my apartment. Most of the products I was used to were to be found in the little neighbourhood grocery shop – though they looked somewhat different and their taste wasn't the same. Now and then I was surprised by packaging that made me think it contained a certain item only to discover later that it was something else altogether. Before the outward journey I had taken a quick course in Russian. But whoever thought that I was in a good enough state to acquire a new language was sadly mistaken. I continued to be confused by the interchange between Latin and Cyrillic letters which, though written identically, sounded entirely different. Nor was I able to memorize the sounds of various letters which only a combination of characters in English or Hebrew sounded close enough, such as the 'che' for Tchaikovsky or 'tse', or 'shche'. Not to mention the letters that look like the numbers 6 and 61, the first softening the letter preceding it, the second giving it a harder sound. Only the 'sh' that looked and sounded as if it had come straight from Hebrew seemed 'user friendly' to me.

The elderly couple who owned the grocery shop didn't know a word of English and despite their show of geniality and their desire to assist a new customer, the help I got was fairly limited. The English–Russian phrase book was only a very partial solution to my inability to communicate.

The small shop mainly stocked beers, wines and bottles of vodka. In a corner was a counter with fruit and vegetables but my focus was on the huge selection of sausages and salted fish. Now that I didn't have to speak to anyone, certainly not kiss anyone – women included – my morning menu had changed and consisted of an omelette with various kinds of sausage in it, salt fish, and a rye bread that was both full grain and very filling.

After this satisfying meal I would make my way by metro and foot – and on particularly cold or rainy days by taxi – to my office. I loved the metro ride, enjoyed looking at the passengers. Most of them didn't have the Slavic faces I was expecting to find and there were even some dark-skinned people from the Republics of the former Soviet Union. I couldn't but notice the civilized behavioural code, the outcome of either an effective education or of a totalitarian regime. People talked quietly, boarded the train in silence, got out calmly, everyone minding their own business. Young people gave up seats to their elders and the handicapped, a courtesy I too benefitted from when a young woman got up and offered me her place – a gesture I found to be a tolerable indignity.

I preferred not to change trains and not to wander around the metro's tunnels. Though in the army I had been quite a good navigator, in St Petersburg's labyrinth of subterranean passageways I discovered that these skills of mine were worthless. I was never able correctly to guess the direction from which a train would be coming or its route of departure, where to go in order to catch the other line, or on which side of the road I would find myself after climbing up from the depths of the earth. The signposting in Russian hardly helped. Instead, I got out at the city centre station and walked from there to the office. But with the arrival of autumn and the sharp drop in temperature, I discovered that the distance between Nevsky station – on the blue line 2 from my house – and the office, made walking far too painful an experience.

Though the heating in the office building worked, it wasn't enough to warm up the frozen expanse. I switched on a heater to thaw my feet, lit the kettle, and made myself a cup of coffee to thaw my insides; there were days when I didn't even take off my coat.

Only once I'd got a bit warmer, did I work at the computer. Getting on line took two or three attempts and when I finally made it I began to search for tenders in various places that were of interest to us, leafed through catalogues, requested and offered prices. Three tenders and three price bids a day was the target I set for myself. No less. We request your best possible offer for a heating system, I wrote when a Russian firm caught my eye in a catalogue or on the internet. And when the offer was received I forwarded it to merchants all over the world and added a very small percentage in commission which I was also prepared to waive if the customer pressed.

I made small deals with Russian manufacturers, bought goods from them and sold these on, mostly to buyers in the ex-Soviet Republics. After a while I began to participate in tenders for goods in Western countries as well. I was also willing to absorb a small loss so long as the books showed a profit and I could demonstrate to the authorities in Russia that my stay in the country was justifiable and even rewarding. Now and again I also managed to make genuinely profitable deals and got a real kick from doing so.

I got to my office at nine in the morning and counted the minutes until midday when lunch began to be served in the restaurants. I often ate at the Babi Saabi, a Japanese eatery close to my office which attracted very few tourists. The food was to my liking and after the futile hours in the office on my own I was happy to see live faces. It was also warmer there than in the office. I didn't talk to the other diners. From time to time I spotted Canadians there, but nobody knew anything about the national identity of my cover story and I didn't feel the need to either strengthen it or put it to the test.

Further down the street was an Italian restaurant. Once I was eating there when a group of Israelis came in. I barricaded myself behind the pages of a magazine, fearful that someone might recognize me. Of course I would have denied being me but then I would be just like the troubled couple who were counselled to have a romantic meal and took the recommendation a step too far: her knife fell to the floor, she bent to pick it up, and he jumped on her. The counselling worked for them, but they'll never go back to that restaurant.

Returning to my cold office I would usually find that at most just one email had arrived in my absence.

I idled away the time till four or five in the afternoon, and then went back home. There too the heating wasn't particularly effective, and I was forced to kill quite a few hours in the cold before going to bed and lulling myself to sleep. Mostly I spent this time reading or in a small, neighbourhood restaurant on the far corner of my street where I regularly had my evening meals.

The restaurant, it seemed, was once the living room of its proprietor's home. Now a door linked the small kitchen at the back of the restaurant to their apartment. There were only six tables, lined up in two rows, and I usually sat at the innermost table, away from the window from which a cold draft blew in.

The proprietor, cook, and waitress, was Mrs Vashkirova, a big-bosomed lady who, for my own amusement I nickname *La vache qui rit,* an allusion to the laughing cow that appears on a range of French cheese products. I hadn't yet understood the phenomenon which gave rise to so many Russian women having such large bosoms whereas their sisters in northern European countries are for the most part relatively flat chested. Vashkirova succeeded in learning my culinary preferences by trial and error. It took about ten evening meals for me to sample the majority of the dishes on offer. With the little Russian at my command I managed, during this period, to ask for more salt and less oil, as well as some other refinements until finally my desired fusion of ingredients was achieved. Because the dishes were prepared especially for me, I waited longer than the other customers, a delay that suited me fine. I found it pleasant to sit in the cozy restaurant, redolent of cooking aromas which were far removed from the smells that used to come out of my mother's kitchen. The place was generally half empty, so no one was bothered by my occupying a table for a good hour or more. I even began to bring the book I happened to be reading to the place.

I was never a speedy reader, not even in Hebrew. I like to mull over the nice expressions I come across, ponder their meaning, try and imagine the hero and what I would do in his place – and even the writer and what I would have written had I been him. For many years, in planes, trains, hotels, and hideaway apartments, I'd been reading only in English. And yet, wading through a book still took me an inordinate amount of time and was a huge effort.

After my divorce from Orit, and after I had made my way through the 'big bores', I chose to read at random great tomes such as Thomas Mann's *The Magic Mountain* and Norman Mailer's *The Naked and the Dead* which I had previously not dared to take on. Now I considered plunging into Russian literature and perhaps learning something more about the country in which I was due to spend the next few years.

Along Nevsky Prospekt I found a couple of bookshops that sold English translations of Russian literature. I armed myself with classics which I hadn't yet read such as Dostoyevsky's *Demons* as well as translations of young writers whose names I hadn't heard of till then. I would start reading at home after getting back from the office, then go to the restaurant and read at my regular table until Mrs Vashkirova served my food. I ate at a leisurely pace, sometimes turning over a page or two as I did so. Back at the apartment I continued until I felt tired enough to fall asleep. I enjoyed this routine little more than I had in Tel Aviv.

Some of those who came to the restaurant were regulars, perhaps residents of my building or of the neighbourhood that stretched beyond the end of my own street where simple, cheap, cube-shaped blocks had been built during the Khrushchev era with smaller apartments, smaller rooms, and lower ceilings, than in my Stalinist building. The locals who were drawn to the restaurant were ordinary middle-aged people. Some came alone, others with their partners. All of them clearly preferred the cheap dishes prepared by Vashkirova to having to cook in the tiny kitchenettes of their apartments.

Sometime after I, too, became a regular, I began to notice one of the diners – a woman who always sat by the window reading and making do, more often than not, with a bowl of soup or even just a cup of tea. Despite the dim light in the restaurant, I couldn't help noticing the loveliness of her features silhouetted against the background of the window illuminated by the street lighting. Even from the distance of a number of tables I could see the beauty of the straight nose, the well-defined jaw line, and the high cheek bones. This was a quiet beauty, not drawing attention to itself but aware of its fine attributes. It was recognizable even from the upright way in which the woman sat, from the elegance with which she crossed her legs – despite the thick fur boots she wore – and from the pleasant but distant smile she directed at Vashkirova when the lady of the house offered to serve her. She looked as if she was my age, coming up for forty.

When she glanced up from her book, as if thinking about what she had read, the street lamps twinkled in her eyes – eyes that looked oval, Asiatic. Her neck was always wrapped in a soft scarf, a fur hat always on her head. This gave her a transient appearance. Yet she continued to sit, slowly sipping the soup and reading, without looking at those coming into the restaurant or those in the street who walked past her window.

About a week after I first noticed her, two men, who looked as if they didn't belong to this part of town, caught my attention. They seemed too animated and jovial to be eating at such a humble restaurant. The pair, sitting with their backs to me, were a few years younger than me, they were well dressed and I saw that other diners were also glancing at them with interest and then looking away.

When they'd eaten and were waiting for their tea, one

of them turned to the woman, sitting at the next table. I didn't understand all he said or all of her answers, but I saw the blush in her cheeks and, from the rapid way she turned her face away from him and back to her book, I guessed that the young man had made some kind of advance and was turned down. His friend tapped his back fondly and the two laughed. She continued with her reading.

When they finished drinking and had paid, the two men got up to leave, at which point I could see their handsome Slavic faces. The one who'd approached her was powerfully built and particularly good looking. Apparently having no intention of giving up, he went to the woman's table and exchanged a few words with her. She looked directly at him and answered dryly, words that were meant to put an end to his overtures. He took out a visiting card, wrote a number on it and offered it to her. When she didn't reach out for the card he placed it on the table and left with his friend, giggling in embarrassment. I heard the powerful roar of an engine being turned on, and through the window watched a Mercedes jeep drive away at speed.

Moving slowly, the woman picked up the card and without looking at it, or pausing in her reading, she delicately tore it in two and dumped it in the ashtray. She continued to read, obviously aware of the looks she was getting from the other diners. So she too doesn't like sharply-dressed, rich youngsters, I noted to myself in appreciation as I also went back to my book.

I was apparently so preoccupied with Varvara Petrovna and Stepan Trofimovich that I paid no attention to the woman making her way out of the restaurant.

22

The small restaurant was unusually full. My regular table was taken, as were the two tables near the windows. I was a bit surprised that in a neighbourhood restaurant such as this there were no families with children, only couples and a group of middle-aged people apparently celebrating a birthday. I sat at one of the tables in the middle, the only one that was free. Shortly afterwards the woman came in. She surveyed the scene, clearly embarrassed, and lingered at the entrance.

I would have been happy to ask her to join me but she didn't look in my direction and I didn't know how to go about inviting her without appearing too forward.

The good-hearted Mrs Vashkirova leapt to the rescue – mine and hers. Without consulting me at all, she attracted the woman's attention and signalled her to sit at my table.

The woman's manners were a little bit more refined than those of the large-bosomed cook. She looked bashfully at me and at Vashkirova and asked if it was OK with the 'gospodin', the gentleman, meaning me. Of course it's OK, Vashkirova told her, pointing first at the chair facing me, then at the woman and then, without pausing for my response, drew the seat away from the table in readiness for the woman to sit down. I nodded, somewhat belatedly, and blurted a clumsy 'Da, da'.

Hesitantly, the woman approached and asked if it was OK.

It's OK, I answered.

She thanked me with a pleasant though somewhat restrained smile.

The table had been laid for four and although Vashkirova offered my guest the seat opposite mine, the woman placed her bag and coat there, gently pulled away the second chair, and sat down to my right.

American? she asked keeping the enquiry to a minimum.

Canadian, I answered, Paul, and offered my hand.

She shook it quickly, smiled, and took her book out of her bag.

I very much didn't want our short acquaintanceship to end with this brief exchange. Paul Gupta, I said after a brief silence, and felt ridiculous, like a poor imitation of James Bond and the way he invariably introduces himself.

When she looked at me with her beautiful eyes and said, as simple courtesy required, Anna Petrovna, the surprise in her expression highlighted for me how clumsy I'd been. Bond's image had always seemed to me exaggerated. I couldn't, and had never wanted to, resemble him.

Why on earth had I introduced myself in the first place, I wondered. This, after all, wasn't a 'getting to know you' encounter. It was a solution to a seating problem in a restaurant. And indeed Anna herself seemed guarded, and limited the contact between us to a minimum.

But it was too late. I couldn't suppress the pleasurable feeling that flowed from my palm through my arm and to my heart simply from the touch of her hand – soft and surprisingly warm for someone who had just stepped in from the bitter cold outside. Her almond-shaped green eyes with a brown fleck, were remarkably beautiful.

The very subtle smell of a pleasant perfume drifted towards me. Unable to resist, I lifted the hand that had held hers up to my nose. An alluring fragrance of some sort of cream had been passed on from her to me.

She clocked my hand movement and concealed the slightest of smiles without even taking her eyes off her book.

When Vashkirova returned to the table, Anna ordered her usual bowl of soup and returned to her book. I, too, immersed myself in my reading. Dostoyevsky in English was hard going and my progress was very slow. In two weeks I'd managed to read only half the book's one thousand pages.

My roast and her soup arrived at the same time. As we put our tomes down on the table, each took a peep at the other's. To my surprise she was reading Saul Bellow's *The Adventures of Augie March*.

Demons? she asked, spotting the title on my cover.

I nodded.

She thought for a moment. With or without the chapter 'At Tikhon's'?

I don't know, I said

You can see if you look at the very end. Are the last words 'bloody psychologist'?

I turned the heavy volume over. No, the last sentence is 'our city's doctors rejected the assumption that this was a case of insanity.'

Pity, said Anna. It was usual for that chapter to be deleted in editions published in the Soviet Union but I hoped that it would be restored in newer editions.

So I'm reading a thousand pages and when I've finished won't know how the story ends?

Anna's giggling made her eyes sparkle and around them numerous thin, laughter lines formed but despite these lines, she looked ten years younger. Her spoken English was good, surprisingly good.

No, no, she reassured me. The end is an end. But the deleted chapter is about Stavrogin's confession which Tikhon doesn't accept.

I asked her to explain.

Stavrogin tries to confess that he once raped a small girl but the priest refuses to accept his confession on the grounds that repentance can only be achieved by prolonged inner struggle not by a single act.

I can see that you are a long way into the novel, she said, and by now you must have gathered that, through Stavrogin, Dostoyevsky tried to create the ultimate Russian image of the exiled revolutionary. Stavrogin was both a genius and wicked, and Dostoyevsky made him humble so as to make possible a religious absolution.

I started at her in astonishment. No, I said, I hadn't. Perhaps further on I would have understood. I saw the germs of his pride and hatred of man but never thought that it would end in confession, even humility.

Your understanding wasn't bad, Anna grinned, a note of appreciation added to her smile. Are you trying to understand Russia through its literature?

It is one way, I answered, seeing as I'm already here. And are you trying to understand America by reading Saul Bellow?

Perhaps, she answered. It's amazing how the Russian soul so differs from the American. Here they write heroic tragedies and there – heroic comedies.

I haven't read *The Adventures of Augie March*, I said ruefully. I would have been delighted if I could have demonstrated a grasp of literature similar to hers. I'm familiar with his *Seize the Day*, which is fairly tragic, even if there is something a bit comic about the hero finding himself at a stranger's funeral where he bursts into bitter tears lamenting his fate.

Yes, she said and then was silent for a moment, as if debating whether to continue the conversation. In the brief interlude she sipped at her soup.

Augie is searching for his destiny and freedom, becomes addicted to life – but won't descend to the tragic depths that Stavrogin does. He won't murder. His morality won't allow him to cross red lines, she said finally.

For a moment we were both left lost for words, and Anna suggested that we eat before my roast and her soup got cold.

We ate in an almost forced silence. Anna interested me a great deal – her beauty, the solitude in which she was enveloped evening after evening, her rejection of the handsome young man's advances, her literary understanding – who was she, what was she? An author? A literature lecturer? A woman waiting for her husband to return from abroad? And where does her very good

English come from – aside from her habit, as in Russian, of not using the definite article and so causing occasional misunderstanding? And yet I knew that the more I dug the more she too would ask questions, and I had no interest in unveiling my story.

We finished eating, Vashkirova cleared our plates, I ordered coffee, and Anna asked for tea. As we again picked up our books Anna asked if I was a tourist. The question surprised me a little. It was hard to believe that she'd not noticed me before now so why would she think a tourist would eat in a neighbourhood restaurant like this every evening for several weeks.

I have a trading company here, a branch of a Canadian company, I told her.

More and more American businessmen are discovering Russia, she said, and I corrected her – I'm Canadian.

Yes, of course.

May I ask what you do, seeing that you know so much about literature?

I run a small bookshop, not far from here. Mainly works in Russian but there are also a few shelves of books in English. This, she said pointing at her book, is from my shop.

Good to know, I said happily. I've been searching for English books but the only ones I found were in the city centre bookshops.

She didn't react and didn't invite me to visit her shop.

By the way, you said Gupta? Isn't that an Indian name?

That's right. My father was Indian. I was pleased that

the dark shade of my skin hadn't yet turned white beneath St Petersburg's cloudy skies.

Anna gave me a somewhat searching look.

Yes, I can see that there is something Indian about you.

And then an urge to be mischievous grabbed me and took our relations one step beyond the necessary.

Forgive my asking, but am I seeing something East-Asian in you?

I didn't think it was so obvious, she smiled. I had a Tatar grandfather.

The eyes, I said. Though actually they are more like Sophia Loren's.

And in a note to myself I added that so far as I could remember Tatar eyes were not Asiatic-looking.

Anna's face lit up. A Western woman would certainly have denied the comparison, but she was as happy as a kid in a sweetshop.

But Sophia Loren is gorgeous! Are you talking of Sophia Loren as she is today, in her seventies?

For me there is only one Sophia Loren, the one from my childhood. She is really beautiful and your eyes are very much like hers.

Thank you, thank you. I think you've made my day, said Anna, using an expression that sounded odd coming from her. And, as if to signal that we had crossed the boundary she had set for herself, she turned her beautiful eyes away from me and back to Augie March, leaving just a remnant of a smile of satisfaction in the corners of her mouth.

We sipped our drinks in silence, each absorbed in their

reading. When Anna finished her tea, she signalled to Vashkirova, handed her the exact change, then got up, put her book into her bag, and formally offered me her hand to shake.

It was very pleasant.

For me too. Thanks for the company.

I thought of getting up and helping her on with her coat but she indicated gracefully that there was no need and went towards the door, walking the few steps in her upright manner. She made her exit without looking back, leaving behind only a slight trace of the fragrance of her exquisite perfume.

I remained sitting in the restaurant for quite some time. I was enchanted. This beautiful and clever woman had become even more mysterious. I tried to imagine her at work, but couldn't. There was something else about her, something that wouldn't permit her to sit for hours each day in a small bookshop.

23

THE NEXT MORNING I was surprised by a new feeling stirring within me. I couldn't yet give it a name but the vague unfocused sense of expectation with which I had been wandering around over the previous few days was beginning to take shape. As I waited for the sausage and onion omelette to cook, I noticed my fingers drumming a melody. I used to think that the songs buzzing around in my head and the way my fingers responded, were a sign of some kind of disorder. Mostly it was the last song I'd heard, sometimes even the tune of a cell phone that had sounded off near me. Seems like I've swallowed a radio, I once said to Orit when she asked where the music my fingers were strumming on her thigh was coming from. But at some point this radio had gone silent. That morning it sounded the first notes of revival.

The hours in the office passed more quickly. I felt less alone and less cold even though the day itself was chillier than those that preceded it. A company from Tajikistan and another from Dagestan decided to join the party by asking to buy a canning production line which I'd offered at a slight loss to me – altogether a thousand rubles below the Russian manufacturer's price. Accepting the suggestion of my Mossad controllers, I even included an annual inspection in the price. This gave me cover periodically to visit these Republics, where Iranian influence was significant, and to tour the shores of the Caspian Sea, Iran's unguarded back door. I quickly forwarded a contract and the details of the Letter of Credit required by my bank, advanced the time of my weekly briefing to HQ, and announced, with a degree of satisfaction, the opening up of the Tajiki and Degastani markets.

At lunchtime, the thought of returning to the neighbourhood restaurant momentarily crossed my mind – I didn't after all know whether or not my beautiful bookseller also ate there during the day. But I quickly realized that I was being overly enthusiastic and held my curiosity in check till the evening.

That night I learned that I had to delete the word 'my'

and make do with just 'beautiful bookseller'. Anna was already sitting at her regular table by the window with a bowl of soup and Saul Bellow. When I entered, she glanced at me briefly, smiled a tentative smile, acknowledged my presence with a slight nod of the head, and promptly returned to *The Adventures of Augie March*.

Seeing that she was immersed in her book all I could do was to make my way to my regular seat, which this time was free. I forced myself to disregard the feeling of slight disappointment that had somehow sneaked in. Realistically, nothing that had happened the previous day could possibly justify my hope for a continuation of some sort in my relations with Anna. A set of circumstances had led to us sitting together and the conversation we'd had was the minimum to be expected given those circumstances. Nor did the interest that Anna had shown in the *Demons* go beyond what a Russian bookstore owner was likely to exhibit in such a situation. And in any case, her curiosity was not about me but about the book. I recalled that yesterday Anna had also maintained her boundaries and shown no interest or provided any information that went beyond basic good manners. The fact that she was alone gave no grounds for optimism. She had spurned a suitor who might have been seen as more fitting than me with his Mercedes jeep the price of which was undoubtedly equal to the profits made by a small bookshop after decades of trade. The fact that she'd shifted the iceberg creature inside me was an altogether different story and one that must not cause me to lose sight of the direction and purpose that I was here to pursue.

Only after I'd finished consuming my roast, reading the same page three times over without remembering a word, did it enter my mind that Anna, as befits a principled woman whose presence was forced upon me the previous evening, wouldn't make a move towards me even if she wanted to. If, indeed, she was at all interested, she would surely hope that I would make the first advance. What a fool I am! I can at least suggest that she join me to drink the tea/coffee each of us is about to order.

But as these thoughts raced through my mind Anna was readying herself to leave. As she stretched to put on her coat, I noticed that she was wearing a thin, close-fitting sweater that exposed the outline of her breasts. If I can see them from where I'm sitting, I thought to myself, they can't possibly be small.

As she turned towards the door, our eyes met. She nodded her head in my direction, completed her turn, and went out.

The following two evenings Anna didn't turn up. I tried to shove her into my missed chances drawer where, because of a certain clumsiness on my part, many lost opportunities had accumulated over the years. But thoughts of Anna forced themselves on me and made me lose my concentration. So as to avoid wandering aimlessly around my office or through the streets, I crossed over to the Zheton, the casino on the other side of the road. I read the name of the casino in Russian, practising the new and strange letters, the ZH that looked like a multi-legged cockroach, and the N that looked like an H and the E that looked like an error in the diagonal of an N.

I was one of the very few customers – after all it was the middle of the day. Yet again my passport was photocopied and I was asked to smile into the camera in the wall. I was then able to enter the gaming room, disturbing the peace and quiet of some workers playing poker around one of the tables. The only game I knew was roulette: I decided that I would not allow myself to lose any more than five hundred rubles but, after an hour's worth of systemless yet successful gambling that had the workers gather around me in appreciation, I stopped, a pile of jettons worth more than a thousand rubles to my credit – the price of a good meal in a fine restaurant.

For the first time since moving into the neighbourhood I headed north until I reached a large, square, brown building that almost bordered the banks of the Neva. In my guide book it was listed as the 'former courthouse' and since it was square and very ordinary I didn't bother studying it with the same interest as I did the rest of the street's buildings, all of them very beautiful. I noticed that security cameras were peering out from every corner of the structure, as well as from above the side entrance which abutted a small, enclosed car park. Curious, I walked past the heavy wooden doors at the front and paused to read what was written on the iron plate attached to them. It took me time to connect one word to another. I understood the word 'federalni', thought that the second word 'Sluzhba' meant office or ministry, but couldn't decipher the last, very long word. I did, however, manage to link the first letter of that word to the first letters of the previous two, and all of a sudden

244

the initials FSB leapt into my mind. The Federal Office of Security, the successor to the KGB.

The situation was so bizarre that I burst out laughing. Other pedestrians passed by on their way from the Neva to the city centre, some wearing brown uniforms. None of them entered the building, none paid any attention to me, and I simply kept on walking towards the parapet that runs along the length of the Neva. I took a moment or so to observe the branching of the river into the big and small Neva, trying not to let on that I was in any way connected to the office building across the road.

When I got back to my own office, having taken a substantial detour, I telegraphed my findings to HQ. Considering the unreasonableness of cancelling the rental agreement, I recommended that I stay put. Perhaps due to the blunder of the security department in not knowing that Russia's counter-espionage HQ was in Liteyny Prospekt, or perhaps because of my emotional state, HQ agreed to my recommendation but instructed me not to dare go past that building ever again. I, in any event, had no intention of doing so.

On the third evening Anna was sitting in her usual place by the window, and as usual she looked amiable, remote, and pensive. When she nodded her head in my direction a lock of hair fell over her eyes and she pushed it back with a slow movement of her hand. The small creature burrowing in my iceberg informed me that I was far from having to place her in my drawer of missed chances.

That evening and on the evenings that followed I tried

to ignore her. I had every reason in the world to expect nothing from her. But when the restaurant became overcrowded again and she was forced to sit at the table opposite mine, I noticed the merest light movement of her tongue – the tip of her tongue – that protruded slightly, wetting the corners of her mouth. That movement tore into me like a pile of ice picks.

I am forty years old, I thought to myself. I'd been with a woman for more than half of my life. I had been in love with my wife. Since we'd parted I'd felt almost nothing, certainly not towards women. What on earth could make the barely visible tip of a tongue wetting the dry lips of a strange woman so alluring. Beautiful, it's true, but nonetheless strange. Or make the slow movement of the hand spontaneously brushing away a lock of hair that insisted on slipping down from her brow and across her oval eyes, so captivating? I had no idea. But the hidden organism within me knew and went berserk, threatening to bring down the walls of the iceberg that were now thinner than ever after it had been burrowing into them so continuously.

As I got up to leave Anna stopped me with a slight gesture of her hand. I found a copy which includes the chapter 'At Tikhon's'. Would you like it? Without waiting for my reply she took the thick volume out of her bag. Does it interest you? She looked at me, as if curious to know why I hadn't yet responded.

Yes, yes, of course. It's so nice of you to have made the effort, that I…

That's OK, it's my job, remember? An amused

expression spread over her face at my enthusiastic appreciation. It was no trouble at all. One email to second-hand book dealers, and a copy soon arrived in the post.

I took the book from her, barely touching her outstretched hand.

How much did it cost? I asked, placing the book on the table, searching for my wallet.

You don't have to pay me, it's a loan.

I insisted.

I can't take the money now. I have to enter it in the accounts and give you a receipt. We'll do it some other time. In the shop, perhaps.

I left the restaurant with the address of the bookshop and with that feeling of joy once more sneaking its way in. So there we are. It wasn't just me thinking about her all this time. She was also thinking about me, and she even went to some trouble on my behalf.

At home I skipped the two hundred pages left in my own copy of *Demons* and went straight on to read about the last meeting between Nikolai Stavrogin and Bishop Tikhon in Anna's copy. I didn't fall asleep until I'd finished the chapter. Tomorrow we'll have something to talk about.

But the next day a dispatch from the European front company awaited me in the office. Upon receipt I was to set up an encrypted contact with HQ, which I did. We want you to be in Makhachkala when the equipment arrives, and attached is all the information you need concerning the city, wrote my controllers. Shortly before that they had received my report about the closing of the deal with the Dagestanis and the shipment of the production line to a fish canning plant in Makhachkala, on the shores of the Caspian sea.

The directors of the plant had written to say that they would be happy to host me. Because the equipment was arriving that night and would be assembled in the morning, they advised me to come as soon as possible. A guest suite had already been reserved for me from that evening on the owner's estate.

I didn't want to appear to be overly keen but at the same time I also didn't want to compromise the cover story that enabled me to be present while the equipment was set up. So with much regret I booked an evening flight, which meant not seeing Anna.

24

I TOOK AN instant dislike to the luxurious limousine waiting for me at the airport and politely but firmly refused to taste any of the local drinks loaded into its bar, 'not even the Smirnoff'. After a short drive we stopped outside a large iron gate and were waved in by a uniformed armed guard. Only the light of the moon lit up the otherwise hidden, well-kept gardens between the gate and the large building. The dull light illuminating the residence of the owner of the canning plant, gave no hint of the grandeur inside. The same man was also the proprietor of most of the shrimp fishing vessels in Makhachkala as well as being the owner of an indeterminate number of other businesses in Dagestan –

in other words he was the head of the local Mafia in whose home the guest suite had been made ready for my arrival.

I was at a loss to know what entitled me to such honour, as I was greeted by the sight of enormous dazzling chandeliers, Persian rugs, statues of lions, and two shiny wooden staircases leading up from the entrance hall to the guest floor. Immediately after I'd placed my things in the suite, a servant escorted me to a reception room where the host himself was waiting, attended by a phalanx of servants. The portly bald man was called Mahashashli. He turned out to be a very pleasant individual in mid life assuming, that is, that his rivals would allow him to live out his natural span. The little bit of hair he had left was dyed blond and his eyes, to my surprise, were sky blue. The remnants of the long years of Russian involvement in Dagestan had somehow sneaked into his gene pool.

His very limited grasp of English prevented us from having a real conversation as did the copious quantities of caviar, shrimps, and other sea food that were served. He managed to ask what a man like me was doing in Leningrad – that's what he called the city – and also to clarify the purpose of the lavish entertainment I was getting: he wanted us to sign a new contract at a price ten per cent above my offer. I would get the entire one hundred and ten per cent from his company but return the extra ten per cent to him personally. I, of course, would be losing nothing, while he in this way would go on building his empire. And after this deal, he said, there would be many more. If the production line succeeded, he would need at least another ten such lines. Each at 110% of the price I offered.

Mahashashli said all this with a slight smile, though the colour of his eyes had changed from sky blue to steely grey and it was obvious that a 'no' from me to his proposal was not an option. I didn't think that he would have tried to harm me. At most I would have found myself outside his palace in the darkness of the forest and wouldn't have ever seen a single penny of my money.

Fortunately, there was no possibility of my seeking authorization for this convoluted deal which almost certainly would not have been approved by HQ. I also had no chance of turning it down. As soon as I agreed Mahashashli ordered more hard liquor and more caviar to be brought to the table, leaning over to ask whether I preferred a dark-haired woman, a brunette, or a blonde to come to my room that night.

When I said I was tired and would fall asleep immediately, my genial host said that in that case the woman would merely massage my shoulders and back and then, if I so wished, would go. But he still insisted on knowing if I wanted her to have black hair, or be a brunette or blonde. What sacrifices a man makes for the sake of his motherland! I said to myself. I went for a brunette but got a blonde. And in a strange and surprising way I felt as if I was being unfaithful to Anna.

After my visit to the port of Atyrau in Kazakhstan a few years previously, Makhachkala and its harbour were no surprise in terms of their seediness, poverty and the stench that rose from the fish processing plants and from the markets and roadside vendors on every street corner who looked more like vagabonds than vendors. Nonetheless there was something picturesque about the catch of fish being unloaded from the vessels and into crates, the old and rusted boats themselves, the mass of masts, winches, and nets, the shouts from the deck to the dock; something touching about the small fishing craft manned by doleful-looking fishermen squeezing their way in between the tall ships in the harbour.

Having struck his profitable deal the previous night, Mahashashli didn't join me on my visit to the canning plant. Instead, I was accompanied by some of his assistants. The plant turned out to be a row of sheds and rusty makeshift buildings and the stench around it was unbearable. A large proportion of the shrimps had rotted in their crates having never even reached the refrigerated storage rooms. A group of labourers were working on assembling the new glittering canning machines which looked decidedly out of place in this otherwise dingy plant.

While still in my office I had gone through the instruction manual for assembling the production line and was able to exhibit a bit of know-how, check on the way the locals had assembled it, and even make a number of intelligent comments.

After the visit I asked my minders to leave me alone, but on Mahashashli's orders at least one of them stayed with me at all times. As a result, the gathering of vital pre-operational intelligence in line with the instructions I had received was accomplished in the company of a bodyguard with a pistol poking out from beneath the short sheepskin coat he was wearing. To be honest, this suited me down to the ground. The very sight of his Mercedes opened all the gates for us and no one asked any questions. The guard spoke a little English and readily answered most of the questions of interest to HQ. He was even happy to photograph me against the background of the port and its ships – useful in the event that at some point we might want to use the port of Makhachkala as a stepping stone to Iran.

In the absence of hotels, and not wanting to offend my host, I remained in the guest suite in his palace for another night. As a brunette accompanied me to my room, Mahashashli took the trouble of whispering in my ear that the manager of the escort agency had been fired after having in error sent me the blonde thinking that that was what foreigners preferred. I could only hope that his ground flesh would not be mixed in with the shrimp paste soon to be canned with the help of the new equipment I had supplied.

But today you are not tired, right? I want to find her in your bed in the morning! he said, parting from me laughing like a drunkard though his harsh eyes again testified to total sobriety.

I assumed that the sexual deviancies of the ageing Mafioso included watching my activities in bed on CCTV and for sure recording them for some possible future use. But the real reason for my sending the woman on her way at the end of a pleasant massage were my thoughts about Anna.

When I left in the morning with the driver to return to the city, we passed the brunette walking along the roadside. I asked the driver to stop but he refused.

She walk because no sleep with you, he said, and continued to drive on at speed.

After an absence of two evenings I returned to the restaurant. I heard a car door slam and when, a moment later, I reached the entrance to the restaurant I thought I could see Anna approaching from the end of the street. A car was parked with its light on a little behind her. Then it reversed and disappeared. Despite the cold I decided to wait for her. I watched her upright somewhat dreamy strides coming towards me and felt my heart pumping. When Anna's pensive look caught sight of me an engaging smile swept across her face.

It's cold she said. Why didn't you go in?

I was waiting for you, I said simply, and she instinctively turned her head round in the direction from which she had come and then swung it back towards me.

Have you been here long?

I just arrived, and saw you coming.

I thought to ask about the car but it would have been tactless. Instead I filed it as a question somewhere at the back of my mind.

I read the chapter 'At Tikhon's' I said, but haven't brought the book back. I didn't come here straight from my apartment. Is it OK if we sit together and talk about it?

Of course, Anna answered, flustered. Of course. I

prefer the window, is that OK? I agreed and we sat at her regular table.

Mrs Vashkirova smiled in satisfaction when she saw us sitting together and asked if she should bring our usual dishes and whether, for a change, we would like to have some house wine. Shall we? I asked Anna. She happily consented.

With a flashing smile she turned from being a beautiful, sad woman into a gorgeous, joyful, young girl. Once again her beauty made me feel as if I'd been pierced to the heart. But we were here to talk about the book.

Have you understood that Bishop Tikhon sees that for Stavrogin there is no difference between the crime and the confession? she said after a while.

How can that be? I asked.

Because Stavrogin wants to confess in exactly the same way as he commits his crimes. It is his way of controlling his existence.

But he will go to the gallows if he publishes the confession.

Going to the gallows, like committing the crimes, is an expression of Stavrogin's existential nihilism and this was something that Dostoyevsky was unwilling to accept. This conjunction of existentialism and nihilism only became acceptable after his time, she explained and I didn't really understand. It seemed to me that only Russian or French intellectuals talk that way.

Our food arrived, bringing our literary conversation to an end. I poured us two, rather full, glasses of the red wine and clinked my glass with hers.

What shall we drink to?

To Dostoyevsky and his admirers? she suggested.

To his admirers, I agreed, which means to us.

She gave me a look of approval and took only a sip of the wine which was tolerable but no more than that.

Have you seen Dostoyevsky's grave? she asked.

I didn't know it was in St Petersburg.

It's in a church at the far edge of the city, and I recommend a visit. She didn't suggest going with me.

Anna slowly drank her soup in silence and I waited before asking the question that I'd thought of asking since I first laid eyes on her.

You...are single?

You too, she said in a mixture of question and assertion, tilting her head to one side.

I got divorced a few years ago, I said. It really did feel as if years had passed since then.

Children? she asked, still not answering my original question.

We didn't have any, and that, it seems, was the reason we divorced, I told her, adding a slice of my real life to the legend.

Again there was silence. And then, apparently finding it difficult to get the words out, Anna said, my husband is dead. He was killed in a traffic accident a few months ago.

All at once her story and her demeanour linked up and at that very instant I understood the cloud of sadness and solitude that hovered above her – the dreamy, even weary, quality there was about her. That also explained her being in this neighbourhood restaurant almost every evening. I was now sure that the matter of the car disappearing in reverse which, in terms of timing could well have been linked to her arrival, was nothing more than pure coincidence and nothing whatsoever to do with her.

Children? This time it was me asking.

We didn't have any either. In today's Russia people are not in such a hurry to bring children into the world.

I think that's so in all northern countries, I replied.

Especially here, she said. In other countries it's because of people's careers, here it's because of political and economic uncertainty. In this country after the collapse of the Soviet Union nothing is certain, especially not the economy.

Here, in Russia, this giant of a country, nothing is for sure? I wondered to myself. Everything's relative. True the communists came and went, the USSR vanished, millions paid a heavy price for it all, but hundreds of millions remained as they were. What would parents in my country, where the economy is the last thing on anyone's mind, say? In that tiny country where surviving even the seventy years that the communist regime endured cannot be guaranteed?

I find it really strange that you and the Europeans and the Americans choose to open companies here, Anna concluded as I continued thinking my thoughts.

Strange? I said, regaining my composure. There are thousands of millionaires who got rich only because of the breakup of the Soviet Union. Prices here are still low enough to make a huge profit by buying here and selling in the West. In front of every classy hotel I've seen a fair number of expensive cars – Porsches and BMWs, Mercedes or Jaguars, with the oligarchs' drivers standing by dressed in suits and ties. This is a sight I haven't even seen in any city in Canada or the USA.

And this opportunity, despite being cut off from everything you are familiar with, makes it worthwhile for you to be here?

There wasn't much that was worthwhile left for me there after the divorce. My parents died, I sold the farm, the few friends I had went their separate ways to various places in Canada and America. Reading quietly at home, which is what I did there, is something I can do just as well here, I said, trying to effect a smile.

Yes, that's how I spend my evenings too, Anna said, reminding me that I was not alone in this club of solitude. I wish you success, she said, suddenly bringing to a close this particular conversation, by asking Mrs Vashkirova to bring the tea.

After the wine I didn't want to drink the insipid local coffee that reminded me of the thinly-ground and tasteless Elite coffee I used to drink back home. So I too asked for a cup of tea.

We drank in silence. Suddenly it seemed to me that my presence was a nuisance, preventing her from reading. Before I'd finished drinking my tea I paid and got ready to leave.

You weren't here these last few days, Anna said.

A short business trip, I answered. I sold some machinery and had to be there while it was assembled.

'There?'

In Dagestan.

Dagestan! I've never been there. You are certainly on the lookout for exotic places to travel to.

Wherever the dollar takes me, I said, assuming the mantle of the businessman.

And I live here, in rubles, she said, and in her eyes I saw a streak of sadness.

As I got up to go, she took her book out of her bag.

25

HQ EXPRESSED ITS satisfaction with my report on the Dagestani deal and the anticipated follow–up, as well as with the initial briefing I had sent about Makhachkala. They asked me to begin looking into the possibility of becoming a partner in one of Mahashashli's fishing fleets. I explained that this meant dealing with the Mafia but that didn't bother HQ. The Russian Mafia wasn't the Sicilian Mafia, I was told. In Russia – and certainly in the Republics – it's simply the group that replaced the collapsed central authority and takes care to ensure the maintenance of order, for which, of course, it gets a payoff. In any case, the possibility of being able to sail the Caspian Sea in a vessel of our own, perhaps even reach the shores of Iran, seemed too attractive a proposition to resist.

When I went into the restaurant the following evening I didn't see Anna and, after pausing for a moment, realized that I couldn't simply allow myself to sit at her vacant window seat and so turned to my usual table. When she did arrive she smiled at me, waved, and promptly sat down by the window. I literally felt a physical pain, as the sense of expectation, or should I say of hope, plunged from my heart to the pit of my stomach. Apparently, for her, our encounter the previous evening amounted to no more than concluding a minor discussion of a literary issue. And any way, what on earth do I have to offer her?

I'm not particularly good looking, neither tall nor well-built. Recently, since I stopped working out and my job no longer demanded that I be in good shape, I'd put on a few excess kilos. I hadn't shown any particular grasp of literature, I'm not an amusing or exciting conversationalist, or even a particularly successful businessman, seeing as I had to go all the way to St Petersburg to give my commercial activities a boost. The fact that I too am a solitary soul with a streak of sadness is no reason for anyone to be attracted to me. Perhaps the reverse is true.

But then I realized that the question of my chances of attracting her didn't really bother me so much. I had a capricious wish to be with Anna. It wasn't even a sexual desire. I wanted to gaze into her beautiful eyes, let my hand skim her smooth black hair with its sprinkling of grey, and kiss her dry lips.

I was – I had to admit – in the early stages of falling in love. I wasn't of an age when one suddenly falls in love, but something about this beautiful and sad woman touched me to the core.

Before love happens a magical web is slowly woven. And Anna's thinly spun and invisible threads of magic had been gradually closing in on me. I knew that if not severed while still tenuous, those threads, like a spider's web, would turn into the most enduring bond imaginable.

Anna's beauty was of the quiet kind, the kind I loved. But that was not the only thing about her that captivated me. A woman's beauty is an advertisement. But with Anna I felt that the content was more beautiful than the packaging.

I had her book with me but only handed it over as I was leaving and she didn't invite me to join her. Despondent, I walked out into the cold of the night.

We continued to eat separately, restricting ourselves to a casual, passing 'hello'. I tried to suppress the awakening inside me in case the ties became too burdensome and prevented me from devoting myself to my work which had begun to show signs of life; following in the footsteps of the Dagestanis, the Tajikis had also at long last opened a letter of credit and invited me to visit them – a turn of events that pleased HQ a great deal and me less so.

And then, one evening, before she had finished her meal, Anna came over and sat casually in the chair opposite mine, keeping her legs to the side of the table.

This is a bit embarrassing, but I'll ask you anyway. My husband and I had – have – a subscription for two for the Philharmonic. The next concert is tomorrow evening. I haven't found anyone who wants to go and it's a pity for such an expensive ticket to go begging. Are you interested?

She said she couldn't remember the whole programme but the concert was dedicated to the works of Tchaikovsky and there would be passages from the third, fourth and sixth symphonies, plus a few other lighter pieces, and would end with the overture to the *1812* which I 'surely like'.

With pleasure, Tchaikovsky is my favourite classical composer, I said, trying to curb the eruption of joy I felt.

Anna looked happy. We'll meet at the entrance to the Mariinsky Theatre?

If you want, but I'd be happy to pick you up.

Better we should meet there, she said. At eight fifteen?

Eight fifteen it is. But only on condition that you allow me to pay for the ticket.

Her face fell. Why bring money into it?

OK, we'll talk about it some other time.

We'll see each other there, she said, the look of happiness restored to her beautiful eyes.

The Mariinsky Theatre has four huge white columns straddling its green façade, while on either side of it other, non-symmetrical buildings in the same colours looked as if they had been glued on to it. Anna waited next to a doorman at the entrance to the building, tickets in hand, and as soon as I saw her I realized that I wasn't appropriately dressed for the occasion. She was wearing silk gloves, a white fur coat, white leather fashion boots, and her make-up gave her eyes an even more elongated and beautiful look. I was wearing a simple suit, an ordinary tie, and a dark raincoat. From a brief glance I could see that the men and women around me had all come in evening clothes.

Realizing that a regular handshake would be a bit phony, I reached out to her with both hands as if intending to clutch both of hers. She placed her satiny hands in my open palms, then sidled up to me and kissed me on both cheeks. Her scent enveloped me and made me feel a bit dizzy. I felt that the brush of her lips on my cheeks, however formal it might have been, was a step forward in the possibly imaginary relations with her that I had conjured in my mind.

Anna, acting quite naturally, slipped her arm into mine and led us into the theatre's foyer. Surprisingly, both the entrance and the lobby were modest, lacking any decoration.

We have time for coffee if you would like to drink real coffee, she said, a hint that she had noticed the face I'd pulled when drinking Vashkirova's brew.

Not made from potatoes this time? I asked and she giggled charmingly.

Whatever variety you might desire. From Jacobs to Blue Mountain to St Helena and Segafredo. Sorry that I'm not an expert, there are certainly other kinds I've never even heard of.

I'm also not a connoisseur when it comes to taste, not of foods, or wines or coffee, I hurried to cover her embarrassment, which quite possibly wasn't embarrassment at all but rather a slightly ironic remark about those for whom the quality of coffee is an important consideration.

The aroma of the fine coffee mingled with the fragrance of her hair and her alluring perfume as we stood at a raised round table sipping our drinks, I my coffee and she her Belgian hot chocolate. By the looks of it she didn't keep an especially strict diet contrary to what I'd assumed on the basis of the portions of soup I'd seen her eating.

You had a good day at the office? Anna asked.

Normal day, emails, quotations, tenders.

As it happens I'd been engaged for a few hours in a coded correspondence with HQ after they'd sent me an impossible set of instructions for the gathering of intelligence about Tajikistan. They had asked for reports on security agencies and security arrangements at the airport – controlled by senior Iranian personnel – in the sort of detail which I didn't think I could provide after a short business trip.

And how was your day? I asked, trying to quickly divert attention away from my activities.

Very few buyers, she said. I spent most of the time searching for some old books that a few of my regular customers are looking for, including first editions that are no longer available on the open market.

I must come and visit you there, I said, and immediately regretted it, guessing what would come next:

And I'll visit you sometime too.

If you're interested in seeing a boring office, I said trying to put her off the idea.

Would you like to go over the program? she asked and to my great relief let go of that troublesome topic.

The first work was to be the piano concerto in B flat minor. Anna told me that this was a fairly rare performance of it. Even though in the past it had been thought of as a perfect piece of musical writing, she explained – in fact the first of Tchaikovsky's compositions to be received as such – it is nowadays considered over-sentimental, and is almost never played.

We went into the concert hall at the sound of the first bell and there the real magnificence of the place became apparent: tier upon tier of boxes, their fronts inlaid with gilded wood and in the middle a large ornate box bedecked with gold engravings dating back to the days of the Czars. The splendid curtain also remained hanging as it had done at the time of the Czar and everywhere around there was an almost unimaginable wealth of dazzling baroque.

When, after a short while, we settled into our seats, the woman to Anna's right turned to her, expressed her condolences, and glanced at me briefly. It occurred to me that, for season-ticket holders, the seats and the neighbours are usually the same, and that it was obviously uncomfortable for her to be seen with another man. But when the conductor and pianist entered, the audience greeted them with loud applause. Anna looked straight ahead at the stage, and the conductor signalled to the pianist and the orchestra to launch themselves into the concerto. I couldn't help but feel exhilarated by this romantic and passionate music. Perhaps, being next to Anna, this is what I was bound to feel, our elbows sharing the same armrest, touching each other. But Anna was not swept away, not by the gushing music, as she described it, nor by the rub of my elbow.

My musical knowledge was limited – guitar lessons,

music lessons at school and listening to the radio station, *The Voice of Music,* during the long hours driving from the Arava or Jerusalem to Glilot, the Mossad's HQ near Tel Aviv. Back then I did very much like Tchaikovsky, particularly as it happens, because of that romantic and harmonious lightness.

When the orchestra began to play the Forth Symphony I could see that Anna was trembling. I noticed this during the first movement which, as she told me, describes abortive attempts at fleeing from tragic reality into the world of dreams, as well as in the second which deals with escaping into the past. It was only when she whispered this, whilst I was having trouble connecting the 'composer's intent' with the arabesques I was hearing, that I became aware again of the fact that next to me was a woman wronged by fate, a woman who had lost her husband only a few months earlier.

During the interval we sat at a table in the foyer, and Anna happily ate a salmon sandwich. All I wanted was another cup of coffee. When I asked how she knew so much about music she told me that at one time she'd been a student at the St Petersburg Conservatoire where Tchaikovsky had studied a hundred and twenty years earlier, though in his time it had been in a different place. She also said she knew every one of his works and was familiar with practically every chapter of his life. Did you know that the new Conservatoire is right here, it's that brownish-grey building across the street. I spent some wonderful years there and I love it very much.

You play? Compose? I asked

I used to play the piano and also compose, but that was years ago, Anna replied, her eyes lowered. Now my connection to music is through concerts and what I listen to all day long in my shop.

Did you ever think of becoming a musician?

I thought of becoming a composer or a pianist, but when I realized that neither of these was going to materialize I went to university to study at the Institute for Russian Literature at Pushkin House because I wanted to be a poet and a translator as well. Now I am a bookseller and have a subscription to the Philharmonic. What's left are the memories of dreams, she said sadly, then asked me to excuse her for what she'd said.

No, no, I said, placing my hand on her palm, it's really OK. I want to hear about it.

But Anna shed her expression of sadness and said, so let's talk a bit about the *Pathétique*.

The *Pathétique*?

The Sixth Symphony which we're about to hear. This was Tchaikovsky's last before he succumbed to cholera here in St Petersburg and died. In this symphony you can trace virtually the entire story of his life and glimpse all his talents and weakness. From gross sentimentality to the peaks of melodiousness and majesty.

And all in one piece? I wondered.

Just as all are to be found in the life of one man; a man who was both ridiculed and admired, who was a homosexual yet was married to an admiring and crazy young woman. A wealthy widow was his patron yet she refused to meet him face to face. Life showers us with the good and the bad; and we take a bit, avoid some of it, and for the most part, whether we like it or not, are hurled into this centrifuge, right? she asked. And when I didn't reply and only smiled to myself, she asked again, is that not so?

A particle accelerator more than a centrifuge, I said. At the end there is a crush.

When we returned to our seats a couple sitting in the row behind us leant forwards and expressed to Anna their sorrow at the death of her husband which they'd only recently become aware of. For years we've been seeing each other here once a month, and it hurts, Anna explained to me in a whisper.

Immediately after the *Pathétique*, another ten or so woodwind players came onto the raised stage clutching their silver and gold wind instruments. The orchestra played the overture to Tchaikovsky's *1812*. I was particularly moved – not so much by the familiar passages but by that part in which only the large string instruments with their deep bass tones filled the hall with a resonance that made my whole being quiver. I held Anna's hand. She didn't push it away, aware of my emotion and, indeed, encouraged it. But as we left the hall, she told me that anyone who knows anything about contrapuntal music could weave together the Marseillaise and the Imperial Russian Anthem and write such roaring and nationalistic marches.

I suggested that we take a taxi back together, surely we didn't live far from each other if we regularly ate at the same neighbourhood restaurant, and the prices of the few taxis that still ran at this time of night were crazy. She agreed.

Anna directed the driver. As we passed the main avenue close to my apartment she told him to turn into a side street shortly after which we came to a halt. We were indeed not far from my apartment but the buildings here were large, square, ugly blocks. I asked if I could accompany her to her door.

Anna hesitated and taking advantage of her hesitation, I paid the driver, and sent him on his way.

Anna lived in an enormous twelve-storey, brick building with five or six entrances. I estimated it to be no more than a kilometre from my house. The further away the construction was from the main avenue, the more the euphoria of victory over the Germans subsided, the economic failure of communism became more apparent, and as the great leaders gave way to lesser ones, so the buildings became drabber and drabber. The small lift dipped slightly as we entered it and then ascended at a snail's pace.

In the limited light, as Anna busied herself with the key, I saw peeling walls that projected shadows and stains. The door creaked a bit and Anna went in first to put on a light in the bleak entrance to the apartment.

Books. That's what I saw all around me. In the entrance hall and in the small guest room further down the hallway. Bookshelves from floor to ceiling, inside cupboards and behind glass panels.

Perhaps you should keep your coat on until the heater warms up the room, Anna said, directing me into the living room and to the two-seater of the standard three-piece suite that took up most of the room. She lit a small electric fire and drew it close to me. Even in such a small apartment the building's central heating system clearly wasn't up to the job.

Anna seemed edgy and embarrassed.

I'm putting on the kettle for tea, I'm sorry but I don't have any coffee in the house, neither I nor Mikhail drink coffee. Didn't drink. I mean he didn't drink and I don't drink, she said, getting all tangled up with her words.

It's OK, Anna, I'm not cold and in any case I don't feel like drinking anything.

But we have to have something, she decided, and disappeared into the small kitchen which I could see on the other side of the hallway.

The walls on which there were no books were covered in old and fading wallpaper, the sort that disappeared from apartments in Israel many years ago. The wooden floor was also scratched and worn.

On the table facing me there was a picture of Anna with a mustachioed man in some garden or other. She looked much the same as she did now. The man was tall, well built, with slightly Asiatic features that reminded me of Stalin. Feeling somewhat uncomfortable, I got up and scanned the books, most of them in Russian, a small number in English. Displayed between them were some certificates which informed me of the man's full name, Mikhail Starzav, from which Anna's family name, Starzava, also derived. Only now did I understand that she was named Petrovna after her father.

You also read German? I asked noticing that among the books on the shelf were the works of Heine and

Schiller and more modern writers such as Heinrich Böll and Thomas Mann.

Just a little, came the answer from the kitchen.

I prefer to read what I can in the original rather than in a translation, she added as she arrived bearing two cups of tea and a small plate of biscuits on a decorated tray. You know what they say, the poetry gets lost in translation.

Was your husband also a book person?

More than me. Mikhail taught literature at the university here. What I know comes from what I learned at the Institute for Russian Literature, then at the Institute of Philology and now as a bookseller.

No small achievement, I said.

As she sat next to me on the sofa and drank her tea, she became less reserved and a bit less fidgety. I could well understand what she was going through, letting a strange man into her dead husband's apartment for the first time. But I also knew that I didn't want to let go of this woman with whom I was falling in love.

Anna asked about my musical preferences, she wanted to put on a record, to break the silence a bit. When I said *Swan Lake* and *Sleeping Beauty*, she stood up and on her way to the record player, stretched out her hand and brushed it affectionately against my cheek.

If such joyful and charming music is on your list, she said, you must be an incurable romantic.

We didn't ask any questions as we finished our tea or when the few words we exchanged ran out. The wall clock had long since struck twelve. We got up, suddenly held hands like two youngsters, and stepped slowly towards the bedroom.

I don't want to put the light on, OK? Anna said and I mumbled my agreement.

A double bed filled the narrow bedroom and in the dim light that filtered in from the hallway I could make out a cupboard against one wall and, on the other, pictures that were something of a blur though I did make out a figurine of Jesus on the cross, something I thought unusual in Russia.

At the foot of the bed Anna stopped, turned towards me and moved her lips close to mine. She was the same height as me and we arched our heads to the left and to the right until our lips met with ease. I couldn't avoid recalling Orit's observation about the advantages of an equivalence in height, and then quickly suppressed the memory. Anna's kissing was light at first; I didn't feel her tongue but clearly heard the beat of her heart and of mine as her breasts pressed against me. I also felt the stirring in my loins as she pushed her hips close up to me and her kisses became more passionate. I saw that her eyes were closed as she sucked at my lips and her tongue began to slide in through them. Her dry lips welcomed the wetness of our tongues, hers introducing the taste of a different world into my mouth, a world that totally vanquished me.

As I stretched my hand towards the buttons of her blouse she said, I'll undress myself. She stepped away, turning her back to me. I too undressed.

Sorry that it's so cold, she said, as she slipped under the quilt and I didn't know whether she meant the temperature of the room or the reserved way in which we were doing things.

I joined her under the quilt, dismissing from my mind any fantasies I may have had of quick sex. Anna was half with me and half in some other place. Again I kissed her and again she responded by kissing me cautiously, her tongue continuing to insinuate her other world into my mouth. I caressed her shoulder, her back; her skin was covered in goose pimples and quivered slightly to the touch of my palm. I kissed her brow, her eyes which opened to me in the dark, her neck.

Anna, Annushka, I heard myself saying and she, at the sound of my endearments, pressed her head into my shoulder. I held her in my arms, a prisoner of the softness and scent of the new body. Nothing from my past had prepared me for the silkiness and loveliness of the ripe and relaxed body now in my arms. From the depths of her being came sobs that she tried in vain to suppress.

I'm sorry, I'm so sorry, she said. It's so difficult for me.

I didn't suggest leaving. I wanted her so very much and in a way that was entirely different from my desire for her only a little while earlier. Anna was now embedded in my heart, in my soul, I wanted to be good for her.

I stroked her back, the tips of my fingers running up and down her spine as she trembled to my touch.

That's nice, she said, and her naturally deep voice became even deeper when whispering. Even though your hand is still cold.

Your skin is so soft, I said, as the goose pimples vanished.

When she drew away from me a little, I placed my hand on her soft, heavy breast, one finger circling her nipple which began to harden slightly. Again she kissed me, her kisses covering my face, and when my hand slid between her thighs she whispered, you don't need to, I'm ready, come to me.

Her scent on my fingers was different from the female smells I'd experienced before. She lay on her back, and when I entered her I was surrounded by a warmth and a softness that was out of this world. Anna sighed, a sigh of sheer pleasure.

Potikhonechku, she said, which I understood as 'slowly' or 'gently' or 'carefully'.

I didn't want to, nor could I, be otherwise. I was overcome with love and affection.

Do I need to be careful? No, Anna whispered and, to my shame, after less than a minute of gentle movement I came into her wet softness.

It was my turn to say sorry, but Anna didn't let me utter a word. She filled my mouth with kisses and only said, stay, don't move, please stay.

I remained inside her, entrapped, for a while in her embrace. As I left her body I was overwhelmed by a sense of despondence but she continued holding me and wouldn't allow me to move away, her beautiful eyes gazing into mine and she said, 'my love'.

And this time it was I who pressed my head into her shoulder.

26

I hoped to make amends for my lacklustre performance later that night when I was drained and less excited but Anna gently told me that it would be best for me to go. She didn't want her neighbours to see me leaving her apartment in the morning so soon after her husband's death.

She suggested calling a cab which I didn't want to do, preferring to make my way on foot, even though she claimed that it was dangerous. I knew from a briefing by our intelligence people that regular taxis didn't run in St Petersburg late at night and that the only ones available were private and controlled by the Mafia, a group I preferred not to make myself known to. I got dressed without taking a shower and bent down to kiss her. Anna sat on her bed, her hair dishevelled and then, wrapped in the duvet, accompanied me to the door and again kissed me. I left her apartment quietly and strode into a bleak and deserted street.

I was shivering as I walked through the narrow alleyways and past the huge, silent, residential buildings. I didn't know whether the tremors running through me were due to the dry, intense cold, the freezing gusts of wind that blew in every time I crossed a road leading to the sea, or whether to what I had just experienced with Anna. I felt as though the iceberg inside me had split apart, and that chunks of it had plunged into turbulent waters, creating a whirlpool of differing emotions within me.

Magical threads still connected me to Anna's soft body. The inviting warm embrace of the wetness inside her, the taste of her, her scent, her voice, her gentle touch, the noble manner in which she accepted the hurried way I'd come. They all combined to produce a storm of sensations that I felt not only in my groin but in my entire being.

As I continued on my way, I felt saddened by my performance, disappointment in myself, remembering how, whenever Orit and I had sex, it went on for a long time. I had no idea what the future held for Anna and me. Would she want to see me again? And if not? The love I felt had settled in my heart. I couldn't think clearly. I walked as if intoxicated. Two drunks, curled up in the entrance to one of the buildings heard me approaching and tried to haul themselves up and come towards me. But something about the way I was walking apparently put them off. Perhaps they saw me as one of them, and so it ended with them merely mumbling some unintelligible words as I passed by.

I don't know how long it took me to get home. I paid no attention to what time it was when I reached Moskovsky Prospekt. It was only when I passed Vashkirova's restaurant that I knew I was nearly at my apartment. I was still trembling so much that I couldn't slide the building door's magnetic key into its slot and then had difficulty inserting the key into the lock of my own front door. I even had trouble undoing the buttons of my clothing. I fell onto the bed fully dressed and with my overcoat still on, wrapped myself up in a blanket and didn't wake up until lunchtime the following day.

The alluring scent of Anna's wetness, now dried all over my loins, remained with me as I undressed. I pleasured myself with that intoxicating smell for quite some time, passing it with my fingers to my nose. For a moment I even considered not having a shower so as to keep the aroma of her sexual musk. This feeling might not return so quickly. Perhaps not at all.

The bickering with HQ over the Tajikistan intelligence gathering instructions continued all day. I was asked to go there without delay, apparently because of the expected arrival of some senior members of the Iranian Revolutionary Guards. Reluctantly, I booked myself a flight for the following morning. In the meantime, I counted the hours till my return to Vashkirova's restaurant.

Anna waited for me at her usual table, and as I entered gave me the most enchanting of her smiles. She removed the bag from the seat beside her. I leant over to her, she tilted her head slightly, and I kissed her cheek, not her lips as I had wanted. She noticed that and smiled coyly.

I felt so stupid all day not being able to contact you – I don't have your number either at home or at the office and as I waited for a call from you I realized that you too had no way of getting hold of me by phone. We didn't even exchange numbers. Terrible.

A split second before I allowed a sense of joy to engulf me, Anna added: I was worried about you and angry with myself. How could I have allowed you to go off at night and on foot, and who would have known if you hadn't got back safely: there is after all no shortage of drunks and hooligans around here.

So that's what worried her. Not a yearning for the man who'd been with her the previous night at the concert and in bed. And indeed there was perhaps nothing to yearn for. I'd behaved like an overwrought pupil both in the concert hall and while we made love.

Why are you so quiet, Anna asked as she brushed her hand against my cheek and the lump in my throat melted away as if it had never been. I only had to be sure that it wasn't draining into my eyes and turned my head away from her in case, despite my strenuous effort, an unwanted tear should surface. But Anna held my chin and redirected my gaze towards her.

Our eyes locked. She looked very earnest, and a glimmer of anxiety appeared in her beautiful penetrating and, for once, lustreless eyes which were peering straight into me. The laughter lines in the corners of her mouth had also vanished.

Paul, I don't know how to tell you this, she began after a while. I didn't think that anyone new would come into my life after Mikhail. I was prepared to live out the rest of my days alone. It didn't occur to me to go looking, and I certainly didn't think that I would find someone who could occupy a place in my heart. She clutched my hand and waited for a moment as if trying to calm herself down.

I don't really understand what happened between us yesterday. I didn't plan to take you home with me after the concert. It happened, it seems, because we both needed it to happen. I'm glad it did. I've had the first hours of happiness since my husband died. But it's not part of where I'm heading. I don't know what your hopes are for the future, and perhaps it's important for us to talk about it.

She's had hours of happiness? With me?

I don't think I'm ready to talk about it, I said. You do something to me that I don't yet know how to describe. I know it mustn't be a fleeting romance. I feel it can't be a fleeting romance. But I don't even know how much time, from a business point of view, I will want to stay here. It never crossed my mind to link my future to a Russian woman.

And what *are* you ready to talk about? Anna asked quietly.

I really don't know. And perhaps it's too early to know.

Indeed I didn't know. An attachment to a woman here would be a millstone around my neck so far as my operational capability was concerned; it would put the cover story at risk, infuriate HQ and would, inevitably, be severed when I returned to Israel. And yet, I wanted her.

We had a lovely evening, I said, which, to my regret, didn't end in a particularly successful way and I'll be happy if it doesn't mark the end of our relationship.

Stop being childish about our night together. I'm a grown woman, Paul. I'm not searching for what a young girl would look for. I was happy with you yesterday. And I also don't want it to end, but it's important to me that you understand that I, too, don't know where it could lead.

So we're on the same page, I smiled ruefully.

Vashkirova served our meals, adding a bottle of house wine without even bothering to ask.

I poured the wine into the two glasses. Let's drink to uncertainty? I proposed.

We'll drink to our friendship wherever it may lead, Anna responded. Once more wiser and more sensitive than me.

As we sipped our wine my heart ached. Friendship? I don't just want the friendship of this beautiful woman. I want her love. But there was no point in my saying so.

You are morose again, Anna said and looked at me with compassion. I want to hug you, she whispered, stroked the palm of my hand and clutched it tightly.

We ate in silence. Suddenly we were in such a different place from where we had been just the day before, at this very time. But the path on which we had taken our first cautious steps appeared to be a dead end. Hopeless.

Is your office closed this weekend? Anna suddenly asked.

Yes, I answered, intrigued.

How about us going to visit the graves of Dostoyevsky and Tchaikovsky?

She saw the look of hesitation on my face.

Or we could just wander around the city; there must be plenty of beautiful places that you still haven't seen.

I'm flying out tomorrow morning, and it looks like I won't be back until the beginning of next week.

Again? What a pity!

The business world makes its own demands, I said and thought I sounded like an absolute phony as I said it. What am I trying to do, impress her as a hustling businessman?

Where to this time? she asked.

Tajikistan, I said, and her almond eyes became almost round at hearing my answer.

Tajikistan! And what did you lose there?

I didn't lose, I found. Another big customer who wants me to be there when my equipment arrives.

Shame, but it will at least be warmer there. Didn't you catch a cold yesterday?

I was shivering all the way, but nothing more than that.

I didn't think Anna would invite me to her apartment again that night and indeed she didn't. I knew it would be untactful to invite her to mine after she'd explained how she wanted to avoid speeding up our relations and had toasted our 'friendship'.

And so we parted at the entrance to the restaurant with a kiss to both cheeks, each going their separate ways. I felt that her heart, like mine, was heavy.

With great difficulty I returned to being a spy. A twin engine Tupolev plane belonging to Pulkovo Airlines flew me to the small airfield on the outskirts of Dushanbe, the capital of Tajikistan. As we came down to land I took a series of photos through the plane's window of the buildings to the right of the landing strip. From the gangway, with only the camera's lens peeping out of my coat pocket, I took a number of wide panoramic shots of the entire terminal area. Then, from the window of a vintage bus that took me and the few other passengers to the arrivals building, I sneaked a few more pictures of the area where the executive jets were parked. That's where the distinguished Iranians would be landing were they to arrive in a private plane.

At the front of the airport's central terminal was a statue of an astronaut, with the control tower rising skywards from the building's upper floor. Once in the arrivals hall I continued with my covert filming, while trying, also at the same time, to memorize the details and find the VIP lounge. If HQ decides it doesn't want to hit the aircraft itself, it may be possible to get at the senior Revolutionary Guards in the VIP area. But I couldn't find such a place. I left the terminal building and asked for a taxi that would take me to the In-Tourist Hotel in the city centre.

Dushanbe turned out to be a not very large city with its older neighbourhoods built in a way that made them resemble a series of small family encampments with a courtyard at the centre, an idea I'd come across in the hutongs of Beijing. The post-World War II Soviet influence could be seen in the clusters of four-five-and six-floor residential buildings dotted across the town. There wasn't a proper 'downtown' and most businesses were conducted from offices in Dunaki Street which is where my hotel was also located.

The company that had bought the canning production line from me was in the Industrial Area, a little out of town, and there I headed in the afternoon. I set aside the following day to continue the gathering of intelligence data and planned to get to the governmental buildings, the parliament, and every other site the Iranians were likely to visit.

Within two days I had practically all the intelligence information that would be of interest to HQ, including data relating to the extent of Iran's penetration of the country and the activities of the security services. Iranians were everywhere, taking control of businesses, buying real estate, signing contracts with governmental agencies and with leading private companies. Dushanbe – itself a Farsi name meaning Monday, named after the Monday market held there when it was still a village – was turning day by day into an Iranian satellite. The owners of the canning plant, who thought it appropriate to exhibit a pro-Russian position in their conversations with me, were happy to enlarge on this trend, and on the helplessness of the authorities and the security services to halt it.

I'd concluded my meetings and intelligence gathering activities by mid-afternoon and, because I was booked on an evening flight back to St Petersburg, spent the few hours left to me strolling the streets close to my hotel. In one of the alleyways, Hebrew lettering momentarily stopped me in my tracks. I found myself in front of the Bukharian Synagogue. Like most of the houses it also had a courtyard with an additional building in it. One was used as a synagogue in the summer and in winter worshippers used the second building for prayers. I was mesmerized by the Hebrew lettering, the like of which I hadn't seen since leaving Israel, and had forcefully to tear myself away, leaving the place in a great hurry.

27

THE IMMEDIATE EFFECT of my unexpected encounter with the synagogue in Dushanbe, made me decide to visit the Grand Choral Synagogue in St Petersburg immediately after my return. I knew that in so doing I was committing a serious breach of security for which there was no justification. What's more, going to a synagogue in no way chimed with my beliefs or my way of life, even in Israel.

My delight at the very sight of the building came as a surprise to me: a magnificent brown and white structure topped by a grey dome no less impressive than the great churches gracing the city. When I reached the guard at the entrance to the enclosure I hesitated for another moment or so and then, based on nothing more than a whim, decided to enter.

Where to? asked the guard in Russian.

I'm a Jew, I answered – also in Russian. *Ya yevrei*, and felt an inexplicable pride well up within. The guard gestured for me to enter.

I wasn't wearing a yarmulke and so sat down on the bench at the far end closest to the entrance. The hall was impressive. There were two rows of pillars on either side supporting the upper tier reserved for women, and reaching all the way to the high-arched ceiling from which there hung a huge chandelier. The Holy Ark straddled the entire eastern expanse of the hall and its yellowish walls gave me a sense of warmth. Suddenly I felt at home. A strange emotion for someone who, at most, finds expression for his Jewishness through its nationalist and cultural aspects. However, in their absence, I was drawn to the synagogue and the synagogue reached deeply into the void within me. I sat there for a long time, not daring to go into the centre of the hall or to approach the Holy Ark. It took an effort on my part to tear myself away from the place. Enough, I said to myself. I've finished re-charging my internal batteries and there are limits to my transgressions.

I agreed to Anna's earlier idea that at the weekend we should visit the graves of Dostoyevsky and Tchaikovsky. We met in Vosstaniya Square in the middle of Nevsky Prospekt. Do you know how this square came into being? Anna asked me. The Czar wanted to build an avenue from Nevsky's place of burial to the Admiralty building. But two teams of road pavers advancing from two different directions strayed from the planned path and met up here.

The clouds covering the sky blocked off the little heat there was and Anna suggested we walk to the Tikhvin Cemetery in the Alexander Nevsky Monastery, where Dostoevsky, Tchaikovsky, and many other of St Petersburg's great men of letters are buried. Why on earth are we travelling around on the metro and on foot and not by car, I thought to myself as we made our way towards the cemetery.

But I knew perfectly well why I didn't have a car. In briefings before my departure it was pointed out that having a vehicle increases ones embroilment with the authorities, and the grey uniformed traffic police, the DPS, are stationed at every crossroad and constantly carry out spot checks on cars. The purchase of a car also adds to the expenses that have to be officially accounted for, and the metro, tramways, and buses, make travel around the city easy. But I had no idea why Anna didn't have a car and when I asked her she said: actually Mikhail and I did have one. Most of the time he was the one driving and after he died I sold it to ease my financial situation. I don't miss it.

Just missing him, I thought to myself regretfully.

Ahead of us was a relaxed hour's walk before we got to the Alexander Nevsky Monastery. As we strolled along, Anna delighted me with her great knowledge of the poets and authors who'd written about her beloved St Petersburg. Alexander Pushkin, she said – making sure to mention his first name in case I didn't know it – did indeed describe the city's aura in great detail. But of all his works about Peter the one I love most is *The Bronze Horseman.*

You must have seen the big statue of Peter the Great on a horse in Senate Square, she said. The poem's hero, Yevgeny, has a great love who drowns in a flood. Yevgeny remonstrates with Peter for having built the city in a place prone to flooding. You know that this whole area was one big swamp, don't you? And that's also the meaning of the word 'Neva' in Finnish. A swamp. In any case, poor Yevgeny goes crazy, and in his delirium he is pursued through the city streets by the statue of Peter.

I said nothing about this savage confrontation between man and the state which Anna had taken the trouble to explain to me. After a long silence she continued with her enlightening account.

Nikolai Gogol – again informing me of his first name – though a Ukrainian, did most of his writing here. His *Tales of Petersburg* – perhaps you've read some of them – described the disparity between how things in the city seem and the true nature of their reality; a divergence that can lead a person to dream of things that cannot be, go crazy, and die.

Why is the wise Anna telling me all this? Is it perhaps her only way of describing the literature written here in Petersburg or is she trying to hint that something in me, and perhaps in her, something in my dreams and maybe in hers, is beyond realization. That the reality differs from what we see, think and feel. That the state will rear its head and stand between us and against our love.

We had reached the Monastery and chose to go first into the cemetery. In the burial grounds to the right, alongside the families of the nobility and close friends of Peter the Great, the city's most renowned architects and composers had also won the right to small family plots. We stood facing Tchaikovsky's large tombstone crowned with a big statute of the composer, behind him a huge angel and a cross, and in front a woman obviously reading from his compositions. Alongside Tchaikovsky were the more modest graves of Mussorgsky and Borodin.

We waited for a group of tourists to leave before approaching Dostoyevsky's grave. Behind a small fence a grey tombstone was topped by a cross and below stood Dostoyevsky's finely sculptured bust. The inscription was weathered and almost illegible. We stood there, holding hands.

Dostoyevsky was subjected to many transformative experiences before writing *Crime and Punishment,* Anna said. And if you read the book in depth you will see that St Petersburg's contrasts, its inequalities, form the background to Raskolnikov's deeds.

The thought of Raskolinkov, the murderer, and the realization that Anna had avoided using the word 'murder' and made do with 'his deeds' flashed through my mind. But before I was able to delve more deeply into that she continued her peroration.

Have you read *The Double?* I said I hadn't. There too Dostoyevsky presents St Petersburg as a city in which the imagined is truer than reality. Something of the hero splits off from him and turns out to be more successful than he was. As a consequence the real character becomes crazed.

I couldn't but think about myself, Yogev Ben-Ari, losing control over his double, Paul Gupta, who proceeds to usurp my place in the world. I was overwhelmed by a sense of deep distress.

On the two weekends that followed we again toured the city. Autumn's blaze was at its height, the trees were changing colour and I was so visibly roused by the splendour of the green, yellowish, red and purple foliage, that Anna had to ask me if in Quebec trees don't change colour. Coming to my senses and somewhat embarrassed, I explained that the sight had simply triggered feelings of nostalgia for what I'd left behind, a sentiment for which I got a big warm hug.

She showed me the romantic 'winter canal' and its roofed passage – between the new Hermitage and the theater – which arches over the waterway and allows one to look at the Neva, its contours reminiscent of Venice's Bridge of Sighs.

We stood there gazing at the canal and the tour boats passing beneath us between the walls of the palace, while she continued to pepper me with allusions to the literature in which St Petersburg features so widely.

It's true that only part of the story took place here in St Petersburg, she said. But you know what happened to the woman who wanted to live the dream, everything – the husband as well as the social status and the lover. What she got was all of its shards, became miserable and made her whole family miserable in its own way.

Even my limited literary knowledge was enough for me to understand that she was talking about quite another Anna, Anna Karenina. This was one of the novels that I read during my Tel Avivian nights of solitude after Orit and I separated. I, as it happens, had identified with entirely different characters in Tolstoy's novel. Dolly, Kitty, and Levin, who were prepared to give up on love to keep the modest family happiness intact; ready to live with its flaws and limitations and not impose such levels of misery on others for the sake of that dream of love. As I was telling her all of this I described myself hibernating in Canada's long, icy-cold, winter nights.

Levin was really the character in the novel who most

reflected Tolstoy's ideals, Anna said. Village and religious life. I am sure that Tolstoy was in love with Anna, but look at where he landed her – either he, or her infatuation – under the wheels of a train. And even now that train continues to speed ahead at full steam.

I couldn't but see her words as a clear-cut warning to me about the inevitable end to our love. But family love was, after all, what I too had hoped for, with Orit, and what Anna had yearned for with Mikhail. That expectation failed us both. Perhaps the way back to that happiness has to include another tempest of love. With Anna, and despite the speeding train.

Pass through the cloud and you will see the sun again, I said to Anna citing an old American Indian saying. She glanced to her left and right as if looking for something or as if she was afraid of someone, and then, surprisingly, gave me a snatched kiss on the mouth.

On weekday evenings we met at Vashkirova's restaurant, ate together and then bid each other goodbye. Occasionally, at Anna's behest, we substituted Vashkirova's menu with that of a restaurant in the city centre. After all, Anna remarked, eating is not solely about filling the stomach. There are lots of lovely restaurant on the banks of the canals and in the main streets, so from time to time it could be nice. And it was.

We went wherever Anna's fancy took us. Once she chose a restaurant called Chekhov, decorated in the style of an aristocrat's 19th-century dacha, with a piano player sitting in the middle. One Friday evening we went to the Fyodor Dostoyevsky restaurant which also tried to re-create the atmosphere of the 19th century and on Friday nights offered a special dish of shellfish that didn't satisfy me at all. I also didn't like the round tables with white tablecloths, the chandeliers, the immaculately-dressed waiters, or the location inside the small and pricey Golden Palace hotel. There was a casino there which attracted wealthy types and the place was swarming with their security people.

We both enjoyed the Dickens, a bar-restaurant brilliantly designed to resemble an English pub with shiny mahogany tables, green and red leather couches, a display of English football club scarves on the walls, and every drink imaginable.

In the spring, when the ice in the canal has melted, we'll go for a night cruise and watch the river's bridges open to allow ships on the Neva to pass. It's the most romantic sight in the world, Anna said. But I knew that for me Anna was the most romantic sight in the world and that the coming spring was the thing furthest away from my mind.

Since that cold night when I had left her apartment neither of us had brought up the subject of spending the night together. My fear that what Anna was offering was just her friendship distressed me more and more as my need for her love intensified.

I was acutely aware of the literary warning signals that Anna kept on offering – cautions that I, in fact, didn't need. I knew, without her having to tell me, that this was a love that had no future. But now that I loved her so much I could no longer make do with a fleeting romance or with just her friendship.

*

The time has come for you to pay me a visit to my shop, don't you think? Anna asked one day. I hoped that this question would be postponed for as long as possible and so delay the prospect of her visiting me in my office. Wouldn't the bookshop have closed by the time I finish at the office?

But you're the master of your time, aren't you? Come in the morning, or finish early. And if you can't, I'll open up specially for you. What are your plans for tomorrow morning for example? she asked.

We agreed to make it a date. I found Anna's shop without any difficulty, not far from Vashkirova's restaurant. No wonder that that is where she goes after closing up. The shop was small and, like other neighbourhood stores, was set up in the columned portico of a residential building.

Anna welcomed me at the entrance, more animated than ever and visibly happy. I realized that up till then I'd mostly seen her in the evening and certainly never as early in the day as this. Her skin looked fresh, her cheeks were slightly flushed – make-up presumably – her lips high-lighted with a red colour that suited her clothing – a tight-fitting, woollen blouse that accentuated her breasts. There was also a little light make-up around her eyes which shone with joy.

I couldn't restrain myself from saying, you look utterly gorgeous this morning, and the excited Anna kissed me on the mouth and invited me in.

Though true that Anna herself was always neatly

dressed, the order and cleanliness of the shop nonetheless surprised me. The place resembled more the neatness and spotlessness of a library than a bookshop. I made some reference to this and Anna, somewhat embarrassed, told me she'd arrived early and tidied up in honour of my visit. But what do you think? she asked in a tone of childlike expectation.

It's cozy and warm. Just a pity that I'll never be able to read all these books in Russian.

Though my Russian had progressed a little because of the few contacts I had in the course of my daily life, my reading skills hadn't improved at all and my writing skills were non-existent.

I'll translate for you, Anna said happily, placing her arm in mine and taking me for a tour of the shelves while explaining what was on them; this is the poetry section. Pushkin, Lermontov, Mayakovsky, Yesenin, Yevtushenko, Anna Akhmatova…and quickly adding a nugget of information about each of them.

Did you know that Pushkin was killed in a duel?

No, I didn't.

Yes, this romantic writer got involved with beautiful married women, and men got involved with his wife and it would usually end in a duel. In this contest, the last one, a French officer who'd wooed Pushkin's wife shot him. It all echoes in *Eugene Onegin*, his satire on Russian society in the days of Nicholas the First.

She told me about Pushkin's poetry which she 'admired' and about other poets she was less fond of.

Yevtushenko, for example, is more highly thought of

among Jews and in Israel than here because of his poem 'Babi Yar', she said, and my heart skipped a beat. I'm sure you are familiar with it, she added.

No, doesn't sound familiar, I said, and Anna quoted the first lines of the poem – which I'd read in translation and knew well – and told me about the Jewish common grave that had stirred the heart of the poet. Ilya Ehrenburg also wrote about 'Babi Yar', she added. But he had the direct support of Stalin who admired his anti-Nazi articles so he allowed him to be pro-Jewish.

My heartbeat only returned to normal after we'd finished going through the poetry section and Anna began showing me the works of the great Russian classical authors – Tolstoy and Dostoyevsky, Chekhov and Gorky, all the way to the outstanding writers of today.

Not many shops stock Solzhenitsyn, she said, pointing to the works of the regime's famous opponent who'd gone into exile in Vermont and returned to his native land on the eve of the collapse of the Soviet Union. I stock him not because I have a particular liking for the opponents of the regime but simply because he is a wonderful writer. It's funny, you know, here in his time, he was considered a dissident and in the West was viewed as a reactionary, a nationalist and an anti-Semite.

Anna glanced at me then continued.

I also have a lot of literature in translation from all over the world. You'd be surprised to hear how much demand there is for it here, and she led me to another bookstand. Here you'll find all of Goethe, the whole of Rilke, Heine, and here the moderns. And on the other side

Shakespeare, Milton, Chaucer. Russians love all the great western classics.

I couldn't put my finger on what it was that seemed strange to me about this shop other than its pristine orderliness. Perhaps it was the sheer volume of 'the complete works of' so that the shelves were lined with clusters of vividly coloured covers and the books were of the same height. There were only a few shelves on which this uniformity and variety of colour schemes was missing – those were the shelves with English and German classics stacked in no particular order, more like the kind of display I was used to in bookshops.

A lady came into the shop asking for a particular title. Anna had to search for it on the computer and I said that I had to get back to my office.

Next time we'll go to your office, Anna called out as I headed for the door, and I just muttered that there was nothing interesting there for her to see and left.

In the weeks that followed, Anna didn't deviate from her clearly expressed view that we were just 'friends'. Her friendship was indeed dear to me but as time passed my desire to love her, embrace her, sleep with her again, simply drove me crazy. All day long my mind was filled with thoughts of her beautiful face, her easy smile, her eyes, her white body, her sensuality when we made love. But I knew she needed time and the hope of her love continued to fuel me in my every encounter with her.

I knew that I too needed time. I continued to go over in my mind why this love was doomed, and why I must not allow myself to take it further. But the magic web already had me in its grip and I couldn't, of my own will, detach myself. The strands around me became tighter and tighter from one rendezvous to the next and I became its consenting captive.

I followed my beautiful jailer even when she rattled the keys of the prison gate; a rattle I heard once again when we went to Peterhof, the imperial estate nestled on the shores of the Gulf of Finland. We toured the beautifully kept gardens, with their ponds, their gilded statues and amazing array of fountains that reminded me of Versailles. I stood on the steps facing the statue of Samson tearing open the jaws of a lion, encircled by an array of cascading water. The gilded Samson was a giant when compared to the lion, a sight that utterly amazed me. Anna, perceptive as always, smiled as she asked: Is it his strength, his courage, or the folkloric Jewish tale that appeals to you? Droplets of water from the fountains around the shiny statue helped to disguise the beads of sweat the question provoked. All three, it would seem, I said.

A bit over the top, isn't it? she asked as I studied each of the other figures around us. It's possible to be entirely happy in a small apartment without all this grandeur, don't you think? Small and well heated.

Could we in this magical city – or in any other place – in fact dive beneath the whirlpool of illusion sweeping us up, and be rid of the bonds of steel that were binding me, surfacing over clear water and one day find happiness in a small well-heated apartment?

Anna remained enigmatic about everything relating

to her personal life. In our long conversations in restaurants and cafés, on our tours of the city's bridges and canals, and even at Vashkirova's, she told me about her childhood, about her studies, but said little, if anything, about her husband.

It's still too painful, she said, and you wouldn't want to see me crying, would you?

And I, consistent with my cover story, responded in the same vein. In doing so I relocated our farm in the Arava to a ranch in Sainte-Agathe in Quebec, a few hours journey from Montreal. I also had to substitute the cultivation of summer crops in the desert with the vegetation more common in northern climes. I described apple plantations, maple trees, and fields of wheat, told her about the tractor I'd started to drive when I was only thirteen, and spoke about my parents. The story of the hardships experienced by Eastern European immigrants who came to Israel, was turned into a tale of the difficulties endured by an Indian who emigrated to Canada. His love affair and subsequent marriage to the daughter of a local rancher whilst he was a student at the university of Montreal and the sudden death of his father-in-law, led him to settle down among French-speaking Québécois farmers.

And they accepted him?

He never really became 'one of them', I replied, transposing the foreignness of my father. At home we spoke English – my father didn't know any French – and his feeling of being an outsider rubbed off on me. I was a small child when the Bloc Québécois came to power and made French the only official language. My father then sent me to a kindergarten and subsequently a private school for English speakers. One by one, the members of the English-speaking community left the region, including the small numbers of farmers among them, but he continued to live there, modestly, working hard, always in the shadow of my lovable mother who acted as a go-between with their neighbours.

And why didn't you stay on the farm? Anna wanted to know. Isn't that more attractive than going into business?

I loved the farm, but I was different from all my peers in the area, both in looks and in language. I didn't have any friends there and didn't want to stay. I also wasn't able to buy another farm and my father was still a healthy man. It made no sense for me to hang on until I could take over from him so I decided to study business administration rather than agriculture and didn't return to the farm.

Tell me about Montreal, Anna asked. There must be something magical about it if you left the farm to go there. We were sitting in a small bistro on the banks of the river after Anna had explained to me that the word 'Bistro' comes from Russian and means 'quickly'. It was evening, and the skies over the Gulf were lit up by the last rays of the setting sun. Apart from us, there were only two other couples in the place. On every table there was a small candle burning and we sat there holding hands. Anna's almond eyes gazed at me with the inquisitiveness and eagerness of an adolescent expecting her knight in shining armour to transport her on his horse to an unknown land.

Yes, there is something magical about Montreal, I said.

During my childhood I went there with my parents and also visited Quebec city, the capital, with its citadel and impressive ramparts, and many other cities as well. But when I got to Montreal as an eighteen year old, a young student, I fell in love with it.

Tell me more, I want to know with whom and how you fall in love, she smiled at me.

For some reason I felt that I had to go into detail, that I had to set Anna's mind at rest. The earlier brushing up of my cover story enabled me to do this.

I remember my first tour of the city exactly, I said, gazing to one side as if recollecting the visit, avoiding her piercing look and the need to lie directly to her face. I was a young man who'd just left the family home. I rented a room in Cumberland Street in Notre Dame, a lower-middle-class neighbourhood. It wasn't particularly close to the university but it was an area where I could afford to pay the rent. I lived in the attic of a family whose children had already left home. The houses in the street were two storeyed and small, red bricked – all in the same style and yet different from each other – with well-kept lawns and rows of colourful flowers at the front. I walked the length of the road with mixed feelings; sadness at having left my parents' home, tinged with excitement about the move and the euphoria of a tourist on a trip abroad.

And since then being a tourist abroad is something that you love to do, Anna added, words of empathy that regained my direct attention.

My description to Anna of my first encounter with Montreal wasn't that far off the truth. It was based on the legend I'd formulated in that city immediately after its inception in India fifteen years earlier, and since then I had indeed travelled a great deal.

I took the metro to the city centre, and got off at Côte-Sainte-Catherine station. These were the last days of summer twenty odd years ago, I told her, adjusting the dating to make it consistent with the age a student who hadn't served in the army would be. On one side of the street was a young man playing the violin, a pouch at the ready for the dollars he was given by passers-by. A bit further ahead was a thin young girl playing the guitar, singing and tapping her foot, ringing small copper bells attached to her ankle. Crowds of people passed by the street's huge shop windows and on every corner there were street painters drawing young women sitting in front of them. I stopped at Place Ville Marie crammed with youngsters sitting around the fountain in the middle of the piazza. Many others stood listening to a childrens' orchestra, each child dressed in the red uniform of cadets from the fire fighting service. In line, waiting their turn, were a group of young naval recruits in blue uniforms, white berets, and gilded swords. When the reds left, the blues marched in and performed a number of amusing foot drills which were loudly clapped by the onlookers. To my great surprise almost all the navy cadets were black.

There too, Anna commented, only those who have nothing enlist in the army. It's the same here. But go on, please, you're a wonderful storyteller.

I remember continuing on to the old city, to Place Jacques-Cartier, a narrow elongated piazza between the two sides of an ancient paved roadway leading from the port to the hills behind the city. Horse-drawn carriages carrying tourists trundled along the paved upper area of the square which was also an assembly point for dozens of bikers. Further down there were loads of youngsters sunning themselves on a lawn, some bare chested, some with guitars, many feeding the pigeons walking at their feet. I felt as if I was in a film. And then, suddenly, the bells of the church pealed and I was shaken. I knew at that very moment that there was no way back for me to my parents' farm.

Anna unexpectedly leant over and kissed me on the lips. With these last few words I'd described to her exactly how I felt when I reviewed my cover story before leaving for St Petersburg in the knowledge that there was no way back.

And you stayed there, in Montreal?

No, I replied. I felt like a stranger there. After my studies I moved to Toronto and throughout my marriage that is where I lived. It was only after the divorce that the urge to leave surfaced and I returned to Montreal. But it's not a place for someone alone, I said, transposing my isolation in Tel Aviv to that of an English speaker in Montreal.

You went back to the love of your youth, Anna said. I can really imagine you, just eighteen, in the solitariness and magic of a foreign city. And now, twenty years later, you're doing it again.

Twenty plus, I corrected her. Then I was a teenager with his entire life in front of him, Annushka.

Did you notice how, when we talk, we're echoing the titles of a couple of books? O Henry and Émile Ajar, she smiled and squeezed my hand more firmly.

G'enry, she'd said, O G'enry and it took me a moment to understand the Russian pronunciation of O Henry's name.

And now what? She looked at me encouragingly. Perhaps not all our life, but a big slice of it is still in front of us, isn't it?

I liked the fact that she was talking about 'us'. We sat facing each other, she on a sort of velvety sofa pushed up against a wall and I on a wooden chair. I moved to sit by her side on the sofa. We embraced and kissed each other for what seemed like an eternity. This time at your place? she asked, and I trembled. That's it, Anna's made up her mind. At least about one more night of love.

This time at my place, I said, concealing my excitement. And you'll have to excuse the mess.

The life of a bachelor, Anna forgave me in advance.

With the money from the Mossad and the need to be seen as a relatively successful businessman, my apartment was a few notches better than Anna's. The building itself, though crude and dreary, was nonetheless soundly built. In addition to its good location, the apartment was big, renovated, and well furnished. For a short while I felt uneasy about being 'better off' than her, and nervous about the untidiness. When Anna went to shower, I quickly tidied up the bedroom, straightening the bedcover despite knowing that it would, in any case, be thrown aside again pretty soon. I managed to stuff my scattered clothes

301

into the wardrobe and arrange in one pile the American newspapers in the living room – my main source of information for what was happening in Israel. I placed the *Toronto Star*, which I got daily, at the top of the stack. Anna came out of the shower, wrapped in my bathrobe, her hair wet. Strange how a male dressing-gown makes the naked, wet body of the woman concealed inside so desirable. I reached for the robe's belt as Anna asked, aren't you going to have a shower?

I didn't plan to but if you think I need to…

Leaving someone unsupervised in my home was against the most basic rules of caution. But with Anna my cover story somehow became an integral part of me. I turned into the young half-Indian who'd left Sainte-Agathe in Quebec for Montreal, who had nothing to hide, and was now doing business in St Petersburg. Besides, there wasn't anything in my apartment that could incriminate me. What's more, I trusted Anna. When I came out of the shower she was waiting for me in bed, under the cover. The bathrobe was draped over the back of the chair.

Do you mind putting out the light? she asked as she had done when we were in her apartment.

I slipped into bed beside her, into my bed, and this time was greeted by the smell of my shampoo from her hair and the scent of my soap from her body. The warm water had been good for both of us and we slowly enjoyed every inch of the other's body. Her skin after the shower was soft and smooth, her breasts heavy and pleasing. This time Anna allowed me to go down to her thighs and pleasure her, the salty taste captivating me, as did the sound of her light sighs that could be heard as if coming from a distance. She also stroked my cock until she pleaded with me to come in to her. My excitement wasn't what it had been the last time round but I was nonetheless still very aroused and when, after a short while Anna wanted us to change position I had to tell her that it was a bit late for that.

She remained in my bed, and in the middle of the night we made love again. This time I was, at long last, really drained and was able to make love to her slowly, as she wanted me to. Let's try spooning, she said, and I groped a bit under her full buttocks until I was able to penetrate, my one hand trapped under her body, the other embracing her and stroking her breast. I upped the pace of my movements and soon felt a series of quivers running from her fingers to her arm. Anna pleasured herself with rapid movements and after what seemed like a very long minute I heard her come.

No, don't say anything, she whispered. Just hug me and let's sleep.

Just before daybreak her internal clock woke her up. Her hand stroked my face, my chest, and slipped down to my penis. I moved towards her and we again made love in the way I wanted to and then in the way she wanted. It was good for us both.

Annushka, I whispered, as she lay beside me, panting. She wrapped herself round me, covered my face with kisses and said, I have to go.

Are you some sort of a siren, a mermaid who grows a

tail if she sleeps with someone in the light? I asked with a smile.

I don't want you to find an old, flabby, fat woman by your side she answered sounding sad. I wasn't waiting for a man to come along and since Mikhail's death I haven't been taking care of myself and I've got fat.

You look beautiful, I said.

With the help of a corset and a push up bra. It's a pity you didn't know me before.

I didn't want to imagine a youthful Anna. This most feminine of women beside me, beautiful and in full bloom, was everything I wanted. But I felt the need to apologize for my own body which had also lost its youthfulness and in doing so comfort her a little.

I also didn't have this paunch until a year or two ago. But we are not children, Annushka.

Aren't we? Since I was eighteen I haven't felt like I do with you, and offered me her lips in a long lingering kiss.

Don't get up, she ordered, and went to the shower.

By the time she'd reach the beam of light from the bathroom, a poised, white woman with large buttocks and firm thighs, I was already yearning for her return. I too was a teenager in love. And when I thought about it, it seemed to me that maybe even way back then in the Arava, I hadn't experienced love in this way. I'd grown up with Orit, she was there when I'd first experienced sexual arousal. Now it was different. Suddenly, for the first time in my life, a woman wanted me. A beautiful, mature woman. And for the first time in my life I felt worthy of a woman's desire and her love had made me worthy of being loved. She could, after all, have chosen whomever she wanted. And she picked me. Childish, perhaps, but I even felt a sense of pride, and this, together with a feeling of contentment, caused me to tremble. A broad smile spread through my whole body.

Anna returned from the shower fully dressed. I'll go by my house to put my make-up on, and then to work. Shall we meet tonight at Vashkirova's? Yes, at Vashkirova's, I said, retaining that smile of happiness, pride and wonder at what I'd experienced.

She called a cab, kissed me, and went downstairs.

Still naked, I watched her through the window. The chill I could feel on my back was at odds with the warmth in my chest. As she stood there in the mist of early morning I was already missing her, again full of desire and apprehensive about how I would protect this love. Then the cab arrived and with Anna inside, it disappeared into the dawn of a new day.

28

THERE WAS A dispatch from the Mossad. The front company was asking me to check price quotation number 2007, meaning that I had to activate the secret communication system because HQ wanted to relay something to me in code.

After the previous evening and night, this was a saddening return to reality. I wasn't my own master after all. I typed in the password and up came a regular commercial letter. I locked the door and typed in an additional password which reversed the message's lettering.

HQ informed me that the intelligence I had gathered formed the basis for two planned operations for which I would have to return to Makhachkala and Dushanbe. They also wanted me to open up for them two additional locations in Caucasia and along the shores of the Caspian Sea. The outline of these operations had already been prepared and I would have a role to play in them – at the very least as the one who receives, briefs, accompanies and assists the operatives. But some important pieces of intelligence were still missing, principally in relation to the conduct of the security forces, the locations where there were permanent roadblocks, and I had to hurry.

A feeling of rebelliousness welled up inside me. What about the long period of rehabilitation which they had talked about? I asked myself, my mood defiant. And what, all of a sudden, was this idea of me taking part in the operation? Hadn't it been agreed that I would no longer take part in that kind of activity?

Before sitting down to write my reply, I remembered that I was supposed to give an account of the night Anna spent in my apartment. Strictly speaking my report should also mention the few moments she was alone while I was taking a shower, explain who she was, what she meant to me, how we'd met, and who'd initiated the relations. In other words, all the information that the security people would want to know to be convinced that this wasn't some kind of a trap. These were sensible, set procedures, yet at the same time very irksome so far as I was concerned.

While thinking about this, terrified by the prospect of a possible intrusion into my life and my love, I reconstructed in my mind the story of our liaison and answered my own questions – the sort of questions they would undoubtedly be asking me. I don't know if she was a customer at Vashkirova's before I started going there, but it would seem that she was. We ate there many times without approaching one another. She was brought to my table by Vashkirova, almost against her wishes, because the restaurant was packed and while sitting with me was uncommunicative and embarrassed. Then came the conversation about Dostoyevsky's *Demons* all of which was perfectly reasonable given the nature of her work. Then she went back to being alone and didn't attempt to establish any form of contact with me. She brought me a copy of *Demons* with the additional chapter, but that was entirely predictable seeing as she owned a bookshop. Sitting with her later on was my initiative as was the conversation that followed. She remained withdrawn and distant after that as well. The concert was the only event that she proposed, but that was done in such a natural way and her understanding of the music was so profound, it was obvious that this was her field. People with seats next to hers at the Philharmonic knew her and knew about the tragedy that had befallen her. It was I who suggested escorting her home and going up to her apartment. She was the one who asked me to leave her apartment and subsequently restored our relationship to one of 'friendship'. And yesterday night – that was so natural, for God's sake.

It could be said that it is surprising, even strange, that such a beautiful woman – who I saw with my own eyes turning away a suitor – should want me. I am now a man of forty, not at my peak. Even at my best I was no Apollo. Nor could her desire for me be based on my being a western intellectual. I knew a great deal less than she did about every subject we touched on. Perhaps the very fact of my relative inadequacy was what prevented her from being turned off me at the beginning, and then slowly it happened, an adult friendship that gradually developed into love. And not for a moment could I say with any certainty that on her side it was also love.

A further thought. I found it odd that she sent me off to shower in my own apartment. But who knows, perhaps she felt that after a day's work my body odour was unpleasant? Perhaps that's what lovers in Russia do? Also something about her shop didn't seem quite right to me. Everything looked too new and spotlessly clean – but maybe that's the way bookshops in Russia are, like a sort of pharmacy? And anyway, her knowledge was so profound – clearly she lived her life with books and among books. And there was the matter of the car that perhaps had brought her to the vicinity of the restaurant. But her connection to the vehicle was purely circumstantial. I didn't see her get out of it.

This was how I conducted my self-interrogation with respect to our relationship. I decided not to write anything about her. A procedure is a procedure. But there is life. I don't believe that every operative who brings a woman to his apartment reports it. This was the first time in my apartment and only the second occasion on which I'd slept with her. I am not prepared to accept such interference and my relations with Anna are too precious for me to allow a stranger to intrude into them. And who on earth knows whether there will, in any case, be a continuation of these relations?

But the very fact that I had transgressed compelled me to respond to HQ's demands. I informed them that I had to establish the commercial cover that would justify frequent trips to these godforsaken countries and that I was starting to do that as of now.

There will be a few lucky traders in these Republics who will shortly be getting offers at prices lower than they could possibly have dreamed of – a temptation they won't be able to resist. This time my aim was to buy and sell agricultural machinery that would require maintenance. My plan was based on the belief that my farming experience would enable me to be the person taking on the maintenance work as well, and that if I added periodic inspection every few months to the quotation, that would provide me with the necessary cover to visit these places frequently.

I decided first of all to approach my amiable Mafioso from Makhachkala – to him the deal would look even better on paper after I added his twenty per cent since the money going back to him would be sent directly from the offices of the company in Canada and wouldn't show up in the books here.

This time I was equipped with Anna's number at the bookshop and phoned her immediately after transmitting the message to HQ and before beginning my search for a suitable item of agricultural machinery. She didn't answer, which surprised me. Just before I went out for a late lunch I considered going to the shop instead of eating at either the Japanese or Italian restaurant in my street. I tried her number once more and this time she picked up the phone, breathless and excited.

I heard the ringing from the door and got to it just in time, she said. You won't believe it, but when I got home I went straight to bed again and simply didn't want to get out of it. I thought about our night together again and again in my mind, each and every movement, and couldn't bear the idea of getting up and going to the shop. I so want to see you again.

At Vashkirova's?

What about coming straight to my place? I'll make us dinner.

Wonderful cooking smells greeted me as I climbed the stairs to her apartment. I don't know how to distinguish between various spices, but I did smell steak as well as some kind of fish, stewed fruits and what afterwards I discovered to be cumin and cinnamon. Anna opened the door for me wearing an apron over her clothes, her hands wet. She kissed the tip of my nose and said she had to get back to the kitchen and that I should make myself comfortable.

The kitchen table was tastefully laid in the living room, with a tablecloth, cutlery and matching napkins, fresh flowers in an old fashioned vase and white candles flickering in an antique three-armed bronze candlestick.

I went into the kitchen behind her and wrapped my arms around her waist. She tilted her head back and rubbed her hair in the furrow between my neck and shoulder. Very slowly, I moved my hands up and gently cupped her breasts in my palms, kissing the nape of her neck as my stiffening cock caressed her buttocks.

You know I won't be able to resist, and the food will get burned.

Can't you simply turn it off for an hour?

It's obvious you were never a woman or a gourmet chef. I can, but it will be spoiled. Do you think you can control yourself for a while?

She asked this in a tone of voice that implied she was ready to accept 'no' for an answer. But I couldn't ignore all the effort she'd made, so I stopped brushing myself against her.

I'll try, can't promise though, I said.

I'll compensate you for it afterwards, she said. Meanwhile have a whisky.

On the worn sideboard were two unopened whisky bottles, one Irish one Scotch. I poured myself a glass, sank into the sofa and let the good feelings brought on by the drink swirl around in my head.

Anna came into the room with a tray and a smile that expressed triumph. Let's sit, she said.

Her food was very much to my taste. I don't know if this was due to the Russian cuisine, her talent, or love, but everything was incredibly delicious. From the soup in which, apart from the fish, there were dumplings, vegetables, and even cherries, to the filet steak, one of the tenderest I'd ever eaten, the pastry puffs filled with all sorts of vegetables, and all the way to the steamed fruit that adorned the plates – it was simply wonderful. And with every compliment Anna's face beamed with joy.

I couldn't possibly have imagined how generous she would be in 'compensating me' when we went to bed. Though she once again insisted on the lights being off, she knew even in the dark how to reach all the exquisitely sensitive spots in my body which I didn't even know existed. Orit and I were children who grew up together, I thought, and at a certain stage, certainly so far as sex was concerned, we stopped growing. What we had was good enough for us and we didn't learn anything new. Anna, on the other hand, gave me an appetite for new experiences with my body and hers that thrilled me from the tips of my toes to the roots of my hair.

I made love to her slowly, as she had asked me to, and wanted her to guide me to those hidden spots that gave her pleasure. I remembered Orit and the discovery of such a spot, which was the key to long years of great pleasure. I immediately banished her from my thoughts.

Anna directed me, at first shyly, and then I felt her yield at the touch of my fingers. In the dark I'd come to know her soft body, now exuding all the aromas of the kitchen, very well. I'd learned to recognize the sounds she made, to know when it was good for her and when I should intensify my movements. As excitement overcame her she lapsed into Russian and I was forced to guess at some of what she was saying. But when I quickened my movements a bit more she suddenly said, don't move, don't move, I'm so nearly there, but it needs to be exactly right and your rhythm is chasing it away. I didn't move. Anna adjusted her dance around my cock and around the bone at its base and then sounded a few thin moans and suddenly also a loud scream, very different from Orit's deep 'oi' that once again returned to my consciousness. And then, all at once, she let go and stretched herself over me. Don't wait for me any longer, she whispered, and immediately after feeling me spill into her rolled herself to my side, gasping. A moment later she held me tightly in her arms and asked with a smile: Where have you been all my life?

When we'd cooled off, Anna switched on a small bedside lamp, leant on her elbow, her face and body towards me, pulling the bedcover up to her shoulders. Are you prepared to tell me about your wife? she asked in a loving tone.

I felt that the time for this had come. Her silence about Mikhail was no doubt connected to his death, and she had, after all, said that it was a subject that would make her cry. Divorce is different.

I transposed the story of our lives from the Arava and Jerusalem to Toronto, and in carefully measured words I came close to telling the truth. All I did was to turn my travels into business trips. When I got to the bit about the fertility treatments Anna tensed up. I told her first about the loss of spontaneity, when my wife's temperature indicated an imminent ovulation and I would 'hurry home from wherever I happened to be in Canada or the United States', and about the monthly disappointments. I told her about the decision to try insemination and, further down the line, IVF. I talked about the hormone injection, the dashes to the hospital at the time of ovulation, the painful suction of the ova and the production of sperm, the days of tension when we we barely spoke to each other, and then the disappointments. I gave her every detail but one: the occasion when a viable embryo had formed and when, by a cruel twist of fate, my wife had chosen that moment to separate from me and give up our possible parenthood. But I knew I was incapable of explaining this. I could not come up with any justification for such a decision. I didn't think that after so many attempts at bringing a child into the world a woman would forgo a sound embryo – even if she was by then sick and tired of her husband. At the time, Orit's reason didn't make sense to me and my inventiveness was unable to come up with a similar argument. I was incapable of fabricating the sort of crime and its punishment that life had thrust upon me. The taking of life by me, the punishment for which was the taking of the life of my embryo.

But there was no need for that. Anna cried. At first soundlessly, just tears trickling down her face, then she pressed her head into my shoulders and sobbed. It was clear to me that this wasn't a response to my story. She wasn't crying for me. I hugged her in silence and only after a while did she tell me, her voice breaking, about abortions she'd had as an adolescent and then as a young woman, including one performed by an unqualified doctor which was particularly bloody. After that, she said, she didn't think she'd ever be able to give birth.

Though we made love again that night it was the lovemaking of two utterly defeated people. Despite lasting for a long time it barely helped us to comfort ourselves. There was no joy in it. Even if our love was to overcome all the obstacles that my nefarious work placed in its path, I thought sadly, we would be doomed to live together as a childless couple.

Once again Anna asked me to leave before dawn, so that her neighbours wouldn't see me.

To me this was a sign of her unwillingness to link her fate to mine. And what if she was willing to do so? What possible chance did I have of getting HQ's permission to bring an unapproved local woman into my life? What would happen in three or four years' time when my stay here came to an end and I would be told to return to Israel? What chance did I have of concealing my real work from her? And if she did know, would she stay with me? I didn't want to, nor was I prepared to, conceal the truth from her. Not if we were to develop true bonds of love. I had already paid a high price for that.

So what do we do now? I was already dressed and the cab now on its way.

I think that perhaps it would be preferable if we didn't meet again today, Anna said to me. The last couple of days have been too dizzying, too emotional, and exciting. I feel as if I'm on a roller coaster. And please, don't ring and don't come here or to the shop. After I've had time to think, I'll get in touch with you. OK, my love?

A blast of cold froze my limbs and not only because of the door I'd opened to the chilly night air. She hugged

315

me and held me tightly with tears flowing down her face.

Enough, my Annushka. It's difficult enough anyway, I said. I turned round and made my way down the stairs.

29

ANNA'S TIME AWAY from me lasted much longer than I expected it to. At first I felt as if was in mourning. The thought that she would, in the end, decide she didn't want me was like a knife twisting and turning inside me, making it hard for me to breathe, turning my limbs into deadweights. I couldn't live without her. After two, three and then four days, the idea that perhaps it was better this way came between me and my grieving. We'd both be saved a great deal of trouble and distress. I then began asking myself how I'd stumbled into this relationship that so didn't suit my situation. And why was I allowing myself and Annushka to harbour these groundless hopes? After a week of not hearing from her I began to get used to the bleak idea that this had been a brief and beautiful episode in my life, pleasurable and enchanting, which had come at a time when I needed it more than anything else, and so it had to remain.

And yet, I hoped with all my heart that she would ring, a call, which were she to make, would, I knew, rock my entire life.

In the meantime, without much enthusiasm, I continued with the task of establishing the cover for trips to the former Republics of the Soviet Union in the

Caucasus and on the shores of the Caspian Sea. I gained exclusivity for the sale of a combine harvester, and was also successful in obtaining a motorized sprayer, as well as other, smaller, items of equipment.

During one of those evenings, as I was sitting in my apartment tired and lifeless, somewhat like my father in his last years but twenty-five years younger than he then was, a short news item appeared on the TV about a failed assassination attempt by the Mossad in Singapore. According to the commander of the Singaporean police, whose announcement in English could just about be heard through the Russian dubbing, the accidental discharge of a bullet had injured one of a group of Mossad agents who fled from the area with their wounded colleague. Who were they after, and who was it that had failed? Udi? Levanon? They were undoubtedly at the planning and command level. And who'd participated in the operation itself? Was it the younger bunch of operatives, Josh and his mates? I was filled with a mixture of emotions; sadness, anger, sympathy. I could clearly imagine the sense of frustration felt by the commanding officers – Udi and Levanon were both close to my heart – and the pressure they were under from above. Even more than that, I could feel the disappointment of the operatives with their own performance. An accidentally discharged bullet, for heaven's sake. These are professionals! But professionals also have stupid accidents. And who knows more than me that the 'professional' does what he does because he has to. His job, when all is said and done, is to serve his homeland, not to kill.

At least I'll be doing what I've been ordered to do, I thought. The next morning I arranged a tour of the Caucasus taking the route leading from Russia to Iran. Two days in Turkmenistan, a couple of days in Uzbekistan, one day in Tajikistan on the way to Kirgizstan, and from there a flight back to St Petersburg. All in all, a journey of three thousand five hundred kilometres, including a stopover in Moscow. When a week had passed since my parting from Anna, I took off on this seven-day trip. I recorded a message on my answering machines. If Anna called she would know that I was gone.

I left St Petersburg on a cold, grey day at autumn's end. When I returned the city was covered in white. The snow filled me with a childlike feeling of delight which vied with my keen urge to get to my answer phone as quickly as possible and find out if there was a message from Anna.

You silly thing, couldn't you call to say goodbye? I heard her saying lovingly on the machine in my office – which is where I went straight from the airport – and my heart jumped with joy.

I called her straight away. There was no answer at the shop, nor did the phone at home pick up. In the office I arranged the mountain of material that my trip had produced – contracts, exclusivity agreements, price quotations and proposals for joint ventures, tenders, drafts of letters of credit from local banks that needed to be approved by my bank. The people of the Caucasus were hungry for business with Russia and the West and, much to my surprise, I came across a number of traders with commendable commercial abilities.

I locked the office door from the inside and sat down to write a very long report to HQ. My condolences for the mishap in Singapore, I began, and trust that the trauma is already behind you. I hope that what I now have to tell you will be of some little comfort. I gave details of the connections I had made and the deals I had cooked up, drawing particular attention to those of my new business partners who also had links with the Iranians and could be instrumental on our behalf – be it for the purposes of entering Iran or be it in order to extract people from there and recruit them. From time to time I tried to reach Anna but there was still no reply.

On the answer phone at home there were three messages from her. The first said, I'm missing you, I'll try and catch you at the office tomorrow, get in touch when you get back this evening. In the second, after she'd heard the recorded message on the office answer phone, she said, pity I didn't know. I too have to travel to visit my elderly mother in Moscow and I could have taken advantage of your absence to go there while you are away. In the third message she simply said, I'm leaving for Moscow and can't wait to see you again.

The next day she called. Compared to her somewhat emotional phone messages she sounded fairly formal, leading me to assume there were customers in the shop. She didn't explain anything, only asked to pick me up from my office so we could eat in one of the restaurants in town. After a brief and unsuccessful attempt by me to wriggle out of that particular arrangement, Anna showed up at the office at five o'clock in the evening.

After my trip to the Caucasus I had bought a new set of thick files and put a sticker on each of them along with the name of one of my customers – of which there were by now dozens. The files took up the entire cabinet.

Ahead of Anna's arrival I arranged the catalogues by subject matter on the open shelves, stuck labels on a number of closed drawers on which I wrote Letters of Credit, Banks, New Customers, and Price Quotations. I also managed to put some additional furniture and ornamental accessories into the office, and on a further outing to a nearby street, literally at the very last minute, I bought a coffee machine that had caught my attention a while back, and only finished installing it a moment before Anna arrived.

My office door was slightly ajar and her light knock opened it still further. She peeped in bashfully. I turned towards her from my letters, overwhelmingly happy at the sight of her. She stood there at the entrance looking ill-at-ease, wearing a white fur hat, a white scarf round her neck and a white fur coat. Against her milky white complexion, those almond eyes of hers – a fine black streak of make-up beneath them and highlighted lashes adding to their length – looked liked two gondolas in a frozen sea. But this sea unfroze as she hurried towards me, hugged me, and planted a kiss on each cheek.

What's that supposed to be? I asked reproachfully, and she laughed a little laugh and then wholeheartedly responded to my kiss.

When she stepped back from our embrace, Anna looked around and gushed, nice, nice. Still holding on to my hand, she edged herself away from me, scanning the cabinets, the shelves, the catalogues, the files and, finally, the sitting alcove and the coffee machine. I could even say quite impressive she then said.

Annushka, I thought you'd come to see me, not my office, I said as if reproachfully. She was clearly disconcerted. I did come to see you. The office simply impressed me.

Then she looked straight at me, clutched both sides of my head and said, I missed you very very much. Though it was good for me with you, very good, I didn't imagine that you had so penetrated my very being and that I would feel so empty without you. And that without you I would feel so deprived.

And suddenly, as if to lighten the atmosphere, she quipped, Houston, we have a problem.

I laughed and added my confirmation. Yes my darling, we have a problem. I planned to make a bit of money here from the budding economies in the area and go home quietly. I didn't plan to fall in love.

Paul, she castigated me, be serious. What's going to become of us? I'm not built for fleeting adventures. You also don't strike me as being that type.

It was obvious to me that I couldn't make a commitment. I wasn't planning on staying here and if she's thinking of moving on with me it's Canada, not Israel, that she has in mind.

Why not let time decide, Annushka, I finally said.

Because I know time's decision, she replied. Before we even know it, we'll find ourselves embroiled in such an intense relationship that we won't be able to live without it, and what are you suggesting, that only then do we begin to figure out how to deal with the situation that you and I are in?

I thought about the natural, mature and direct way in which she was describing things. As they were, without uncalled for pathos. Perhaps that's why she'd arrived at my place so hesitant, didn't respond passionately to my embraces or kisses. Perhaps this was also the reason for her almost formal tone during the earlier phone conversation.

Look, neither of us have answers, Annushka. I also don't believe that in affairs of the heart one can allow the head to decide. The head will make its plans, but the heart will choose its own path.

She looked at me, subdued, serious, as if thinking about what I had said which was, in reality, so very trivial.

So what's left is for us to go and eat, I added. And we'll take it from there.

Live for the moment, eh? As if there was no tomorrow, the smattering of a smile crept into her pensive look. Let's go. Just know that I'm confused from head to toe. I feel great desire and I'm very frightened.

I kissed her again and for a moment I thought of making love to her there, in the office, but I could see she wasn't in the mood.

Anna had reached the same point in her path to making a decision as I had, I thought. But for her, apparently, the head rules the heart more than it does for me. I put on my coat, switched off the computer, took

Anna's hand and we went out into the snowy city whose skies were aglow with the colours of sunset.

From the wide Neva, gusts of wind blew into Liteyny Prospekt. But Anna walked slowly, brooding, only bothering to tighten her scarf and ensure that her hat stayed firmly on her head. For her this was a tolerable winter reality. I adjusted my pace to hers, even though my feet were clearly inclined to make a run for it and flee from the cold. Anna even paused from time to time to look at the shop windows from which I learned a bit about the kind of clothes and home decor she liked.

The Japanese restaurant Babi-Saabi was on the next street corner and I hoped that our arrival there would, at least temporarily, halt our icy stroll.

I don't want Japanese food, but I'll drink something hot, Anna said, and we went in. A speedy waitress who recognized me handed us a menu. I asked for a plate of sushi, Anna ordered a cup of tea.

We exchanged few words. As we gazed at one another and desired each other, the gravity of the situation we were in became increasingly apparent to us both. When Anna took off her white fur coat, exposing the tight-fitting woollen blouse I was already so familiar with, I felt unable to contain my love and my passion any longer. The softness of the blouse made it difficult for me to restrain my hands from caressing the finely shaped curves. A sad and frustrating state of affairs.

We left the restaurant in silence and, in order to escape the freezing wind, went into a cross street where the cold was tolerable. We walked without saying a word, hand in hand, leaving footprints in the blanket of soft snow that had painted the road in a festive white, a joy we couldn't share.

When we crossed the Fontanka River and passed the now leafless, sad-looking gardens of the summer palace, a witheringly cold gust of wind again blew in our direction. I embraced Anna and she squeezed my hand tightly. Only when we reached the confluence of the River Moika and the Groiboedov Canal did the ancient palaces shelter us from the wind. A few pedestrians were scurrying homewards from their offices and almost no cars drove by.

A series of small, beautiful bridges stretched across the canals close to the point where the waters met. We walked onto one of them, an ancient arched bridge paved with slippery black cobble-stones. A pale light shone from the ornamental lamp-posts set on its four corners, the snow glistened and the frozen waters of the canal sparkled back. We leant on the steel railing embossed with faces and leaves, small golden globes decorating the railing's upper level, and gazed around us. Large mansions, a red-and-white four-storeyed house, a brown fortress, and a yellow palace with white stone porticos that dominated the approach to the bridge, had seemingly all fallen into a slumber of silence on this wintery evening. But the night lights illuminated the gables and cornices of the buildings in all their infinite wealth of beauty.

It's very beautiful, your Petersburg, I said.

When I came here as a student, Anna told me, I fell in love with the bridges, the canals, the alleyways, the palaces, the student life at the Conservatoire and after that at the Institute for Russian Literature. Those who love the city as much as I do, simply call it Peter.

And you do love it, your Peter, I noted, more as a comment to myself than a query to her. We both knew that her love of the city was weighing down one side of the scales on which our own love was balanced so precariously.

We were also both aware that this question meant looking ahead at an impenetrable future that was likely to come between us with all its might.

Yes I do, very much, Anna laughed ruefully as though saying, what can I do? But nothing here is what it seems to be. Here, this church, she said pointing to the ornamented building we could see on the other side of the square. It looks as though children have coated its walls with chocolate and stuck sweets into it and plastered its domes with colourful liquorice and jellies. But it is also known as The Church on the Spilled Blood because it was here that Czar Alexander the Second was murdered.

As if to stave off the obvious next question about where we would live our lives, if indeed we were to live them together, she told me about the evolution of the city's names.

When I was born it was Leningrad, the name given after Lenin's death. But my parents still knew it as Petrograd, its name during the First World War. The Germanic suffix Burg was replaced by a Russian ending. And now it's again Sankt Peterburg, as Peter the Great named it when he founded the city.

He regarded himself a saint? I laughed and Anna quickly corrected me. He named the city after Saint Peter. She said this in all seriousness reminding me that she was a Christian, perhaps even a practising Christian. The northern part of the city is still called Petrograd, she continued, and many say, as you do, Peterburg, especially the Jews, who do not like saying Saint, or Sankt.

Anna spoke through the white woollen scarf which prevented the freezing air penetrating her throat and from time to time she moistened the dry corners of her lips with her tongue.

The beauty of her almond eyes, her Sophia Loren eyes – all that could be seen between the hat and scarf – made my heart throb and enveloped me in a wave of love. I gently removed the scarf from over her mouth and kissed her. As usual we searched for the right angle until our tongues penetrated each other's mouth and once again became hooked to our marvellous but hopeless love. Like two teenagers we said 'you are mine', to each other and again I had to pinch myself to believe that this wonderful woman was indeed mine. Then, once more, we sank into one another.

A moment later I absorbed the powerful blow to my upper back and Anna's handbag was snatched. I chased the burly thief, kicked him in the back and when he stumbled, turned round, and offered me the bag, I grabbed his arm and hurled him to the ground. He tried to get up but I kicked him in the ribs. He stormed back like a bull, I moved, and kicked him in the nose. He was left bleeding on the ground.

Anna's eyes reflected the fear I had not succeeded to allay, and she fled towards her house via a circuitous route with me at her heels. The moment we closed the door behind us she pounced on me and engaged me in wild and furious sex.

When we'd had our fill and calmed down, Anna said she wanted me to move in and live with her. I want you this way every night and every morning, want you as part of my life, she said. Next morning I woke up in her bed feeling better than I had for years. We made love, and Anna wanted to hear me say that I would never leave her.

I'm here to stay, Annushka, I said, hesitantly at first, but when the expression in her eyes did not show satisfaction, I relented and said, repeating her words, I will stay with you and won't ever leave you, never, never ever.

Anna swooped down on me with kisses of happiness and again we made love with no holds barred, as if ingraining in one another our oaths of loyalty.

Afterwards I sent my report to HQ from my office about my acquaintanceship with Anna and my intention to continue with the relationship and signed the report 'for your information'. Not 'for your approval' as was the requirement.

I was shaking from cold and sweating at the same time. My throat was dry and I went to make myself a coffee with the new machine which I had not yet ever used.

This morning I committed myself to Anna from the depths of my heart. And in my eyes this commitment was more meaningful than any other, I thought. Nonetheless what would happen if HQ was to say 'no'?

30

A SHORT WHILE after sending the message I returned to my apartment, packed a suitcase with winter clothes, toiletries, slippers and a few books. All the while I was shaking and felt cold and sweaty at the same time. I swallowed a couple of aspirins, ordered a cab, and moved to Anna's apartment.

To my surprise her place had already been emptied of Mikhail's things and on 'my side' of the wardrobe were hangers and empty shelves which the few belongings I had brought with me didn't fill. There was new bed linen with clearly visible folds from the original packaging. There was a big bunch of flowers in a vase on the living room table and the photo of Anna with Mikhail had disappeared. Only some time later did I find it high up on one of the bookcase shelves. It was obvious that Anna had done everything she could to give me the feeling that this was a festive occasion and to give us both the sense of a new beginning.

And I didn't even think of bringing flowers or a bottle of wine, I said, lamenting my poor manners. But Annushka, aglow with joy, gave me a big hug and told me that she'd already managed to prepare another meal for us which she hoped I would like.

I loved the food, I loved her. But all the while I was

nagged by the thought that during those very moments in Israel, where the winter is green and grey, a group of people were exchanging views about my message. I reckoned they would almost certainly be meeting this evening, and if Udi is very busy then they'll get together tomorrow morning and discuss my fate and the fate of my love for Anna.

You're not here, my love, Anna said, aware of every nuance of my expression. The move, it's difficult for you? You're not at peace with it?

If only I was as much at peace with everything else in my life as I am with my love for you, my Annushka. The words were on the tip of my tongue but didn't pass my lips. All I said was, it's certainly harder for you my darling.

Is that the impression I give? she asked, surprised, and pounced on me, hugging and covering my face with kisses. You can't even imagine how happy I am.

Her face indeed beamed with joy whereas I couldn't get shot of the cloud hovering over me. I was never a good actor. Even my instructors on the course at the Mossad used to complain about that.

This time Anna surpassed herself with the cooking. She served us a thick chestnut soup with various vegetables, nuts, sour cream and brandy. When I dug my spoon into its depths and my nostrils were filled with its incredible aroma, I discovered there were also bits of roasted goose in there. The combination of tastes was so wonderful that I almost regretted it being wasted on someone like me who ordinarily makes do with shwarma and tahini.

Guess what I've got for us? Anna asked when she'd had her fill of my compliments.

I've absolutely no idea, I said.

I've ordered a home movie system. It'll arrive tomorrow, together with a large collection of films.

Anna caught on to the expression on my face as I surveyed the small apartment. I know it's a bit crowded here, but I've thought it all through. The screen will be here – she pointed to the wall with the outside window – and we'll change the lounge area here so we can sit facing it. We don't want guests, do we? And for us the two-seater is big enough, we can get rid of the armchairs. She gazed at me, her eyes sparkling with happiness and hope.

Wouldn't it be more sensible for us to move to my apartment? I asked. Though my place had only a bedroom and a study in addition to the living room, it was bigger, much more comfortable, refurbished and well equipped. I didn't think that from HQ's point of view it would make much of a difference whether we lived together in my apartment or hers. What was forbidden was the relationship itself.

I don't want anything bigger, she answered. I want us to be very very near to each other all the time. I want you to want to hurry home from your office, and I'll hurry back from my shop, and that our evenings together stretch out into the night.

The thought flashed through my mind that it was as if the home movie system was already screening a Spanish soap opera. I suppressed a smile.

I'll rush back to **you,** my beautiful one, not the movie

system, I said, giving the expected response, and the words sounded a bit forced and theatrical. I had never uttered such expressions of love. And almost none of any other kind. My love for Orit was so self evident, so big was the void when she left, and so unbridled was my love for Annushka.

And I've already chosen a film for us for tomorrow unless you want something else from the selection that I've ordered, she added, and seeing my quizzical look, said, *Doctor Zhivago*.

It's very beautiful but sad, isn't it?

But it's so beautiful and sad that it's almost like our lives? And it's got in it all the history I want you to learn, from the 1905 Revolution till the October Revolution, and all the places and things in Russia that I want you to get to know about, Moscow, the Urals, Siberia, workers, farmers, intellectuals.

She put her arms around my neck and we sunk into a very extended kiss that only ended under the new flannel sheets.

A moment after we'd satiated ourselves and were lying in an embrace, and a moment before my eyes closed, the discussion about us in Mossad HQ popped into my mind. Fifteen years with Udi, now head of the Operations Division, dozens of operations with Levanon who replaced me as head of the division's Planning Department, and a deep understanding of the way in which the office worked, made it possible for me to imagine such a detailed and live scene.

A long time later, when I was sitting in the small room

close to Udi and Levanon's offices, poring over the transcripts, memoranda and logbooks of the operations linked to me, I was surprised to discover how close my imagined discussions were to those that had actually taken place. There were also moments of collegiality during those long and nerve-racking periods of waiting in Udi and Levanon's offices for messages from operatives in the field, when they were willing to share with me various additional details. They told me of the frustration they felt when they realized they had to do something to stop me, or of a move they and those under their command planned to make on me in the streets of St Petersburg. The parallel campaign of discussions and operational orders, reconnaissance and operational logs secretly woven against me, without my being able to know anything about it, became increasingly clear. I was pained, angered, and at times utterly bewildered. The written words turned into voices, the names became those of living people, and the dry language of transcripts was transformed into a real and yet phantasmagoric event played out before my own eyes.

It was Ariel, my young controller who first received my message. He was alarmed by the probable implications of my living with Anna and immediately called a meeting at Division HQ. Those present were Udi and Levanon, Alex, who was with me in the operation in Kazakhstan and now headed the desk for Russia and the former Soviet Republics, Eli, the security officer, and Ilan the division's psychologist. Udi asked Ariel to read out my message to the assembled forum.

Re: An Acquaintance. The restaurant where I usually eat in the evening is also frequented by a single woman. We got to talk. She is a widow and owns a bookshop. The relationship became closer and last night I slept in her apartment. We are both interested in continuing the relationship and it's my intention to do so. I shall, of course, maintain my cover. For your information.

I want to emphasize a number of points, Ariel said. The first is that Yogev defines the relationship as one of 'acquaintance' which is a fairly neutral word. Secondly, that there are relations of intimacy between them, which is not so neutral. Thirdly that they intend to continue this relationship, and fourthly that he didn't, in fact, ask for approval but simply 'informed' us which in my view doesn't bode well.

Let's stop talking about 'Yogev' Udi said, and, as we do with every other operative, use only the alias. So from now on only 'Paul' please. Any more comments on the message?

We know the state he was in during his last period in Israel, Ilan said. He was shattered by his wife leaving him and, so far as we know, he avoided any involvement with women while living in Tel Aviv. We hesitated quite a bit before coming up with the suggestion that he settle in Russia but thought in the end that the move away would enable him to rehabilitate himself. Possibly that is what is now happening. Getting into a relationship with a woman may signal a kind of re-engagement with life.

Does this tell us that he is getting back to normal? Udi asked.

It's hard to know. Paul is very good at putting things in compartments – as he did with his targeted assassinations – and rationalize it in a way that fits in with his perception of himself as a man of integrity. This is an attribute that makes rehabilitation possible. The fact that he slept at some woman's house and wants to continue is a good sign. But it very much depends on who she is. Couples get together in all sorts of places and situations and it's difficult to know if it's really a sign of a new beginning, or just the coming together of two losers.

Udi, as always, was already thinking ahead:

Levanon, would you take him back into the planning department and have him involved in operations? he asked.

In the last operation he was almost caught and we suspended him from such activities. But if he's in a slightly better state of mind I definitely prefer him to the people I now have. With all his limitations, and he has some, he never screwed up an operation, which you can't say about the teams of youngsters.

I was happy to discover that Levanon, who more than anyone else knew my operational limitations, chose to praise my abilities. But the transcripts showed that not everybody at the meeting was on my side.

From a security point of view there's a problem with him staying there, said Eli. If it was just a fuck, so be it. But he says that it's his intention to continue the relationship. Can anyone say what he's inadvertently divulging there and what his lady friend might do with it? Let's face it, if he gets to be interrogated it will be a disaster.

He's got fifteen years of operations floating around in his head.

Is the KGB still that intimidating? Udi turned to Alex.

It's not called the KGB anymore but, of course, you know that. It split into two, there's the security service which deals with external affairs, as we do, and the Federal Security Bureau, the FSB, which looks after internal matters, including preventative intelligence. But it's the same meat with a different gravy. After all, they couldn't throw tens of thousands of workers onto the streets. Their methods haven't really changed, nor have their objectives. Every foreigner is suspect and closely watched. That includes phone tapping, faxes and emails until its shown that there's nothing on him or her. If there are real grounds for suspicion then the scrutiny becomes even tighter with surveillance, bugging, photographing and break-ins.

Ultimately they can put a whole team around him and in the end they will expose him.

Ilan, can you assess his response if we instruct him to end the relationship? Udi asked.

I don't have enough information for such an evaluation, the psychologist answered. My gut feeling is that if she's someone who's lifted him out of his depression it won't be easy for him to give her up.

I'm not in favour of making things difficult for him, Levanon intervened. We've known him for fifteen years. He's a balanced and responsible guy; perhaps too balanced and responsible, he won't let any information slip out.

And I think we need to consider getting him back here

in light of the possible damage of him staying, Eli repeated his view.

OK my friends I'm dictating an answer, Udi said. Write this down Ariel:

A permanent relationship is against the regulations, and has to be avoided. There is to be no relationship on a permanent basis and no living together. Please make do with the necessary minimum, and break off the relationship gradually. The security risk is real. Your return to Israel is being considered in light of the dismal results of the last operation in Singapore. You're needed. Thanks for opening up the area. Now we're looking for someone who can replace you.

That's it, Udi said and looked around at those present. I think I took all your comments into account and prepared him for the possibility that he will be returning.

And please add, he said to Ariel, that he should let us have the woman's full name and every other detail he knows about her. The address of the apartment, the address of the shop and even her ID number if he can. And I'll sign off on the message, not you. Alex, when the details come in start activating sources in Russia to find out about her. But with the utmost caution because every suspicious activity will put him at risk as well; so *dir balak*, be careful, he added in Arabic. Use only trustworthy and reliable sources.

An email from the European company indicated that there was a message from HQ. The fact that Udi was the signatory was only a small comfort; the pill was bitter and hard to swallow. I could live with the 'necessary minimum'. Nobody could possibly know what the 'necessary minimum' for me actually was. I could also quibble with the meaning of 'permanent basis'; we weren't getting married and no one had given me a guarantee as to how long this love of ours would last. The term 'gradually' was also a nebulous term. How long was this 'gradualness' supposed to last? Months? A year? But Udi, with all the appropriate cautiousness, and with all the wriggle room he had left me, had made his intent very clear. 'Not to live together'. That was unambiguous. You can fuck her but then go home, or send her home. If push came to shove I could also live with that. Couples of our age and in our circumstances don't always and immediately move in together, and after an initial spell of being in love, the body can also do without daily contact.

But the tidings 'a return to Israel is being considered' were hard to digest. I thought – and so did HQ in the past – in terms of a stay of about four years in Russia. Not four months, or six, until they found a replacement. The reality of a possible return, of the transience of my stay here and its dependence entirely on the mercy of HQ, was what hit me hard.

What really cut me to the quick was the realization that I wasn't master of my fate or of my time, nor of my choices in life, the places where I would live, the people I would meet. Above all else I wasn't master of my love. That harsh truth dawned on me before I grew bitter about being a pawn on the Mossad's global chessboard, about every plan being essentially open to unilateral changes

337

dictated by HQ's needs, and about the attempt to return me to operations without asking what I might have to say.

The very idea that my love for Annushka was subject to the Mossad's say-so, that the amount of time I spent with her would be limited by its edict, and the dark and sudden shadow of our imminent separation, aroused a recalcitrance in me that grew to the point where I felt my heat would explode.

I couldn't pull myself together and the time for going back to the apartment neared. I knew that Anna was able to read me like a book, that I couldn't pretend to her that all was well and that moving into her apartment had made me blissfully happy. Nor could I contemplate making her sad yet again.

For a while I dithered about whether I should inform HQ that I wasn't prepared to comply with their demands, or leave things ambiguous. When I'd finished the bitter-tasting coffee, it was clear to me that there was no room here for ambiguity. I didn't want to break the rules but nor did I want to give up Anna. That was the simple truth and that I had to clarify. The focus of my life was now here, with Anna. My preference was not to make a choice. However, even though the Mossad had been the centre of my life over the past decade and a half, if I have to choose I'll choose Anna. And yet, I still didn't want to say this too bluntly because that would be a clear violation of the orders I'd been given. As in the army, there is a difference between refusing to obey a command and not carrying out an instruction to the letter.

Udi, I began and wrote quickly: I'd prefer to be brief

in describing the difficulties I've had making a decision. Anna Starzava is the only ray of light in my life right now. And despite all the love I have for you and my loyalty to you, I am not able to give her up. This is not a matter of a lax interpretation of the 'necessary minimum' or 'gradually'. As long as there is this love between us, I want to be with Anna – and do my work as best I can. Please don't force me to choose – I've already lost one great love and you know precisely why and how. Also, don't think about returning me to Israel in the near future – I'm really in no fit state for operations now.

For a moment I still hesitated about the matter of Anna's name. They had, after all, asked for all the details about her, whereas I felt that if I passed these on that would be tantamount to siding with the Mossad and the hourglass of our love would be turned upside down. But I knew that if I concealed her name, warning bells would sound. My hope lay in appeasement.

The moment I'd sent the coded message I felt that the die had been cast. The 'not able' and the 'I want' would be understood by HQ to mean 'not prepared to' and 'intend to'. The 'don't think about returning me' would be translated as 'I don't intend to return' any time soon. They wouldn't be prepared to live with such a direct refusal and would try to force me to accept their diktats. For my part, I'd given some pretty broad hints as to the choice I would make if they forced me to do so. The ball was now in the Mossad's court.

I didn't feel that a load had been taken off my mind. Rather, I felt like someone whose fate was once again in his own hands. I knew that the ultimate outcome couldn't be good. Even if the Mossad accepted the capriciousness of my late-in-life love affair, there was the possibility that at some stage or other I would have to bring Anna into this tangled web. How could I do that to her? How could I bring her into the murky world of lies, cover stories, and forged identities when she was holding on to me as someone who'd taken her out of darkness and into the light? But I'd cross that bridge when I got to it. One war at a time was quite enough.

By the time I got to Anna's, the new system had been installed and a DVD of *Doctor Zhivago* was in the machine ready to be played. This time we ate in the kitchen, a cream of vegetable soup with all sorts of spices that gave off a wonderful aroma. I couldn't quite understand when she'd had the time to cook, just as I hadn't really understood her readiness to invest time and energy in cooking and in me. In fact, I didn't at all comprehend the love this wonderful woman had for me. Apparently I had breathed new life into her and didn't know what it was about me that had earned it.

Anna was as impatient as a child and wanted us to move to the living room to watch the movie. So impatient was she, that she didn't sense the cloud of gloom that had enveloped me. For a moment I was happy not to have to explain or conceal it. But then I nervously recalled that this was how the rift that eventually led to the unavoidable crisis with Orit, began. Exactly this way; a secret that was concealed in my heart and darkened my countenance, a loving woman busy with her own things who didn't notice my melancholy and the chasm simply becoming deeper and deeper, foreshadowing the earthquake. But what could I have done then? Put her in the picture and for sure bring on the earthquake immediately? And what could I do now?

We spent three hours on the sofa made for two, facing the big screen, watching Dr Zhivago's loves and agonizing doubts. There were tears in Anna's eyes, tears that made me kiss her head. Julie Christie and Geraldine Chaplin were beautiful and sad, and Omar Sharif was charming; his indecision touched my heart. The tragedy of the wars and revolutions seemed to me more relevant than ever. At that very moment I was preoccupied with my own private war. I felt the lie, the pretence as I would a malignant growth, a growth that was spreading within me and filling my existence. With the shadow of exposure hovering, I couldn't really give myself over to Annushka. The lie, whether it was sustained or exposed, would kill my love. And I now knew that another death of a love of mine would be my own death.

At the end of *Dr Zhivago*, Anna remained nestled in my lap, her eyes red from the stirring final moments.

I had thoughts about the last scene: when we spoke about music I got the impression that you actually don't really go in for grandiloquence and nationalism, I said.

But the end, with the girl who was born out of this forbidden love, so moving, and highlighting all the things that are really important! Don't you think that poetic justice was done to this love? Just think about how much

341

faith in love and its fruits Pasternak and the director had when deciding to end it that way, knowing that every kind of disbeliever in love will see it as nothing more than sentimental kitsch.

I couldn't but hear the plea of a childless woman behind these words, not to mention that I too was childless.

That's true, I agreed, but that's not what I was talking about. What I had in mind was the shot of the big dam and Tanya's pride in her proletarian boyfriend. For my taste that was a somewhat grandiose and nationalist ending.

Boris Leonidovich Pasternak a nationalist? Anna looked at me with an expression that verged on rebuke. Did you know that in Zhdanov's days he wasn't published at all and that since he couldn't publish *Doctor Zhivago* in Russia he had to do so in Italy instead? Uri Zhivago's attempt to run away from the war and find refuge for his family in a place that the wars and the revolution hadn't destroyed is a stand, not only against war but also against the Russian experiment to create a new man. Look at how, despite the revolution, the civil war, and terror, Pasternak succeeds in dealing with what is really important in life – love and family. A man torn between his wife and his beloved – that is more important to him than everything else happening around him. More important than all the revolutions and ideals. Don't you think so? There were those who saw it as a political novel – but anti-Russian. Russia, after all, forced Pasternak to give up the Nobel Prize.

I haven't read it, I said.

And I've read it at least three times. First in foreign editions and then here when its publication was allowed at the end of the communist period. And I've seen the film many times, there are whole dialogues that I know by heart. She sank into thought.

But you know, she added after a while, if there is something patriotic about it, that's not necessarily bad. It's the novel of a poet who, because of his love for his country, is pained by Russia's reality. Russian patriotism is innocent, not nationalistic, a simple love of the homeland. Even if the head says 'no' the heart remains devoted to it. The highly welcomed glasnost and perestroika succeeded only partially in weaning us off this.

Who knows this more than I, I thought, and said nothing. Perhaps there is such a thing as a love of the homeland that doesn't have anything to do with nationalism. My own patriotism was a 'negative' concept: I didn't think my country was more beautiful than any other or that my people were better than any other. I simply thought that we had no choice other than to live in our own country. For more than half my life I'd made sacrifices for my country because of my concern about its fate, my worry about what would happen to the state if not enough of its sons enlisted into combat units and the Mossad, and were willing even to kill and be killed in its name. I was not a patriot because of love for my homeland, certainly not because I thought that it was in any way superior to other countries. Something inside me, in my education, in my family's story, prevented me from shirking what I regarded as my duty, and placing the responsibility on the shoulders of others.

The fact that I loved the country, the Arava's landscapes, my own village, the things my father and his friends had achieved there, was merely a bonus. But what remained of this love? What had I left behind me in my country? And what remnants of the commitment I had towards it still existed? Was I now not writing off all these years of sacrifice, exactly as Orit had annulled all the years of our love? And was I left with nothing, not even a past?

On our way to bed Anna asked what I wanted to watch tomorrow, but I couldn't think.

There's a film that fits in well with our situation, Anna said, filling the silence. *Un Homme et Une Femme*, remember it? Claude Lelouch?

I suppose I saw it twenty years ago but no, I don't remember, but it's fine with me.

It's so easy with you, Anna said happily, with you everything is 'fine'.

How could I possibly tell her that nothing on my side was at all 'fine'. My thoughts wandered from the film to Anna, to our love for each other, to the lie inside me, to the ambiguousness of the past and to Mossad HQ where, perhaps right now, my defiant message was being discussed. What slippery slope would I be sliding down tomorrow morning?

31

WHEN MY REPLY was received at HQ, Udi cancelled the meeting convened by Ariel and announced that he would discuss the matter at his weekly session with Netzach later that day. Levanon was asked to join him. After a brief review, during which the Mossad's chief was shown the exchange of message, his position was crystal clear: Paul either completely backs out of the relationship with the woman or you return him to Israel, and the sooner the better.

I don't have anyone to replace him right now, Udi said, but the chief was adamant: send someone who'll learn what our man does there and later on that person can pass on what he knows to whoever you find as a successor. And if that doesn't work out, then I prefer losing the network of contacts that Paul has built up in Russia and the former Soviet Republics rather than finding myself with an operative on the loose or being investigated by the FSB.

Levanon asked for permission to speak: I'm sure that Paul won't harm the security interests of the state in any way. I've been with him on operations where he really disagreed with the decisions and was sure that it was possible to achieve the aim in a different way – without going to any extremes – but after having his views heard, and once the final decision was taken, he carried it out.

Not always to the very end, Udi noted.

That's true, but he did to the point at which the

operation was being executed. Whether it was then two bullets to the head as he did, or three as we are drilled to do is less important.

What are you trying to say? the chief interrupted the finessing of nuance.

I'm trying to say that if Paul is allowed to carry out the mission his way, he'll do it. And 'his way' means, apparently, with the woman. In my experience at least, this won't be the first time that something like this has happened to an operative.

When I try to picture the situation, Udi said, I can easily visualize assignments that he fails to perform because he can't hide them from the woman. This certainly imposes serious limitations on his ability to act. Perhaps not on a day-to-day basis but suppose, for example, that there is a situation in which we require support or operational intelligence on Christmas Day.

In a nutshell, it's as I said, the chief ruled. Get him back home. I, after all, met with him when the post was offered. He'd cracked up completely. And something that is cracked can either get glued back together again or fall apart. In my view what has happened here is a falling apart. And however much sympathy you may have for the guy, and I too am sympathetic towards him, we cannot allow ourselves to have a completely cracked operative in Russia.

And if he accepts our diktat? Levanon gave it another try.

Then let me know and I'll eat my hat, the chief answered. But it's not going to happen.

*

When the message came back to me from Israel I was completely prepared for the decision. Though Udi tried to soften things he couldn't refrain from noting the bottom line.

I go back to what was said in yesterday's message, he wrote. A permanent relationship is against the rules and has to be avoided. There is to be no relationship on a permanent basis and within this rule you are not to live together. Netzach demands that the breakup is immediate and if it is difficult for you then you must return to Israel at once. And that's unrelated to our need for you here in matters connected to Levanon's activities.

In due course I was to discover the extent to which Udi had wavered before writing the message. How, together with Levanon, he'd searched for the exact phrasing that would enable me to reconsider my position without feeling threatened or humiliated and how, among the scenarios they conjured up between them, they'd also raised the very chain of events that actually took place. 'If it is difficult for you,' he wrote. Nice of him, I thought. Nice that he at least considered the possibility that this was not some childish game but was, in fact, a relationship that would be difficult to disentangle. However, this was of no comfort. The Mossad chief's hands-on involvement was a sign of the importance which the organization attached to this situation and a clear indication that they weren't about to back off. The chief's codename, Netzach, means 'eternity' in Hebrew; evidence, perhaps, of his intention – like that of his predecessors – to secure a place in history.

I hoped it wouldn't be at my expense. Since it indeed was 'difficult' for me to immediately break off the relationship – 'you must return to Israel at once' was the only other option they'd offered.

In my mind, the wording of the reply came to me without a struggle. Over the previous few days I'd taken a close look at myself, at my love, my life of lies, at the damage that life of deception had done to me. I weighed all this up against my oath of fidelity to Anna and my loyalty to the Mossad and the state, and the answer that popped out of the fog was clear.

Dear Udi, Levanon, and all of you who cherish a memory of me, I started the letter and continued: I won't weary you with the difficult twists and turns of the thought processes I have gone through, nor describe the enormity of my love and its meaning for me. The option you have left me with is no option at all. I cannot part from a woman who has breathed life back into me. Though it saddens me, I understand that you are unwilling to accept this. With that the path we walked together has come to an end.

It's my intention to leave the office as it is now, and the keys will be sent by post to our company in Montreal. You can collect them at the service office there. There are no pending transactions just now, and everything is documented, so it's possible to continue from where I left off – especially the ongoing deals with the former Soviet Republics. I am circulating a notice that I'm going on vacation. New Year and Christmas are just around the corner – I'm sure you know that for the Russian Orthodox the birth of Jesus is celebrated about a week after New Year – so that my announcement will be well understood and I hope that by then you'll be sending somebody to re-open the office here.

And now for what is, in my view, the main point and one which it's important for you to know: I have found no way of telling Anna about my real identity. For you that is perhaps important from a security point of view but for me there are also other considerations. My marriage collapsed because of a failure to tell the truth, and I don't intend to risk that happening again. The only way left open to me is to turn the lie into a truth. To become Paul Gupta and erase Yogev Ben-Ari altogether.

There is nobody waiting for me in Israel. I'll not be in touch about my mother's care, I hope that Orit – and perhaps you – will do that. I have not stopped loving our complex country, but I have nothing there to make me come back, and here I have a woman who means everything to me.

When you get this message I will be making my way out of here. I have great respect for the work you do and the reasons why you do it. I ask that you don't look for me, try to stop me, or attempt to persuade me to change my mind. I've been sleeping on this – or more correctly having trouble in sleeping because of this – for many days and nights, and am entirely at peace with my decision. Farewell.

After the 'dispatch' I stayed sitting in my armchair for a long time. Perhaps someone will 'get the message' understand what I mean, think again, and get back to me urgently. I owed them these last moments of grace even though my preference was for no response. After all, if they agree and approve my staying with Anna it will merely postpone the day of judgment. And then I'll face the same decision, if not an even more difficult one. And the lie will be greater, the confrontation with it will be unavoidable, and the crisis will be even more dangerous.

On the other hand things being as they are now, perhaps there will be no crisis. Perhaps as Paul and Anna continue to live their lives, as the fledgling and all embracing love enables me to build my new home, my life's new reality, so these lives will find fulfillment and won't be in need of what there was before we met. Mikhail's Anna will fade into oblivion as will the Yogev who once belonged to Orit, to the village in the Arava, to the Mossad and to the infant that never was.

The DVD of *Un Homme et Une Femme* was already in the machine ready to be played when I got home. But Anna, holding on to me tightly, welcomed me with a long lingering kiss saying that we hadn't made love the day before and she wanted to make up for that now. She'd already made sure the food wouldn't burn.

I couldn't have expected a better answer to the questions that, despite everything, kept coming into my mind after the decision I had taken and felt like drops of acid oozing into my gut. Only then, in fact, did I give any thought to the possibility that this was the biggest decision of them all. I had, of course, taken decisions in the past that greatly influenced my life. Some that also put it in danger. The paratroopers. Orit. The Mossad. The targeted assassinations. But in those instances I'd opted for tributaries of the main river along which my life ran. It was a river that flowed from my childhood in the Arava village to the army and marriage, and continued into the delta of possibilities that life throws up, but that takes you on in the same direction until it reaches the open sea. I had leapt out of that river. If I failed to find an alternative source of water, I was condemning myself to agonizing and prolonged death throes.

Anna asked me how I wanted us to make love and did everything she knew to please me. She'd discovered how much I loved her hands stroking my balls while her mouth pleasured my cock and how I adored having it enveloped in her breasts or in the lips of her vulva as she rubbed it through them. She offered me all her magic with its flavour of a different love from a different place and a different time. I allowed myself to wallow in pleasure, and when I came and saw her smile of satisfaction, her eyes filled with joy at my happiness, I knew for sure that the new source of water was here with me. I was no longer a fish wriggling in the sand. I was like a sailor who had reached a magical mooring place. But I knew that I would have to fortify it and fight to defend that haven.

I saw yesterday, and again today when you came home, that you are not happy, Anna said. She was leaning on her elbow after pulling the blanket up to her shoulders. I know that you don't like talking about your work, and I remember how you flinched when I entered your office. That's OK. The life of each one of us is like a table with drawers and the more we have done in life the more drawers there are. We don't always want to open them all or have others be party to what's in every one of them.

I was surprised by the analogy Anna had chosen. 'Drawers' was a common term in the Mossad to describe the transitions we make between our lives undercover and our lives at home, and I didn't think it was much used outside of that world.

I wanted the new table we are now setting up to be a happy one, she continued. Even if, underneath, some of its drawers are filled with sadness. And I was thinking of how I could make you happy and hope that I have succeeded even if only a little little bit. *Tchut-tchut*, she said, slipping in a word in her enchanting sounding Russian.

Annushka, Annushka, I said, gathering her head in my arms. I so want a cover to conceal all the drawers and that at some point we'll be able to forget that they ever existed. And the cover you are embroidering for us is so exquisite that I cannot imagine what I have done to deserve it.

Suddenly Anna hummed a melody from the *Sound of Music* 'But somewhere in my youth or childhood I must have done something good,' and looked straight into my eyes. I kissed her forehead.

So you can also sing?

In the first year at the Conservatoire solfège was a compulsory subject which taught us to sing the notes of a scale. We actually performed *The Sound of Music*. At the time that was thought to be very subversive, almost akin to identifying with imperialism, and was only allowed because of its anti-Nazi stance.

After we'd showered and eaten we sat and watched *Un Homme et Une Femme* and now it was my turn to end up red-eyed.

Anouk Aimée reminded me of Anna – the same quiet beauty, the same kind of femininity. But Anna's almond eyes made her even more beautiful. There were other similarities between the man and woman on the screen and the two sitting on the sofa, similarities which wreathed my heart in a ring of pain.

A woman whose stuntman husband had died in a film-set accident, and a man whose wife committed suicide when she thought he'd been killed in one of his car races. Their love story was woven together very slowly in the shadow of a past that constantly preyed on them, in somewhat the same way as it did in our love story. Anna's husband had also died in an accident, I remembered. And though I was much less charming than Jean-Louis Trintignant, I carried a drama on my back that was no less oppressive than that of the character he played in the movie. It was my race that killed my wife from the inside and also killed what could have been our child.

Would I ever be able to start a new chapter in my life without a terrible skeleton rattling around in my cupboard? Would this skeleton ever allow me to build a new life?

After we had made love again and with various thoughts floating through my mind as I began drifting off to sleep, hugging Anna's body 'like spoons' the way she liked it, a sudden shudder coursed through my body. What was the Mossad doing now?

My message, I could well imagine, had unleashed a storm in the inner sanctum of the Mossad. I visualized Ariel running in a frenzy to Udi's office and on his way summoning Levanon and perhaps also Alex and Eli; Udi reading the message and immediately calling Netzach on the phone and the head of the Mossad convening an urgent meeting in his office in the middle of the night. An operative has deserted. What other interpretation could there possibly be of the move I had made? Though I hadn't gone over to the enemy, I had given notice that I was breaking off contact and staying with a local woman in the country to which I'd been posted. And what's that if not desertion?

At the meeting, I imagined, the atmosphere of an operation, of crisis, a sense that something must be done and quickly. Perhaps somebody like Levanon would get up and say, wait a minute guys, he's not about to do anything damaging tomorrow. Allow him time to understand by himself what he's done, give him a chance to find a way out of the movie he's cast himself in. Another week or two, the blood will drain from his dick and circulate back into his brain and he will be in touch. But even if there is someone who dares to defy the air of operational activity, he will be silenced. He thinks he's macho, we'll show him what it is to be macho. I remembered Orit furiously stating 'so they muder us and we murder them? Always retaliating.'

What can they possibly do? Send someone here tonight to talk to me? Unlikely that they will decide on something more momentous than that. More likely nothing will be done till tomorrow. After all they won't want this somebody to arrive directly from Israel. And if it's to be one of the people in Europe he'd first of all have to be well briefed. What do they know? The addresses of the office and my apartment. Not Anna's address, though to my regret I gave them her first and family name in partial response to their demand when I still hoped that the storm would blow over. I could only hope that this would be useless information in a city as huge as St Petersburg with its five million inhabitants. Nonetheless I would somehow have to deal with this.

I should go now, tonight, to remove the rest of my things from my apartment and tomorrow start looking for some other anonymous place for the two of us. But how will I explain that to Anna?

32

THE HEAD OF the Mossad wanted Udi first of all to make the most of the existing regular channels to contact me before reaching any new decision about the matter. But the emails sent to me by the European office remained unread. There was also no response to their calls to my office, my house, and my mobile which I'd left on the table in the office to avoid it being used to locate me.

Twenty-four hours had passed since my last message

to HQ and the discussion there about me. Alex's men in the department for Russia and the former Soviet Republics had meanwhile managed to check St Petersburg's computerized databases and found six Anna Starzavas. In Russia as a whole there were hundreds. There were also many males named Starzav. Conceivably Anna was the wife of one of them and as such not separately listed in the databases. Not a single Anna Starzava linked to any kind of bookshop was found and the number of bookshops was huge. Alex himself relayed a specific briefing to one of his agents, a former KGB man who was asked to check details about an Anna Starzava from St Petersburg. He was told to be extra cautious and had as yet not got back to Alex with any answers.

Eli, the security officer, put together a document summarizing all the operations in which I'd played a role going back to the time when I first joined the Mossad. Though each operation took up just one line, the document was three pages long. A second nine-page paper prepared by Eli itemized all the operations I had any knowledge of. When, much later on, I was allowed to review these documents – attached to the transcripts of HQ's discussions about me – I discovered that most of these operations had been erased from my memory.

Netzach, already in his third year as head of the Mossad, had created a relaxed, businesslike atmosphere around him, made all the more so by his famous sense of humour. None of that interfered with his razor-sharp and at times far-reaching conclusions.

Have there been occasions in the past when you were

not able to reach him in the course of a twenty-four hour period? he asked

No, though besides the weekly arranged contacts we've not tried to reach him more than three or four times since he's been there, Udi replied.

And you've tried all the possible channels? the chief asked to make doubly sure. Udi confirmed that they had.

Well, keep trying. Independently of that and from this moment on, we'll work on the assumption that he has broken off contact with us. As a first step I want you to send someone to his office and apartment to see what is going on there.

Has there been a referral to somebody on the other side?

Alex reported on the enquiry that had been passed onto the ex- KGB agent codenamed 'Cotton Field', to find out details about the woman.

We chose him because he assumes his controller is an American businessman and our damage assessment indicated that this was the best possible option and wouldn't be traced back to the Mossad, he explained.

But it could arouse the suspicions of the CIA, Netzach said, clearly dissatisfied. And the results?

For the time being there are none, Alex replied, blushing in embarrassment from the obvious rebuke. He reported on the large number of Anna Starzavas that there were.

Concentrate on the addresses that are close to his apartment, the chief ordered. Overall damage assessment? he asked turning to Eli.

The security officer began to delve into the detail, passing over a copy of the two lists to the chief. Netzach cut him short.

Stop! The fact that he killed Arabs in all four corners of the globe doesn't worry me, even if he tells the Russians about it. Their killing rate is eight times greater. I want to know about the operations he took part in and those he knows about mounted directly against the Russians, or those that, if the Russians knew about them, would damage us.

There were the rocket transporters in Kazakhstan, Eli replied skimming over the list, and a few disruptions in the supply of missiles and radar equipment from Russia to target countries. That's what I see from a quick glance over the list of operations he was involved in. As far as 'knowledge' is concerned – his attention reverting to the second document – well, that's already much more problematic because he knows about quite a few sensitive operations in a number of countries linked to Russia.

I want full details, the chief interrupted him yet again. These could be critical to our final decision. For the moment we continue to work on the assumption that he's a 'love deserter'. Nice term? he chuckled. Include it in our lexicon of expressions. If it turns out that he knows too much or can cause too much damage we'll begin to relate to him as a deserter in every sense of the word.

Meetings in the chief's office were recorded and fully transcribed. This enabled me, even with the passage of time, to enjoy the special atmosphere in which they were held. Except that the 'subject' on this occasion was none other than me.

So I'm sending someone out today, Udi said.

I want us to reconvene here no later than tomorrow night with the results of your man's surveillance, Udi. I want a real damage assessment from Eli, and Alex – see if you can push for replies from your 'Rice Field'.

'Cotton Field', Alex corrected him instinctively, and I could imagine the roars of laughter from the others in the room.

I can still tell the difference between rice and cotton believe me, said the chief accompanying them out of his office. But I have the feeling that before we're done we're going to become seriously constipated because of this KGB guy of yours.

My apartment was already empty by the time Don, one of the division's operatives who'd been in Germany for a number of years, had winged his way to St Petersburg. HQ took care to send someone who'd never met me. That way I wouldn't be able to identify him as he sniffed around the house and office, or hide from him before he'd had a chance to approach me.

In two taxi rides, I had moved all my personal belongings from the apartment: the rest of my clothes, books, towels and bed linen, the rest of my toiletries, shoes and overcoats. I also took one photo – a couple embracing on a railway platform. Of all the pictures that I'd brought with me and hung in my apartment this one was dearest to my heart, even though the image was redolent of my former life.

Anna joyfully accepted the completion of my move to her apartment and straight away found a prominent spot for the photo in our bedroom replacing that of her dead husband – next to the figure of Jesus on the cross. The only clothes I was able to bring with me to Russia were those bought in Canada, and here I'd done very little shopping, but the side of the wardrobe cleared for me in the bedroom soon filled up and I had to leave some of my things unpacked.

So perhaps we really should move to your apartment, Anna said.

I have another idea, Annushka.

From the smile on my face Anna understood that she would like what I was about to propose. She sat on my knee, her eyes looking straight into mine. I'm listening, she suppressed a grin.

Let's rent a new apartment, a big one, more suited to us. And let's open a new shop, more spacious, with a foreign books section which I will manage.

Paul! Anna beamed. You really mean what you're saying, don't you?

I usually do mean what I say, I told her, and she put her arms around my neck, pecking my forehead, cheeks, and the tip of my nose.

But the money Paul, she suddenly became serious. And I don't know if it's even possible. I think all the bookshops belong to big chains – I'm sure you know some of them, like Dom Knigi – and are controlled by the oligarchs.

The city is full of small shops of every kind, I answered.

That's how it seems. But if you scratch beneath the surface you'll see that after the collapse of the Soviet Union those people took over everything and nothing happens without their consent. Everything belongs to the same group of people you saw with their up-market jeeps. Perhaps here and there you can still find private shops, like mine. But in a good location they will be more expensive and I don't have the money for that.

As if I'd been sprayed with icy cold water, I suddenly realized that from a financial point of view I hadn't planned my escape. Covering one's tracks costs money. So does a new apartment and a new shop. Though I had my company's credit cards and there were substantial amounts of money in the firm's bank account, I had no intention of making use of these funds.

The money I had on deposit in Israel from the sale of my parents' farm and my half share of the house, were primarily intended to pay for my mother's care. A quick calculation showed me that these funds were yielding profits that exceeded the average salary in St Petersburg, and that there was more than enough money there. I hadn't planned to use it, but I could draw on the account there if I absolutely had to. I only needed to find an alternative trustee to the Mossad's financial department which was currently taking care of all of that. And if there are places to rent that are not yet in the hands of the local Mafia, that's where we'll open our shop I thought to myself.

We'll find such a place, and I have a bit of money, I said.

From the expression on your face I can see that when you say a bit, that's what you mean.

I have enough for an apartment and a shop in the centre of town and at some point our business will have to start making a profit.

And what about your business?

From now on you'll be my business.

No Dagestan and Tajikistan?

The office in Montreal will continue to handle the deals here and over there, I said.

And we won't ever have to part?

Not even if you wanted to. I'll be with you, behind the counter.

The colour hadn't yet returned to Anna's cheeks. I want to find out tomorrow at the municipality what the implications are, she said. The shop is registered under Mikhail's name and I have to see what kind of bureaucracy is involved. Do you want to experiment tomorrow and work in the shop while I'm at the Town Hall?

With my feeble Russian? I would prefer to search for an apartment and a shop for us.

But I want to do that with you!

OK, so in the morning I'll deal with closing down my business and in the afternoon we'll start looking for an apartment and a shop.

Paul aren't you being a bit hasty? You can't close your business down like that. There's no guarantee that a more expensive shop in the centre will keep its head above water. Perhaps we should start by opening up a foreign books section in the shop here?

The shop is yours and Mikhail's, Annushka. Let's start a new life. You without Mikhail's shop and me without the company in Montreal.

You really mean it, don't you? Anna's beautiful eyes pierced mine.

Never been more serious in my life.

The look of deep concentration on Anna's face had made her brow crease and her nostrils slightly widen. Now that expression of seriousness gave way to lines of laughter in the corners of her eyes and lips, she broke into the happiest smile I'd ever seen. My heart was filled to the brim with love for her.

And you'll no longer be sad like you've been over the past few nights?

A few more nights and that's it, I said, and Anna erupted into a mix of laughter and tears.

I was so afraid that I wasn't making you happy and that you would leave, she said hugging me.

I promised you, never, never, never.

During the night it occurred to me that if the Mossad was trying to prevent my desertion it was likely to try and restrict my activities by freezing my accounts in Israel. I decided to be proactive. The next morning I called Orit from an internet café from which one could also make overseas calls. I could hear the shock in her voice. And immediately afterwards I could also hear a note of unconcealed joy. Her voice sounded as if it was coming from another world, distant and dissociated, a voice that I could remember but couldn't feel anything towards.

After the required few words of civility, Orit said that she of course couldn't ask me where I was.

I could just say that I'm wearing a heavy overcoat and that everything here is covered in snow, and that would be true. But I'm about to give you an address, I said, to her surprise, and went on to talk about the matter which had led me to break the long period of absolute silence between us.

Can you still access our joint account?

I don't know. It's been a very long time since I made any transactions on that account, she said.

But you didn't remove your name from it or cancel your signing rights, did you?

I don't think I did anything about that. I simply opened a new account.

Great, so please write down what I'm about to tell you.

Orit said she needed a moment to find a pen and paper and in the background I could hear the boisterous sounds of the little baby girl I'd seen and the wailing of another infant. I visualized them, three thousand miles to the south and thirty degrees warmer than here, and my heart trembled. A whole life, another life that was mine and could have still been mine, leapt at me from the receiver. A life that had been erased and which I had blotted out. A life which had been pushed away and which I had suppressed. And this telephone link seemed ethereal, impossible, confusing, and at the same time moving.

I'm back, Yogev. Yogev? I could hear her voice, sending yet another shockwave through my heart as I understood that the voice was addressing me. I'd only been 'Paul' for about six months since leaving Israel for Montreal and in that short time the Yogev that I had been for forty years had been almost obliterated. At first I didn't respond. Only after a third 'Yogev' did I manage to pull myself together. My two selves were facing each other from either end of a virtual umbilical cord connecting me to my past, a link that could be severed by the slightest of electrical disruptions. I mumbled the rest of the instructions as if caught in a daydream.

The money I got for my parents' farm and the funds I got from you for the house are in our joint account in a savings plan. I want you to cancel the plan and transfer the sum to an account which I'm going to tell you about right away. Leave two hundred thousand shekels in there to support my mother's ongoing upkeep.

There was silence at the other end. Orit?

I hear you, her voice came across a moment later, the tone hesitant and uneasy.

My salary goes into the same account. There's a standing order that transfers most of it to the hospital department where my mother is and to Madeleine, her carer. I want that to stay as it is, and I also want you to leave for my mother's benefit the funds that have accumulated there.

Yogev, is everything OK? Now her voice sounded really worried.

Everything's OK Or, I said without thinking, and from the other end I could hear a stifled cry.

Is that all? she asked, in a choking voice.

Apart from my not having yet given you the bank

information, I said, and read her the details of the account I'd opened in Montreal. Since I was presenting myself in Russia as a Canadian I couldn't very well allow a direct transfer of the money from Israel to here. Orit went over the bank details in a mechanical and still audibly strangled tone of voice.

Can I ask you please to do it today if that's possible? And if you are going to the Sapir Centre this morning, then to do it this morning?

I'll go there now if it's so urgent for you.

Thanks, thank you. And I also wanted to know if by chance you've heard something from my mother.

I visit her about once a month. She looks the same but now doesn't communicate with anyone.

I wanted to cut the conversation short. The FSB most probably listens to every call to Israel and it was best that I get away from the place quickly before a surveillance team arrived and linked the conversation to me. And yet, something inside me was shaken by the sound of her crying.

You want to tell me what's happening with you?

Oh, Yogev, Yogev, things are not easy here. Not easy with two children – you know that we had another little baby girl?

I muttered something vague.

Well, there are dreams and then there is reality. And I don't know how in touch you are but we had someone killed in Gaza, Shmilo's son. Did you know that there are rockets and military operations all the time? And overall the country leaves a lot to be desired.

I kept quiet and tried to remember Shmilo's children, but couldn't. He came to the village in the 1980s and his children, it would seem, were born after I was enlisted into the army.

Orit was also silent for a while. And what about you?

I'm alive, I said. And it's bloody cold here.

That's not terrible as long as you're not killing anyone there, she said. And with that the call was cut off. Orit? The Shin Bet? The FSB? Somebody took fright at these words.

I hurried out of the place and took a cab to a branch of one of the banks in the centre of town. There I opened a new account that required me once again to produce my full ID and fill in endless forms. The Russians want foreign currency but are still slaves to the totalitarian bureaucracy which remains part of their way of life. Happily, bank officials were more polite than other governmental clerks who continued to stick to the communist tradition of service. No metro ticket seller, for example, could be bothered to explain to me how the multiple journey magnetic card worked and so I continued using the single trip tokens.

When I'd finished at the bank I went into another internet café and after a few minor problems – not understanding the instructions in Russian on the screen, and Google insisting on linking me only to local websites – I transferred the details of my new account to the bank in Montreal with the instruction to forward the whole sum sent from Israel to that account.

Up to the time I'd arranged to meet Anna, I sat in a Coffee House on Nevsky Prospekt, giving myself a chance to calm down from the exertions of the morning and in particular from talking to Orit. That conversation had suddenly re-injected my former life into the here and now. For the first time I realized how fragile my new identity really was, and the ease with which it could be uncovered as a fiction. Then Anna arrived, her head wrapped in a grandmotherly kerchief against the cold. She giggled at the amused look I gave her and said, like a babushka, yes? And it wasn't till she'd removed the head scarf and bent to kiss me, that Orit and the Arava contracted and returned to that drawer that I didn't want to be opened ever again.

In the afternoon, together with a new real estate agent, we began to view apartments and shops for rent in the centre of St Petersburg. Because of the prices, we very quickly decided to look at places a bit further away. I knew that in a few days time I would be able to afford even those exorbitant rents but had no way of explaining my sudden wealth to Anna and I didn't want to come to the attention of the authorities. As much as possible I also wanted to get away from the hustle and bustle of the centre, from tourists and from the prying eyes of the Mossad who would most probably be arriving any time now.

Annushka, let's make it as simple and as distant as we can. Here, in St Petersburg, of course, don't worry, I hurried to add when I saw the look of concern on her face. But just as it's difficult to find an apartment in the centre it will also be difficult to find a shop here. And I saw in advertisements that new big residential complexes are being built on Vasilyevsky Island.

That's where the university is, you know? I studied there and I'll be able to show it to you, she said happily. But the areas where they're building, on the western side of the island towards the Gulf of Finland, were a wilderness then. We called them *golod*, from the Russian for hunger. Only those who had nothing went there.

Vasilyevsky is the biggest of the islands in the Neva delta on which the city is built. In the estate agent's car we crossed the one bridge that separates it from the Hermitage and the city centre, and I could see the imposing buildings of the university among which, apparently, there were also a scattering of governmental buildings since the people in brown uniforms outnumbered the student population. We drove on along Bolshoi Prospekt, a wide thoroughfare that led to the new housing estates in the western part of the island.

Close to the water's edge, alongside a harbour created by the small river that cuts across the island, rose a few clusters of huge steel and glass apartment blocks. Each one was painted in a slightly different colour – one blue and glass, the second brown and glass and so on. In each cluster there were a few high-rise towers of twenty storeys with lower buildings next to them. Walking in one of the estates we found there was a wide avenue within the complex with shops, cafés, and a hint of gardens-to-be.

In the sales office, a young real estate agent agreed to accompany us to view the available apartments.

We were like a young couple. I had never been a spontaneous, light-hearted type and I could never freely express my emotions. But Anna had changed that in me.

Her happiness at looking at apartments made coming to a decision a bit difficult. But it clearly wasn't necessary to cast the net too widely. Satisfying her, and indeed me, was easy. The various estates were similar to each other and offered a choice of apartments for both sale and rent. The rental prices turned out to be high, much higher than what I'd paid in Moskovsky and similar to the prices in the centre. They ranged from one thousand dollars a month for a small apartment looking directly on to the next building, to a few thousand dollars for a big one with a sea view. Without the Mossad's reimbursement of the rent this wasn't going to be easy but I decided to do it anyway. In the end we agreed on a nice three-roomed apartment on nearly the top floor in one of the new buildings facing the sea.

The sunsets you will see from here make it worth double the rent, the agent said. A rounded balcony stretched the length of the sitting room. I didn't know if a balcony in St Petersburg was a practical thing to have, but Anna was already planning the pots of herbs and flowers she would grow there. What attracted me was the huge expanse of glass, half of which was a door and the other half a window we could sit by and gaze at the promised sunset. A side window overlooked the rest of the buildings in the complex. Beneath it was the avenue of shops, and beyond that, as far as the eye could see, the rest of the city's buildings.

When we got back to the agent's office to sign the contract I asked that it be in his name. Anna and the agent were surprised but I told them that on my declared income I would have difficulty explaining the high rent to the tax authorities. In exchange for a not inconsiderable commission, the agent quickly agreed and the deal was closed before Anna had a chance to say anything. Covering the trail, mine and hers was, I thought, vital.

I'm beginning to understand how western capitalism works, Anna said to me on our way out. First of all there's the speed of closing the deal and then the property is hidden from view. Nice, very nice.

Yes that's part of the capitalist game, it suited me to agree with her.

Anna remained happy throughout the whole evening. She wanted us to go out to a show and we found tickets for an evening of jazz that embarrassed me for its cheap take-off of Americana. It wasn't enough for the members of the band to dress up as Americans, they also had to try, in the few words spoken, to sound like blacks from New Orleans. But that didn't disturb Anna and she continued to enjoy it well into the night.

On our return she called her mother and sister and for the first time told them about me. My mother is fairly apathetic she said, it's an age thing. My sister, though, is happy for me but also worried because you've come here for only a limited time. Usually we barely manage to talk to each other once a month, but she wanted to know everything and I promised to update her soon. You see, because of you even my family relations are improving.

Don's first report reached the Mossad that same evening. In accordance with the instruction given by the head of the Mossad, Udi asked to come up to see him with the results. It was almost midnight before the chief was free to meet him.

We can't deduce much from the fact that both the office and the apartment are in darkness and locked up, Udi said. And we also learned nothing from Don's initial check on the six possible addresses for the woman.

Right. But I don't want us to sit here like a bunch of lemmings, the chief retorted. First of all I want to block all his options of partying at our expense, and it's a pity we haven't already done this. We must block his credit cards and close the company bank account.

I don't think he'll live it up at our expense, Udi said. He's not the type.

Come now, what are you, a child? You think that someone who deserts the Mossad for a roll in the hay would shy away from dipping his hands into our pockets? Desertion costs money. You need an apartment, there are other expenses, and to keep hold of such an ass you need a certain standard of living, fur coats and vacations. Do you really need someone to explain that to you?

The full transcript didn't censor the freewheeling comments of the chief and I could imagine the serious-minded Udi swallowing hard before going into the detail: we can block the credit cards because we had them issued for him and the company's account in Canada can be closed as well but only if we dispatch his controller Ariel, who also has signing rights, there at once. In Russia we can't do it because he opened that account by himself.

So get going with what is possible and tell your man

in St Petersburg to be vigilant. We'll give it another couple of days and then decide. And let Alex give his cotton picking peasant a kick up his ass. How long can it take for him to find out from his friends if this Natasha Romanova is one of theirs or not.

Anna Starzava, Udi corrected the chief.

Lucky us! I was already afraid that she might be a member of the royal family.

Udi looked at him, puzzled.

From the House of Romanov, the chief said impatiently. The last Czarist dynasty. Go on, get to work, it's already nearly tomorrow, he laughed.

As soon as he left the chief's bureau, Udi summoned Ariel from his house. Get here with a bag and enough clothes for three days, he told him. He then instructed the night secretary to book a seat on the first available flight to Montreal. When the eager controller arrived at HQ in the middle of the night a ticket for a flight via Vienna was already waiting for him.

Get to Montreal, find a place to stay and go straight to the bank, Udi wrote in his instructions to Ariel. To close the account you'll need to show your power of attorney and that's being arranged for you right now in the documentation department. Report to me by phone as soon as it's done.

33

THE VERY NEXT day we arranged for a removal company to take all our belongings to the new apartment. Once everything was arranged we began looking around to see what was still needed. Anna's apartment had furniture for only two rooms and in any case we both preferred a more modern style. A quick visit to the bank revealed that the money transfer had not yet arrived. But I trusted Orit to do what I'd asked of her, relied on the bank in Montreal to carry out my instructions, and had enough cash to satisfy Anna's expectations without having to tap the company account for a loan. And indeed with every piece of furniture that Anna took a fancy to and I agreed to buy, she became visibly happier.

Towards evening, after a new living-room suite had been delivered to the apartment, we decided to stay in. From the huge window we could see a sky of astonishing beauty. Layers of low-lying dark clouds covering the wintery heavens were painted rosy pink by the setting sun. Streaks of orange coloured the gaps between them. Across the city, the lights were being turned on. We stood at the small window overlooking the shopping thoroughfare, spotting street billboards as they lit up and following the fading colours of the sunset as a mist rising from the sea drifted ever closer and slowly shrouded the city's gardens.

We hadn't turned on the light before sunset and now found ourselves in pitch darkness, standing at the window spellbound as the city donned its night-time finery and was slowly covered by a blanket of fog.

Come to me, Anna said, and I stood behind her, rolled her pants down and inched my way into her. With delicate movements she adjusted herself to the position, her forehead and the palms of her hands resting against the window. When Anna said 'glass will break' it took me a moment to understand that the definite article was missing and that she was telling me to pay attention to the forcefulness of my movements and the shuddering of the window panes.

At that very moment, Don was making his rounds in the neighbourhoods of my old office and apartment as well as exploring the six addresses where an Anna Starzava was known to live. He chose varying times: in the morning and evening and then earlier in the morning and later in the evening. But even if he saw and photographed a few Anna Starzavas he didn't see me and couldn't link me to any of the women.

When, after three days of such efforts, his detailed report arrived, Udi convened a staff meeting.

It's possible that Paul has gone to live at the woman's place and from the various options we have we don't know which of them is the right Starzava. Perhaps the two of them have left St Petersburg and may be part of his attempt to cover his tracks. Here's what I want to do. We need to have a number of fixed vantage points: the office, the house, and the addresses of the various Starzavas. We have to tail women seen leaving these addresses who could be our Anna Starzava and that, maybe, will lead us to him. If he's not working in his office then it would seem he must have some other work. He needs to do something to earn a living. All of that is for you to handle, Levanon, assuming, of course, they're still in St Petersburg.

Udi then turned to Alex. We need a Russian to start investigating the Russian-Canadian, or St Petersburg-Montreal chambers of commerce, the register of companies, and real estate offices, in case some Canadian has rented an office from them, and so on and so forth.

In my opinion this is all much ado about nothing, Alex said. Paul wasn't the Don Juan of the century and without doubt the woman he's shacked up with won't be Ms Russia or Ms St Petersburg. How long will he stay with her before he realizes that he's made the mistake of his life and come back to us on all fours begging for forgiveness? And how long will she stay with him once we've blocked his sources of finance? And even if I'm wrong – where's the damage? I don't imagine he will have introduced himself to her as a Mossad agent.

I was surprised that internal transcripts, taken down by hand by Udi's secretary, didn't omit such personal comments. Apparently, the story of my love affair was on everybody's lips. But Udi, I was glad to learn, stayed out of it.

Enough Alex, we're talking about one of us and I ask you to respect that.

He turned to Levanon. How many available men do you have?

Here in Israel there are, at the moment, four men I

376

could send out overnight. I can increase that number with people from Europe at the expense of their vacation time. Most of the operational teams are due to return here because it's Christmas. In St Petersburg offices won't be open as people are on holiday. In my opinion we'll be running the guys around for no good reason.

Let's be accurate, Alex said. Christmas for the Russian Orthodox Church is the night between the 6th and 7th of January, but the winter festivities get going around about the 25th of December.

What does that mean for high street businesses and offices? Udi asked.

The big party is at the end of the civil year on January 1st. During the Soviet period they wanted to eradicate every vestige of religious practice and symbolism so that became the central and almost only festive event. The Russians go on vacation on the 31st, but foreign tourists arrive towards the 25th of December, and that's when the winter festivities begin in St Petersburg. Now there's a return to religion, so on the night between the 6th and 7th of January there are Masses and they're on holiday on and off during this whole period. Sometimes this even continues until the 13th – the Russian New Year.

If that's the case get the four guys ready to leave tomorrow, Udi instructed. What about intelligence? He turned to ask the division's head of intelligence.

We prepared the initial material for Paul when he was about to leave, said Moshiko, and we also briefed Don before his departure. Since then Noga, one of my department workers, has put together a well researched dossier with the help of satellite photos, some video clips of St Petersburg which she got hold of, photographs that she found on various websites, and sightseeing routes around the city taken from guide books. Together with Eli we also prepared a detailed briefing on the various security forces there.

It should be regarded as a semi-target country, you understand? Udi clarified. It may be that St Petersburg looks like Paris or Amsterdam but it has to be treated with the utmost care, like operating in a soft target.

That's clear, Moshiko said, that's also what the briefing says.

Udi summed up: I want the guys to get an intelligence briefing before the end of the day and be prepared to leave tomorrow morning. Levanon, see to it that they arrive separately from different countries and that they stay in different hotels.

I'll send them in two pairs, Levanon said. A European arriving on his own at Christmas arouses suspicion.

During those three days Anna and I also found the shop we wanted to rent. We looked for somewhere on our island, preferably reachable on line number 7 which passed close to our apartment.

In the end the find came out of the blue and in a charming location. Between the wide Bolshoi Prospekt and Sredni Prospekt – the middle avenue parallel to Bolshoi – the cross streets go by numbers. Streets Six and Seven have been linked up to form a spacious pedestrian zone with two rows of trees in the middle. And all along it there are shops, restaurants, and cafés. Only two churches on the corner of the street have kept a certain Russianness. The rest could have been lifted straight from the bustling city centres of Western Europe. In the middle of the pedestrian zone, on the ground floor of one of the most beautiful buildings there, we found a bookshop with a sign on it saying for sale or rent. Our joy knew no bounds and we were quick to commit even though the price was high. For the locals, so it seemed, this was their favourite spot. The shop's proximity to the university undoubtedly attracted many students and the owner of the shop promised that this was a place that even tourists came to.

The attempt to register the property in the name of the estate agent didn't succeed this time because it also had to be recorded at the town council, the Chamber of Commerce and the Small Business Authority. I said that I wanted it to be in Anna's name which surprised her but she raised no objection. It's not easy for foreigners to set up a business in Russia.

Carpenters started work. The shop was L-shaped and we divided the space into two sections; books in Russian, which took up the long arm of the 'L', and books in other languages which occupied the shorter arm. Two sales counters were built in the corner between the two, each counter facing a different section. The counters separated us from the customers, but our chairs were close to each other. Books from the existing shop filled a large proportion of the Russian section, but my area remained predominantly empty.

During our time off, Anna took me on trips to the university, where she had spent many happy years. We ended up eating at the very cheap cafeteria in the student centre. However much I put on my tray it was always 150 rubles – less than six dollars. The cheap eatery attracted not only students but also military personnel and government employees who worked in the nearby buildings. Outside Anna pointed to a statue in the square opposite. Andrei Sakharov, she said. You know the name?

I mumbled that it rang a bell but that I couldn't put my finger on it.

He was a well-known critic of the regime. This square has been named Academician Sakharov Square in his memory. But I've heard that his wife, Elena Bonner, was against this. Elsewhere, in America, in Israel, they named far worthier places after him.

I was often stuck in traffic jams near the Sakharov gardens at the entrance to Jerusalem. But I tried to keep a straight face and not allow even a hint of any such knowledge show.

As the New Year holiday approached, we took home various catalogues and, in the evenings, after we'd arranged and re-arranged the new furniture until we were happy with it, and had finished putting away our clothes and kitchen equipment in cupboards, we sat snuggled up to each other and marked the books we wanted to order for my section of the shop. Anna knew that I'd taken courses in Far Eastern Studies and International Relations and that I also knew a bit of Chinese, so she urged me to order Eastern literature and books on political subjects.

She showed no interest in international policy or politics but was pleased to hear me telling her about China. I didn't hide the fact I'd been there but told her that it was part of my studies. Anna had a special way of listening to me, as if she was drinking in what I was saying and my every sentence was breathing new life into her. We spoke a bit about the Chinese literature I was familiar with, and spent long evenings talking about the world's great writers. What is the book you loved most? Anna suddenly wanted to know.

I've never thought about that. I read a lot, I've been reading since I was a child, but I've never gone in for ranking my preferences.

But Anna insisted: a heroine that you loved, a hero you wanted to emulate, a plot that excited you.

A hero I wanted to emulate, who excited me, I answered after a while, someone who pops into my mind from my youth but in a blurry sort of way, is Martin Eden by Jack London.

Not his suicide by drowning I hope, she said.

No, not just that. I remember descriptions of this broad-shouldered character, walking around awkwardly, actually fearful of bumping into things and causing damage. Something about this reticence verging on clumsiness combined with strength, and the writing, greatly appealed to me. I was just a boy, and felt like him. My shoulders were broadening out, I had enormous strength, I didn't know how to talk properly and from the reading I wanted very much to be a bit of a writer and a bit of a sailor and fighter...

You know that he really did commit suicide, Anna said.

Yes, I said. I knew that Jack London was a seaman. I assumed there was an autobiographical basis for the book, and that's what I loved. But mainly I was able to identify with the portrait of a man who didn't understand himself and wasn't aware of the inner drives preventing him from ever being at peace with himself.

Anna stroked my thigh affectionately. And you too are like that. I see that in you, and so dream of tempering that inner struggle of yours.

And which book did you love most? I preferred to divert the focus away from me.

The book I love best is *Love in the Time of Cholera*, the most wonderful love story I have ever read. So many people fail to realize the great love of their youth and spend a lifetime dreaming of that love. Marquez really made me happy when, in the end, he returned Fermina into Florentino's arms. They were both old by then, she a shadow of her former self. And yet love conquered all. It's so moving that people don't stop believing, loving, trying. I don't have a love from my youth that I want to meet again. Yet I do feel that this book is very relevant to my life.

Our love was at its height and Annushka at the peak of her beauty and ripeness. We were neither the youngsters at the beginning of the book nor the elderly couple at its conclusion, but I said nothing. The seeds of destruction were already latent in our love and who could tell how it would end?

34

At dawn the four members of the team took off for Europe and by lunchtime were on their way to St Petersburg with fake IDs.

Early in the morning, Ariel contacted Udi at home. I had problems closing the bank account, he said in his wake-up call from Montreal, and I need to know whether I should come back as planned or stay here until it's all settled.

What, exactly, is the problem? asked Udi, still drowsy.

The day before I went to the bank there was a substantial transfer of funds from Israel to here and from here to Russia and when the market closed the rates of exchange were not final and adjustments to the balance are expected.

A transfer from Israel? Udi was now fully awake. The company account in Montreal that Paul set up was supposed to have absolutely no link to Israel.

And you won't believe the sums involved, Ariel added. Something like a million shekels. Apparently he transferred everything he had in Israel.

Was it sent to the company account in Russia? He's burned the company?

That's it. He hasn't. I have the account number in Russia to which the funds were transferred, and it's not the company account. So at least in Russia the account remains clean.

Have you managed to close down the account in Montreal?

That's not possible because of what I've just explained to you. But I've cut its link to the company account in Russia and blocked all foreign dealings except for what's involved in these exchange rate adjustments.

For the moment that's good enough. When is your flight back?

It's now 1 a.m. here. I have a flight at 7 in the morning to Vienna and land in Israel at 11 p.m.

Come straight to the office with all the paperwork, Udi said. We'll have to do some serious work on it.

A short while later Alex called and the conversation wasn't any more encouraging. Cotton Field's controller met up with his source tonight and was informed by him that 'Anna Petrovna Starzava from St Petersburg was an ex–KGB spy catcher and is apparently employed in the same role by the FSB.'

Was he able to give any more information about her? Udi asked, impatiently. At least so we can say which one of the six listed in the phone book she is?

The paternal name, Petrovna, isn't listed in the phone books, Alex said, Cotton Field was only able to give me what I've now told you.

No address, no description, not something we can bite into?

No, said Alex, the instruction was not to push to avoid it impacting on Paul.

Does the source have encrypted communications?

No, his recruitment is not yet at that level. But he's a businessman who is in Europe every few weeks.

If what he's reported is correct it doesn't leave us much time, Udi said. Is the controller still with him?

Until lunchtime, Alex replied.

So get him a precise list of the essential information we want, and do it urgently. We must have an address, a description, every possible detail. He should tell the man to come to a follow-up meeting the moment he has some answers. Have him give the guy a backhander of some sort to make it worth his while.

Udi quickly left his house for Mossad HQ. The bureau secretary ushered him in straightaway.

Double espresso, thank you, Udi's request was picked up by the recording machine and the head of the Mossad duly ordered his third cup of coffee of the day.

Not the worst news but hardly encouraging either, Udi said as he sat down. For starters, we sent out four people this morning who'll be arriving in St Petersburg during the course of the day.

Up till now you're doing OK, the chief responded.

But that's the end of the good news. Ariel was at the branch bank in Canada where the company has its account. It turns out that Paul transferred large sums yesterday, apparently everything he had in Israel, via the account in Montreal to a new account he opened in St Petersburg.

Son of a gun, the Chief said.

That messes up the Canadian company for having ties

with Israel and prevents the account's closure because of some issues with the exchange rate. It also shows, of course, that he's serious about wanting to cut his links to Israel and live in St Petersburg. And that's only the half of it.

Oh, there's more?

Yes. The source in Russia has relayed information that there is an Anna Petrovna Starzava from St Petersburg who's an ex-KGB spy catcher and is continuing to work in that role with the FSB. But he had no details about her and as you'll recall we know of at least six Anna Starzavas.

Petrovna narrows down the number, not all their fathers were named Petrov, the chief said confidently. And quite apart from that she's not one of the six. Does it seem likely to you that a spy catcher would be listed in the phone book?

If so, it means that right now we are clueless. The 'Field' was instructed to get an address and a description.

Good, at least we're clear about what's happening with Paul, and all those bleeding hearts in your division who think that he's either the most righteous or the most pitiable man of his generation can begin eating their hats, the chief said. The guy has really deserted and, if we take the worst case scenario, has been seduced by a spy catcher and is now in the clutches of the FSB.

Alternatively, this isn't the KGB's Anna and he's just severed his links with us to be with her, what you called a love deserter, Udi replied.

We have to work on the assumption that we're facing a far more serious possibility. At least until we're proven wrong. How many people did you say were on their way, four?

Right, and I can organize a few more who are either heading for home or a vacation.

OK. Let the four make a start with nonstop surveillance of the addresses. Do they have filming equipment?

Yes, they'll cover four of the addresses every day with video, and the other two with lookouts.

Prepare a big team for the beginning of next week, including the possibility of a kidnap. And start planning it.

In the meantime, if he's spotted, you have to wait till he's alone and then approach him and tell him that we demand he come back. And from that moment on – he's not to be left alone anymore. You stay constantly on his tail.

You know the risks involved in this, Udi said. If she's really FSB and if he's really switched sides, when the guys make themselves known to him they'll all be arrested within a minute. And he, of course, will slip away.

Can you come up with an option other than going up to him and speaking to him? Do you think it's right to go for a kidnapping straight away? the head of the Mossad asked.

No, kidnapping from Russia is very complicated. I'm only pointing out that none of the options we have are particularly good.

OK, so it's no picnic. But put the plans for a kidnapping in place and perhaps it will turn out not to be so complicated.

Netzach's secretary knocked on the door to tell him

that people from the foreign relations division were waiting for a meeting.

Keep me informed at every stage; they didn't see, they did see, if there is something from Cotton Field etc, said the chief, summing things up. By the way, how much money did he transfer?

The documents are on the way, but Ariel said about a million.

Son of a gun. That's not only enough for a change of identity, it'll also pay for a sex change.

Shekels, not dollars.

OK, but it's cheap there isn't it?

And wouldn't it be a pity for our Russian lady, him having a sex change?

A former KGB woman? It's more than likely to be at her request.

Udi immediately convened the Division's most senior forum. When, much later on, I had the chance to read the transcript, I could imagine that those involved, having only just managed to get comfortable in their own offices, turned up holding their cups of coffee. The picture is changing, Udi said opening the meeting. There are clear signs that Paul has cut off contact with us and is thinking of settling down in Russia permanently. It's also probable that the woman with him is an FSB spy catcher.

How clear cut are these signs? Levanon demanded.

They are not absolutely clear but the indications are sufficiently strong for us to change our working assumption, Udi replied. We have to prepare for a new situation that at worst could include kidnapping Paul and bringing him back to Israel. And I'm now putting into motion the initial planning stage.

Murmurs that ranged from surprise to dissent were heard around the table. Udi continued.

Start taking notes, I'm dictating decisions. The mission: Locating Paul and returning him to Israel as quickly as possible. Main steps: Round-the-clock surveillance and discovery of his most frequented haunts and contacts; attempting to talk to him and if that doesn't work – kidnap him. Hopefully that's something we'll be able to avoid. Planning Department: Levanon, you now prepare a six-man team ready to leave tomorrow in case Boaz's squad, which is currently in the air, succeeds in locating Paul. If he's not found, this team will leave here on the 1st of the month. At the same time, put together a kidnapping plan. How, where, who, a safe house, transport, and everything else. I want us to be able to look at the initial draft before the end of the day. I also want the team to get a preliminary briefing today.

Levanon's response didn't appear in the transcripts but I could imagine him keeping his mouth shut, chewing on his pen or doodling away as he always did when things took a turn that wasn't to his liking.

Intelligence, Udi continued. Moshiko, I want you to assign an intelligence officer to the mission. He has to be an operational intelligence officer, not an analyst. All the information relevant to a kidnapping operation must be prepared, and there's a lot of it.

Security, Eli. We are going into an operation in an area

with which we are not sufficiently familiar. I want you to assemble everything that we have on the work of the Russian security forces in general and in St Petersburg in particular. Surveillance of foreigners, monitoring of hotels, roadblocks, etcetera.

We did this before Paul went to Russia, Eli said, and in preparing for Don's departure and then for Boaz's team.

That's just the basics, Udi said. Now we have to collect the intelligence required for a kidnapping scenario. I need to know what kind of forces they activate, how long it takes them to put up roadblocks, how they reinforce the checks at border crossings and at airports, and so on and so forth.

Eli took it all down, his lips pursed. The operational air of Udi's succinct and hurried orders didn't leave room for debate.

Alex, Udi turned to speak to the man in charge of Russia and the former Soviet Republics, I want a Russian speaker to be attached to the team. He has to work on his own, searching various sources for information, and be available to the team for any help they may need. Questions anyone?

I've done some thinking about the people involved, Levanon said. To get six to come to a briefing today and keep them on standby from tomorrow morning, I have to screw up five people's holidays. Three who've only just landed and two from Europe.

So do it, and stay behind for a moment, Udi told Levanon. I'll fill you in on the whole picture. Guys get to work, he said, releasing the rest of them.

Udi's secretary, who was responsible for the transcription, left the room and closed the door behind her. Udi and Levanon were now alone.

Tell me, why the hysteria? Levanon asked suppressing his anger.

Udi gave him the details of the information he had.

I don't buy it, said Levanon.

Don't buy what?

Not the story about the money, and not the one about the woman.

The stuff about the money is documented. Ariel has the paperwork, Udi said.

I'm not saying he didn't transfer the money. I'm saying, so he made the transfer, so what? He wants to live with her there.

With a spy catcher? Udi retorted angrily.

That I don't buy. Not only are there six Anna Starzavas in St Petersburg, but think about Cotton Field. No doubt he's some frustrated ex-KGB guy with a pension of a hundred dollars a month and we come and ask him such a question. If he says he knows nothing, or that there's no such worker, we'll go on meeting him once a year and he'll go on getting his miserable hundred dollars from us. But if he says there is somebody like that – there'll immediately be another question and another hundred dollars and he will give a partial answer so that there'll be another round and another hundred dollars – it's all so obvious.

Listen, that's not Cotton Field's profile. He's in fact a fairly well established businessman. But anyway, are you trying to argue that for no particular reason some woman turned Paul's head to such an extent that he transferred all his money to Russia and cut off contact with us?

Levanon was deep in thought. I don't know, he said. But kidnapping? Do you know what a bitch it is to arrange to kidnap him in Russia? I'm sure there are other things that can be tried.

For example?

For example that I or you, not Boaz or Yoav, speak to him. What do Boaz or Yoav mean to him? He will ignore them.

And let's suppose we did that. You speak to him, I speak to him, and he says to us, 'guys, I'm in love, sorry, but this is my life and I'm not about to screw it up again because of you.'

Then he's told that she's a spy catcher.

And he doesn't believe it. Then what?

Convince him, Levanon said. There are ways of doing that.

I'm not ruling out what you are saying, but let's get ourselves prepared for the worst case scenario.

And so, Levanon told me a year later with more than a hint of apology, we began to go after you. And you know the Division. The moment an operation is in motion it's like a semi-trailer on a steep slope. There's no way of stopping it. And admit it. The way things looked from our end, we didn't have much of a choice.

I found that hard to admit. I was left with too many scars from the chain of events that followed.

35

Boaz's team landed in St Petersburg and after a quick check-in at their hotels the four went to meet Don in a restaurant. He provided them with exact descriptions of my office, my apartment, and the addresses of the various Anna Starzavas in town. He gave an account of people's daily routines in these houses and neighbourhoods, the police patrols there, where in the area one needed to be careful of hooligans and places where drunks hunkered down at night. Don also informed the team of where he'd spent time as a lookout, and where he thought the suspicion of residents had been aroused. Then, with Boaz, he toured these addresses, helped him plan the schedule of patrols and lookouts, said his goodbyes to Boaz and set off to fetch his belongings and fly to Europe and from there back to Israel.

In the freezing cold Boaz's men invested many days in what turned out to be pointless effort, which included briefly tailing a number of possible Anna Starzavas. By the end of the New Year holiday they had come up with nothing. In the meantime, Roman, the Russian speaker Alex attached to the team, was also of little help. Even if the operatives reached our block on Morskaya, the street which ran along the length of the sea shore, they wouldn't have been able to find anything. They gravitated towards Vasilyevsky Island's attractive pedestrian zone and when, much later, I saw their reports, I realized that they had even passed our shop. We could have been found there, arranging books, putting up tables or labelling shelves. But there was nothing that could help them identify either the shop or the apartment as belonging to us.

At midnight on the 31st of December, Anna and I opened a bottle of champagne. We gazed out of the window of our apartment overlooking a city immersed in revelry and were intoxicated by the beauty of the blanket of snow and the colourful lights that decorated the town. Just then the snow began to fall once more and Anna squealed with joy, kissed me again and again, wishing us both many many more happy years together. How little we then knew.

The next morning we meandered slowly through the snow-covered squares and gardens. From mid-day on, the locals, waking up from a heavy night's drinking, began to stroll together with their children towards the improvised entertainment and amusement stands in the gardens. Couples of *Ded Morozy* and *Snegurochki*, Santa Clauses and their Snow Maiden granddaughters, wandered around in matching clothes, red and white or blue and white, handing out presents to excited children. No words were exchanged, but it was clear that knowing we would never be part of such a family filled us both with a feeling of deep sorrow.

We returned to our apartment and continued, as had become our habit over the previous few evenings, to flip through various book catalogues. In one, I saw a listing of the translated works of Amos Oz and David Grossman, some even marked as essential material for any self-respecting shop. Showing no reaction, I continued to leaf through the catalogue but Anna turned the pages back and asked me what I thought.

I don't have a view, I said, in the most indifferent tone of voice I could summon up.

Because you don't know of them? she asked and looked straight at me.

I've heard of both, but I don't remember details, I replied, not taking my eyes off the catalogue.

As it happens, I remember both *My Michael* and *See Under: Love*, she surprised me. I remember thinking that the first part of 'See Under' about the little boy was the greatest children's literature I'd ever read, no less impressive than Charles Dickens and Mark Twain. But the other parts of the book didn't work for me. It might have been because of the translation and also the fact that I read it in English which then was much more difficult for me than it is now.

I mumbled something, not daring to look at her. I loved the writings of both Oz and Grossman. I had grown up on Oz's books and had even met Grossman once after a lecture he gave about his work.

So I'm marking them to be ordered, Anna said when I didn't respond.

Like the conversation with Orit, the sudden intrusion into my consciousness of Oz and Grossman deeply punctured the cover of foreignness that I was still in the process of constructing around me and only proved to me how difficult the task I had imposed upon myself was going to be.

Are you OK, my darling?

I cleared my throat and said, still without lifting my eyes, I'm OK.

The following day, we opened our shop, even though the signboards had not yet arrived. Many local shops were not open as their owners were still on holiday but Anna and I wanted a trial run. That same day the new, six-man team of operatives led by Yoav arrived in St Petersburg and the search for us intensified. Thousands of tourists streamed into the city for the week between the beginning of the year and the celebration of Christmas. The location of our shop, in the charming pedestrianized street of Vasilyevsky Island, and the fact that it had a section devoted to books from the West, attracted local as well as foreign shoppers and immediately after the signboards were hung we were rushed off our feet.

The signboards were simple as both of us wished to maintain an air of modesty. One signboard had *Knigi*, books in Russian, painted on it, and the second simply read books in English.

Anna turned out to be a born saleswoman, showing infinite patience to customers, and an extensive knowledge which enabled her both to recommend when someone asked her advice and to find a book when a customer had a specific request. I, on the other hand, had a lot to learn and many areas that cried out for improvement. Difficult customers, and there were many of them, I just wanted to be rid of as quickly as possible. I couldn't understand how someone could come armed with a load of questions, have them all answered, leaf through dozens of books in different editions, and then walk out of the shop empty handed. Common, perhaps, though I myself was a very purposeful kind of buyer. I would enter a shop only when there was a defined need, quickly buy what I'd come for, pay, and leave, so I found it extremely vexing to accept such behaviour. The foreigners, naturally, were drawn to my section. However, I usually ran out of answers after the third enquiry and Anna had to come to my rescue. Her beauty led even those who didn't find what they were looking for to leave the shop clutching a book.

At the end of every day, when we'd closed up the shop and drawn the blinds, we sat down to do the accounts and found that the daily takings were going up and up.

A few days later Roman, on a visit to the Small Business Authority, came across our bookshop's registration. Triumphantly, he told Yoav that Anna Petrovna Starzava was the owner of a bookshop on 6th Street in Vasilyevsky. Shortly afterwards Harry entered the store.

I didn't know Harry and he didn't arouse any suspicion in me. There were five or six other customers in the shop at the time and Harry came nowhere near me. Instead, he browsed the bookshelves. I learned later that this young blond guy had been recruited into Yoav's team from one of the European squads and our paths had never crossed. From his appearance I couldn't even tell that he wasn't Russian. Some time after he first spotted me he went to Anna's section, observed me from a different angle, and then left. Once outside he confirmed Roman's findings.

Yoav left Harry to keep an eye on the shop. He himself walked past it, convened the team for a meeting at McDonald's on the corner of Sredni Prospekt and reported back to Israel. Following the departure of Boaz and his men from the city at the end of a week's work, Yoav, a relatively young team leader, was the most senior commander left on the ground.

The news of my having been found spread rapidly within HQ. In a hurried consultation between Udi, Levanon, and the head of the Mossad, it was decided to give preference to discovering my favourite haunts before any attempt was made to approach me directly. That way, were I to disappear following such an approach, they would know where to begin looking for me again.

OK guys, this has been easier than we thought it would be, Yoav told his men. Fortunately, there is a match between the information Roman gave us and what Harry saw, and that saves us from having to expose ourselves to the subject. To Paul, he corrected himself. According to the most recent instructions from HQ, we are to follow Paul and Anna who, I assume, is the woman with him in the shop. Our objective, as has just been re-stated, is to find out where their apartment is and other haunts of theirs, if any, learn their routine and, most importantly, discover who their contacts are. Who they meet, when and where. We also need to get photographs of Anna.

Wouldn't it be worth it if someone who actually knows him could give us a positive ID? asked Debbie, one of the female members of the team. Harry, after all, only remembers him from the picture, from the briefing by intelligence.

You're right, and that's why I'm now going to join Harry at the lookout point. In our team you, Harry, and Rosy, don't know him at all. You'll also be the ones who'll keep tabs on him when he goes out. Guri, Nadav and I, will tail the woman.

From now on I want two cars in the close vicinity of the bookshop, one for each team of operatives. Debbie, you're in charge of the team following Paul, Guri, you're responsible for those tailing Anna. There's a Sbarro pizzeria and a Coffee House opposite the shop, two good vantage points. Vehicles can't, of course, enter this street, but there are parking places in Bolshoi as well as in Sredni. In both these streets there are also buses and there is a metro station on the corner of 7th and Sredni. We don't know yet how they move around so get yourselves bus and metro passes.

Debbie and Guri went to rent cars. The rest of the team set off to take up their positions opposite the shop.

Anna and I were becoming accustomed to our blissful routine. Just before nine in the morning we'd leave our apartment and a short while later open the shop. At about 1 p.m. one of us would go out to eat and an hour later the other did the same. At five we closed the shop. To enjoy the city's festive atmosphere, now at its height, we went twice to a Balkan restaurant that Anna loved and on another evening to the monthly Philharmonic concert. Anna was able to exchange both the series and the seating she previously had. I don't want to hear all that gossiping around us, she explained.

Before the concert, the excited Anna took me to the

Conservatoire building opposite the Mariinsky Theatre. Right at the entrance we were engulfed by the sounds of singing and playing coming from the rooms along the corridor. We went up an elegant staircase and with much enthusiasm Anna showed me the classrooms she'd studied in and the grand piano in one of the halls on which she'd practised on 'countless evenings'. Her excitement was so great that we were very nearly late for the concert.

On the evenings we didn't go into town we strolled along the strip of neglected shoreline between Morskaya Street and the sea, sat on the steps of the jetty surrounded by graffiti and beer bottles left by youngsters – who probably made their appearance there much later on in the evening – and stayed until the bitter cold chased us back into our apartment and bed.

Yoav reported our precise routine to HQ, along with his impression that we were indeed running a legitimate bookstore. He hadn't seen any suspicious-looking people coming in or out, nor had he noticed any questionable meetings taking place there. Team members had followed both Anna and me to meals, and observed that we ate alone.

To their credit, it has to be said that I didn't see them or suspect them in any way. When for the second or third time I ate at Sbarro opposite the shop, I knew that I had already seen the two young women sitting at the far end of the Italian restaurant, but that was also true of other diners. On the short bus ride to the shop in the morning I saw nobody suspicious – they might have been following us in a car – nor did I see anyone on the way home when the mists of evening had already gathered.

In retrospect, I was glad that I'd spoiled them with meals at the Balkan restaurant. On the evening of the concert the poor souls must have frozen in the cold outside the Conservatoire and when they stood waiting at the various exists from the Meriinsky Theatre from where, presumably, they followed us home.

At Christmas, Anna asked me if I wanted to get a *Yolochka*, a Christmas tree. I loved learning the Russian words that Anna slipped into our conversations whenever the right English term slipped her mind. I said that it made no difference to me. As the son of a Hindu father and a Christian mother such aspects of religious festivals were no part of my life.

Anna, nevertheless, went ahead and bought a miniature tree, placed it in the corner of the living room and decorated it. I bought her two nightdresses and a silk robe which I wrapped and hid until Christmas Eve, when I placed the parcel by the tree. Anna happily produced her present to me – a white designer shirt. She thought it was high time I dressed like a real businessman even though I was now turning myself into a salesman in a bookstore. This was a flaw in me that even my instructors in the long training course at the Mossad had failed to correct; as a villager who throughout his childhood saw the people around him wearing only working clothes, I hadn't got used to the attire of a business man. When I did wear a suit and tie because there was no other option, my controllers found themselves having to comment on the black trainers that I was wearing.

Anna wanted to go to midnight mass and asked if I wished to join her. If you're going I'll come with you. I'm an atheist it's true, but an atheist in love.

Anna kissed me. How can the son of a Hindu and a Catholic be an atheist? she wanted to know.

Precisely as a result of that, I replied. Two contradictory truths led me to a reliance on science.

But every scientific theory that tries to explain the world is full of holes, she said. The expansion of the universe doesn't necessarily point to a big bang. And do you know why the big bang theory was accepted? Because the Russian scientists who thought that the galaxies simply passed one another and were now drawing away, didn't have the money to come to the West and make their views heard.

Before I'd even managed to voice my reservations about that, Anna quickly continued. Theories about the formation of life from simple chemical substances, such as the Miller-Urey experiment, though based on the work of a Russian scientist and his student, only explain how life could have been created if the substances used in the laboratory were also present in the same proportions in the 'primordial soup'.

I wondered whether communist education hadn't, after all, damaged her in some way.

When Anna also argued against Darwinism, claiming it pushed Lamarck's theory aside, I asked if Lamarck had also been a Russian and Anna silenced me by pushing her tongue deep into my mouth.

French, she said, like my kiss. But I've said enough. Now it's your turn.

I don't have such scholarly arguments, I said bashfully. Science's answers are not sufficient – but are pointers in the right direction, whereas God – as an answer to the big questions – amounts to nothing more than speculation that bases itself on writings we're forbidden to question. In my view it's simply irrational to accept that.

And our love, that's rational?

Not really, I admitted.

Then forget about rationalism and come to church.

And so, wrapped in heavy overcoats against the freezing cold, we found ourselves standing in a long line in front of St Isaac's Cathedral, across the bridge that links our island with the centre of town.

The gigantic Cathedral – a cube-shaped structure of grey stone with a large gilded dome, a row of steps at the front, and brown granite columns – enabled each of the ten thousand people who gathered there with us to enter through its magnificent wooden doors. Once inside we found a narrow space for ourselves on one of the benches at the very back.

I couldn't understand a word of the prayer service, but the magnificence of the building, the singing of the choir, and the moments of utter silence as the priest and monks performed various ritual ceremonies with the candles they held, inspired a feeling of sanctity in me. Anna's presence undoubtedly added to that sense and neither my atheism nor my rationality could explain it.

After the holiday, HQ concluded that the time had come to speak to me and it was decided that Yoav should be the one to do this. He's liable to try and ignore you, he was told during a detailed briefing. Be assertive but at the same time be sensitive.

Despite the cold I was walking slowly on my way to a solitary lunch. The tall, pale-skinned young man of an indiscernible European appearance coming towards me looked like someone I knew. But it took me time to remember where from. I'd been HQ's representative in one of the operations in which Yoav participated as a team member. Though we hadn't spoken then, I was with him during both briefings and debriefings. Another second passed before my brain clocked the obvious. This is no chance encounter that sometimes happens in the course of operational work. In such circumstances there is no option but to ignore the individual and leave him behind surprised and offended. Yoav was here on purpose. He'd come specifically to see me.

I decided to walk on regardless. I thought that that would also send the appropriate message to Israel. I gave up on going into Sbarro and walked ahead paying no attention to him. But he caught up with me and adjusted his pace to mine.

Shalom Paul, he said.

I continued to walk straight on.

Paul, hello, he repeated in a slightly louder voice.

I upped my pace, as did Yoav. He decided on a more direct approach.

Yogev, I'm here on behalf of HQ. Are you prepared to sit down somewhere and talk?

I had to make the situation clear to the young man. I stopped and looked him in the eye.

Were you talking to me? I asked in English.

Paul, let's stop this, he said in Hebrew. I'm Yoav. Perhaps you don't remember me. I've come with a very important message and I'm asking that we sit and talk.

I am awfully sorry but I didn't understand a word of what you just said, I told him and continued walking.

Yoav repeated that he had a message from Israel which he wanted to pass on to me. I continued to ignore him and turned towards the next restaurant along the way. Do you mind if I join you? Yoav asked, switching to English in an attempt to soften my recalcitrance.

If you join me I'll consider that harassment and ask the doorkeeper to throw you out, I replied. Distressed, and wanting very much to pass on the message, Yoav momentarily put his hand on my shoulder and said quickly, it's been decided that you have to return to Israel immediately because Anna Petrovna Starzava is an FSB spy catcher.

Angrily I shrugged his hand from my shoulder but he must have seen the shock on my face as I left him standing there and entered the restaurant.

Even the waiter sensed my agitation and asked if I was OK. Impatiently I nodded as if to say 'yes' and he directed me to a table in the corner. For quite some time I completely failed to take on board what Yoav had said. I'd imagined I would hear a demand to return to Israel but I had to repeat the second part of what he said over and over again in my mind so as to get to grips with its significance.

The words, Anna Petrovna Starzava is an FSB spy catcher, reverberated in my mind. Anna Petrovna is a spy catcher. What are they trying to say? What does it mean? Can it be true? Can they say such a thing just to get me back home? I didn't tell them her paternal name, Petrovna. That they found out for themselves which means they'd set in motion an intensive intelligence gathering operation around me – the grim picture was becoming a little clearer in my mind.

I'd given the waiter an order but the food remained on the table in front of me, untouched. I applied real force to try and focus my thoughts. My immediate inclination was to dismiss what I'd been told out of hand. Where did they dig up such nonsense? Even if it's not simply a cooked-up story there's undoubtedly an Anna Starzava who is a spy catcher. Then, a few dormant instincts of the spy I'd been were re-awakened and again I went over in my mind our innocent first meeting which she most certainly didn't initiate. Our entirely natural conversation. Her reserve. The slowness of the contact that was made between us. And then her love, her full, absolute love, leapt into my thoughts. What are they talking about for God's sake? And besides, what sort of spy catcher runs a bookstore? Something about the shop had slightly bothered me, yes, but why would a preventative intelligence service apply such resources to trap me, a semi-dormant Mossad commercial agent. It's total nonsense, and doubly so in view of the genuineness of her life with me. If there is such a spy catcher it's not my Anna.

406

Without touching the food and unwilling to call the waiter and explain, I left more money on the table than was necessary and left quickly for the shop, very worried. But Yoav was waiting for me.

He had been sitting on a bench by the restaurant and without any preliminaries he stood up and asked, have you thought about what I said? We want you to return to Israel immediately.

Young man, I replied angrily, if I see your face again you won't know what's hit you.

Yoav stepped back. It was clear to him that I meant every word. He didn't even try to follow me.

I couldn't conceal my fury from Anna but fortunately for me there were several customers in the shop. She looked enquiringly towards me and without managing to smile I signalled with my hand that nothing had happened. She delayed leaving for her lunch so she could talk to me, but several customers stayed put, among them one of the two young women I remembered from the restaurant. Now I was able to make the connection. So they want to see what I'll do after the warning. What did they think, that I was about to take Anna and run away? Run off without her? Accuse her of betraying me to the FSB?

In fact, the presence of the operative – later on I learned that this was Debbie – made me calm down. I was now in operational mode, self controlled and calculating. I made a sign to Anna that she should go for lunch. She apparently saw that I had calmed down but when she returned a short while later I suspected that she too hadn't eaten anything.

The hours before the shop closed restored my peace of mind. There had been a mistake in the office, and I didn't intend to pay for that. I also decided that I wouldn't change my routine in any way. I must have appeared so calm that even when there were no more customers Anna didn't ask what had happened to me. I didn't want us to spend an entire evening at home and said I was still hungry. Anna was also ravenous and so once more we took Yoav's people to a good restaurant. I noticed a couple who came in a short while after us. I had only a vague recollection of their faces from the previous week, but in the days that followed I saw them again and again. They were Harry and Rosy. Yoav kept himself at a distance and I didn't see him again. I also didn't know whether the other operatives realized that I was already able to recognize them and had accepted that their presence was known to me, or simply hadn't noticed that I'd sussed them out?

It wasn't the knowledge that they were around me that was disturbing but its implication. That the Mossad insisted on returning me home. I felt my hands were tied. I didn't want to escape alone and couldn't do so with Anna, revealing this crazy tale to her and, so it seemed to me, then losing her.

A number of days passed without there being any development. What other plans did the Mossad have?

Yoav's team didn't continue to follow us beyond the time allotted, and one day they all disappeared from view. I assumed – an assumption that proved to be correct – that others were filling in for them. And then, waiting for me, was yet another surprise.

36

AT FIRST HE simply tried to ignore me, Yoav said in the meeting that took place in the Mossad chief's bureau. For Yoav to be in Netzach's presence was a huge experience but he managed to deliver his report of what had happened to him fluently. I'm sure he recognized me, he said. Although there was no one else around, he seemed to be behaving the way we are taught to when suddenly encountering an acquaintance during an operation abroad. But he continued to ignore me and in the end was aggressive and threatened to have the restaurant's doorman deal with me.

But you managed to deliver the message to him? Udi repeated what he already knew from an earlier briefing to make things clear to the chief.

Yes, though it was brief. I told him that the Mossad demanded he come back because Anna Petrovna Starzava is a spy catcher.

And how did he respond? the chief wanted to know.

He shrugged me off and went into the restaurant, saying nothing. But you could see the look of worry on his face. I think he was in shock.

Tell us about Rosy, Udi said.

Yes, Yoav continued. We sent one of the operatives whom he doesn't know into the restaurant and she reported that he ate nothing. There was food on the table, but he didn't touch it. And afterwards, on the way back, once he'd had time to digest what I'd said, he not only ignored my demand, but also threatened to beat me up.

It's not the sort of thing you internalize in half an hour, the chief said. And your team continued to sit on him and saw nothing unusual?

Debbie was in the shop when he got back, and saw nothing out of the ordinary. Later on he'd clearly identified us, linked the faces he saw on the days before with those that appeared on the days after, and still continued to maintain his regular routine. He either doesn't realize the seriousness of the situation or he's playing a game.

I want to play devil's advocate for a moment, Udi said. What if he's already realized that Anna is who she is and he's toying with her? Perhaps he'd already had some slight suspicions and what Yoav told him confirmed them, and now he has to continue the game until there's an opportunity for him to escape?

It's a bit farfetched isn't it? the chief said.

But it could also explain why he ignored Yoav and the team. That way he was actually protecting them. If she's a spy catcher and he's under some sort of surveillance, Yoav's team would have been arrested if Paul had not ignored them.

But he really was in shock, Yoav said.

One doesn't contradict the other, Udi insisted. And I'll tell you something else. Perhaps him leaving the office and opening the shop was intended to distract the FSB from what we were doing?

Look, we do live in an extremely manipulative world, a world of reverse psychology. But it seems to me that you've gone too far with your assumptions, the chief said. Our working assumption has to be that he's made up his mind to sever contact with us and stay with her despite knowing that we've found him and despite hearing from us that his girl friend is a spy catcher. What's the new team reporting now?

We've sent out a very young team. They've come straight out of the course. They're practically the only ones that Paul doesn't know. This is, in fact, their first experience of real work but some of them are graduates of the Shin Bet operational unit and some learned the ropes in the police undercover unit. So there aren't any real novices among them. In any case, they've been instructed to keep their distance from him. Gonen, the commander of the team, reports that Paul and his partner are keeping to their routine.

OK; that's to say, things are not OK, Netzach commented after thanking Yoav and asking him to leave the room. If, a week after Yoav warned Paul in the clearest possible way he's still carrying on as usual, then we have a problem. We cannot allow this situation to continue for too long, nor can we simply leave him there. We've reached the point where we have to start deciding on kidnapping options.

I just want to say that the fact that Yoav's team got back in one piece shows that Paul hasn't defected, Udi said.

When I read this remark of Udi's in the transcripts, and despite everything he did to me afterwards, I couldn't but appreciate his attempts, at that stage, to protect me.

You may be right, but not necessarily so, Netzach told him. He has perhaps crossed the line but hasn't turned into such a SOB as to cause the arrest of his ex-team mates. A sentimental deserter. And perhaps it's also clear to him that if he betrays the guys, the next team will put a bullet in his head and that he's better off keeping quiet.

Nonetheless, I'm still for having one more go at convincing him before we decide on a kidnapping, Udi suggested. Look, Yoav doesn't have a common history with him, he doesn't owe Yoav anything. I don't believe that he would ignore me or Levanon in the same way. It's worth a try.

I agree, the chief said. Where is Levanon?

He should be getting back from the Gulf tomorrow evening.

On what documentation?

His French documents.

Let him buy a fur coat and fly to Russia. I don't want you to do it. You've now got three or four teams abroad haven't you?

Five.

So you continue running your operations. Levanon's in the Gulf working on a delegation from Venezuela isn't he?

Udi confirmed that he was.

Has he got to be there till tomorrow evening?

Most of the work has been done and the rest is planned for tonight.

So let him leave tomorrow morning. He can sleep on the plane. Have him briefed in detail.

I also want to try something else in the meantime. I want to slip our Russian, Roman, into the shop to have a bit of a sniff. Mainly around Anna.

Just as long as he doesn't also fall in love. Oh, I forgot to ask Yoav if she's really worth all of this.

He didn't say anything, so apparently he wasn't particularly taken by her, Udi replied.

I didn't notice Roman as he walked around the shop. He'd possibly arrived while I was out for lunch. In any event, his report which I read a long time afterwards exonerated Anna: Anna Petrovna, Roman wrote, gives the impression of being an experienced bookseller. I approached her pretending to be a student of comparative literature seeking material on existentialist writers from different periods and various countries. She suggested I read Ibsen and Kierkegaard to get an idea of the origins of existentialism in literature and philosophy and pointed in particular to Peer Gynt's dictum 'unto thine own self be true'. It's difficult to imagine an inexperienced sales-woman, or someone working undercover, being able to cite such a thing – although she didn't mention its source – *Hamlet*. I only found this out when I looked up the quotaion. Then she referred me to Heidegger and his *Dasein*. She also, of course, suggested I read Nietzsche and then took me to a shelf of French books picking out Camus and Sartre. Despite that maybe seeming obvious, she did, for example, know the difference between Sartre's idea of freedom in his philosophical writings and in his trilogy *The Roads to Freedom*. She was extremely knowledgeable about existentialism in Russian literature but that, I suppose, is no big deal.

My impression is that this is a genuine literary woman

and a skilled and learned book seller. I allow myself to add, Roman concluded, that she is also very pleasant.

I warned you, the chief told Udi on the phone when he'd read out Roman's report. Don't let the guy anywhere near her, I don't need another love sick adolescent on my hands.

But just a minute, what about what the report actually says. It sounds pretty convincing, doesn't it? Udi tried to assert himself. But the chief wasn't persuaded.

The Russian educational system is possibly less screwed up than ours and the lady maybe very knowledgeable. And maybe, by chance, she might have studied literature and philosophy before enlisting in the KGB. None of that must be allowed to delay Levanon's travel plans.

Meanwhile, in response to the clarifications passed on to him, 'Cotton Field' reported from his sources in the FSB that Anna Petrovna Starzava, an employee of the organization, had opened a shop with a man suspected of being a spy.

I hope that puts to bed any doubts you may still have, Netzach said to Udi. And stop operating like someone suffering from heartburn. Change gear and hit the accelerator. We have to cut short all these interim steps and produce results. I want to see him here in two weeks, tops. We are playing with fire.

For over a week I didn't see any of the Mossad people anywhere near me. I'd almost managed to suppress the memory of my traumatic encounter with Yoav, and after

I'd convinced myself that a mistake had been made in the Mossad, I returned almost completely to my routine. The temperature in the second half of January plummeted to minus twenty. Even those who dressed in the warmest clothes felt stabs of freezing air piercing their eyes, threatening to remove them from their sockets. Every bit of exposed skin ached and only those who absolutely had to, came into the shop. Over the previous two days the weather had also been very stormy and Anna and I brought food from the house so that we wouldn't have to go out to a restaurant. We took advantage of a time when no one was in the shop to eat. It gave us a new sense of intimacy and we considered making it a regular habit during especially cold winter days. But on that particular day Anna fancied a hot soup and went out to a nearby restaurant. I sat at my desk eating the sandwich we'd made at home.

Immediately after Anna left, in came a tall man wearing a woollen coat that went down to below his knees, fur overshoes, and a fur hat with ear muffs. His mouth and nose were covered by a scarf and a pair of shades protected his eyes. He looked around and then slowly unwrapped the scarf. As he ambled towards me he removed his glasses and then his hat. Only at that moment did I recognize him. I felt a breach opening in my heart.

Levanon smiled. A smile that communicated such closeness and warmth that it could have made me lose control of my senses altogether. I felt the empathy and fondness slipping through the breach, diving down into my gut, and my stomach muscles tightening to fend off the sudden and disarming invasion of my being. From his expression it was clear that he'd noticed the look on my face tighten.

I'm here in friendship, he said in Hebrew tinged with a French accent that mimicked a well-known Israeli TV comedian and would have got an automatic response from virtually every Israeli. I was almost seduced, just a second away from responding in a similar accent and then regained my composure.

I beg your pardon sir?

Levanon smiled and sat on the edge of my desk, towering over me. Hi Paul, he said, stretching out his hand.

My hands kept holding on to the sandwich. There was no offer of a handshake from me.

Yogev, after half a year of not seeing one another you don't even shake my hand?

Sir, I don't understand a word you're saying. Do you mind getting off my desk?

As he told me later, this particular sentence prompted a great many laughs when Levanon repeated it at HQ on his return. He said that momentarily he'd even asked himself whether this wasn't a case of mistaken identity and that perhaps there was simply an extraordinary resemblance between me and an innocent bookseller in St Petersburg that had misled everybody.

The desk, from which Levanon did indeed elegantly remove himself, was my last defence, if not the actual battle field on which my future would be determined.

Levanon decided to take maximum advantage of the

lull in the shop. He came through the gap between my desk and Anna's, sat in her chair, and pulled it towards me.

What do you think you're doing? I asked raising my voice. But Levanon was quick to silence me.

Cut the bullshit Paul, he said now raising his voice in turn and then switching back to Hebrew. You don't want to return to Israel, you insist on staying here, you want to claim that Anna isn't a spy catcher – OK, but let's talk about it. Stop evading the issue because if you do the next stage will be much more painful.

I shook my head. I wasn't about to give in and yet he'd managed to take the wind out of my sails. Sorry, sorry but you have to leave, I said.

I knew that Levanon was right. I knew he'd come 'in friendship', that talking things over with him was the correct thing to do and that, if the Mossad was indeed determined, then the next stage would be twice as painful. It was also right for me to hear what he had to say about Anna. But I wasn't capable of conducting this dialogue. I felt I had to hold on to Paul's persona, the Canadian businessman who'd opened a bookstore in St Petersburg with his sweetheart. If I allowed the smallest of cracks to open in the wrapping around this persona it would crumble completely.

Levanon's handsome face now had an expression of real pain on it. Even of empathy.

Enough of these games, Yogev, he quite literally pleaded. You're up to your neck in it. We have reliable sources who've told us that Anna Petrovna Starzava is employed by the FSB as a spy catcher. They have information that you are a spy. She was assigned to you and I don't know what happened after that.

I said nothing and Levanon took advantage of my attentiveness. It's possible that she was convinced by your cover story and stopped spying on you. It's also possible that she's still spying on you. She may have already exposed you and the only reason you're not in jail is because they're trying to recruit you. And perhaps she's really fallen in love with you independently of her assignment. Perhaps you both think you can spend the rest of your lives here. But that's not going to happen, Paul, Yogev, whichever you prefer. We are determined to bring you back home, because we can't allow ourselves to let you fall into their hands. I hope you believe me. I haven't dived fifty degrees – from plus thirty in the Gulf to minus twenty here – just to trick you. And it would be a thousand times better if you leave of your own accord. You can regard the last sentence as friendly advice, even a friendly pleading.

There was silence. I knew I didn't have much time. Customers could come in at any moment. Anna could come back. I neither wanted to, nor could I, respond to his appeal, however sincerely meant. The transition back and forth between my two worlds seemed impossible to me. At that moment the only chance I saw was to entrench myself behind my cover story. I knew that this was something that happens even during the training course when a trainee is told not to drop his cover under any circumstances. He's arrested and interrogated but then, when he's released from the police station, he fails to realize that the exercise is over and refuses to abandon his cover. Like the Japanese soldiers who emerged from their holes in the ground thirty years after the war had ended. I also knew of a case in which this phenomenon required psychiatric intervention. To say nothing of operatives who fell in love with their new identity and who, when they returned home and had to give up their cover, suffered serious mental problems.

Perhaps they'll buy this pretence in Israel, I thought. Perhaps they'll agree that Yogev Ben-Ari has been expunged together with everything he knew and poses no danger. Even if they don't buy it, it will clarify for the Mossad just how adamant I am. I'm staying here. What can they do, turn me over to the authorities? Certainly not. They won't kill me. That's well beyond the red line. As for kidnapping me, if they truly believe that this is a rescue from the jaws of the FSB, that will be really difficult for them to do.

Look, mister, you seem to be a nice guy, but you obviously have mistaken me for somebody else. Now you must leave. If not I will have to call the police.

Levanon concealed a brief smile. He too understood the boundaries of the game and knew that I certainly wouldn't call the police. He slipped his hand into the inside pocket of his coat, momentarily startling me. Instinctively I got ready to grab his hand and punch him in the face.

Levanon froze, appeared serious for a moment, then smiled again: your instincts are still good. But I just wanted to give you something. He slowly pulled out a small bundle of pictures from his pocket and placed them on my desk. Take them, refresh your memory a little.

The first was a picture of Levanon and me on Victoria Peak, high up on the mountainside above Hong Kong. Udi had taken the photo on the observation deck overlooking the city's skyscrapers and the bay. You remember Zaif? he asked. Two bullets of yours and the third that I had to fire to complete the job? That's the only reason why, today, the Syrians don't have another chemical weapons plant.

I didn't touch the pictures and Levanon picked them up.

You must realize what an effort was made to send me the pictures from Israel so that they would arrive at the same time as me, and yet you ignore them? Have some manners man. He laid them down on my desk again, one after another. The next shot was also of the two of us together, this time in a local restaurant in Seoul. Here it was Rashid Nuri with the prostitutes, remember? You fired three into his back and I two into his head.

When he put a photo on my desk taken by the pool in a hotel in the Emirates he asked, remember Mustafa Quader?

Next were pictures from Kazakhstan. Remember the missile transporters? If it wasn't for us being there the Iranians would long ago have had intercontinental rockets with nuclear war heads.

In another picture, I saw myself on a golden sandy beach surrounded by palm and coconut trees with my back to a turquoise sea and a speed boat. The Seychelles, in case you've forgotten, Levanon said. You brought down two Arabs, one carrying a shoulder missile and the other the launcher. You fired and hit the target from a distance of a few hundred metres and saved a plane carrying hundreds of passengers. Then you saved me in the committee of enquiry because I shot at the rest of the group without any real justification.

I breathed in deeply. I felt how these images, rolling out fifteen years of operations were, picture after picture, delivering powerful hammer blows at the suit of armour I had wrapped around myself. And for some reason one recent picture in particular hit home; a Hanukkah party at the Division. Led by Udi, all my acquaintances were there, smiling on the other side of a lit candelabra, some of them holding a doughnut. Apart from Anna, I thought, this is, after all, my only family. A family to which I am connected by blood, though it was a different kind of blood connection.

From the expression on his face it was clear that Levanon understood what I was thinking.

Yogev, the country owes you a great deal. You did so much for it. Why are you destroying everything? Come home.

I don't know where this conversation might have lead to had a customer not entered the shop at that very moment. As the cliché goes, a picture is worth a thousand words, and these had shown me the extent to which my new façade had failed to cut me off from my past.

Get up, I said to Levanon, my lips pursed. He slowly rose from Anna's chair, gathered the pictures, returned them to his coat pocket, and moved to the other side of the desk.

I am still here, he said as the customer came towards me. At that very moment Anna entered the shop almost running.

Bozhe moi, my God, it's cold outside, she said, laughing and rubbing her hands together.

I was too bewildered to deal with the Russian-speaking customer. Before even taking off her coat Anna leapt to my rescue by signalling the customer to come to her. Levanon, meanwhile, wandered between the bookshelves and when Anna was free, went up to her and asked in French whether we stocked modern Russian writers in French translation. Anna answered him in a French that wasn't at all bad. Levanon was surprised, even confused for a moment – he hadn't really intended to put his cover to the test.

I, too, was surprised. At the beginning of our acquaintance I'd spoken to her about my complex relations with the language of Quebec and she hadn't said a thing and had continued to talk to me in English quite naturally. My cover story would also have been undermined a bit if she'd insisted on switching to French – the Mossad was content with the four years I'd spent studying the language in high school and invested time and effort only in improving my English.

Though translated Russian literature was on the borderline between Anna's section and mine, I decided to leave the rest of the dealings with Levanon to her. They remained for a while at the counter, laughing and chattering to each other. Eventually Levanon left with two books by Platonov and Kurkov. He paid Anna and before leaving the shop, tall and erect, managed to sneak a slight smile at me – the meaning of which I didn't even want to attempt to interpret.

I didn't like him, Anna said to me after he'd gone. Rather than wanting to buy, I felt he was trying to find out how much I knew about the translation of Russian books into other languages. Who gets translated, which subjects are more popular, and what are the languages they are most often translated into – and all of it in a sort of artificial light-heartedness. Even his accent was strange. Not Parisian nor from the south, perhaps French Canadian, what do you think? You should know.

I don't think so, I answered, he's suntanned, perhaps from the colonies. I decided not to relate to the question of his accent and not to encourage a conversation about my French.

A few days ago someone else, rather like him, came into the shop, Anna said.

What do you mean 'like him'? I asked, slightly apprehensively.

He was, in fact, Russian, but he too asked questions that you would normally expect to be answered by your professor at university, not a salesperson in a bookshop. Fortunately, I love the existentialists so I could help him. But out of all the books I suggested he bought only Sartre. What a pathetic choice, the simplest and most pompous of the existentialists. At least he bought the whole trilogy. I think he was a Jew by the way, she said, and I held my breath. And this last one as well, she added.

You know how to spot Jews? I asked in a strained tone.

Sometimes. You for example, if you hadn't told me that you are half Indian I would have thought that you were Jewish, she said, briefly glancing at me. But that's OK, she answered the questions that had welled up inside me within a second. I value Jews very much. A wise nation, stubborn, unfortunate, and heroic. I had some good friends at university who emigrated to Israel in the 1990s and I miss their friendship very much.

The raging suspicions that had sprouted quickly wilted like a field of wild plants.

You keep surprising me. This time with your French, I said to bring the discussion about Jews to an end.

French was once the language of the intelligentsia in Russia and there are remnants of that in the educational system, my sweetheart told me. In high school, as well as at university, that was the first foreign language I studied. Before English and German. But I knew it was a language you weren't fond of so I didn't think it right to flaunt it.

You have any other skills I should know about? I asked.

I know a bit of German, and I was a ballet dancer when I weighed twenty kilos less. And you wouldn't believe it but I once trained in judo. If you want I'll show you some exercises at home tonight.

And at home Anna did indeed show me some throws from the hip and shoulder exercises as well as a number of pinning moves on the carpet. It turned into one of the wildest lovemaking episodes we ever had, the only one during which I literally ripped her clothes off as we wrestled with one another, both screaming as we twisted and turned and when I came into her. Behind our screams, and behind our grappling and throttling and the pain we inflicted on each other, was the vague understanding that neither of us wanted to allow into our consciousness. My realization that something in what Yoav and Levanon had told me was right, and her recognition that someone was snooping around us, that there was something bad in the air. The feeling of an approaching end that hovered over our love proved to be a highly intoxicating aphrodisiac. We made love again and again. We moaned in a mixture of pain and pleasure and we cried, our screams and weeping preventing us from voicing what deep deep down in our gut we could already feel.

37

LEVANON WANTS TO know if you have a message for him, asked the young man who came up to me in the street the following morning. In a fit of anger and frustration I punched him in the shoulder and shouted, fuck off you bastard. The surprised lad stumbled backwards and nearly lost his balance. He stopped following me. My answer had been clear.

Levanon watched the spat from a slow moving car behind me. Having understood my response he took off for home. Late that night he presented himself at Udi's house and in the morning both were summoned to see the head of the Mossad.

As far as I'm concerned, our patience with him has run out, Netzach said when he'd heard Levanon's account.

There is a limit to everything, and I don't know what price we'll have to pay for the fact that he already knows we are onto him and are determined to get him back to Israel. It's clear that to kidnap him will now be much more complicated. Have you a plan to show me?

Udi and Levanon glanced at each other in embarrassment. We began to work on one, assigned an intelligence officer and a project manager to the job, but the plan wasn't completed because Levanon left for the Gulf, Udi said.

That's not good enough, the chief responded. Before the end of the evening I want you to present an outline plan to me summarizing every step, I want a team that will begin to train by tomorrow morning, and I want to see a dry run the day after tomorrow. The team must be ready to leave within three days at most. If you need infrastructure personnel in Russia to get apartments, vehicles, a plane, a yacht, whatever – I want them to be ready to leave tomorrow after I approve the plan tonight in principle.

Levanon cleared his throat. I know that we've tried and so far failed to convince him, but I still don't think we need to kidnap him.

And do what? Your powers of persuasion haven't exactly proved themselves, the chief said tetchily.

That's right, but it did something to him. I saw it on his face when I spoke to him about Anna and when I showed him the pictures.

I heard the same thing from that young chap, what's his name? said the chief.

Yoav, said Udi.

Exactly, from Yoav. He also saw all sorts of signs of a response on Paul's face. But the bottom line is that he threw you out of there and saw your guy off by pushing him away, isn't that right?

Nonetheless, I'm asking for permission, in parallel with the preparations we're making for a kidnapping, to also propose some additional options and then you'll decide between them.

What additional options? I won't accept anything that means postponing Paul's arrival here, which as far as I'm concerned has to happen within a week from today at the outside.

Levanon and I spent half the night fine-tuning the various options, Udi said. We both think that what Paul needs to be convinced is some sort of proof that Anna really is a KGB woman and then he'll leave.

What do you want to do, show him the records of the meetings with Cotton Field?

No, we thought of cooking up proof that Anna is what we think she is and not what he thinks, Udi said somewhat uneasily.

In conjunction with the psychological warfare department?

We wanted to do it with our people on the ground.

Let me have a plan tonight for that as well, the chief concluded.

In the evening the head of the Mossad approved the two plans of action presented to him by Udi, Levanon, and the division's head of intelligence. The plan to kidnap Paul, and the plan to incriminate Anna.

I intend to present these to the prime minister at our weekly meeting tomorrow, Netzach said. Prepare a one-page summary for me of the operational order for kidnapping and on another page the operational order for incrimination. To include a paragraph on possible risks and a summary of the known intelligence. And start training, he said in parting.

Udi wavered for a while about who should be the team's commander. Boaz had accumulated experience and knew the territory, but was dark skinned and wouldn't blend in well with the locals of St Petersburg. In the end, however, Udi decided to rely on the icy cold weather that required people to wrap themselves up from head to toe, and assigned Boaz to the job.

Early in the morning, eight operatives reported to the operational squad's training facility. Also present in the briefing room were HQ personnel involved in the operation. Members of the team sat on chairs facing a big screen with Udi standing in front of them.

I want, first of all, to emphasize the sensitivity of the operation and its highly classified nature, Udi began. We are dealing with an Israeli citizen, and not just any Israeli, but one of us and not only one of us but a skilled operative whom most of you know. He is suspected of crossing the line and is now in some sort of contact with the FSB – the KGB in a new guise – and particularly with one of the female workers there. On the face of it, this is a romantic relationship but we don't know what lies beneath the surface.

His audience listened attentively and Udi went on to

present the background to the operation and its objectives.

I don't yet know what we will and what we won't be authorized to do. In the meantime we're preparing for two possibilities, one decidedly less attractive than the other. Kidnapping is in all circumstances a complicated action and in this case five times more so. Firstly, because it involves one of our own whom we don't want to harm. So he's not to be drugged with any fast-acting substances, nor is he to be subjected to violence of the sort that might injure him. Secondly, it's highly complicated because this is a skilled man, at least as skilled as any one of you. Even if he's slightly out of shape it will be difficult to overpower him. Thirdly, because he's expecting us. He knows that we've followed him and that we're determined to get him back home. So it will be much more difficult to sneak up on him, or lead him into a trap. Fourthly, there's the arena itself. Russia is not a target country but you must not treat it as a friendly country. St Petersburg may be as beautiful as Paris or London, but it is neither Paris nor London and there are drunks and Mafiosi who run the city from sunset till dawn. Russia is a police state and that will make every move of ours there difficult – from the renting of a car and an apartment all the way to crossing borders. And fifthly, there is the complication of the female involved being a KGB woman, obviously alert and aware, and our man is liable to be under some sort of surveillance.

Boaz raised his hand. Is it not reasonable to say, in light of what you have just told us that, for example, it will in fact be necessary to use real physical force and a fast-acting tranquillizer?

Questions at the end, Udi said. He saw the serious faces peering at him, knew how justified the question was, but continued.

The second option, incrimination, looks easier because it doesn't involve any acts of violence. No one has to be put in a crate and taken across a border, etc. But most of the drawbacks I noted previously apply also to this option. It involves operating against people who are alert, skilled and who might be under surveillance. That applies to both Paul and his girlfriend. It may be that incrimination requires photography, eavesdropping, or breaking into their apartment. In this particular territory all of these are highly sensitive actions. From a political point of view, the consequences of something going badly wrong and an arrest could be calamitous. You have to bear all of this in mind at all times. And in addition to everything else it's bloody cold there.

Giggles and murmurings of confusion could be heard as Udi sat down and Levanon rose to explain the main points of the plan of action. He switched on the projector. On the screen in front of the group appeared the operation's codename 'Cat in Snow'. The lights were dimmed, and there was, once again, silence.

Levanon explained the main moves in my kidnapping that appeared on the screen. They included seizing me in the shop when no one else was there; as I went out for lunch, provided the street was empty; or on my way home in the dark, if I was alone – as the preferred options.

As for the kidnapping technique, he said, you'll be

practising it during the day with the close combat instructor and we will then make a final decision. But the general idea is to kidnap and bundle him into a vehicle.

When I read about all of this in the transcripts it seemed to me entirely fanciful. Like reading a thriller rather than the operational order for kidnapping me. When I said this to Levanon he told me that for him it was so real that he couldn't sleep at nights because of the stomach pains it caused him. Pains that were not evident in the cold and calculated language used in operational orders.

Levanon went on to present the stages of the getaway plan; first to a nearby safe house then administering any treatment Paul may require, and finally choosing between two main options. The first, a yacht in St Petersburg's harbour for a short sail to Finland, if everything isn't still frozen, and from there continuing the homeward journey by other means. The second, taking off in an executive jet from the city's airport. Our people are already on their way to Russia to organize all of these different possibilities.

Now, as far as incriminating her is concerned, he continued, the objective, he read from the written text, is to produce evidence proving to Paul that Anna is an FSB woman trying to expose him as a Mossad agent. The nature of the action will be dictated by the reality on the ground. It can include photographs, if we find a way of obtaining incriminating photos of her, or recordings if we can find things she has said that can be presented in such a way.

I don't understand, a young operative by the name of Nitza said as she raised her hand. What if there are no situations or statements of hers that can be presented like that?

She only needs to do half the work, Levanon replied. We'll do the rest.

Doctoring her recorded voice plus photomontages, Boaz volunteered, spelling out what was actually meant.

Which is to say that even if she is not spying on him we will show her as doing exactly that? Nitza continued with her question.

Udi got up and spoke to the assembled group. If that saves us from having to kidnap him, then yes. Remember that the mission is to return him to Israel within a week. We have to do it quickly, smoothly, and elegantly.

It's not really elegant, Zohar, the second female member of the team, commented.

Please no gratuitous romanticism, Boaz intervened. Not elegant is when a person has to be beaten up and bleeds or when we are chased across Russia. Incrimination is very elegant. And if there's anybody here who prefers kidnapping to incrimination on the grounds of elegance they're in the wrong place.

Udi signalled to Boaz to take his seat. Everybody will get their chance to respond to the plans. I too think that it's not right to introduce into this the morality of the underworld according to which killing is tops, armed robbery comes a close second, and stealing is the least honourable action. Anyone prepared to kill and kidnap cannot justify having reservations about incrimination. Levanon continue please.

Levanon finished his presentation and was followed

by people from intelligence who gave a detailed survey of St Petersburg in particular and Russia in general, with an emphasis on the conduct of the security services. Eli, the security officer, concluded the analysis by talking about the need to maintain cover. He reminded everyone that the Christmas holidays were over, that this was no longer a tourist period in St Petersburg, that every foreigner attracted attention, and that in going about their work they all had to keep an especially low profile.

Now that the picture is clear, I return to Boaz's very proper question about the use of violence and sedation, Udi said. Here, all we can do is offer guidelines. We cannot possibly anticipate the fine detail of such an operation which ultimately will be dictated by the reality on the ground. So I say two things that you must bear in mind, the room for manoeuvre being down to your judgment in the field, Boaz. One – it is forbidden to cause him irreversible injury. Two, he must be brought back to Israel. Questions?

There were no further questions. The operatives went over to the big hangar next to their training facility and began practising a kidnapping. After a few hours' training, the most effective way of abducting me – either in the shop or while I was walking in the street – began to take shape. By the afternoon they felt sufficiently confident to ask Udi and Levanon to check out the drill.

The classroom desks brought into the shed represented the bookshelves in the shop, the plan of which was sketched on the hangar floor in chalk based on drawings prepared by Levanon. A commercial vehicle waiting nearby represented a car parked at the end of the road in which the shop was located. Naphtali, a short sturdy operative who was not a member of the team, represented me. Two customers, Simon and Kent, entered the improvised shop and made out that they were browsing through the books. Simon asked Naphtali for help. The latter went up to him and as the two were chatting Kent suddenly emerged from behind, grabbed Naphtali tightly by the neck, while Simon punched him hard in the stomach. At that moment, Lavi and Hagai burst into the shop. A sack was pulled over the head of the choked and semi-conscious Naphtali, his hands and legs were cuffed, and the four men quickly lifted and carried him to the door and from there to the vehicle outside. The side door of the commercial van was opened and, as if they were handling a carpet, the kidnappers shuffled their way into the vehicle.

We'll leave the comments for later, Udi said, let's now go on to the street drill.

The exercise of kidnapping 'Paul' while walking in the street included similar elements. Kent strode towards Naphtali and the rest of the operatives advanced a few metres behind him. When they were about to pass one another, Kent delivered a hard blow to poor Naphtali's stomach – only saved from serious injury by his exceptionally muscular physique. Within no more than a second, Simon closed in and grabbed Naphtali tightly by the neck. Hagai and Lavi helped to lift and quickly bundle him into the van. Boaz shut the doors and ordered the driver to go. Then the kidnappers were able to handcuff Paul and Nitza prepared the syringe.

434

The group crowded on to the two benches that had been placed at the entrance to the hangar. Udi patted Naphtali on the shoulder and suggested he drink a lot and apply some cream to his throat. Together with Levanon and the close combat instructor, Udi stood facing the operatives to propose ways of improving the drill.

Though they had quite a lot of suggestions to make, Udi and Levanon concluded by saying that the group had made significant progress, and that these plans for a kidnapping had a chance of success. On the face of it, kidnapping in the street is faster, but in the shop the violence it involves is not visible to the public, Udi commented. Meanwhile, both options are possible. The shop drill is taking you twenty five seconds. The street drill fifteen. We have to cut each by at least five seconds and we will then begin to think about other things that may happen and our responses: someone else coming into the shop, pedestrians getting involved, intervention by drivers passing by, and so on. You have the whole of tomorrow for this by which time, after you've completed the drills, I want to present a fully completed exercise to the head of the Mossad, including even a location that resembles the real one in St Petersburg. I've asked our administrative officer to find us a suitable shop and street in Tel Aviv.

In the meantime, Levanon added, we've made progress with the details of the plan, and I want you to devote this evening to studying it and the intelligence. You have to get to know St Petersburg well before you land there. The intelligence officers will arrive in an hour, so get ready for a long evening. After that, go back home to sleep. Pack, say goodbye to your partners, take the children to their kindergartens and schools tomorrow morning. We'll meet here at 10 a.m. and continue with the preparations until you leave for the airport. Your tickets have already been ordered. You'll be travelling in two groups of three, and one as a couple, to Berlin, Vienna and Budapest. By the following evening all of you will be in position in St Petersburg.

When they got back to their offices, Udi and Levanon found a summons from the head of the Mossad to come and see him.

I've just got back from Jerusalem, Netzach informed them. The prime minister didn't like the idea of a kidnapping in Russia. He said there were some very sensitive negotiations taking place about the nuclear reactor in Bushehr which was about to be completed. An operation mounted by us in Russia would cost us dearly.

So we've wasted a day exercising for nothing, Levanon said.

Suddenly you're for a kidnapping? the chief chided him. And anyway, kidnapping is not off the table, because the prime minister understands the danger involved in leaving Paul there. But he wants it to be a last resort.

We're keeping to the timetable, Udi said. The drills look good. If you want, you can see a rehearsal tomorrow afternoon, and tomorrow night the team will be leaving. By the next evening they'll be set up in St Petersburg.

Great! And another thing, the chief said. The prime minister wants someone senior on the ground. You, Udi, will be the one going. He also wants the fine details to be absolutely clear as well as the limitations on the risks to be taken. So you and I are going to meet him tomorrow at 6 a.m. before he starts his working day.

The prime minister duly received the two of them in his private office in the government building, sitting at his desk. He had been going over the morning's newspaper cuttings.

Udi, right? I remember you, the prime minister said without getting up or offering to shake his hand.

You'll be the commander in the field?

The team has a commander who's with them on the ground, but I'll be there, in touch and within eye contact, and I'll be the one with overall responsibility.

So listen, I want this to be clear. The bottom line is pretty simple. There are to be no screw ups in this operation. Meaning, there can be a mishap with that bandit, what's he called? Pierre, Paul, yes, Paul. With him you can mess up a bit, not desirable but still not a disaster. If you have to, use force against him. That, let's face it, is liable to happen in such an operation. What absolutely mustn't happen is that one of you gets caught or that the Russians even know that you've been there. Is that clear?

Udi nodded.

Great! Then I leave everything else to you.

38

Two days after Udi, Boaz, and their team landed in St Petersburg, the group met up in the apartment Alex had rented for operational use in a housing complex close to ours on the other side of the island. Because of the sensitivity of the operation Alex, who headed the department for Russia and the former Soviet Republics, was also there. With him he brought Boris, a man who'd grown up in St Petersburg and had now replaced Roman as the second of the infrastructure personnel. Udi, Boaz, and the Russian speakers toured the streets of the city in cars which Alex and Boris hired, explored its various sites, and checked out our neighbourhood and bookshop.

I've understood the conditions here, Udi said to his people. For the moment I think the kidnapping option has to be put on standby. True, there is a plane waiting at the airport, but sailing in a yacht is virtually impossible and, in any case, very unusual. So I don't see a way of complying with the prime minister's proviso to absolutely avoid running into any problems with the Russians. I cannot guarantee one hundred per cent that someone won't call the police who, bless them, are on every street corner, and I can't even begin to think about a chase on ice.

What do you mean by 'put on standby'? Boaz asked.

It means that the infrastructure personnel will continue with the preparations, but you and your team will now work full time on the second plan, incrimination.

But they're so sweet together! Nitza said.

Nitza! Boaz rebuked her.

What? the young woman protested. You were with me yesterday evening when we 'took' them to the café. You saw how they were holding hands and kissing, like a couple of young lovers!

Wow, Zohar sighed in a somewhat phoney rejoinder. I also saw them the day before yesterday walking home, embracing each other. She's ever so pretty and he's just so so.

Zohar! Boaz ticked her off as well. Be serious all of you, OK?

Boaz, Udi suppressed a smile, you've got to familiarise yourself with the house, the shop, the area, and I want you now to prepare a plan with your team to bug the apartment's phone line and also to assign people to document Anna leaving the shop. I want photos that can be modified to include another person. Also, when she's in a restaurant, alone or with Paul – we might cut Paul and everything that identifies the restaurant out of the photo and insert someone else into it. We'll see. When you've finished come up to my room in the hotel with a detailed plan for approval.

I have to say that this is not my cup of tea either, Kent said. Udi looked at him disapprovingly, ending Kent's intervention.

Later when I read the summaries of the reconnoitring and the probes, it actually gave me a few moments of satisfaction to see that at least some of the participants had felt outraged by their assignments.

*

Boaz prepared a plan for break-ins, installing wire taps, and taking pictures. He and most of those in his team had already participated in such operations in Europe and this time too, the plan didn't deviate from the norm.

I want to mount observations of Paul and Anna's house over the course of two consecutive days, to learn the routine in the building, Boaz told Udi as he presented his plan. I then want to gain entry into the building to locate the connection box into which all the tenants' phone wires run, identify Paul and Anna's specific line, connect into it and plant a small transmitter that will radio their conversations to the safe house. Alternatively, I want to enter the stairwell to check the lock of the apartment and then go in and hook up to the internal phone line. The pictures will be shot while Anna is followed on foot and from a moving vehicle, including having either a couple or just one person going into a restaurant immediately after her. The plan is no different to an operation in Switzerland, Boaz concluded.

You were still in high school, or maybe even in primary school, when we ran into problems in Bern, so you can allow yourself to talk like that. As for me, the word Switzerland still sends shivers down my spine, Udi told him. But in principle you are right, only you have to be extra cautious about security. If there is any doubt, you hold off.

Isn't it always like that? Boaz asked, feigning innocence.

If it was, there would be no screw ups but also no operations.

Isn't our motto 'zero screw ups'? Boaz laughed.

Yes, but not 'zero operations'. Come on get going now.

And Boaz, Udi continued, as much as you can, go in and out of the hotel wearing a hat and scarf. Though there are Asians and Caucasians in the city, 'I'm a Middle-Easterner' is writ large all over your face.

Locating our apartment within the huge blocks of buildings was not simple. It required following us very closely till the moment we arrived, then gaining entry into the complex to see which specific building we went into, and into the building itself, immediately after us, to discover on which floor the elevator stopped. The team managed to accomplish all these tasks without my spotting any of them.

At night, the temperature sunk to minus thirty and it became impossible to station a look-out on foot to monitor the building's routine. The same applied to a parked car, the windscreen was immediately covered in condensation. Boaz and his team had no option but to keep watch from a car with its engine running. This limited the amount of time they could stay put in any one place so they were forced to patrol the area, risking a possible run-in with a touring police vehicle.

The building's routine revealed that towards midnight the residents were already asleep and that after that time the team could do the work in relative safety. The entrance to the building was not guarded and Boaz's men found the connection box in the basement with its door unlocked. However, Alex and Boris were unable to pinpoint the apartment's phone number, listed in the name of the real estate agent and not ours. They couldn't, therefore, initiate a call to that line while other team members used butt sets to identify the pair of wires leading to the apartment.

Udi was forced to decide between two solutions offered by Boaz: one was to call the dozens of other residents whose names were in the phone book. While they were initiating these calls the team could get a fix on each pair of wires in the basement and, by a process of elimination, identify our line. The other option was to break into our apartment and simply dial out from there.

I don't want to wake up the tenants in the middle of the night while the team is in the basement, Udi decided. Breaking into the apartment is only possible during the day when it's empty. But that also means working in the basement when the building is alive. Neither solution is ideal, he concluded. After some hesitation he authorized a break-in.

The whole team took part in preparing for the lunchtime break-in, and Udi held a briefing session in the safe house. He assigned Alex to Simon and Kent – who were to break into the apartment – and Boris was attached to Boaz and Zohar whose task was to go into the basement.

I'm sorry if it's not to your liking but I want you, Zohar, to dress like a whore and I'm sure that any chance passer-by will readily accept that Boris and Boaz are your clients. Boaz will be with you inside the basement and Boris will wait outside. And you, he said turning to the three would-be housebreakers, if there is any kind of

442

disturbance you've simply made a mistake about which building you were supposed to be in. Alex, you'd better look tipsy which will explain why you got muddled.

The team worked on fine-tuning other possible chance happenings and responses to them. But there were no such incidents either in the apartment or in the basement. Kent and his two men broke into the apartment. Simon called the airport's automated answering service, and Alex searched the place. They're certainly living the high life, he said to Kent and Simon. I've found a season ticket here to the philharmonic and another one for the opera. There's a performance of Pushkin's *Eugene Onegin* in three days time, anybody interested? I somehow doubt they'll be using it.

In the basement, Boaz and Zohar, in order to monitor calls, attached butt sets to the dozens of different wires and finally identified the pair on which they could hear the list of flights taking off and landing.

I must remind you that this was only half the job, Udi told the satisfied operatives when they left the building to go to their cars. Have a rest and then tonight we'll install the bugging device.

Since there was no need to return to the apartment, the teams shuffled roles and this time too there were no mishaps with the plan. The entry into the basement at 1 a.m. was smooth. Boaz, Simon, and Kent connected and concealed the transmitter quickly and efficiently while in the safe house Lavi announced that the reception signal was good. The group dispersed.

Excellent work. Tomorrow's another day, now go to sleep, said Udi. Who's on morning watch?

Hagai and Zohar, who'd taken on the role of drivers and spent the night behind the steering wheels of their cars, volunteered to start the morning following me and Anna from the house to the shop.

The head of the Mossad was pleased to hear that the apartment had been successfully bugged and that a significant number of pictures had been transmitted to HQ. I'm not building my hopes on the telephone conversations, he told Udi. Who knows if they even talk from there and if they do, about what. We won't get incriminating evidence from an order to the grocery store. But tell your guys to come up with the pictures and I want to see what they manage to do in the lab.

The pictures taken in the street of Anna going out to lunch or of both of us on our way to the shop and back, were merely the raw material for the creativity displayed by the technicians in the photo lab and the people working in the psychological warfare department. Computer programs placed her wherever the lab staff wanted her to be. To get the job done, they turned repeatedly to Boaz's team with additional requests. They were supplied with a roll of pictures of the exteriors and interiors of cafés and restaurants near the shop, photos of public gardens in its vicinity, and a row of cars.

In Israel, Anna's 'controller' was selected; a thin, tall, grey-haired man who worked as a teacher in a language lab. Without explaining their purpose, the photo technicians sat him at the wheel of a car and photographed him. In one take he was looking straight ahead and in another to the side at someone supposedly standing next to the vehicle. They shot pictures of him sitting on a bench, standing near a wall, climbing stairs, and coming out of a building wearing a winter coat and a pair of gloves.

The computer editing of these images was truly a work of art. Anna, walking in the street and sitting in a restaurant, was slotted in perfectly. The pictures were printed, enlarged, and photographed on regular film which was sent over to Udi and his people by special courier.

Even the head of the Mossad was pleasantly surprised by the authenticity of the pictures. Listen, I was convinced, he said to Udi on the phone. If he's not persuaded then it means that he's not listening to reason, or not acting of his own free will. If that's the case, we'll have to move to plan B. You're aware that we're approaching the end of the week I gave you.

Yes, I'm aware, Udi answered, but we've made good progress. As soon as the film arrives we'll give it in for developing here at a regular photo shop and I will present him with the pictures in the shop's envelope to allay any suspicion. I hope that within a couple of days this will all be behind us. I'm also continuing to rely on the phone conversations. I think they will be the straw that breaks the camel's back.

I wasn't able to tell with any degree of certainty what was

445

going on around our house and shop but felt shadows increasingly closing in on me. Somebody looking at me for a split second too long; some woman looking away an instant too soon. Here a car slowing down for no clear reason, and over there a vehicle suddenly accelerating. A couple behind a misted-up windscreen early in the morning. An unrecognizable figure stopping when I stopped. Footsteps restarting when I continued walking. Freshly trodden footprints in the snow next to the shop when I came back from lunch. And I didn't want to admit any of it.

As the days since the encounter with Levanon slipped by, I wanted to believe the episode was at an end. Perhaps in Israel he'll report that I am adamant, as Yoav certainly did, and that Anna is simply a pretty bookseller who'd captured my heart. After his conversation with her that surely must have been his impression. And if that Jewish Russian who interrogated her a few days earlier about existentialism is indeed a Mossad man, then they already have two such eyewitness reports. And who knows, perhaps, despite their determination to do otherwise, they'll let me stay. Moreover, it may well be that the anonymous source that supplied information about Anna, will come back and say that he was mistaken. I wanted to believe that, but couldn't. The Mossad won't let me live here, a country which, day by day, is perceived as more and more hostile to Israel.

The days were quiet, the evenings beautiful. But my peace of mind was not restored. Anna, of course, sensed this and tried to please me with her love and her body and to take my mind off whatever was bothering me with romantic films.

My love for her during those nights was different. I loved her in a desperate sort of way. I loved her as if these were our last days together. Anna responded to my sorrowful love, and embraced me with all her heart and soul.

We made love endlessly. The flesh hurt and the soul ached even more. And Anna's words pained me when she said again and again, what's happening to you, my love, why are you so sad when you have all of me, all to yourself, forever. I have never loved like this, she said during those nights, I never will again and I didn't know that it was even possible to love this way. You know exactly where to touch me. When you are inside me, I feel you as a part of me, and when you withdraw I feel I've given birth to you. When you embrace me I feel more protected and peaceful than I have ever felt. You remember that you promised that you would never, never, never leave me? So why, my love, are you sad, why so distant?

I also remembered making such a promise in an earlier incarnation to Orit. That too was a promise I didn't keep. All I wanted to do was cry. I could sense what was being contrived around us during these days and nights, but didn't want to believe it. I was burning inside as Anna melted to the touch of my fingers, had become addicted to her endless embrace when I was inside her, not moving so as to let her squeeze out every drop of good there was. And all that time I knew that the end was approaching, it was tangible, just beyond our door step.

Since the run-ins with Yoav and then with Levanon and his men, I'd stopped lunching in our street fearing that another such encounter could happen in front of Anna. Instead, I'd go to one of the restaurants on Sredni or Bolshoi, not far from our shop. I was on my way back after lunch when Udi climbed out of a parked car and walked towards me. Hi Paul, he said, his face undisguised looking serious. He wasn't wearing glasses or even a hat. The cold undoubtedly pained his shiny bald head, the ears must have considered dropping off, his eyes looked as if they were being stabbed by freezing gusts of wind, but, of course, I recognized him in an instant which was exactly what he wanted.

The way he stood right in front of me, apart from making my heart miss a beat, faced me with a dilemma. It was no simple matter to ignore him in the way you can some anonymous person who comes up to you in the street. But the feeling of unease was quickly replaced by alarm. If the head of the Division is here, the Division is here, and in a matter of a second I could well be feeling an arm around my neck in a stranglehold. I quickly glanced either side of Udi. There were people around but there were no cars appropriate for a kidnapping. They wouldn't try to bundle me into Udi's little car. Their only other option was to point a gun at me, and that was a threat to which I wasn't about to surrender.

Before I could calm down, I was seized by another wave of panic – is it conceivable that he would draw a pistol and shoot me? That's not something the Mossad does. But I wanted to get away from there, and fast. Without responding to Udi in any way, I stepped to one side and, by-passing him, continued on my way at speed.

Paul, I have something important for you, I heard his voice behind me and upped my pace. Again I was able to imagine, as I had a year earlier in Paris, the hands holding me and the shot penetrating my back. But this time all I wanted was to go back to my Annushka. I walked faster and faster and avoided running only so as not to attract the attention of any passers-by.

Udi remained behind me, but not for long. A few metres before the turn into 6th Street, close to the rose-coloured church on the corner, his car halted alongside me. From the seat next to the driver, he opened the window and handed out a small package.

It won't explode, he said. This is for you and it's important. I hoped it wouldn't come to this. I really regret that you have to see what's in here.

I wavered, but refused to take it. The car edged forwards slowly, keeping up with me. When I didn't react Udi got out and again stood in front of me.

Paul, this is something that you absolutely have to know, and it's upsetting. His expression was so sincere, so serious, even pained, that I simply held out my hand, grabbed the package, put it into the big outer pocket of my coat, and hurried on to our pedestrianized street and into the shop.

I hesitated about whether to hang my coat on the hook close to the shop's entrance with the package in the pocket, something that wouldn't escape Anna's notice. Just from

Udi's words and the expression on his face it was clear to me that the package was connected to her somehow. I turned the coat round so that the outside pocket was out of sight.

Has something happened? Anna, who could sense my every mood change, asked.

No, I answered, not looking at her.

Anna needed no more than that to know that something had happened. Clearly unhappy she said, I'll go and eat now. She left me alone, with the small package concealed in my outer coat pocket.

39

THE POSSIBILITY THAT the package might explode in my hands scared me less than my fear of what I might find inside it. They wouldn't, after all, have Udi hand me an explosive device. Anything of that sort would have been delivered by a specially chosen courier in a postman's uniform to ensure that I received it, not Anna. Playing for time, I took out a small penknife and cut away the wrapping. Inside the small package was an envelope bearing the logo of Yarkiy-Mir, a chain of photographic shops with a branch opposite our bookstore. I could barely breathe as I removed the pictures with a trembling hand.

The first was of Anna, snapped from behind, as she walked up the stairs of the restaurant on the corner of Bolshoi Prospekt where she regularly ate her lunch. The shot was taken from a car on the other side of the street. At the edge of the photo I was able to make out the outline of the car's window and the tip of its side mirror. From the photo's extended white margin, where the Hebrew for 'Shining Star' had been written in, an arrow drawn in ink pointed at Anna.

I instantly understood the logic. A team often gives an object some sort of associative codename. Here the first four letters of Anna's family name, Starzava, had given somebody the idea of assigning her the codename Shining Star.

The second picture, taken from the same position, was of a tall, silver-haired man walking up the stairs. At the bottom of the arrow drawn in the margin and pointing at his image, were the Hebrew words for 'The Controller'.

Come on now, really, I said to myself. They write Controller and expect me to swallow it? I thought of chucking the pictures away but had a premonition of something bad and I continued to scan them. In the third photograph Anna was seen leaving the restaurant and in the fourth The Controller was also pictured on his way out of there. In this shot his face was turned towards the camera. I could see his features, but didn't recognize him. Just some man in his fifties or sixties.

The fifth shot was again of Anna, this time in different clothes, walking in the direction of the restaurant. From the strips of heating elements visible across the picture I could tell she'd been photographed from the car's rear window.

The Controller's image was captured through the front

windscreen. He was quite close to the car and the picture, which was apparently shot from the back seat, also included the vehicle's interior mirror reflecting the photographer's own silhouette. I was able to see the controller's features more clearly. They remained unfamiliar.

The next one was snapped from inside the restaurant. The conditions for taking pictures were not good, the shot itself came out a bit dark and indistinct. The caption in the margins 'meeting of Shining Star and Controller' led me to the tip of the arrow. In the middle of the picture, encompassing four or five tables, two images were visible that could well have been Anna and the man they'd dubbed The Controller.

But in the next picture, apparently taken as the photographer was passing Anna's table, the two could be seen clearly. Anna sipping her soup, and the Controller, sitting with nothing in front of him, looking at her.

My hands shook as I went on to view the rest of the batch. Again Anna and the Controller, on another day and wearing different clothes, at a table in some other restaurant. By the Controller's side a cup, Anna's place at the table unlaid. And another picture. The Controller sitting on a bench in a public garden – a place I was unable to recognize – and Anna, snapped from behind, approaching him.

And then again at the entrance to our house. Anna emerging and the figure of the Controller clearly visible behind her.

He'd been in our apartment? I shuddered. When? It

was, after all, rare for Anna to be at home alone. Did she go there during her lunch break, and if so perhaps he's actually a lover and not a Controller?

I was beside myself with pain and didn't know which possibility hurt less. But the final shots supplied me with the answer. The team followed the Controller and photographed him travelling along Liteyny Prospekt, the very street in which my office was located. The picture showed him entering a guarded car park next to the former court house which became the KGB's HQ and now housed the FSB. There could be no doubt about the identity of the square brown building, so different from any other in the street, with its beige façade, its shocking functionality, and its utter lack of any form of décor.

In the last picture the man was seen walking towards the side entrance of the building.

A terrible void opened up inside me. The story the pictures told was so incomprehensible, so impossible to assimilate, that I couldn't think at all. I was sucked into the void, utterly shattered. On this occasion Anna was out for longer than usual which gave me time to pull myself together. I looked at the pictures once more, refusing to believe, searching for evidence that would enable me not to believe, evidence I found it hard to come up with. Their story was conclusive. And it had also been organized in a clear cut way with an ending that was watertight and clear.

And yet that is not how pictures taken by a team look, I heard another voice inside me saying. Someone took care to organize them in a way that would lead me from my initial doubts to the unavoidable conclusion at the end.

Someone knew that I wouldn't believe the first photos and would only finally be persuaded when I saw them together in the restaurant. That I wouldn't know if the man was a lover or a controller – and that I would get the irrefutable answer at the gates of the FSB building. And that same somebody also knew that I would recognize the building. I tried to climb out of the pit, looking over the pictures for a third time, lingering over every single one of them, trying to find flaws, indications that these were nothing but a set of photomontages. But the walls of the pit I was in were too smooth to scale and there was nothing for me to hold on to.

Anna was always Anna. In every picture wearing clothes I was familiar with. The coat, the boots, the hat, and the glasses I knew so well. On the two occasions she was photographed in the restaurant she even had on blouses I remembered her wearing in the past few days.

And the unrecognizable Controller, what could I say about him? In the photographs he wore two different coats. Most government officials had just one such winter garment. He wore neither a hat nor glasses, nor did he wrap himself up in a scarf, unlike all other living creatures who did everything possible to cover every exposed inch of their bodies during these bitterly cold days. The photo in the public garden seemed a bit odd to me. Who sits on a bench in a garden in temperatures of minus twenty degrees? And then it also seemed to me that there was some slight difference – too slight for me to be sure of it as evidence – between the sharpness and colouring of the images of The Controller and that of Anna or the backgrounds that appeared in the various pictures. They could have photographed Anna and then afterwards planted The Controller. But in the picture taken at the entrance to our house the image of Anna was brighter and in the one in the garden with The Controller on the bench, his was the clearer image.

The pictures were developed here. The probability of such a plant was low. Nonetheless, I managed to kindle slight doubts in my mind. Like the little boy in the Dutch legend I succeeded in thrusting my finger into the hole in the dyke. But I still felt utterly defeated.

I tore the pictures into little pieces, packed the shreds into two separate bags and left the shop for a moment to dump them in the nearby public bin. I didn't even put on a coat, and sharp arrows of icy cold wind lodged inside me, burning my body wherever they reached.

I hadn't been willing to hear what first Yoav and then Levanon wanted to tell me, and hadn't wanted to see what Udi had brought me. Like a breakwater, I protected the safe harbour I'd found for myself, stubborn waves of new information constantly crashing into me. But like salty, bitter, sea water the pictures penetrated the cracks and overran me.

I can only compare my emotions at the moment when Anna entered the shop to what I felt when Orit discovered I'd shot Schultz, the Austrian arms dealer, and instructed the lab to destroy our embryo. The time we spent in the shop that afternoon, and in the evening at home, reminded me of the hours when I wandered the Arava in my ATV. And perhaps this was an even more difficult time because I had to put up a front and because of Anna's ability to clearly see through it.

She was silent and so was I. For the first time ever we spent an evening in avoidance, alienation and suspicion. Only deep into the night, as we lay awake in our bed in the dark, each enduring their own nightmare, did Anna touch me, caressing me gently. I turned towards her, and when we made love all the despair and hopelessness we both felt accompanied our every act of passion. Afterwards, I heard her cry and stroked her head. She pressed her face into my shoulder, and I put my arms around her. But we didn't exchange a word.

Udi gave me forty-eight hours to think things over. This was how long he needed to forward to Israel the cassette on which Anna's voice was recorded and get back the 'doctored' version. Between Anna's conversations with her mother and sister, a short call from the FSB's HQ was also recorded giving the psychological warfare staff everything they needed to play with. In their audio lab, the voices of the mother and sister were erased, Anna's words were edited, and questions asked by another man, speaking Russian in a deep bass voice, were inserted in perfect unison. In the safe house, Udi and Boaz, Alex and Boris, listened to the doctored cassette. After the two Russian speakers had translated the verbal exchanges and confirmed the accuracy of the conversation – and Udi had approved its contents – he left the safe house to find me.

Udi came into the shop immediately after Anna had left to have lunch. Two customers were perusing the books, but that didn't deter him from coming straight up to me. Not trying to disguise a thing he placed a small tape recorder linked to a pair of earphones on my desk.

Please listen to this, he said quietly in English, a look of sadness in his eyes. It's urgent. There is a translation after the original conversation which we made here just an hour ago. He stared at me for quite some time and then left the shop.

Almost paralyzed by the prospect of what I was about to hear, I put the tape recorder in my pocket, plugged in the earphones, and pressed the play button.

I heard the voices, clearly recognized Anna's, here and there understood words and sentences. The translation that followed was not professional and obviously done in a hurry. It was in English but in the background I could sporadically hear Hebrew being spoken.

Anna Petrovna, this is Alexei Nikolayevich, the voice of a man was heard saying. We know that you are now alone in the apartment and we decided it would be easier for you to talk to us on the phone than to bring you in to us at HQ.

I'm listening, I heard Anna's tense voice saying.

For a month now, immigration police have been reporting to us on the suspicious movements of various young people arriving from Europe and giving the impression that they are involved in some sort of covert activity. They have been arriving in small groups of two or three at a time. Usually, two such groups, maybe three, arrive on the same day and stay here for about a week. A day after this sort of group leaves a new one, of the same type, arrives. They stay in the same few three- or four-star hotels in the centre of town. Generally, the group rents a vehicle which isn't driven out of town. The majority of observed movements have been in the city centre with a particular focus on the streets around your shop and house. We know this to be true from analysing footage taken from traffic light security cameras. Night-time activity close to your house has also been observed.

Aha, Anna said as if waiting for more.

We've examined their passports and pictures, photocopied at the border crossings and in the hotels. About half are Canadians and the rest of various nationalities. We haven't been able to disprove these identities but nor have we been able to confirm any one of them. Because of the suspicions we have about Paul Gupta, I wanted to know if you've noticed any unusual activity on his part, or meetings he may have had with new people?

No, Anna answered, there hasn't been anything different or unusual. Shop-house, house-shop. And lunches. That's the only time I'm not with him. But I don't think that something happened there.

Have you noticed a more than usual incidence of young people milling around your shop and house?

No, Anna answered. Nothing out of the ordinary.

Keep your eyes open, and report to us if you see something irregular, because something of that sort is definitely going on, Alexei Nikolayevich said. And what about his own behaviour?

There was silence at the other end of the line. Then I

heard Anna saying: He's not been himself for a few days. I don't know what's happening to him but it's clear to me that he's going through something. He doesn't talk, he's not open with me…

This is Anatoly Lenkov, a deep-sounding voice intervened. When you previously told us you reckoned he was embarking on some operation or thought he was recruiting various sources, was his behaviour similar then?

I don't know what to tell you, Anna's voice was heard again.

Try to remember. On those occasions, did he also not talk to you very much and you thought he was hiding things from you? For instance, when he told you about his trips to the Republics, did you also then feel that he was lying, that he wasn't in fact doing business there but was involved in something else?

Something not good is happening to him, that's clear. I have all sorts of theories but I can't tell you what they are, Anna said in a pained tone.

I'm happy to hear how aware you are of the need for security and that, as usual, you don't want to talk on the phone, the deep voice said. So we'll meet again at lunchtime tomorrow and I'll get the details from you then. I'll come myself, instead of Alexei. We'll meet in a new place so they don't think in the Georgian restaurant that you eat with a different man every other day. In the meantime be strong and vigilant.

I'm strong, Anna said, as strong as can be expected in these circumstances.

We trust you, Anatoly Lenkov said, you haven't

disappointed us yet. And tomorrow, when Paul goes out to eat, get in touch with me and tell me the exact time and place. I'll wait for you in the car close to the restaurant you decide on, and when I see you I'll go in straight after you.

I'll try, Anna said in a choked voice, and my tears flowed unstoppably.

If I hurry, I'll still manage to catch Anna with her new controller, I thought to myself. See for myself that this is not some sort of dastardly trick being played by Udi and his people. But where am I to go? I don't know what Anna said to this Anatoly when I went out to eat earlier, have no clue where they finally arranged to meet. And when I see her she'll also catch sight of me, and then what? I felt utterly drained and completely powerless. I sat with my head lowered. A customer approaching me noticed the state I was in and left me alone.

I listened to the conversation for a second time. I tried to find flaws in the sound, indications of it having been doctored, faults I could figure out. There was a slight difference in the sound when Anatoly Lenkov intervened in the dialogue but it's possible he was speaking from another receiver and that that accounted for the difference. I listened again to Anna's voice. It was her, without a doubt, but she was addressing her interlocutor in the singular, a form in Russian one would only use when talking to someone you're close to. The language itself, as well as good manners, required addressing a stranger or someone of a higher rank in the plural. But perhaps this was proof of an intimacy between Anna and her controllers. The same could be said of the first controller who'd addressed her using her private and her father's name rather than her husband's family name.

I had no way of knowing then that Anatoly Lenkov with the deep voice was, in fact, a technician of Russian origin working in the Mossad's weaponry department who'd been asked to take on the role of the third party in the conversation. At the time I couldn't possibly have known that every word he uttered was scripted and that what Anna said about my mood was lifted from a conversation with her sister, a conversation that ended with the sister encouraging her to be strong and Anna promising to try. The editing of the conversations and the doctoring of the recording were certainly convincing.

Before Anna returned, Udi came into the shop for the second time. Now there were no customers present.

Listen carefully, he said, leaning towards me. Alex, from the Russian department, is at this very moment sitting close to Anna and her controller in a restaurant. He's sent me an urgent SMS. Our activity has been exposed, and revealed as being connected to you. You understand what that means as far as you're concerned?

From the expression on my face Udi saw that I didn't understand.

He again pulled out his mobile phone which was vibrating.

Look, Alex is SMSing me again. They've decided to arrest you, he read out from the screen, and Anna will also be investigated. It's possible that the arrest will be immediate. Various thoughts ran through my mind threatening to pierce holes in it.

But Udi interrupted my ruminations. He put an envelope from a travel company with an airline ticket and a passport on my desk.

This is a ticket for a flight to Copenhagen in three hours' time. It's possible that in the next three hours they won't realize that you've gone and won't look for you at the airport. Just in case they do look for you there, you also have a new passport here with a different name and an entry stamp. Leave now. It's your only hope.

I got up and looked at him. I'll leave if you also get Anna out of here.

We've thought about that, and we are making plans to do it. Get in touch with her from the airport and explain that to her.

Shocked and confused I yielded to Udi's hand on my shoulder pushing me gently towards the coat hanger.

Come, we'll continue to talk in the car, he said. Let's go now.

As we came out, I looked up and down the length of the street but saw no sign of Anna. A car stopped at the end of the pedestrianised street and its doors were flung open. Udi lowered my head as, with mixed feelings, I entered the car. He closed the door, got into the front seat and the car sped off.

Boaz drove and Hagai sat in the back beside me.

Perhaps we should stop by my apartment so I can take a few things from there, I said to Udi.

462

You have things there that are worth risking your freedom for? he replied.

It's a bit suspicious appearing like this for a flight, without anything, I said.

In fact, I simply wanted a bit more time to shed some light on the fast moving developments, to try and understand what was happening before deciding what my next step should be.

We'll buy you a travel case, so you won't look any different from any other businessman, Udi said, knowing perfectly well that stopping at the apartment could lead me to change my mind.

Boaz drew up to the entrance to the international departures terminal. To my surprise Udi and Hagai got out of the car with me.

We're also flying, Udi informed me.

Of course. He wasn't going to allow his prey to escape. The two took me directly to the counter of the Danish airline company.

I'm going to call Anna, I announced when we'd gone through check-in, but before reaching border control.

I'm sorry I have to show you this, Udi said, and handed me his mobile. I don't think there's any point in you calling.

On the screen was a new message from Alex: Paul's arrest is planned for this evening, when the two come out of *Eugene Onegin*. Anna will make out she's being arrested against her will. They parted amicably and she's on her way back to the shop.

It arrived while we were on our way here, Udi said, and

I was hoping not to have to show it to you. I don't think there's any point in you calling her. It will merely reveal your whereabouts. They will be sitting on the line and will trace the telephone you're calling from. But even if they don't, she'll hear the airport's public announcements in the background.

The few words on the screen hit me like a succession of hammer blows. Arrest. She'll make out. Amicably. But more than anything else *Eugene Onegin.* How could they know?

I stood there, at a loss what to do. Based on everything Udi had shown me and told me, could I really cut and run like this leaving Anna behind? The voices and pictures were convincing and so too were the words on the screen. Collectively, the efforts made by Yoav, Levanon, Udi and their teams were impressive. But deep down I didn't believe all of that. My eyes saw what they saw, my ears heard what they heard. My head says that yes, Anna is reporting on me to Russian intelligence – as has everybody who's been approached by them since the days of the Cheka, the NKVD, the KGB, up to this very day. But my heart does not believe it. My heart knows that Anna truly loves me and that I love her with every fibre of my being, and that our six months together have been the most exciting, most profound and most real I had ever lived through.

But how could they have known about *Eugene Onegin* this evening, if not from her? I couldn't think of any other explanation. This giant wave crashed into the breakwater with overpowering ferocity and destroyed it. Udi saw my slumped shoulders and put his arm around them. Yogev, he said, calling me by my real name, I know what you're going through. I think I know what's going through your mind. Think about your options and go with the worst-case scenario. We haven't made a mistake. But if Anna has a good explanation you'll invite her to Tel Aviv or Canada or Jamaica. In a few hours' time you'll be a free man, you'll be able to do whatever you want. However, if you make a mistake now, then in a few hours' time you'll be a prisoner and you'll spend the next ten or twenty years in the Lubyanka without Anna. And if you ever get out of there you'll be a mere shadow of the man you once were.

Udi helped me get things into focus. I still didn't completely believe him and felt that there was something fishy about the pictures and the recordings. Even in that terrible and confusing moment I understood that all of this could have been a ploy taken straight from the movies – to get me back home without kidnapping me on Russian soil. Nonetheless, he was right in saying that I had to decide on the basis of the worst possible outcome. So, if there was even a kernel of truth in what I'd been shown, the right thing for me to do was to get out of Russia. After that I'd be able to decide what to do next.

I'm coming, but on one condition, I said. As I told you before, I want you to extricate Anna from there. In an hour or two she'll understand that something has happened to me and will begin to take some action. Perhaps she herself will run off. I want somebody to go to the shop in the next hour, two hours tops, give her a ticket and say or write that I'm waiting for her in Tel Aviv. If you can issue a passport

465

for her, all the better. I have passport pictures of her in my wallet.

We'll give her a plane ticket, Udi said. I'm already instructing Boaz to get going with this. We won't write Tel Aviv but we'll leave her with an international telephone number which she can call and which will reach us. I'm willing to issue a passport for her, but that's not a matter of a few hours, and it will be done in Israel.

I had no more serious arguments for delaying my departure. Nonetheless, I went up to a nearby kiosk and asked for a cup of coffee. The obstinacy I felt deep inside me turned my legs to lead. Udi and Hagai exchanged glances.

Paul, we're going to miss the flight, Udi said. He picked up the case which Hagai had bought for me in one of the airport shops, and with his arm around me we walked towards the border control booth.

By the time the plane took off I was emotionally dead. Udi tapped me gently on the shoulder. Just like an era ago, at the end of the Hong Kong operation, I flinched at his touch. I gazed out of the window until the snow-covered buildings of St Petersburg disappeared behind me. We flew over the frozen Gulf of Finland and in the swirling fog inside me were sharp and painful needles of sadness and regret surrounded by a sea of confusion and uncertainty of a kind I had never ever felt.

40

BOAZ DIDN'T BUY Anna a ticket. She wasn't then in any danger, and the meeting with her new controller never, of course, really happened. Anna was not yet suspected of anything, notwithstanding Alexei Nikolayevich's questions in his phone conversation with her which had, indeed, taken place, and made HQ's doctoring of the call possible. The SMSs that Alex sent to Udi's mobile were planned and scheduled in advance as part of the fictitious and sophisticated presentation which had ensnared me and which I only learned of months later.

What happened to Anna as a result of this plot I found out in detail only years afterwards.

When she returned to the shop and found it abandoned she began to worry. It was hardly credible that I'd leave the shop for no good reason and without even leaving a note. Customers prevented her from leaving the shop to look for me. She called home and got no answer. As time passed her worry grew, and as the hours went by she began to realize, with an increasing sense of apprehension, that something had happened to me. She then linked this fear to Alexei Nikolayevich's phone call and the visits to the shop by Roman and Levanon.

If what he'd said was true, that some young foreigners were hanging around the house and shop in operational mode, then perhaps they were behind my sudden disappearance? Had they kidnapped me? Killed me? she wondered.

Anna closed the shop before five and hurried home. When she discovered that all my clothes and suitcases were there and later also found my passport, she understood that something bad was happening and that she had to do something. In her distress, she called Alexei Nikolayevich. He listened attentively to the story of my disappearance, said he knew nothing about it but would check with HQ to see if they were involved and would issue an alert to the people on the ground. He did indeed issue a directive. He ordered his people to put Anna Petrovna under surveillance. She's agitated and liable to make mistakes, he said, she could also lead us to her missing partner.

Anna spent a long, sleepless night. Every possible scenario went through her mind but she retained hope; that if I'd fled, for whatever reason, I'd think again and return; and that if I'd been taken by force I'd be released or would escape and make my way back to her. She sat at the window surveying the white empty street below from up on high. It snowed, at midnight the heating faltered, but she continued stubbornly to sit there, wrapped in a blanket, gazing out. On the odd occasions when a car stopped outside, or somebody passed by, she opened the balcony door, went out and looked down, her bones pierced by the cold, her feet submerged in the soft gathered snow. But each time she was disappointed and hurried back into the apartment.

Morning found her shivering from the cold, her

forehead burning. But she was determined. It was clear to Anna that I wasn't coming back. It was also clear to her where she had to find me. She waited till the beginning of the business day and ordered a plane ticket to Israel. Not long after that she arrived at the airport with a small suitcase. The instant she collected her ticket at the counter she was approached by two FSB agents who informed her that she was under arrest.

The unmarked Lada swept into the parking bay inside the big building housing the FSB. From there the internal lift took Anna and her two escorts to the third floor. Unprotesting, she walked with them through the long and familiar corridors of the organization's counter-espionage wing.

Instead of being taken to the interrogation room she was led into a spacious conference chamber. She stood at the door and scanned the people sitting to one side of a wide table waiting for her in silence, staring at her.

Among them was 'Mikhail', the man with the Stalinist appearance whose picture had hung in her bedroom. Some six months earlier she'd been photographed embracing him solely for the purpose of putting the snapshot on the living room table in her apartment. Her 'dead' husband was, it turned out, simply a work colleague. His face was expressionless. Also sitting there was Sergey, the bag snatcher. The burly sullen man glowered at her as only a betrayed lover could. Then there was Dimitri, the sharply-dressed good-looking young man who tried to flirt with her in Vashkirova's restaurant. He had a slight, scornful smile on his face. Seated at the head of the table was Alexei Nikolayevich, Anna's controller.

Alexei gestured to her to sit in the chair on the other, unoccupied, side of the table. Her two escorts stood behind her.

For some months now we've been asking ourselves what has been happening to you, Anna Petrovna, the controller began by saying.

In the past, it took you just one, two or, at most, three meetings to expose anyone suspected of spying. When we saw that time was passing and you'd not even established contact with Paul, we helped you. But as for results – there weren't any. It does happen that even experienced spy catchers like you fail. It doesn't happen often because we put a well-oiled apparatus at your disposal that supplies you with a lot of helpful information about your adversaries. But mind battles are mind battles. Some you win some you lose. Up until now we were prepared to accept your failure as something that happens in this game. Do you want to respond to this?

Anna looked straight into the eyes of the man with whom she'd worked for many years, turned her gaze away from him and surveyed the other faces staring at her, some with curiosity, some in embarrassment, some in disgust, and said, no.

So, we'll continue, said Alexei Nikolayevich. I just want to make sure the recording equipment is working.

A technician, sitting out of sight at the other end of the room, with headphones and a tape recorder in front of him, confirmed that everything was OK.

But you decided to go ahead and invited the suspect into your house, out of step with the planned time for such a visit and without getting prior clearance. From that moment on, the blame for what ensued rests on your shoulders. Do you want to say anything about this decision of yours?

You've already arranged a hearing for me to clarify it and I explained, Anna said. I'm sure there is a well-ordered transcript in my file.

Correct, said Alexei, and pulled out a bundle of papers from a slender portfolio lying in front of him. Here, and I quote: To crack this hard nut I had to bring him into my home, to be with him. This is where I asked whether by the term 'to be with him' you meant 'to sleep with him' and you answered in the affirmative, and continued by saying, I feel that he will open up to me only if we develop a romantic relationship. End quote. Do you confirm that?

I assume that's more or less what I said, Anna replied.

That's what you said or that was also the truth? the controller asked.

That's what I said, Anna repeated.

But it's not necessarily the truth, the whole truth, and nothing but the truth. Is that right?

Anna paused for a moment before answering, and then said quietly, nothing about our lousy profession is the truth, the whole truth, and nothing but the truth. Nor is it in our miserable lives. She lowered her eyes, enveloped in a pain that suddenly erupted from within her and threatened to swamp her eyes with tears. She breathed in deeply. Anna had no intention of breaking down here, in front of her colleagues.

Anna Petrovna, we're not insensitive people. We're also sufficiently seasoned campaigners to realize that there are cases in which the 'hunter' falls in love with the 'hunted'. We all know about the Stockholm Syndrome whereas here, where the story is the very reverse, we have the St Petersburg Syndrome, Alexei said, expecting to hear chuckles of agreement from his colleagues. We live at a time when one could even forgive such a thing, he continued. But you asked us to keep our distance, not interfere with your work, not hassle you until you found something and informed us. What you found and forwarded to us were reports that acquitted Paul entirely of any suspicion. Do you want to explain this?

Anna kept silent.

You, perhaps, didn't suspect him, he continued, but from the other side we got reports that the CIA had suspicions about you and wanted information on you. Can you guess why Paul Gupta suspected you?

Who said that Paul suspected me? Anna wondered, and unaffectedly raised her eyes towards her controllers.

So you think that just like that, for no reason, without Paul Gupta reporting on you or asking for you to be checked out, the Americans became interested in you?

Anna's evident distress produced a slight smile of satisfaction on the faces of the others present.

The Americans suspected me? Anna's shock was real, but didn't divert Alexei from the line of questioning he'd embarked on.

Their queries about you leave no room for doubt, he said. We could have forgiven that too, and assumed that Paul was simply a better agent than you. That he succeeded in concealing his identity from you whereas you aroused his suspicion. This too has its precedents in the history of counter-espionage. A bit odd, bearing in mind that you are such an experienced agent. But it happens.

It was clear to Anna and to the rest of those present that Alexei Nikolayevich was merely warming up and that his little act would be taking off very soon. An air of suspenseful quietude pervaded the room.

For a month now we've been monitoring suspicious movements of foreigners and gaining the impression that they were descending on the area of your apartment and shop. To save time I violated security regulations, contacted you, and informed you of this. Is it really your intention to have us believe that, what regular desk staff saw by scrutinizing arrivals and departures at the airport, by observing people staying in hotels, and by following the movements of cars hired by tourists, you, with all your training, didn't see even though it was all happening right under your nose?

In contrast to the rising volume of her controller's voice, Anna answered in whispers. No, I didn't see. I'm sorry. And she was indeed sorry but not for the reasons he could possibly have imagined. If only she'd noticed. If only she'd been able to warn her love and flee with him.

And do you think that the fact that you requested to part from us so as to build your life with your Mr Gupta counts in your favour? he continued. The very reverse is the case. I can only presume that this request of yours was a bit of a cover to conceal that, in effect, you'd already parted from us. Perhaps, who knows, you'd even planned your escape with your man but he and his friends scarpered and left you behind!

This possibility, that hadn't crossed her mind, plunged yet another knife into Anna's heart. Alexei's voice rose even further.

And then, all of a sudden, Paul Gupta disappears. Suddenly. The love of your life. The man for whom you broke all the rules so you could be with him, whose every word you believed, the foreign spy you shared your bed with, suddenly disappears – and you want to tell us that you had no advance warning? You didn't notice that he was planning to leave, there were no mysterious phone conversations, no secret meetings – nothing? Suddenly, just like that? And immediately after I had alerted you of those movements?

Regretfully, that's right, Anna said, her eyes lowered. How could all this have happened around her without her noticing what was going on?

Alexei leant back in his chair, chewed at the pencil in his hand, and looked at Anna for a long minute. And then he again lowered his tone. I might have believed you Anna Petrovna. You are a very persuasive woman. Yesterday evening when you called me, and even during the night when you went out on to the balcony to see if your beloved had returned – she was astonished by the level of surveillance she was under – I nearly believed you. But how, in God's name, how did you know that you had to buy a ticket to Tel Aviv?

Anna suddenly understood how foolish she'd been to call him and afterwards order a ticket by phone. Obviously he'd placed her under tight surveillance, eavesdropping as well as observation. Of course she'd had no chance of escaping.

Even if you'd simply wanted to follow him, her controller looked at her fixedly as if he was himself trying to decipher what was going on in her mind, this would be considered desertion, and you'd sit in jail for it. The law is the law, and desertion is desertion. If you'd absconded for love, they might have been a little more lenient with you. But as it happens, Paul Gupta, or Roger Smith – if you want to know the name in which he left the country – in actual fact flew to Copenhagen. We analyzed footage from the security cameras at the airport, and passengers' names and passport details, and this was his name and destination. It was only from there that he travelled on to Tel Aviv, our sources in Denmark informed us. So how on earth did you know that that's where you had to fly to? Especially given that Tel Aviv was presumably only a transit stop on Mr Smith's voyage back to his homeland?

The slight trembling that had gripped Anna during the night now overwhelmed her. If you're not saying it then I'll say it for you, the controller concluded. You not only knew that he was a spy, you also knew that he was about to disappear. You knew exactly what his escape route was, what his planned stopovers were, and it was there that you planned to meet.

Anna cowered in her chair but her controller continued with his horror show.

And it doesn't end there. We know that the people who took him from here were members of the team who worked here, and that they flew with him to Copenhagen and Tel Aviv. They didn't kidnap him. The security cameras show clearly that he left with them of his own accord. They were here to extract him and shield him from us. And you know what that means? It means that you were Paul Gupta's assignment! Alexei Nikolayevich shocked Anna by saying. Alarmed, she now finally grasped how deep a pit she'd been thrown into.

Through you he gathered intelligence on us, Alexei continued, his eyes narrowing, you collaborated with him, protected him and of course also protected yourself. You knew that if we arrested him then at the end of what could be a short or a long interrogation he would squeal on you. There is no other way of understanding this. You knew where he came from and where he travelled to, you knew what he was doing here, and helped him. The picture is clear, and there isn't a judge who will look at it in any other way. I'll be surprised if you see the light of day even twenty years from now.

The Return Home

41

STRAIGHT FROM THE plane, without having to pass through passport control, I was driven off in a car with blacked-out windows to the Shin Bet – the General Security Service in Ramat Aviv. Udi and Hagai were cordial in saying their goodbyes at the airport where they handed me over to the men from the Shin Bet. With them was Ariel, my controller. Though a little hostile towards me, his assignment was to ensure I was treated fairly. The Mossad had not given up on me quite yet. They questioned me over a period of a week, sometimes for fifteen hours a day. Food was brought in straight from the Shin Bet's canteen and I slept in a room close to the living quarters of the facility's security guards. If I was being watched I didn't notice it. Ariel was present almost the whole time – protecting the Mossad's interests.

The Shin Bet's investigators were interested in every detail of my adjustment to life in St Petersburg; meetings, acquaintances, business dealings. From time to time, when the matter touched on the inner workings of my job – such as the commercial deals I'd struck, or my trips to the former Republics – Ariel would halt the questioning and say, that's a matter for us.

They also, of course, wanted to understand who Anna was and what she knew about me and my work. As far as the investigators were concerned there could be no doubt: Anna was a spy catcher and I was her assignment. The only thing they didn't apparently understand was how it could be that in the course of six months she hadn't had me arrested. Had I crossed over to her side?

Naturally, the picture I saw was different to the one seen by my inquisitors. I didn't know then about the convoluted steps taken to incriminate Anna in an attempt to persuade me that she was working for the FSB. After everything I'd been shown I couldn't completely dismiss the possibility that she did indeed work for them. But although that is what reason dictated, deep in my heart I continued not to believe it. And even if that's what Anna was, I thought, even if, at the beginning, she was assigned to operate against me, I was sure that she began to love me, accepted me for who I said I was when I introduced myself to her, and perhaps even protected me from the authorities.

The fact that I stuck to my cover story would have convinced even a seasoned spy catcher that I was bona fide. Even if she had some suspicions they were at some point allayed and Anna remained with me because a beautiful love story had developed between us. In this situation, even if they forced her to continue spying on me, and even if she persisted in reporting on me and meeting her controller, couldn't we have gone on living together?

When, in response to the investigators, I offered a detailed reconstruction of the sequence of events in our relationship, I again saw how natural its development had really been. In my heart, the feeling of immense loss became ever deeper. Within me the equivalent of a washing machine was spinning, tossing, wringing everything out but cleaning nothing.

I was constantly tormented by questions of what was now going through her mind. Whether she was an innocent bookseller or a spy catcher who loved me, cleared me, and lived with me out of love and with love – what could she possibly be making of my sudden disappearance? She had no grounds for believing that I'd run away from her or from the authorities in her country.

I could clearly visualize her waiting for me in the evening, and at night, searching, calling hospitals, wandering around places where we'd spent time together; at Vashkirova's, my previous addresses, even alerting the police. The images of my Annushka helpless, scared, looking for me, and then sitting, demoralized, in our apartment, uncomprehending, waiting for me in vain, broke my heart.

Udi came to visit me. His handshake was firm; mine was limp. I still saw him as responsible for my painful separation from Anna and for the fact that she hadn't followed me. His attempt to explain why she'd not been given a plane ticket didn't satisfy me. I filed it as yet another lie hurled at me by the Establishment. Levanon also came and saw fit to embrace me, apparently clinging to the memory of the dozens of operations we'd been in together, ignoring his own last undertaking in which we were on opposite sides of the barricade. For them I was like a son who'd been brought back home from a drug-polluted environment in Goa, whereas for me they were the people who'd driven me out of the private Garden of Eden I'd created for myself.

Before the Shin Bet had finished with me I passed three separate polygraph tests, carried out by three different examiners, with slightly varying questions in each of them. How was I supposed to respond to 'Were you in contact with a foreign agent?' I wondered. Even if Anna was indeed a foreign agent, that is not who or what she was as far as I was concerned. I certainly had no contact with her knowing that she was any such thing. How was I supposed to reply to the question 'Did you pass on information about your work to an unauthorized person?' When I told Anna that I was going to Makhachkala or to Dushanbe, was I passing on information to an unauthorized person? Even if I'm a businessman and she's my girlfriend? No wonder they needed to conduct more and more tests. The evidence that I was telling the truth was clearly not definitive.

At the end of that week, the Mossad moved me to a small apartment and I was asked not to leave it until my fate had been decided. Now Eli and Ariel, Alex and Levanon, sat with me, wanting to know details about my work, the deals I'd concluded, and the contacts I'd made.

Perhaps, on top of everything else, I was also suspected of being an agent of the Dagestani Mafia, an emissary of Mahashashli's – who knows? At least that is how it seemed from the way Eli and Ariel spoke to me. Alex and Levanon, on the other hand, tried to project an air of calm, of being happy that I was back home. Even though I didn't yet know of their role in the great deception, I did have the feeling that we weren't on the same side so I wasn't willing to accept their expressions of sympathy.

Behind the scenes various meetings apparently took place to sum things up. About ten days after my return to Israel, Udi informed me that from the point of view of the organization I was clean. However, rather than letting go of me, they wanted me to contribute something from my extensive experience to the younger generation of operatives. He took the trouble to hint that this was not a suggestion I could turn down: as a condition for letting me remain unsupervised, the Shin Bet was insisting that the Mossad take full responsibility for me. And 'of course' I was not to communicate with anyone I'd had contact with while in Russia.

Even though it was already evening, I quickly left the Mossad apartment and set myself up temporarily in a hotel in Tel Aviv. It was winter but the air was pleasant. Along the promenade the sea was stormy and I stood peering into the depths, my heart and soul reaching out to the one I'd left behind somewhere there across the ocean. Droplets of salty water from the waves rinsed my face, blending with my tears.

After that, I wandered like a drunk through the city

streets, battles raging in my mind between actions and prohibitions, possibilities and fears. Before stumbling back to my hotel I succumbed to temptation and committed my first offence: I called Anna from a public phone box. I prepared the precise words I'd say to her. But there was no answer either at the apartment or at the shop. Thoughts about where Anna could possibly be prevented me from falling asleep. In the middle of the night, in the pouring rain, I went to the nearest public phone, getting soaked to the bone in the process. And again there was no answer. In the early dawn, trembling with cold, I tried for the third time. Once more without success. When I got back to my room the phone rang. It was the night orderly summoning me to an urgent meeting in Ariel's office. My assumption that only the phone in my room would be tapped into had obviously been somewhat naïve.

If you want a war that's what you'll get, Ariel said. And believe me we know how to be bad. Anna is passé. Get that into your head. No phone calls, no letters, no nothing. And be thankful that this is the only restriction you're under.

I left his office and Mossad HQ and drove to Beersheba to visit my mother.

I had no expectations and yet my heart bled for her. The small woman, who'd managed to preserve a tiny trace of her beauty, not only failed to recognize me but was absolutely detached from everything around her. She didn't respond, didn't say a word, not to me, not to anyone else.

I felt like someone coming face to face with his own memoir, and finding it to be a sealed book; gazing at the album of his life and discovering it to be empty. This beloved woman was all that was left to me, and she too was no longer a real presence. I was left without Orit who'd erased my youth and young adulthood; without Anna who'd disappeared taking with her the present and the future I so desired. And also, in effect, without the Mossad which had shunned me. My mother was the only link I had with who I'd once been, and with who I now was. And the mother I'd had was also not really here. The shrivelled-up shell that so saddened me didn't embody her. All that was left of what was once my mother was locked in my memories and my feelings.

But was I still what I'd once been for her? And what was left of me when everyone I had loved and everyone who had loved me had gone?

I sat at her side. Could it be that while I was holding her hand and stroking her something was aroused in that debilitated brain or old heart? Her eyes expressed nothing, but the smile that had always typified her was still there.

Her dedicated carer Madeleine was with her. Tearfully, she told me in broken English how my mother was failing from day to day and, because she had no control over her bodily functions, she would soon have to go into a palliative care ward. Madeleine asked if I'd be able to afford this because the cost would amount to more than four thousand dollars a month, excluding her own salary. I said that I could but only then remembered that I'd left most of my money behind in St Petersburg. At that rate the funds I had here in Israel would be eaten up within a year. I'd become an expert at scattering sincerely meant promises that I wasn't able to keep.

An initial check revealed that my Russian account had not been closed down. To me this fact meant either that I wasn't suspected of being a spy in the first place, or that Anna had protected me and concealed the existence of the account from the authorities. Whichever it was, I'd clearly made a terrible mistake in complying with Udi and his men's demands and as a consequence lost the love of my life. Again my guts were churning and I demanded an urgent meeting with Udi.

The conversation didn't get us anywhere. Udi maintained his position vis-à-vis Anna and rejected my insistence that I, or one of his people, contact her and make it possible for her to come to Israel.

Do you really think that the State of Israel would allow a known KGB spy catcher to enter the country? And do you think that Anna herself would agree to come here and risk arrest? She, after all, knows what she is, and it's reasonable to assume that she also knows that we know.

So let's test her, I said.

Yogev, get a grip. If she comes, the Shin Bet's working assumption will be that she's a spy. And there's a high probability that this will be proven right. So would you rather she spend her life here, in an Israeli jail?

I couldn't see a way of turning things round all by myself. The passport in the name of Paul Gupta was in our apartment in St Petersburg. The one in the name of Roger Smith had been in Udi's possession since the flight to Copenhagen. And my real passport was also being held under lock and key by the Mossad. No one's going to allow me to take it and apply for a Russian visa. I was a long way from convincing the Mossad that they had made a mistake about Anna, and the Shin Bet's view of me was also hostile. The feeling of loss was hard and I didn't know how to make the situation any better.

The Mossad helped me to withdraw my money from Russia with the aid of a front man and an intermediate address. My mother was transferred to the palliative ward and I deposited the bulk of the money in a closed account enabling her to live out the rest of her days there with Madeleine at her side. With the money left over I rented an apartment in Tel Aviv not far from the sea and I furnished it with the bare essentials. I hadn't given up on the dream of seeing Anna here, with me. In my mind's eye, I saw us going from shop to shop, completing the furnishing of the apartment to her taste. I saw her smiling happily as I told her again and again that it's OK, it's within our budget.

Returning to work felt like changing gear in an old car without stepping on the clutch. There was, naturally, an intention that I should brief whoever took over from me in Russia. But in the discussions held on this issue, the fact that Anna had visited my offices and knew about my business connections came up, and the idea of sending out a replacement was promptly dropped. I was also chastised for the roundabout link I'd created between my Montreal company's bank and Israel. The way I'd done it had, I was told, tainted the Canadian company and it was decided that it had to be closed down. The many contacts I'd made in the Caucasus and along the Caspian sea sank like a stone in its waters. From my knowledge of the Mossad, I reckoned that in the not too distant future another operative, based in Germany, France, or some other country, would appear on the scene and, for the sake of the homeland, perhaps agree to bed one of Mahashashli's girls, and establish new contacts there. The Mossad never gives up.

Then, for a brief period, they made me an instructor. But it quickly became apparent that my story was known to all the young operatives. I was not a suitable role model for them and this experiment at finding a slot for me also came to naught.

The attempt to return me to operations was a failure that should have been foreseen. In retrospect I'm surprised at Udi and Levanon, people who knew me so well, for even thinking of doing such a thing. You don't send a worn-out war-horse into battle. They must have been in real need to think that, after all I'd gone through, my time in Russia could be viewed as a period of rehabilitation, and that just the smell of battle would reawaken the war-horse in me. I'd never been one and only fought if I had to.

I also don't completely understand the process that left me in the Mossad to begin with. The first thing they should have done after clearing me of the suspicion of desertion and treason, or of being a double agent, was to kick me out and keep me at arm's length. But there were those who thought it was better that I remain under their wing so they could see me in the flesh every day. From there, by way of a predictable bureaucratic lapse, I rolled back into operations. I'd seen many similar cases, including guys who'd not completed the operational course but were nonetheless integrated into the work of HQ. When the need arose they were sent on an operation. After that they continued to be thought of as operatives without anybody bothering to mention any weaknesses noted during the training course. That, it would seem, is the way it is in such dynamic organizations where the tasks taken on are far more numerous than the available manpower.

During those days I was a broken man, lacking any kind of drive. I was free of my interrogators' questions, but again and again images went through my mind of the slow and somewhat subdued course the relationship between Anna and me had taken before it turned into what I thought was powerful love. Now I was fighting the painful question marks that were trying to sneak into it. In my mind's eye were dozens of pictures of Anna with me – laughing, loving, listening, explaining, happy, lustful, weeping – I was absolutely sure that none of them were staged. However, there were the conversations I'd heard with my own ears, and the pictures I'd seen with my own eyes, of Anna reporting on me and meeting up with her controller. The possibility that she'd been with me not because of love but to expose me was too hard to bear.

Then the question of what Anna was thinking and doing, would flash through my mind. A food processor was mincing my insides, pulverizing everything there and turning it into thick, repulsive dough.

Unable to control myself, I continued to consider the events of the love we had and could have had – if, that is, there truly had been such a love, and if, in reality, it could have continued. In the end, during the whole of my stay in St Petersburg, from the moment all the barriers came down, our time of real happiness had been limited to just a few weeks; for me and for the woman who gave me back my youth, and who I knew, with all my heart and soul, I wanted to be with and grow old with until death did us part, that is all there was.

These thoughts tortured me day and night. Frequently, in my sleep, my hand sought Anna's body and my chest searched for the lost spoon. When I found neither I woke up to a reality that hit me hard. I felt cold all over, there was pounding in my chest, and dryness in my throat. I had to get up, drink some water, and calm down. Then I was unable to fall asleep again until the blackness of the night outside had turned into the dark blue of early dawn. And soon after I returned to bed and fell asleep, the alarm clock woke me. I arrived at the office shattered. Anyone looking at me could see I was exhausted but no one could tell that I was, in fact, sinking into a quagmire that threatened both body and soul.

In their hour of need, Udi and Levanon appointed me to be HQ's representative in various operations. The truth is that I felt so uneasy in the corridors of the Mossad, with the judgmental looks I was getting from all sides, that I preferred to be abroad. Most Mossad people are intelligent and hard working; those who serve in operational roles are also courageous and ready to sacrifice themselves; those in positions of command are level-headed and determined. All are lovers of the homeland. But there is one trait with which not all of them are blessed – the capacity to forgive. The ethical code of many Mossad personnel is totally rigid. If someone strays from that code, he is condemned to persistent and eternal infamy. There are almost no cases of disciplinary hearings in the organization. There are only investigations and committees of enquiry into operations that were unsuccessful. The trial by one's friends is conducted by word of mouth, by whispers. It's in the corridors that sentence is served. There they knew everything about my 'attempted defection'. And, just as many years earlier every glance at me in HQ's passageways was one of appreciation, now every look was of hatred. The trips abroad were a godsend.

The thought crossed my mind that the first operation I was now sent on in Europe was merely a dummy run intended to make sure I wasn't a double agent and wouldn't betray the team. Otherwise it's really difficult for me to understand the ease with which the guys reported that they got into the Russian Embassy, photographed the documents, and withdrew without being discovered. I sat in the 'communications centre' in the suite of a nearby hotel together with the telephonist who handled all communications between the team members. My role was merely to give advice and be in touch with Israel in the event of any complications. However, I had attended the team's briefings in Israel and the details of the plan were all well known to me. Had I been a double agent I could easily have handed the team over to the other side.

And so came the second operation and then the third. They went like clockwork. The teams of youngsters were efficient, the preparations were good, communications worked well, and the results were excellent. There was almost no need for me to interfere. In between operations I didn't have much to do. I continued to feel out of place at HQ and as someone whose presence wasn't wanted, even though no one actually said anything. After one particularly sleepless night I simply decided not to go to work that day and my commanders turned a blind eye to it. In the Mossad people are not fired, nobody wants embittered departing employees freely wandering the streets. Such people are hung out to dry at home without being given any kind of role and they continue to be paid until their conscience is pricked and they leave of their own accord. Twice I asked Udi if he wanted me to quit and his unambiguous answer on each occasion was that no, I was still needed.

And, indeed, Udi made a small office next to Levanon's available to me and gave me the title of 'Assistant to the Head of the Division for Methodology'. We work with unrecorded verbal principles, he said. And as one generation is on its way out and its successor takes over, it's worth our while to save the new generation from having to invent types and methods of operations which the previous generation has perfected to a tee. As the person who had had more operational experience than anybody else now in HQ – except for Udi and Levanon, that was indeed the case – I was asked to piece together

490

the principles and write them up as a manual on how operations were carried out.

The months passed by, I wrote what I wrote, and once every few weeks took part in various operations as HQ's representative. 'My' operations were mostly the simpler ones, all the rest were handled by other senior HQ staff.

My new role gave me access to the division's entire archive, including the operational files so that I could extract its operational principles from them. And there, to my utter astonishment, and horror, I came across my file, tagged The Cat. The tag was based on one remark included in the transcript, made by the Head of Division about me settling down in Russia: Yogev is a cat, Udi had said. He becomes troubled by his own reasoning, he confuses himself but in the end he falls on his feet. He looks like a domesticated pet but he's a born hunter. And, somebody else added, asking that his name not appear in the record, he fucks and cries, just like a real cat. Goes to show how wrong even those who'd known me for a long time could be. This cat, who didn't want to hunt anyone, had fallen flat on its face – for the second time. The separate file on the operation conducted against me in St Petersburg was labelled 'Cat in Snow'.

No one was farsighted enough to think of the possibility that as a result of my free access to the archive both The Cat and Cat in Snow files would fall into my hands. And so, before anybody became aware of this lapse, all the material relating to me and Anna was mine to read: transcripts of discussions, records of internal phone conversations, operational orders, reports of intelligence gathering rounds, debriefings, memoranda, operation log books.

When I found Cotton Field's reports they seemed to me to be utterly fatuous. As Levanon had commented at the time, obviously he would say that she was a KGB woman, and so guarantee himself additional debriefings and further payments. So, it was on this they based their whole thinking? On a slippery ex-KGB guy? On the basis of this flimsy evidence they decided to destroy my life?

But before I'd done anything with these feelings, I came across Udi's reports from St Petersburg, the material about incriminating Anna, and the outrageous web of deception that had been woven around me. I was dumbfounded. Not because I hadn't sensed it – after all something about the photographs and cassette had seemed strange. What astounded me was that the Division had invested so much in a psychological warfare operation, a method that wasn't at all part of its usual routine. Also shocking were some of the small details I now discovered. How could it possibly have occurred to me that at the time they'd broken into my home, Alex had seen the tickets for the opera, and that that was how *Eugene Onegin* became part of their plan, a part that finally broke me? I remembered what Anna had said about the death of Pushkin, that if it hadn't been so tragic it could well have been woven into a satire of his. I felt I was an actor playing a role in the Theatre of the Absurd.

Appalled and consumed by regret for having bowed to rationality and not gone with my gut feelings, I again demanded an urgent meeting with Udi.

He was unnerved by the very idea that in addition to all the other operational documents I'd also gone into the files related to me. Before confronting me, he gave an order to transfer all these files to the archive in the Bureau of the head of the Mossad to which I, of course, had no access.

Don't twist things, I fumed. Fortunately for you, in a weird kind of way, going through the files has enabled me to see things from the Mossad's point of view and to understand what would have happened if I'd refused to cooperate. You would have tried to kidnap me and God only knows where we would all have ended up. Me, you, the team, and Anna. So I'm not going to war because of the way you chose to make me come back to Israel, even though what I should do before anything else is to turn your desk over. I haven't the strength for that right now. All I want is for you to admit to having made a mistake and enable me to go to wherever Anna is or, alternatively, bring her here.

I respect your assessment of Cotton Field's information, Udi said keeping his cool. But the information per se isn't the determining factor. It's what his controllers say that counts. In their view he is credible and reliable, something that's been proven by many other reports of his. Enough Yogev, he said, almost pleading with me. We've been here before and your request was rejected. Nothing new has happened since then and everything you have discovered is known to us and was considered by us. It's nearly a year since you left St Petersburg, and face it, Anna has not made contact with you in all that time. Tel

Aviv is full of thirty something, single women. Pick one, change path, and start living again.

Can you hear what you're saying? I asked, losing control. If she's looking for someone she's looking for Paul Gupta in Canada. You go and change your woman, whom you only see at night, when she moves to the other side of the bed.

It's a pity Yogev. I'm ready to take your yelling but the organization won't be willing to tolerate your foolishness. This story is over. Do yourself a huge favour and end it, both in your head and in your heart. Don't think for a moment that I don't understand how much it hurts. I also know what love is and how painful it would be if I were forced one day to part from the woman who moves to the other side of the bed when I finally get there at night.

I left his room shamefaced, annoyed, and enormously frustrated. But inside me a new understanding began to emerge. Involving the Mossad was not going to work. I was alone in this.

The emotional baggage I was carrying in my heart did its job. Gone were the quiet hours I'd spend with either Udi or Levanon waiting for reports from the field when they felt free to divulge some nuggets of information about the operation against me. I ended all social contact with them as well as with all the others involved, and asked to be excused from attending Department Heads' meetings. I did my work and created a closed-off enclave for myself within HQ.

And at night I began to plan how to get Anna back. Even if she'd been forced to move apartments or sell the shop in the absence of the rent I used to pay, she's surely to be found somewhere in St Petersburg. And even if I were to be prevented from travelling and my phone conversations were tapped, nothing could stop me from recruiting an assistant, a Russia immigrant, and sending him there. I would instruct him to find her, explain what had happened, and help her to come here.

I located such a person, an immigrant who had arrived in Israel many years before, a solitary man who lived in my building. I spoke to him a number of times trying to understand what type of person he was, in the course of which he showed a willingness to work for me in Russia. However, before I really put him in the picture, I realized what a dangerous situation I'd be exposing him to if there was even the tiniest grain of truth in the Mossad's assumptions about Anna. I had to construct a more sophisticated plan and find a more experienced person to help me.

Weeks passed and then, in a chance meeting with Alex in the corridor, I found out what had happened to Anna. Have you heard that your girl friend is in jail? the paunchy little bear-like Russian casually asked me.

Stunned, I listened to the summary report from Cotton Field which described Anna's attempt to leave Russia so as to be with me, her arrest at the airport, her subsequent trial, and the heavy sentence imposed on her which she was now serving in a Moscow prison.

The unvarnished account distressed me so much that Alex asked me to come into his office and sit down, telling his secretary to get me a glass of water. He sat facing me, looking serious and pale. Did you really not know anything about this?

Nothing, I confirmed, and sipped the water.

We've only known for a month or so because Anna Petrovna is no longer on our required intelligence list, he said, and I choked at hearing the name I so loved. There was a round of meetings with Cotton Field last month, and it was only by chance, in a conversation with his controller, that he mentioned this. The controller just noted it in the margins of his report and it was also ranked by us simply as a rumour that was apparently circulating among the Field's sources.

My Annushka. Paying the price for loving me. And the SOBs knew and kept their mouths shut.

Alex saw the expression on my face as I got up. Listen, he said, I don't know if I was supposed to tell you this. But by then I was already out of his room.

Come, I said to Levanon as I passed his office. He got up immediately and followed me. I opened the door to Udi's room, and instructed Ariel, who was sitting there with him, to leave us alone. And close the door behind you.

Immense anger was flowing through my veins.

I won't settle accounts with you right now but the day of reckoning will come, you can be sure of that. I've only just found out about Anna. Turns out you not only screwed up my life but hers as well. Neither of you will have a moment's peace until she is here, is that clear? As far as I'm concerned she's another one of our hostages being held by the enemy. And that should also be the way you see it, because it must now be clear, even to you, that she protected me and is paying the price.

Udi continued sitting at his desk, Levanon was still standing at the door, and I too remained on my feet. They exchanged glances but didn't look directly at me.

I don't know how you're going to do it. Whether it will be in an exchange of prisoners, understandings between the prime minister and Putin – or maybe you'll work out a plan for breaking into the prison. This Division has already done things like that. And don't, not even for a moment, think that I'm now in shock and that tomorrow I'll be over it. I'm going to turn the whole world and his wife upside down until Anna is here.

Yogev…

Don't you Yogev me, I cut Udi short. I'll stir up the sort of trouble you've never even dreamed of, including going there myself, to get her out.

Yogev, I'm not going to try and calm you down right now, Udi said, but there isn't a single move we made that cannot be explained or that I don't stand behind. The fact that she's in prison doesn't mean that we were wrong, perhaps the very opposite. Think about it. And I suggest you don't resort again to threats of any kind.

He looked me straight in the eye. Not a muscle on his face moved. There is a draft indictment against you for treason and spying. We prevented the Shin Bet from handing it to the Public Prosecutor, but that means nothing. For the indictment to be sent to the Prosecutor all that needs to happen is for us to lift our opposition. Even your being here with us is a response to their insistence that you be kept under our constant supervision. This move of ours was intended to demonstrate the extent to which we trust you. Don't play with a fire that can easily and completely turn you to ashes.

From the look on Udi's face, and from the quiet tone in which he spoke, it was clear to me that what he'd said was the truth. For some reason I wasn't that surprised to discover what my position was. But I understood that the ruthless game of chess that began in St Petersburg a year earlier had not yet ended. I attacked with a pawn and was taken by a knight. I tried to counter with a bishop and was threatened by a rook. I didn't have many more pieces left in this game and the queen was vulnerable.

Levanon put his hand on my shoulder. Since we received the information we've been in two minds as to what to do with her, he said. We thought of telling you the moment we found a way of doing something. We've already sat with the head of the Foreign Relations Division and even with the head of Nativ, the organization responsible for bringing Jews from the Soviet Bloc to Israel. We've also brought Gedalyahu, head of the department dealing with hostages and missing persons, into the picture. We still don't have a clear plan. However, as Udi said to you, he continued in dulcet tones, don't threaten and don't do anything stupid. You could easily disappear in the wing where 'X' prisoners are held, and after the sentence you'd receive for espionage you'd get out of jail in ten to fifteen years. Our organization is much stronger than you are, and more powerful than any system that could supposedly help you.

I knew that despite all their vacillations, Udi and Levanon, in acting against me, had done what they were ordered to do. I knew that they would do the same again.

I left Udi's office, picked up my few belongings from my room, my passport from the documentation office, left the gates of the Mossad behind me, and never returned.

42

NO ONE CAME running after me or applied pressure on me to return. It was clear to both sides that the breach between us was beyond repair. My interpretation of Anna's arrest was difficult to argue with. She and I had been sacrificed, the Mossad and the FSB were the sacrificers. The details weren't relevant. There was only one possible conclusion to be drawn. In light of this bottom line there could be no lingering doubts.

From then on my communications with the office went through Gedalyahu. On one occasion I met the person in the prime minister's office responsible for hostages and missing persons. He wanted to hear a firsthand account of 'Anna story'. Gedalyahu was in touch once a week to update me on what was being done. For the most part he had nothing new to tell me and I assumed that this was the office's way of maintaining contact and keeping abreast of what was happening to me and what state of mind I was in. I also assumed that my phone was being tapped and that I was under some sort of surveillance. The office turned over responsibility for me back to the Shin Bet, and any judge receiving a request from them to allow phone tapping or filming under the heading 'suspicion of espionage' was bound to grant such a petition. The other way of keeping contact with me was via my salary which, for some reason, kept on being deposited in my bank account on the first of every month.

Gedalyahu gave me to understand that the state was adopting Anna as 'one of ours', and that she was being treated no differently from any other missing person or hostage. Anna's case is not clear cut, he said. It's a bit awkward for us to go to the Russians and say she's 'ours' – were we to do that she'd get twenty years instead of the ten she's already been sentenced to and would never be allowed out of Russia.

This was the first time I'd heard that Anna had been sentenced to ten years. I felt dizzy. Gedalyahu was surprised that I didn't know – this detail was also included in Cotton Field's information.

Believe me we are doing everything possible to get her freed but it's complicated, Gedalyahu told me. We only have fragments of information as to what the Russians know or think. The 'Field' says they know you got to Tel Aviv but assume this was only a stopover. According to him you are listed by them as being a CIA operative.

How come? I remonstrated, as I saw Anna's release slipping from our grasp.

No one understands why. As far as the Russians are concerned Tel Aviv, like Copenhagen, was only an attempt to mislead them. If Anna's release is at all possible it will be in the context of a deal between them and the CIA. Not

500

long ago we brought the CIA into the frame, and there's a chance that they will ask for her in exchange for Russian spies held in the US. But they're not going to do that without making us pay. Right now they're talking about another big gesture from us to strengthen Mahmoud Abbas, and even Hamas, by agreeing to a further release of Palestinian prisoners. And for your information, because of this demand the prime minister himself is now involved in Anna's case. In a nutshell it's very very complicated.

I believed Gedalyahu that it was very complicated, indeed too complicated for me to be able to just sit back and do nothing, waiting for a move which might never happen. I began to plan my own private rescue operation. It was no longer a matter of activating some Russian immigrant to establish contact. It had now become an operation in every sense of the word.

The hundreds of intelligence files I'd helped create in the distant past and which I'd reviewed ahead of missions I'd planned and approved more recently, enabled me to work in a very organized way. I made a list of exactly what I needed to know and how I was to obtain this information, starting off by dipping into unclassified sources.

Alex had said that Anna was being held in a Moscow jail. I soon had a full file on Moscow and its prisons that I found on various internet sites, as well as clearly defined pictures from Google Earth. First of all I needed to find out which one Anna was in. I would also have to look at exits from prisons. Did the inmates work beyond the boundaries of the jail itself – in factories, in various forms of forced labour? And if they did, how were they taken there and what sort of surveillance were they under while working? Were they let out of jail on 'home leave' as prisoners in Israel were? Russia was, after all, still a police state. But if they were allowed short stays out of prison – how much time did a prisoner have to serve before being granted such leave and what kind of surveillance were they under while out? It was clear to me that my best chance of rescuing Anna was to kidnap her when she was outside the prison and not from inside it.

With the help of various organizations of immigrants from the Soviet Union, I located some who'd been jailed in these very same prisons, and arranged to visit them making myself out to be a 'government official'. My aim was to find out what the security arrangements were in these places and what the prisoners' daily routines consisted of. I even found one woman – a 'refusnik' who'd been in the women's prison in Moscow and, decades later, was able to dredge up astonishingly detailed memories of her time there. But she was an exception. The majority of immigrants I questioned had been in Soviet jails a long time before, and the answers I was given were contradictory and confusing. Whereas my 'refusnik' and the internet referred to Novinskaya prison as a women's prison, there were others who insisted that it had been closed down many years earlier and that all political prisoners were now incarcerated in Lefortovo prison. The most worrying detail I learned was that all jails in Moscow were no more than detention and interrogation centres, and that once sentence had been passed the accused were sent to a *Zona*, a name denoting a prison in a remote area. In this context, two of those I talked to even told me the same sad joke: They say that the Lubyanka – today the headquarters of the secret service and where, over the years, opponents of the regime were detained and interrogated in the basement – is the highest building in Moscow. And do you know why? Because from there you can see Siberia.

Knowing where Anna was being held was, of course, the precondition for any operation. The immigrants I talked to said that this probably wasn't classified information and that I could perhaps discover where she was by sending her letters and addressing them to a number of prisons. I knew that her mail would be read by the prison authorities and I considered, therefore, sending her postcards with a rented mailbox as a return address and a name and contents that only she would be able to fathom.

If that didn't succeed I would need inside information. That was only obtainable if I could mobilize a male or female guard working in one of the jails to help. I thought that for a decent amount of money I'd find someone willing to supply me with information about both her whereabouts and her movements. But to get hold of someone like that I would have to track down a male or female guard on their way home from the prison.

In the absence of information about where she was being held, all I could do was plan the abduction and getaway in the most general of terms. I'd need transport and an apartment; I'd need to check the fastest routes out of Russia, to the Republics, and identify unmanned border crossings or those that could be bypassed. And even when I had found out where they were, I would need to gather intelligence from the field before I could mount the operation. That would take quite some time.

I thought about making a getaway by plane directly from Moscow or the surrounding area, a possibility that would be relevant if Anna turned out to be held in an area close to the city. Such a plan would necessitate access to an airport and a small plane. I had a vague memory of a group of brave 'refuseniks' who tried to do just that and failed. It didn't mean that I too would fail, but it did mean that I'd have to invest a great deal of time and effort in the planning.

After I typed the word 'Moscow' in various internet aviation sites, up came the names of airports I'd never heard of not far from the city. Myachkovo, Bykovo, Chkalovsky. Enlarging Google's satellite photos gave me an initial idea about these airfields. I chose a small private strip used mainly for short flights in light aircraft and started working on it. Clearly, to know if this was a realistic option I would have to go there and gather information about the fencing around the field, its security arrangements, working hours, and aviation companies using it. And then as the time for putting the operation into practice approached, I'd have to bribe a pilot, perhaps also tackle the field's security guards and risk an aerial chase.

Of course, everything would have been much easier were I able to ask the Mossad for help. A small question put by Alex to his sources in Russia could have unearthed where Anna was being held, whether she ever left the jail and if so, when. One little passport, with a picture of Anna, would have enabled me to sneak her out of Russia before anyone noticed she was gone. But there was zero chance of me getting such assistance. At some stage I thought of turning for help to my friend Mahashashli, but I rejected that possibility out of hand: he would profit a good deal more by handing me over to the Russians than by helping me.

Slowly, slowly, as I uncovered the information, the various options crystallized and I began to fine-tune the scheme. The semi-psychological stages in the planning of every operation were known to me and I experienced them this time as well. At first the idea one has appears to be unfeasible. As the information is assembled, it begins to look possible. But then, as you start to fine-tune the chosen plan and need to gather the small but essential pre-operational intelligence details, once more it slips from your grasp, appearing impossible to implement. It's easy enough to say 'bribe a female prison guard'. But how, in practice, do you track down such a person? Bribe a pilot who flies there? But how do you find one? It's very simple to say 'bypass the border with Kazakhstan' but how and precisely where does one bypass it? Even without help, however, the plan was possible. The risks would be mine. It's me that the jailer, the pilot, and border guard might hand over. It's me who's likely to spend years to come, close to Anna, but in a nearby prison.

I remembered how, years earlier, I'd crossed the border from Russia to Kazakhstan, just before we liquidated the drivers of the missile transporters. That led me to assume that if I prowled around the border I'd again find passable gaps. Were I to wait in my car outside the prison gates, I'd be able to spot a female guard and follow her back to her house. Were I to sleep in a hotel close to the airport, there'd be a good chance of my meeting pilots there and forming a working relationship with one of them. Afterwards there'd be all sorts of other obstacles but in the end I'd succeed.

I was in the mood for action, a very different mood from the one I'd been in for a whole year. At night I imagined Annushka's face as I stopped my car alongside her just as she was walking out of the prison gate on 'home leave', if such a thing existed; or setting off for work, holding on tightly to her few bundled belongings. I'd open the door and say, Annushka, *zahadi* – get in. And I could see her face as we reached the next street, and imagine her pouncing on me with hugs and kisses and her expression when I told her a plane was waiting for us on the runway. Hold on tight, I'm going to drive right through the fence. Or when I told her, we're on our way to Kazakhstan, Annushka, do you want to sleep first? I have an apartment here.

For the first time since my return to Israel I masturbated, imagining Anna's face, filled with passion, biting her lower lip, her eyes closed, her black hair streaked with grey spread out like a hand-held fan, and she was the most beautiful being on earth. I pictured her firm thighs, her slightly rounded buttocks, those shapely shoulders, and her soft, ample, pendulous breasts. And those eyes of hers, wide open, with love. Eyes that said everything I wanted to hear with one caressing, yearning, lustful, look.

I felt like someone fighting his last war. The war over his last love. Orit was my first love and I knew that Anna was the last. There wouldn't be another.

I gleaned whatever I could from sources in Israel. To find Anna and draw up a detailed plan I had to be there, in the field. Only in that way could I find prison guards and through them discover where Anna was. I would then have to familiarize myself with the region in which the jail was located, discover the routes I could take from there to a nearby airfield, or those that led to the border, and rent an apartment along the way. I had a lot to do. The old horse did indeed smell war, and the wind of battle was certainly coursing through his veins.

All I had was an Israeli passport. Through a major travel agency I obtained a visa for Russia and bought a ticket for a direct flight to Moscow. At Ben Gurion Airport, shortly after I passed through passport control, two Shin Bet agents came up to me and I was arrested.

You're playing with fire and you think that you can control the height of the flames and that you yourself won't be burned, the senior Shin Bet investigator summoned to the airport said to me.

I don't care about getting burned, I said, or for that matter, igniting a fire, even if what I've done is made known to the Russians.

Apparently you also don't care about your girlfriend, the investigator retorted. Your chances of freeing her were very small. Anyone you turned to for help would have handed you over to the authorities. They'd have taken the money, and then betrayed you. Meanwhile your girlfriend would never again have seen the light of day. And nor would you. And by the way, her chances of getting out early aren't at all bad. The only thing you were about to do was to spoil that chance.

I'd said nothing to my interrogators about my plan to free Anna. Where had they got their information from?

What difference does it make where we got it from? We knew about every move you made and all the people you questioned. At your trial all the material in your computer will also be presented as evidence. The police are confiscating your computer as we speak.

The Shin Bet had been listening into all my conversations, were aware of all my meetings and, apparently, everything stored in my computer was also known to them.

What are you detaining and questioning me for anyway? I protested. I'm allowed to travel to Russia and even if I wanted to commit a crime there that's none of your business. The only ones whose business it is are the Russians.

We don't have to prove that you've committed any new crimes, the investigator replied in a quiet, firm voice. We have plenty of those to work with from your past. Did you know that the polygraph test didn't show that you were telling the truth? And even without that we have enough to throw you into jail for a very long time.

So get on with it, I said, refusing this time to succumb. Let me go now, and issue an indictment against me. I don't believe there's a judge who'd be foolish enough to buy your crude attempts to incriminate me.

You're not going anywhere. An order prohibiting you from leaving the country was issued a long time ago and you should thank me if, instead of your going straight to jail, I can arrange for you to be put under house arrest while we straighten things out between us.

This is quite a police state isn't it?

The investigator didn't respond and left the room. A few minutes later he returned with Udi who, it transpired, had been watching the conversation on CCTV.

I'm here to sort things out, Udi said, and not as head of Division which I stopped being this week. You can look upon me as a friend, if you want.

With friends like you…I said and stopped. A bout of foolish curiosity got the better of me: Levanon?

What, my replacement? No, Micha actually. He was recalled from Tzomet to be my deputy a few months ago. Levanon is his deputy.

This was the very last thing that should have been of interest to me at that particular moment, but I was happy to know that the likeable, chubby, blond-haired Micha, champion of interpersonal relations, had got the job. For just a moment my mind went back to our days together in Hong Kong and Seoul, remembering the tour company he opened for us in the Seychelles and then his leaving us to join the division responsible for recruiting agents where he quickly climbed to the top.

Udi didn't respond to my earlier pique and we went back to what we'd been discussing. It was agreed that I be placed under house arrest until a contract was drawn up between the Mossad and me regarding the continuation of my activities. The Mossad still saw me as its man and the pay slips I got were proof of that. The Shin Bet once again dropped their insistence on dealing with me, but this time my passport was confiscated.

After a week of wrangling, Udi told me that he'd arranged things with the Mossad. It's OK. They're willing to give up on the indictment and agree not to restrict you. But your passport will remain with us, and the expectation is that you will stay in the Tel Aviv area and have no involvement with the subject of Anna. It is in any case being dealt with, and all you can do is spoil things. Do yourself a favour and believe me. Please.

At least they won't be able to prevent me from thinking about Anna day and night.

And then the Mossad discharged me and I had to begin working for my living. Udi said that this had also been one of their considerations in the decision to let me go. In their view I had too much time on my hands in which to plan idiotic schemes and would now be preoccupied with the difficulties of earning a living.

I soon realized that there were very few things I knew how to do. A first degree in East Asian Studies and partial command of Mandarin Chinese were perhaps good for a young guy of twenty-five but not for a forty-something man. A second degree in International Relations was also of no value to someone not about to start an academic or diplomatic career. I felt that agriculture would suit me best. But from the enquiries I made it was clear that no famer would take me on as a hired hand. The Thai workers did a good job and cheaply. I even offered my services to farmers on the border with Gaza but to no avail. I didn't really see myself working as a hired hand on my parents' farm but curiosity led me there.

The journey to the Arava was like watching a film. It was as if I was day dreaming. When the Dead Sea came into view it looked smaller than I remembered, its colours more beautiful. Shades of turquoise locked between ponds of blue separated from each other by embankments of dry earth that stretched all the way to Jordan. The soil of the Arava was grey and crumbly and there were warnings of sink-holes all along the route. In several petrol stations I discovered new restaurants and cafés. But I didn't allow that to delay me. Though I wasn't short of time and knew that this visit of mine wouldn't alter the course my life, an inner feeling of unease made me up my speed. The Mazda 3 I'd hired – after the car that I got as head of department was taken away from me – didn't really help matters, as it insisted on sticking to its own plodding pace.

The entrance to the village looked different but I couldn't put my finger on what it was that had changed. The electric iron gate was shut, the remote control that I'd used in the past had got lost somewhere, and I had to wait until another vehicle arrived to let me in. I drove around the village's outer perimeter roads. The vegetation had grown tall and almost completely obscured the houses in the original village, and those built since were also already cloaked in green. New sheds had been added to each farm, and everywhere I looked I could see living quarters that had been built for the Thai workers. On the eastern side of the village I came across a large group of them playing billiards on the terrace of a club set up especially for them, a table covered by empty beer bottles at the side.

I drove along the village's inner road to my parents' house which was hidden from view by a new packaging shed. In the car park were cars I didn't recognize and two tractors. My parents' house had also changed. What was once a small Jewish Agency-built home had become the residential wing of the house and along its front a new and large extension had been built which, I soon discovered, included a spacious guest room and a modern kitchen. My parents had always opposed the idea of a 'water guzzling carpet', but now grass had been planted in front of the house and I missed the smell of the old fruit trees which had always welcomed me and had been felled so as to make room for the lawn. Two ancient palm trees on either side of the new gate had me momentarily pining for a bygone era. Everything else looked unfamiliar and strange.

Yehiel welcomed me warmly as his wife and children danced around us. When he heard that I wanted to go back to farming he immediately offered me work 'at a very high wage' and said he'd arrange a room for me in the guest room free of charge. I thanked him but preferred not to accept his generous offer. After he told me about all the renovations on the farm I said my goodbyes. I knew I had to start a new life rather than trying to hold on to the remnants of my former existence.

I decided not to pass up on the opportunity of visiting Orit. I felt sufficiently detached to do this without risking more heartache. She was happy to see me but she too seemed distant. I didn't feel I was doing her any good, especially in light of her little daughter's repeated questions, who is this, *ima* who is this and, is this your boyfriend? Orit didn't answer, and I didn't know what she felt towards me.

She was tired, thin, a bit more grown up and a bit different from the Orit I'd known. Precisely in what way she'd changed I couldn't say. She didn't mention her husband and I didn't ask about him. I had the feeling he wasn't living there, a feeling that grew when the little girl sat on my lap and constantly tried to attract my attention.

I remember the last time I held her, I said to Orit, and we both lowered our eyes. For each of us my father's Shiva seemed eons ago.

I told her a bit about what had been happening to me in words that didn't disclose anything. The work in Russia has come to an end. I've also stopped working for the Mossad altogether. I'm free now, looking for other work, perhaps farming.

Had these words been said at a different time, in a different reality, they could have steered our lives along a different path. But they hadn't and now it seemed that for her as well as for me that was an abstract, intangible, earlier existence which could not be resurrected. There'd been a death between us.

Orit for her part offered almost no information, and this conversation also died. It seemed to me that she no longer had any feelings for the half lifetime we'd spent together. I left saddened that the woman with whom I'd experienced most of the significant events of my life – until the arrival of Anna – could fade out of my existence in such a way leaving only a big void inside me.

Afterwards I went to the small cemetery, took the gravediggers' hoe out of the shed and cleared away the dry overgrowth around my father's neglected grave. When I was done, the sun had already begun to set and I sat myself down on the tombstone. It occurred to me that this was a situation in which I was supposed to talk to him. But the words didn't come, and all I could sense was yet one more heavy stone on my chest. What could I possibly say that would please him? I was angry with myself for having such primitive thoughts but promised, him or myself, that I would return and plant flowers there. Then I rolled the great big stone inside me along with all the other parts of my body back to the car.

I returned to Tel Aviv and decided to advertise my services as a gardener, the nearest thing to being a farmer I could think of. I placed ads in a number of nearby streets, and the response was surprising. Within a short time I had about ten gardens to tend in the neighbourhood. It was work that filled my days and gave me a nice income.

I enjoyed gardening in much the same way as I had once enjoyed working in the fields. I loved going into a neglected garden, rooting out the thorns, wild grass, and plants which had once been sown with great affection and hope and had since died. I had a passion for digging up a whole area – my arms and hands quickly got used to the pick and hoe – then planning the garden and planting it. I felt strong again. Plants that took root, greening carpets of grass, and flowerbeds that produced fields of colour, filled me with contentment. In the evenings I read. In the winter I looked out of the window at the sun setting between the clouds over the houses across the street; in spring, when the sun descended over the strip of sea visible from my balcony, I remained sitting there. In the summer I turned the balcony light on and read deep into the night. And then I went to sleep with Annushka, trembling as I imagined her in her cold damp cell, my eyes moistening.

I'd spent an entire year in the office after my return from St Petersburg and I found it hard to believe that almost two years had passed since I left it. In that time the perennials blossomed, wilted, and blossomed again. I'd uprooted seasonal flowers and planted new ones, replacing the flowers of winter with those of spring and summer's bloom with that of autumn. My life went on and remained unchanged at one and the same time, like the ebb and flow of life in our country, a place which appeared to be stumbling from bad to worse. The launch of an unsuccessful war in Lebanon to the north, helplessness in facing up to Hamas in the south. But who was I to talk of helplessness? Who was I to say anything about weakness and failure? I was planting and uprooting flowers during that whole period, and feeling utterly redundant.

The fire within me at the time of the first Lebanon war hadn't left even a dying ember. Being released from the Mossad meant returning to my unit in the reserves. But I was past the age for combat duty. I wasn't called and had no desire to volunteer when war broke out there again. I didn't even have the strength to get angry with what I was hearing on the news. And, of course, I also lacked the strength to organize another kidnapping operation at a time when the whole of the country's attention revolved around its newly taken hostages. Almost everything took my thoughts back to St Petersburg and Anna.

The sorrow at the death in Lebanon of Uri Grossman, son of the writer David Grossman, which linked private to national grief and saddened so many people, returned me in my pain to the conversation with Anna about Grossman's and Amos Oz's books. When the besieged inhabitants of Gaza breached the border with Egypt, it reminded me of the many monuments erected in memory of the heroes of the Siege of Leningrad. In Victory Park, opposite my apartment, there were a number of such monuments. A leader who didn't know history, I thought, and doesn't understand how a siege creates myths and heroes on the opposing side, should at least know something about biology and realize how the more fertile womb slowly changes the demographic balance. 'A hollow leadership', David Grossman's words echoed within me. The whole nation can hear the voices but the leaders are deaf. There is nothing new under the sun except the people who are in pain.

And every week, for two years, if his call didn't come first, I called Gedalyahu, head of the Mossad's unit for hostages and missing persons. I'd ask for an update, remind him of my existence, of Anna's existence, and of the fact that I wasn't giving up on her. Gedalyahu could only promise that 'it's being worked on' and I, a stowaway in the pained and ever growing family of people whose nearest and dearest are being held or are 'missing', could only hope that he was telling the truth.

Epilogue

43

MY PHONE RANG early one the morning. It was Gedalyahu.

Yogev, are you awake?

I am now.

So sit up and listen.

I'm listening, I said, sitting up in my bed.

Anna Petrovna.

My heart skipped a beat, all trace of sleep gone.

What's happened to her? I asked apprehensively.

Nothing to worry about. Listen. As we hoped, the Russians offered to release her in exchange for some of their spies detained in America. In return, the Americans asked that the Russians put pressure on Hamas and are demanding that Israel increase the number of Palestinian prisoners due to be released. The prime minister agreed to the American demand and the US in turn has accepted the Russian proposal. During the night, the Russians put her on a flight from Moscow to Berlin and a number of Russian spies were flown out of New York. Understand?

I mumbled some kind of a 'thank you'.

Don't think that anyone's doing you a favour here. The Russians wanted their people back and the Americans wanted us to move our ass a bit to prevent Mahmoud Abbas from being toppled and to ensure that the big deal progresses. During the last few rounds of negotiations it became clear that if we didn't up the number of freed prisoners and the Russians failed to push Hamas nothing was going to move. So everything's been put together now and Anna is the beneficiary. It's true that I put in a word, perhaps even gave them the idea. But you, me and Anna are minor players in this show. This is the first part of a big game; there must be no leaks. Even when it's all done and dusted everyone will have to keep their mouths shut. Get it?

He didn't wait for my answer, and nor did I completely understand. I tried to assimilate the bottom line. Anna is being freed.

An hour ago, the Americans and the Red Cross transferred Anna, just as she was, to an El Al flight bound for here, he continued. You are welcome to come to the airport and take her under your protection, if you want. No one knows what to do with her. Yogev, are you with me?

I didn't answer. A stream of tears flowed from my eyes, and a sharp pain sliced its way through my chest. I could barely breathe.

The special document given to me by the Mossad got me through passport control and I headed for the gate at which the El Al flight from Berlin was due to arrive. I waited at the top of the passenger walkway attached to the plane. The passengers began to emerge. Businessmen, a few families, people returning from holiday. Most of the travellers came out all at once and the numbers then tapered off.

An elderly-looking, thin woman dressed in tattered clothes came into sight at the far end of the corridor, stopped close to the last bend before the walkway's connection to the terminal building, and set down a big plastic bag at her feet. She stood there looking bewildered and as her eyes searched for the exit she spotted me coming towards her.

Annushka? Annushka?

Her hair was grey, her shoulders visibly bony under the threadbare coat, her posture stooped. As I got a little closer what I recognized first of all were her almond eyes which now had large black rings under them; eyes that were open so wide as to stretch right across the tormented face. For a brief moment there was a glint, a flicker of recognition, and then it was gone. A two-edged sword embedded itself in my heart – one blade of love the other of pain.

What have they done to you, my Annushka? I ran towards her and cradled her head in the palms of my hands. Her eyes were dead, simply two gaping hollows. Then, from the corners, droplets of tears began to flow.

When I hugged her I could feel the fleshless bones jutting out. Holding her close to me in an embrace I could see the many white hairs interlaced with the remnants of black. Her cheek bones protruded and her face was etched with wrinkles. She was a different woman, a shadow of the woman I'd loved so much. In an involuntary movement, her tongue wet the edges of her chapped lips and the sword, already sheathed in my flesh, was drawn and stabbed me once more. I brought my face closer to hers, wetting her lips with my tongue, pulling her towards me, kissing her with all the pain pent up inside me during all those long bleak years I'd been without her.

She responded apprehensively, hesitatingly, unsure of my love.

I had no desire to force myself on her.

My Annushka, at last, was all I managed to say before I choked up, lifted the plastic bag, gently wrapped my arms round her scrawny shoulders, and led her slowly down the long passageway to passport control. She had absolutely no energy, and very nearly collapsed in my arms. Her feet, clad in a pair of ungainly overshoes, barely carried her.

Her eyes darted from side to side, finding it hard to absorb the dazzlingly bright light, the array of colours, and the multitude of sounds all around. Some twelve hours had passed since the circular prisoner swap in which her name had been included a long time ago, and she was unexpectedly taken out of her cold damp prison cell, dressed, and driven off to the airport.

Waiting at passport control was a Shin Bet agent who escorted us to the other side of the counters. I'll leave you alone now, he said, but tomorrow you have to come to us together with her, OK? We can't do without the minimum of debriefings.

Do you have a suitcase? I asked as we went past the luggage carousels, and Anna smiled in embarrassment.

They let me out just like this, even the clothes aren't mine, apparently they belong to another prisoner who was jailed not long ago. There wasn't time to look for my things in the storage room. They gave me a bit of money and I bought a blanket so I'd have something to cover myself with if there wasn't anywhere for me to sleep.

Didn't you know I'd be here?

I knew nothing. Even when I tried to follow you I didn't know if you'd really be here. I had theories and I had hopes but you left without saying a word.

Annushka, my poor thing, I halted again and held her tight, covering her head with kisses. Without knowing anything for sure, you simply tried to follow me? And how did you know to come here? I was confused.

You disappeared, I didn't think our people would arrest you without saying anything to me, and I thought that perhaps your friends had kidnapped you, and that this was the only place where I could find you again. And then I made some mistakes…

My Annushka. I don't know if I'll ever be able to atone for that moment of weakness when I believed them, and not you. What a price you've paid for that lapse of mine!

Only then did her words sink in, and my heart dropped. Our people, she'd said. Our people; arrested you. If so, then she really was one of them, as the Mossad had said. As I hadn't dared to even suspect. On our way to the car, the feelings in my heart ran wild, collided, and shattered into fragments of fear and doubt; the fear that she'd been sent to entice me as part of her job; the belief that she'd fallen in love with me and duped her employers; the catastrophe that my innocent love had brought on her and very nearly also on me and my colleagues. And all of these were overshadowed by the big questions that had completely preoccupied me from the moment I saw her at the gate: Did I still love her, and if so, how much? Did she still love me, and to what extent? We had a long way to go before we could get back to the way we were.

When we came out, the bright light hit the car and Anna shielded her eyes, eyes that had barely seen sunshine for three years and had never been exposed to anything as dazzling as this. Very slowly, like a baby peeping through the fingers of its hand, she let the vistas in, and only when we'd left the airport area did she remove the protective hand from her eyes.

She stared, wide-eyed, at the gleaming freeway, at the interchanges, at the green fields and the city's houses rising up in front of us, and didn't say a word. As we flowed with the traffic along the Ayalon highway, I saw Anna looking in wonder at the structures surrounding it, a mixture of old buildings and newly erected skyscrapers. And when we passed the Azrieli Towers, the highest of them all, I could see her turning her head back, gazing at them in amazement. What sort of visual image does a Russian who doesn't know a thing about Israel have of the place? A desert? Camels and tents? A Jewish shtetl? Will Anna be able to live in this hot, harsh country?

We drove west along Arlosoroff Street and I began to talk. I explained that this was the Israeli style of building, functional, not the grand façades of St Petersburg, and avoided adding that here the buildings' interiors weren't neglected. I turned at Hayarkon Street in the direction of my building.

I tried to decipher Anna's expression as we parked under the new building, went up in the elevator to the sixth and top floor, and then finally as we entered the spacious but sparsely furnished apartment. I saw the look of relief on her face when she realized that there wasn't another woman in the apartment.

This place is longing for a woman's touch, I said to remove any lingering doubt she may have had, and so am I.

Anna dropped to her knees, bursting into bitter tears, relieving the mass of doubts she'd lived with not only over the previous twenty-four hours but during the three years of her imprisonment. I too went down on my knees at her side, embracing her. I am not a woman any more, my love, she wept. Not only is my soul dry, but so too is my body. It was hunger.

For me you are more of a woman than any other woman could ever be, I said, wiping away her tears. And what am I if not an emasculated man? I gave into them over there, and I even allowed them to quash the plans I'd devised to rescue you.

What tortured me more than the conditions in prison, Anna said quietly, more than the cold, the damp walls, the thin mattress, the bucket full to the brim with faeces, the rats, the hunger, the drug addicts sharing my cell, was the question of why you left.

Her eyes, which could have looked at me reproachfully, were lowered. I wanted to care for her, to offer her sustenance, a shower, a change of clothes, but I knew that her desperate need to understand why I had disappeared was paramount. And I, who'd been hearing a voice inside me asking the very opposite question – what made her come to me in the first place – waited with bated breath for what she was going to say next.

I imagined that in the end the ex-KGB agent your bosses sent to find out who I was, told them that I was an FSB agent and that you were then promptly ordered to come back home. But I didn't know, nor could I understand, why you'd agreed to their demands. Did you believe that I was still spying on you and trying to trap you, I asked myself? Could it possibly be that you'd not yet realized that even had I known you were a spy I couldn't have betrayed you because I loved you so much?

The answers she was giving me began to dissolve that huge lump inside me.

That was something I couldn't believe, she continued, and I imagined that they had kidnapped you. After all, from their point of view, the moment you didn't go along with them, you became a deserter. And if you'd deserted and were living with an FSB woman you were definitely a traitor. All I knew were the details given to me by the counter-espionage division after they'd arrested me. They said you'd left accompanied by two escorts, that you'd used a fictitious name, that you'd flown to Copenhagen and from there to Tel Aviv. But was a gun pointed at your head? Did they threaten you? Did you resist? Perhaps what I was told was true and you really had cooperated with them and left of your own free will? These thoughts killed me. What especially hurt was the possibility that you'd used me in your spying activities. That was also something they said. Was it conceivable, I asked myself, that you got involved with me as part of your assignment, and not because you found me attractive?

Anna told me about Alexei Nikolayevich's horror show on the day she was arrested. The image projected by the look of torment on her face was an exact reflection of my own interrogation, of the suspicions that were hurled at me, the doubts, and the pain. It was as if it was me speaking in whispers through her chapped lips.

I tried to recollect what had happened between us, she said. I knew it was me that had approached you and yet, even knowing that, what went on in my head was simply terrible. I knew that you never asked and that I never said a thing about the counter-espionage division. But I couldn't avoid the thought that perhaps, just as I'd been given a task, which I hadn't carried out, you too had an assignment. I could only hope that just as my love for you stopped me from executing my task, the same was true of you…

My heart, cleansed of its doubts, was overflowing with love. As she spoke I held her hand, stroked her head, and swore to her that I had had absolutely no idea of who she was and that my love for her was the most complete love I'd ever felt.

But I saw it coming you know? she said, once she was able, like me, to put that part of the riddle to rest. During those last few days you weren't yourself. You were frightened and desperate, like an animal hunters had closed in on from every side. I tried to radiate an air of 'business as usual' but you couldn't conceal the despair in your eyes.

I had to remove the dark cloud hanging over my hasty departure, a retreat that had led to Anna spending three years of torment in prison. Tearfully, I told her about the appeals I'd rejected, the pressures and threats, and then about the pictures and the cassette.

But you know that they lied to you, don't you? she asked. What they showed you were photomontages and a tampered-with cassette. Once they got my reports that you were a bona fide businessman, they just about stopped using me, even though, because of that ex-KGB guy, the suspicions didn't altogether disappear. There was just one phone conversation, towards the end, when they suspected that some CIA agents were milling around our neighbourhood, and I denied it.

She paused for a while, reflecting, while I held her hand and stroked her. When she resumed, her voice was so low that I had to read her chapped lips which, from time to time, she continued to moisten with her tongue.

After you'd disappeared, I realized that what they'd claimed wasn't just hot air, that there really had been some people wandering around our neck of the woods – your people. But when I think about how stubborn you were in not responding to their demands, I cannot really be angry with them. Our guys would certainly have poisoned you for such behaviour.

I was poisoned, my beautiful Annushka, I said, clasping her anguished face, its Asian features now more pronounced, its colouring paler than I remembered. Words can also poison, so can voices and pictures. You, perhaps, are not angry with them, but my fury knows no bounds. First of all I'm angry with myself, that I believed what they'd said. But I'm mad at them as well.

A while later we sat on the balcony of my apartment. In the spring sunlight more wrinkles showed up on Anna's skin but the beginnings of a sense of relief and feeling of warmth permeated her body and seemed to soften the creases and to loosen her taut muscles somewhat. Her hand was held in mine, and she allowed herself to close her eyes, getting hooked on the sun. The hint of a smile began to appear in the corner of her mouth. My love for her was so great that I wanted to cry.

Her head tilted slightly to one side and she fell asleep. I opened the sun shade over her and went inside to make us something to eat. The continuation of Anna's story and what she knew about me came bit by bit in the course of the day.

You knew all the time? I asked when she woke up and slowly drank some of the fruit juice I'd brought her.

I knew, Anna replied. We knew about you before you arrived. An informant of ours in the CIA – they apparently know everything that goes on in your camp – informed us that an agent using a Canadian cover, by the name of Paul Gupta, was about to set himself up in St Petersburg. Somehow our people didn't understand that our informant was reporting the arrival of a Mossad agent, someone hadn't read the small print, and we thought that you were from the CIA.

Perhaps we should go in, I suggested. The neighbours' balconies were too close. As I held her arm, she continued to talk as we walked inside.

The first time we met I suspected that you were Jewish. You said you were half Indian and that origin possibly matched your appearance. But to check it I threw all sorts of comments at you about Jews, Judaism and Israel. Over time I became familiar with your expressions and was able to detect even the slightest hint of anxiety. My suspicion grew when I saw that you were circumcised but then I looked into it and discovered that in Canada circumcision was very common.

That's also what I'd have told you if you'd asked I said. And when did you know for sure?

I came to the conclusion that they were right on the day you hit Sergei, she answered, and I didn't understand.

I hit somebody?

Sergei, the man who snatched my bag.

He…I didn't need to continue.

I'm so sorry, my love, but that wasn't planned. He was in the team following us, and couldn't restrain himself when he saw us kissing. Apparently he was in love with me, and decided to attack you. The snatching of the bag was an attempt to make it look like a robbery. In the past Sergei was a professional wrestler, and when you ran after him and insisted on tackling him I trembled at the thought of what lay in store for you. If he could, he'd have beaten the living daylights out of you. When I saw you thrashing him I understood that there were things you were hiding from me…no one, unless there're very highly trained, can get the better of Sergei. And no lonely, sad, Canadian businessman who reads Dostoyevsky is that highly trained. I might have come to the conclusion that you were a Jewish CIA agent, but during the night, she added, I realized you were an Israeli.

Before I could ask, Anna supplied me with the explanation. When you slept at my place that night you murmured '*lo* Orit, *lo*' and '*lama* Orit, *lama*', and the words became etched in my memory. I connected this to what you'd already told me about your wife during the previous night we'd spent together. The following morning I checked and discovered that this was Hebrew, and the whole picture became clear. Then I had to make one of the most difficult decisions of my life, she smiled, and with that smile the Anna I had known returned and had momentarily settled herself down in my apartment.

She hardly touched the meal I'd prepared for us – convenience food that couldn't, of course, compete with the rich array of her soups. We went down to the sea front together and on the way we bought some clothes which she put on immediately, discarding those she'd arrived in.

It was the beginning of spring and a mass of people had come to the seafront to celebrate the end of the rainy season. The lively sights around us fascinated her; bicycle riders, balloon salesmen, couples walking at speed along the promenade, restaurants teeming with life all along it, parasols, swimmers, surfers, and people playing paddle ball on the beach.

I didn't imagine it like this, she said. In fact, I didn't imagine anything. Only you. And for the first time, at her own initiative, she hugged me and pressed her head into my shoulders. I wanted to believe that she was once again trusting me and my love.

Marozhina? Anna asked and pointed at the ice cream stand. With a huge cone in her hand, the withered woman in front of me, returned for a moment to being a little girl.

We continued to walk and when Anna felt tired we went back to my apartment where she fell into a deep sleep. Towards sunset again we went down to the seafront and Anna asked to be left alone for a few minutes. She stood on the shore-line, hands crossed, hugging her shoulders, and gazing towards the horizon. She didn't move even when the tide came in and the sea occupied more and more of the sandy beach and swept over the shoes we had just bought. Birds circled above her, seagulls squawked, and still her eyes were set beyond the skyline and towards her native land. I remembered myself standing just like that, very close to the very same spot on a wintery night immediately after I'd been released from the various interrogations I'd had to endure, my heart yearning for her. What was Anna yearning for?

As the sun descended below the horizon, leaving only the shades of twilight behind, Anna signalled to me to come to her. I held her outstretched hand, and we remained silent. The colours of night began to gather in the northern and southern skies, while in the west the purple of sunset hung on. Now the soles of my feet were also sunk in water and when I hugged Anna to shield her from the westerly wind I could feel her back trembling under my embrace. She turned her face towards me, a smile on her lips, her eyes filled with tears. I could feel the pain of her parting from what lay over there across the sea, but didn't come close to guessing its enormity. My heart ached for her.

Suddenly, in a somewhat theatrical movement, she stretched her hand towards me. Mila Ivanovna Pirova, she said, and you are?

Yogev Ben-Ari, I answered, confused. It had never occurred to me that Anna was not her real name. But I want to go on calling you Annushka.

Anna's eyes shone as they looked right into me. Anna or Mila, Petrovna or Ivanovna, Starzava or Pirova, it really doesn't matter what the KGB called me and which name it forced me to live with. Actually, she reflected, it also doesn't really matter very much what my parents called me, what my father's name was, or what Mikhail's family name was. I want to be known by your name, she said, and tried to pronounce it but with only partial success. She made Ben-Ari sound like Bain Ari. I tried out Mila, but the name didn't arouse a feeling of intimacy. Millie sounded a little better but I stayed with Annushka.

At intervals during the evening Anna continued to tell me her story. There's a bit of truth in what I told you when we met, she said with an ironical smile. She really was a widow, she was widowed ten years beforehand, and her husband was, indeed, killed in a road accident and his name truly was Mikhail. But the 'Mikhail' in the pictures in her apartment was a colleague of hers at work, and photos were taken just for me to see.

Why didn't you have pictures of your real husband? I wondered, a question mainly prompted by professional curiosity.

A long and difficult story. Our life as a couple wasn't good, and during one of our many separations I threw out all the photos of us together.

They really didn't have children. Anna had had an abortion beforehand, and when she became pregnant by Mikhail they were too young, were living the boisterous lives of students, and felt that a child would be a burden.

We were sort of opponents of the regime, she said. I was afraid of going to a government-run hospital, and putting myself in their hands. With the little money we possessed I had an abortion done privately by an unlicensed doctor and bled for weeks on end. I didn't think I could ever give birth but relations with Mikhail had anyway deteriorated and I had no desire to bring a child into our quarrels and into the double life I'd been forced to lead. I deeply regretted this for a long time even after Mikhail's death.

She looked straight into my eyes as if trying to read my mind. I thought this was the right time to tell her the truth about the embryo of mine that had died, but felt that this wasn't the question Anna was asking, that this wasn't the response she was looking for from me, and kept quiet. She tried to say something else, but didn't.

We returned home holding hands but our souls had

been sundered and we found ourselves engaged in a Sisyphean effort to repair the damage.

Later on I learned from her that what she had told me about the Conservatoire was true, as were the stories about her higher education at the Institute for Russian Literature and her love of music and books.

So how did you fall into the arms of the KGB? I asked in astonishment.

Don't you know that half the population of the Soviet Union was in the KGB? You were either an informer or you were being informed on.

So you decided to be an informer? I asked in a slightly tremulous tone of voice.

No, in fact people informed on me. Gorbachev started with his reforms, which were strenuously opposed by the communists and the KGB. I, then a young student, was a keen supporter of the reforms. I was arrested while participating in a demonstration and was given a suspended sentence. A few years later, when the conservatives and the KGB attempted to mount a coup against Gorbachev and detained him in his dacha, I took part in organizing the demonstrations against the attempted coup, was squealed on, and again arrested. Added to the suspended sentence, which they threatened to enforce, I was facing going to prison for many years. The KGB proposed that I become one of its informers and I refused. Then they brought Mikhail in – at that time my boyfriend who I was thinking of marrying – and told me that he too was due to be jailed. This was in 1990. We were in our mid-twenties and when the interrogators said I'd come out of jail 'a wrinkled old woman' I broke down. Which is the way I did indeed emerge from there, she said, smiling sadly.

I kissed her head as we sat together on a wide rocking chair bathed only in a halo of light which illuminated the large window.

And then you agreed, I whispered.

Yes. I thought, so I'll say yes, I'll save Mikhail's skin and my own, and then I'll simply ignore any one I see with some banned material, or anything else. But it didn't work out that way. When they knew about someone and it was up to me to supply the proof and I didn't succeed in doing so, they threatened to jail me. More than once a 'comrades' court' was arranged and each time I was given 'one more chance'.

Nor did I put up much of a fight. By then I no longer had any dreams left. I had dreamed of becoming a pianist and understood that I wouldn't be one, she said in a tearful voice. I dreamed of being a poet, and realized that this too wouldn't materialize. I'm a realistic woman, and back then I was a practical young person. I heard the way talented people played music and knew how real poets wrote. I knew I didn't possess those gifts.

Men were attracted to me but I knew that there were women who were more beautiful than I was. All I wanted was a husband who would love me. And this dream, too, was shattered. We got married and tried, but the love died, as love does, without drama, just with pain. I wanted a baby and was forced to forgo that wish as well and live my life without. I didn't have many desires left, nor did I have the will to stand up to the KGB.

She waited for my response. In the world of spying, as

in the world of crime, there is a clear hierarchy. Agents of my sort – we call them 'operatives' – are mostly contemptuous of every kind of informer, the collaborators. My only response was to tighten my embrace.

In the Yeltsin period, and when the KGB was supposedly dismantled, I thought that I was free of all that, she continued. But the FSB told me that I 'belonged to them' and that given my failure against internal subversion I was being transferred to the counter-espionage division because I might perhaps have less sympathy for foreign spies. After all, I was a patriot. But the change didn't work out with you, again a sad smile spread across her face. When you appeared you awakened a dormant desire in me, a hope I had already stopped believing could be rekindled. Suddenly I was prepared to fight for a dream that had been brought back to life. For love, perhaps a family. Now she too tightened her embrace.

But weren't you in danger when you produced no results on various suspects?

Of course I was. The methods didn't change and as you can see nor did the people. The higher command and the name changed, that's all. And on quite a few occasions I did come up with the goods.

You…

After the dismantlement of the KGB I didn't work as a full-time agent. I worked in a large bookshop on a part-time basis, with the books I loved. If there was a suspect they would call me. I'd work on him for a while, finish, and then return to my beloved books. The management of the shop could not, of course, refuse.

The tormented woman's eyes closed. I understood her hesitations and her actions so well. I completely identified with her.

You're very tired, and there's only one bed, though it is a double, I stroked her head. If it doesn't suit you for us to sleep together, I'll sleep on the couch in the living room.

If you want an old love in your bed, one who's aged thirty years in the space of just three, and who has nothing to give, I'll be very thankful, Anna said, looking down at the floor.

I've been waiting for you night after night, I said, and tonight there won't be a man on earth happier than me.

My darling, she said sadly, thank you, though you don't yet know what a wreck you're getting.

Like spoons? she asked when I embraced her, in bed, and I trembled with love.

44

THE LIGHTS AND sounds of the city that never sleeps streamed in through the bedroom's large window and cast a pale light across the darkened walls. Step by step during the night, between bouts of snatched sleep, hugs and caresses, Anna completed her story, a mirror image of my own spying mission – the view from the perspective of the opposing camp's counter-intelligence that every spy would give his eye teeth to get hold of. The person behind this chain of events and who steered them with quiet confidence was now lying next to me in her gaunt nakedness almost asleep as she talked.

The counter-espionage team tailing me had followed my footsteps to Vashkirova's restaurant. When it became apparent to them that I ate there regularly, the decision was taken to bring Anna into the picture. She was not allowed to approach me, the idea being that she would arouse my interest but that it would be me who approached her so avoiding my becoming suspicious.

There were young women who could perhaps have tempted you but would have aroused your suspicions, so they decided on me. They thought I was approximately your age and that it would be easier for you to open up to me. But you ignored me for an entire week, she said complainingly, which is when we decided to bring in the 'suitor'. Do you remember the two who came to the restaurant and one of them approached me? They were our people. We thought this would kindle your interest in me and you would make some sort of a move – but you did nothing. You can't imagine how unattractive I felt because of you and how angry I was with you … I'm just joking. The truth is that you got a great deal of professional credit for this and it was decided to mobilize additional resources to crack your cover.

A week later we sent people to the restaurant to occupy all the available tables so that there would be no alternative other than for me to be seated next to you…

I'm surprised Anna, why did your people invest so much in me?

The counter-espionage division wasn't happy about

the thaw in relations with America. Catching an American spy would provide them with excellent ammunition that could be used against the various groups of liberals and that made it worth their while to invest in you. When I saw you were reading *Demons* I was pleased. I was familiar with the book but I leafed through it again before the conversation with you. After that evening I thought I'd thrown out enough bait for you to bite at. For professional reasons I stepped back, but you too did the same. What kind of gentleman did that make you?

I remembered her unease and reserve after the evening we happened to sit at the same table with our books, and my sense that it would be very ungentlemanly of me to use the seating problem as a way of continuing the contact with her.

One evening I thought that I'd already been exposed, she continued. When Alexei dropped me off near to the restaurant and you suddenly appeared – I was sure you'd seen the car and that the operation would collapse. But you didn't say a thing, and this strengthened my feeling that you were an innocent businessman, unaware of such subtleties.

I did notice, I told her now, and was in two minds what to do about it. But I wasn't convinced and decided not to ask. By the way, did you also go to such great lengths when we went to the opera?

Anna caressed my face. Are you angry? You have every right to be. Everything I told you about my studies at the Conservatoire was true. And my views about Dostoyevsky really are my own. But yes, I prepared for our visit to the opera. About ten unfortunate people didn't go to the opera that night. A number of counter-espionage personnel went to their homes and took the tickets away from them. Those sitting around us were from counter-espionage. And all of that for them to say a few words to me about the death of my husband which would sound genuine to you.

That was amazing, I was forced to admit. I think there's a thing or two you can teach our Shin Bet. They want to interview you tomorrow.

Please no! Anna said, looking frightened, as she curled up like a beaten dog that'd just absorbed another blow. Please no! I can't and don't want to see anyone else involved in this field. I don't want to speak to them, brief them, be asked or have to answer any questions, please, I'm begging.

I will try, Annushka, I will do whatever I can so that it doesn't happen. No one's asking you to supply information. I think there are simply some formalities that need to be completed concerning the exchange of prisoners.

No, no, please! Her anxiety was so great that in my mind I began quickly to run through the list of people I could approach to save her from this ordeal, among them those who certainly owed me no favours given the way I'd ended my service. Anna won't go there, I ended up saying to myself. And it doesn't matter what I have to do to make sure of that. Again I was promising something without yet knowing how to make good on the pledge, but I knew that this was a promise I would most definitely keep.

After Anna had calmed down, she returned to the point at which she'd halted.

After the concert, when I took you home, that wasn't in line with the instructions. I thought you'd want to know. Although we did want you to visit my place and be convinced of my story, there was no plan for you to sleep with me.

She noticed the quizzical look in my eyes.

I was never forced to go to bed with anyone, if that's what you were about to ask. Not ever. And I didn't go to bed with you to trap you. Though it wasn't love at first sight, I did see a chance of love there. And I wanted you. Simply the desire of a single, lonely woman.

I felt relieved when she'd said all of this so explicitly.

After that night I felt that I was beginning to fall in love with you, and realized that this was going to be a complicated story. I took time off to think and that's why I also asked that we not meet for a while – do you remember all of this?

I remember every minute, I answered.

But I couldn't take the separation. I hadn't yet been convinced of the suspicions around you. This was long before the incident with Sergei and the night when you talked in your sleep, but I knew that in the face of the counter-espionage division's suspicions such a love had no chance. I even tried to warn you with stories and poems describing St Petersburg as a place where reality is misleading, where things are not what they appear to be and about those in power killing off our love. But I so wanted you to be with me, at home, in my bed, that I didn't go beyond these warnings.

And by the way, I also prepared myself for those conversations, she looked directly at me. In the bookshop I read the poems, the stories, and the articles about the city's literature. I'm not the scholar you might have thought I was. I didn't know everything, and looked for the things that might be a warning to you.

Anna stopped talking, as if waiting for my response.

I did actually wonder what it was you were trying to say to me, what you were trying to warn me of, and why. What you knew about me. It didn't cross my mind that you yourself had begun to fight big brother.

I didn't yet know that I was actually starting a war with them. I was just frightened. At that stage I was still buying your stories about Montreal and Sainte-Agathe, she said and the slightest of smiles was visible in the corners of her mouth.

You still remember the names? I asked, surprised.

I have every reason to remember. We sent one of our people in Canada to verify your stories and everything turned out to be correct. The descriptions of the town, everything. I'm sorry I made you talk, but that was my job, we had to check you out. And you were fairly convincing.

Only 'fairly'?

Yes. I remained puzzled about your French. It didn't sound entirely plausible that even after you'd completed a degree course at a Montreal University – and I assumed that it was at McGill and in French – you nonetheless felt it necessary to wander off to an English-speaking region. But your answers were enough to enable me to try and get the counter-espionage division off your back and in my reports I cleared you. This was after another night of love between us and I very much wanted to believe that this love had a chance. But in further questions to our source in Washington he was insistent, claiming that you were a senior operative who was stationed in St Petersburg, for the time being in a dormant capacity.

There are things I wanted to ask, if you have the strength to answer, I said after a little while.

Ask, Anna said stroking my face.

Your apartment, I said. It didn't look like the apartment of a woman like you.

What do you mean by 'like me'? she asked indulgently and I allowed myself to say: beautiful, wise, who's also interested in music … for example, there wasn't a piano there and the furniture looked old.

For a moment I was worried – perhaps it really was her apartment, and I'd offended her? But Anna soothed my nerves: A couple of KGB pensioners lived there, and were moved to one of the Agency's dachas. Most of the books were theirs and at the time no one thought about a piano. They also didn't think you'd be visiting the place quite so quickly.

I thought there was also something strange about the shop, I continued to say.

The shop, too, was part of my cover story, Anna admitted. It was decided that you were a hard nut and that additional resources had to be invested in cracking you.

So they set up a shop for you?

Right. They moved out some people who ran a

544

stationery shop reasonably close to your house and mine – a location that would also help explain why I regularly ate at Vashkirova's – and turned it into a bookshop. This, after all, was my profession so I could be seen to be skilful and it also linked in with your love of reading. And you only called in once, and even that once was something I barely managed to persuade you to do! she rebuked me affectionately. Do you realize what an effort all this was? Finding a place, moving out the owners without them causing any problems, furnishing it, bringing in the books, putting up signs, and staffing it when I wasn't there. But it's interesting that you felt something. What disturbed you about it?

I really apologize, Annushka, I smiled back at her. Everything there was too organized, many sets of 'all the works of', no specific reason I guess, just a feeling. And what happened to our shop?

My heart warmed at the memory of the love with which we'd set up our own bookshop and the hours we'd spent there.

It was dismantled after you left. I, after all, was arrested immediately following your departure. The books in Russian were in any case theirs, and only the foreign language stuff was ours, but no one supplied me with details.

And another thing that bothered me, Annushka, you might think it an odd question, but when you were in my apartment and insisted I should go and have a shower…

Anna held her head in her hands. How I wish I didn't have to talk to you about this, but I don't want there to be any secrets between us. Yes, I sent you off so I could conceal a listening device in your apartment. I hid it in the living room, under the sofa, and activated it just before I left early the next morning. I'm so ashamed about this … if it comforts you just a tiny little bit, they wanted me to place a hidden camera in the apartment and I refused. They'd already accepted that there were relations of intimacy between us and so went along with my refusal.

And I did something else that was awful, Anna continued to draw a picture for me of the other side of the coin which, were it to be used as a spies' security manual would undoubtedly become a bestseller. My visit to your office. The purpose was to gather information about the place and the lock on its door. In particular, my people wanted to know if there was CCTV or an alarm system installed there. The information I provided enabled them to break in afterwards.

As she told this story, Anna burst into tears. I'm so ashamed of myself, her voice trailed off. I was, after all, already in love with you. That was the night I asked you to move in with me and never leave. It followed those two weeks during which we didn't see each other. The moment you came back from your trip they summoned me to return from Moscow where I'd been visiting my mother. My controller was at my side and forced me to call and arrange to meet you in your office. But still, how could I have done such a thing?

I remembered the formal tone of her voice that time. But I also remembered how I'd passed on her name to avoid HQ getting upset with me and concealed the rest of her details from them. What an inhuman game we were forced to play, I thought, and again wiped away her tears.

Many many times I asked myself whether I should tell you the truth, Anna said, so we could fight together. But I was afraid that you'd leave, frightened that you wouldn't understand and stop believing me, scared that you'd confess and my dilemma would become even greater.

I kept silent in light of the heart-breaking mirror-image which Anna continued presenting to me. I couldn't possibly have imagined then that her dilemma was far more acute than mine. For me she was a passer-by in the snow. A lover who might become an obstacle to me carrying out my assignments. For her I was the assignment itself.

And by the way, the fact that you rented an office a hundred metres from our HQ was a huge gamble and whoever was responsible for that is either a genius or an idiot, Anna said when she'd recovered. There were those who thought that you were eavesdropping on us from there or photographing people entering and leaving. On the other hand, there were those who, precisely because of this choice of location, regarded you as innocent. What kind of spy, they'd say, would open an office under the very nose of the local interior security service. Their break-in revealed that there was no eavesdropping or filming equipment there. Then, once all the files in your office were photocopied, and all the email correspondence was forwarded to counter-intelligence's commercial department, and after even your company's bank account had been carefully checked and found to be OK – they became convinced that you weren't even someone's front man.

You won't believe it, Annushka, but there was no genius involved. Just one idiot, me, who didn't check out the street, and a security department that didn't have in its possession the addresses of the other side's internal security service.

She burst into peals of heartwarming laughter, which once more brought back to me the Anna of St Petersburg.

There was so much love in this wise woman. She not only exposed me and concealed the discovery from her employers, but managed to hide it from me as well. Her desertion in the cause of love made her a willing participant in the fictitious world I had created and which I'd tried to present as real. So much love was required to live this lie together with me and hope that the revolving sword overhead wouldn't annihilate us both.

I kissed her and embraced her thin and trembling body and we very very nearly made love. But neither of us was yet ready for that.

Your trips to Dagestan and Tajikistan also reinforced your cover story, Anna continued. After all, at my HQ they only considered the option that you were a CIA agent. And what could a CIA agent possibly be looking for in the Republics? That almost tipped the balance and there were those who were persuaded that our source in Washington had been misled. In fact, they almost left you alone, and didn't mount any further operations against you.

So we could have lived happily till this very day?

No. Because among you there were people stupid

enough to ask some ex-KGB guy for details on Anna Starzava. Didn't they understand that an ex of this sort would be a double agent and would try and play both sides against the middle? Didn't they realize they were putting you at risk? They knew about it at our HQ within twenty-four hours, and the suspicions intensified. It was only because the ex-KGB was not handled by someone with an Israeli identity, but instead by a handler with some sort of Canadian identity, that they continued to think you were from the CIA and not the Mossad. I, however, was instructed to continue working.

In an odd way this worked to our advantage, Anna said. A few days before that ex-KGB double agent informed us that interest was being shown in Anna Starzava, I sent an additional report clearing you. That was on the morning after the incident with Sergei and the snatched bag when I asked you to move in with me and you, my love, agreed. You went off to your office, and I realized that at counter-espionage's HQ you – and I – had new enemies who were doing everything they could to incriminate you. That's because what I'd understood from your fight they, Sergei and his friends, had also understood. I had no option other than to write an unambiguous report in which I even included your sleep talk, except that I reported you as saying things that strengthened your cover story.

But, as you know, the intelligence world is a world in which everything is manipulation upon manipulation? My report was the first manipulation. The second was when they decided not only to accept my conclusions but also to inform me that I must sever all contact because they no longer had any interest in you.

How could I possibly have done that? she asked and looked straight at me. Fortunately for us, immediately after that came the third in this trilogy of manipulations: the report by the ex-KGB agent that your guys activated, saying that there was interest being shown in me. In light of his report our counter-espionage division decided that the interest in me was based on my connections to you and that it was necessary to continue trying to expose you.

Anna spoke in an amazingly well-ordered way, and yet I didn't entirely manage to follow what she was saying. I was still shocked by the fact that on the very morning that I stumbled to my office and sent my tepid report to HQ in Glilot about my acquaintance with her, she, for her part, had turned in a report clearing me of all suspicion.

She continued, and all of a sudden her tone was cheerful: And then I came up with the strange request to move to another apartment and open a shop together with you. For them the suggestion came at exactly the right moment. The pensioners and the owners of the shop who'd been moved out were pressing to move back in. So my people agreed. On condition, of course, that I would continue to work on you. By that time you were considered to be a bit of a legend – how come that nothing you did exposed you as being a secret agent?

It was so important to them to crack your case, she said, that someone was even sent to Makhachkala to get Mahashashli to talk. He was happy to cooperate, explained the revolving deal between you, and said that you'd refused to sleep with the escort girls he'd offered. My bosses took this to mean that you were a highly-skilled spy who didn't fall into traps. To me it indicated that you already loved me before the concert. I was made a very happy woman when this report came in.

She cuddled up and then, raising her eyes towards me, said: Do you want to make love? I think I can now.

And so for the first time in three years, once more *potikhonechku*, slowly and very carefully, truly like two hedgehogs, I knew a woman and she knew a man. I didn't have expectations and there were no disappointments. Not for Annushka either. We just wanted to find out if we could once again love and the sweet response that came with the first rays of the sun, gave us renewed feelings of strength.

Anna, leaning on one arm, swept aside some strands of grey covering her face, and ran her fingers through my hair. There are things it's easy to know, she said. For example, that the rain is the first rainfall of the year. And there are things that are not easy to know. For example, whether a rainfall is the last of the year. There could, after all, always be another downpour. A short while after I met you I knew that you were the last rain. No one would ever quench my thirst for happiness as you had done. When you left, I knew that I'd entered a dry patch that could only end by my being with you again. And now I'm sure I was right.

And I knew then that I, too, had been right in my fight for my last love.

45

WOULD YOU LIKE to go for a walk on the beach? I asked. And Anna, whose youthfulness appeared to be making a comeback, nodded enthusiastically, and announced that she was now hungry. I wasn't sure that I could find any nearby restaurants that would be open at such an early hour of the morning, but in the event there was no need. Anna, who'd begun to behave like a housemate, found enough bits and pieces including bread, tomatoes, onions, cheese and eggs for us to have something cooked. While the ingredients were being fried, she had a shower. By the time she emerged, wrapped in my bathrobe, very thin and grey but refreshed and exuding the scent of my shampoo and soap, the morning's coffee was also ready and we sat down for breakfast. For the first time I believed that we had a chance.

I apologize for all the various interrogations I subjected you to even after we'd moved into our own apartment, Anna said after satisfying her hunger. You were very convincing but I had conflicting information.

Interrogations?

Yes, but for my own benefit. I wanted to know who the man I was in love with and with whom I was fighting the powerful forces ranged against us, really was. I was questioning you about religion and about Amos Oz and David Grossman. Tell your commanders that you are a good actor. That even though you almost choked, you didn't break your cover.

By then I wasn't acting, I replied. I perhaps had a few genuine responses, but for me almost everything connected to Israel was in a drawer so hermetically sealed that there was almost no chance of it getting out. And if it did, then the drawer together with the whole table would have fallen apart.

Later on Anna told me that she realized I had deserted when I closed my office, and when we moved to our new apartment and I asked the real estate agent for it to remain registered in his name. It was clear to her that I wasn't hiding from the tax authorities in her country or mine, or from the FSB – known for recruiting every estate agent as an informer – and that I was, in fact, hiding from my own employers. Added to this was the new bank account I'd opened, which was something else she kept secret from her people.

I again believed we had a chance when Anna, wearing my track suit, asked that we go for a bit of a run on the beach. There, under the blue skies of Tel Aviv, her new home, she sped along raising her arms above her head and breathing the clear Mediterranean air of early morning deeply into her lungs.

I was left with one more riddle that I wanted to solve. I knew why I'd fallen in love with Anna, and was aware of every step of the way. But why had the wonderful Anna fallen in love with me, nobody's Don Juan as Alex was quoted saying in one of the transcripts in the Cat Snow file?

A cool and pleasant breeze blew in from the sea as we

strolled along the promenade hugging one another. It was then that Anna responded to my question, a question I'd had great difficulty in phrasing and had only finally done so in a twisted and somewhat sheepish way.

The personality of a spy who is sent alone to a foreign country has qualities one can easily fall in love with, she said, raising her beautiful eyes at me, revealing a hint of the sparkle I'd once known. I've learned this from the spies I caught in the past. One has to be made of steel to be able to survive under cover in enemy territory knowing that failure means spending the rest of one's days in jail. I had respect for the agents I succeeded in catching in the past but with you it was different and even worked the other way round.

The blank expression on my face obliged her to spell it out.

You were so solitary and sad when I was assigned to your case, sitting evening after evening at the same table, with the same dish of food, all by yourself – reading. So different from the profile drawn for us of a CIA agent setting himself up in St Petersburg; the expectation was of a tall, handsome, slightly arrogant man, making new contacts, going to the right social events, running up against people in the army and politicians. There are solitary men, there are sad men, there are men who read, and there are men who can arouse a woman's sympathy. But I haven't ever come across solitary, sad, spies who read Dostoyevsky.

I couldn't stop myself from smiling. More than once I'd heard that 'I didn't look like…' which in fact was an important working tool for me in the world of deception in which I lived.

At that stage I still didn't believe that you were a spy, she continued. But when I included in you the traits I'd seen in other spies, and which are not visible to the naked eye – courage, composure – that, of course, increased my curiosity a great deal. And then, at the concert, I discovered that you were a sentimentalist. Your musical naivety, the way you trembled during the *1812*, only increased my fondness for you. I wanted to know what it was like to be touched by you. And when I dared and tried, it was made all the more wonderful by the gentle way you made love to me. It's so beautiful when a man who is strong knows how to make love gently. You became very anxious about 'your performance' that first night. But sometimes all a woman wants is tenderness.

And then came the fight with Sergei which solved the mystery for me and made everything come together. Solitary, sad, wise – and tough and knows how to fight? On that very same night I also discovered your ability for passionate lovemaking. Such combinations are rare. I didn't want you to ever leave.

Without planning to, we reached the port and Anna looked in amazement at the shops and teeming cafés along one side of the boardwalk, and the harbour on its other side. In a café overlooking the sea we sat under the shade of a parasol having yet another ice cream. I was too agitated to talk. Anna had no way of knowing the extent to which, after Orit's departure, I needed proof that I was worthy of a woman's love.

In those years I was able to supply anyone who asked for it with cold and prosaic points of view on love. Love as a product of a biological need to reproduce, love as chemistry. I could provide descriptions of the hormones responsible for desire, infatuation, and lasting love, and felt deep inside that they all evaporated and left me empty and drained. There was no romance in the way I understood love during those years. Until, that is, Anna appeared on the scene, and I became immersed in the love story with her like a teenager, and was swept away by it like a man drowning.

I was silent, swamped by feelings of gratitude. I hugged her until she sighed with pain.

Be careful. There's already no flesh to protect my old bones.

A procession of kindergarten children walking in pairs, holding hands, came down to the promenade. Some of them followed the nursery teacher in silence, others chatted to each other, there were those who looked curiously at us, and two of them were rolling about with laughter. Anna's gaze followed the children with an expression on her face that I was unable to decipher. I assumed that, like me, she too was thinking of what we had missed, but deep in her eyes was concealed a remote smile.

Are you in touch with Orit? she suddenly asked, and I took the question to mean that it was her turn to express her fears.

I saw her once. There are chapters in life that are closed for ever, and there are those that have been paused so as to be renewed.

*

When we got home the sun was already high in the sky. I called Gedalyahu and asked him to use his contacts with whoever it was necessary to avoid Anna having to present herself and be questioned.

It's not up to me, he said, and gave me the phone number of the relevant man from the Shin Bet as well as equipping me with a number of suggestions which immediately helped.

Those are the rules, the man said when I called.

She was released in the framework of a deal, I replied, using Gedalyahu's argument. In fact, she 'belongs' to the Red Cross. There isn't a single clause in the deal that allows you to question her. And if there were, I would advise her simply to say nothing. What would you do then?

She wants to live here, doesn't she? The man tried his luck.

The Red Cross certified her as a refugee. She can't be deported. Leave her alone. Drop it.

I'll get back to you, the man said, and I never heard from him again.

You don't have to go for questioning, at least not for now, I gave Anna the news, and she responded with a sigh of relief that came from the depths of her heart. She took off my track suit, lay on the bed, and after almost two days spent between sleep and wakefulness she fell into a deep slumber. I sat at her side and looked at her. She seemed peaceful now, the long walk in the sun had even turned her face slightly red; her hair, with its streaks of black, white and silvery grey, having been washed, nestled in waves on her shoulders, strands of it gliding down her face. Though her cheeks were hollow, their fine bone structure, the well-defined jaw, and the straight nose, still belonged to the face of a very beautiful woman. She was wearing one of my vests from which revealed her bony shoulders, and her sunken breasts were virtually invisible. Her buttocks were almost fleshless and her thighs thinner than her knees. The fragile body only made me want to hug it, which is what I did. I slid behind her, drew close up, and wrapped my arms around her.

Like spoons, Anna said in her sleep.

In the evening we went to a beach restaurant opposite the house. I wanted us to have our dessert on the chairs in the sand next to the restaurant's orange lanterns, as close as we could be to the lapping waves and the whispering sounds of the sea.

Do you want us first of all to wipe the slate clean of all our professional secrets so we can turn over a new leaf? Anna asked on our way there as our feet sank into the soft, cool, sand. So there won't be any more skeletons in our cupboards?

No Annushka. I loved you without knowing anything about you. Simply because of your inner and outer beauty and the solitariness and sadness you conveyed. Yes, you too.

Of the beauty nothing is left, Anna said ruefully. But the silvery grey hair, the lines, the leanness of her body, the eyes that were still beautiful despite the black rings beneath them and the loss of their sparkle, merely heightened my desire to take her into my arms and hold her tight. I kissed her forehead and then her lips.

You will always be the most beautiful and the most loved woman in my life, I told her. And no, I don't want this past to follow us. Not these episodes from the past which life dragged us into, just as a flood plucks trees out of the ground where they had put down roots. It's quite enough that this past hovers over both of us. But I do want to know what you were like as a little girl. Did you wear your hair in plaits? Was the skirt you wore part of a school uniform? And what kind of pupil you were. What you liked doing at school and what you didn't like doing there. Were you sporty? When did you learn judo? I haven't yet listened to you playing the piano. I haven't yet heard the poems you wrote. I want to know about your first kiss. I want you to grow again in my heart, going back all the way to your childhood. There are many things we need to complete and in the meantime you won't ask how many people I killed and I won't ask how many spies you hunted down who are now rotting in Russian jails. When the time comes for these things to be known they will become known.

Anna rose from the chair dug into the sand, walked up to the sea, her gaze once again directed at its depths, beyond the waves. The wind blowing in from the ocean slightly ruffled her hair and her face pointed towards an undefined spot on the horizon. I, too, got up and stood next to her. Anna had never thought about this country. For her this was a penal colony, a place of punishment. I think I have never loved as much as I loved her at that moment. But could I be for her a home, a love, a family? Will we ever be more than a defeated man and woman holding on to one another like fugitives from a flood? I looked out into the encroaching darkness and saw, on the horizon, the lights of a ship.

46

ANNA TURNED TO me and clutched my hand.

Yogev, she said in hushed tones that were almost drowned by the roar of the waves. We have to go there.

I thought she too was referring to the ship, perhaps she had in mind some untried possibilities awaiting us across the ocean, and didn't answer.

I have to go to Russia, she said, as I remained silent.

My heart skipped a beat. I didn't understand. What did she mean? Was she talking about her mother and sister who'd stayed behind?

I didn't want to say anything to you about this before knowing that you accept me as I am. But now that I do know, I can tell you.

A strange feeling began to well up in the pit of my stomach, the kind that knows a moment before the brain does. Anna continued.

When the spells of dizziness and nausea began after I was locked up in the women's prison, I thought it was because of the food there and the conditions. When I didn't have my period, I thought this too was connected to the tension, the malnutrition, the hard labour. One of the prisoners suggested I get myself checked and I did. The test was positive.

You were pregnant, my darling Annushka? I asked embracing her, the profound feeling of a missed opportunity gnawing at me from within. We could have had a child! Suddenly I was seized once again by that desire that had begun to develop amid the village pathways, disappeared together with Orit, and hesitantly flickered back to life every now and then with Anna.

It was a terrible pregnancy. The morning sickness turned some of my cell mates into enemies, and the prison authorities didn't excuse me from the hard labour. I passed out almost every day. The prison doctor pressed me to have an abortion, as did a few good souls among the prisoners. What kind of life can he possibly look forward to, they argued against my protestations. He'll grow up in an orphanage tainted by his jailbird mother.

So you gave up Annushka? My voice trembled, its tone a blend of sadness and hope, understanding and fear.

No, no, I didn't give up, but it was very tough. Especially the birth.

If that's so, there was a birth, I bit my lips and only with great difficulty restrained my questions. Anna had to tell the story at her own pace.

I was frightened that they'd kill him at birth, or say he'd been stillborn and take him away from me. I refused to have any kind of anaesthetic or be given pain-killers. I wanted to see him born, to know he was alive, to be sure that they knew that I knew. The pains were hellish. There wasn't an ounce of strength left in me.

And what happened? I couldn't hold back.

What happened is what happens at the end of every

normal pregnancy, Anna's eyes shone. Paul was born.

Paul?

What else?

And what – what's happened to him?

The possibility that I'd had a child and that he was dead assaulted me from within like a blind bat colliding with the walls of my stomach.

I had no milk, they didn't allow me to get any food supplements nor did they let me off going out to work. I took him with me, with him crying and me crying. And during rest periods he tried to suck at my empty breast, his face becoming contorted as he bellowed and I wept bitter tears together with him, utterly lost.

And he? I asked, impatient.

And he – a sweet, loving smile spread across Anna's face lending it a wonderful glow. He's *molodets*.

He's great, I did my own translation, and stopped myself from rushing her.

After a month he began to be curious about his surroundings. Seeing him able to recognize me was a moment of sheer bliss. After two months he started to smile. I almost fainted with happiness when I realized that this strange grimace of his was actually a smile. It was so wonderful to see that, despite everything he was turning into a little human being; inquisitive, able to understand.

Anna's smile was one of dreamy, distant, happiness.

The first syllables. Mama. That was worth all the suffering. I told him how brave you are, and loving, and how much you wanted a child like him; if only you could also say it yourself, say that you love him and that you will never leave him. Tears welled up in her eyes. I, after all, knew that soon he'd be a year old and they would take him away from me. Prisoners such as me are not allowed to stay with their babies after the age of one.

I thought of every possible way of passing a message to you about his existence. I stuffed notes in the food I sent back. I asked prisoners who were already entitled to be visited to make the story known to every Paul Gupta and every Roger Smith in the world, but mainly in Canada and Israel. I imagined that neither name was really yours. But I knew that were the matter to come to the notice of the authorities, the name you used here and the name under which you fled, the light would dawn somewhere, the counter-espionage division would get to know about it and some double agent or other would pass the information on to your people. But you didn't appear.

His wailing when they tore him away from me and my crying – I went wild – he was petrified and screamed. I hugged him and curled up with him in a corner, completely crazed. They fired an electric shock gun at me and he was only taken out of the cell after I passed out.

I felt weak at the knees. Had my child, our child, been taken away and was now lost?

From her pocket Anna took out a photograph which, until then, she had kept hidden and handed it to me.

I managed to remove this from the wall when they dragged me out and took me to the airport, she said.

I held it up to the little light there was emanating from the orange lantern beside us. I could make out a small child, who appeared to be of a darkish complexion, and was dressed in a sailor suit. He had a dummy in his mouth.

Paul, she said, looks a lot like you. He's just over two years old and is in a state-run orphanage in Moscow.

I insisted on him coming with me when they suddenly took me out of jail to fly me here. I screamed, wouldn't let go of the car doors, refused to get on the plane without him. Their explanations didn't interest me – that the deal was being done simultaneously in a number of places around the world and that there was no way of delaying my departure. They put me on the plane by force. Handcuffed.

The representatives of the Red Cross promised me that they would take care of whatever procedure was involved and that the minute I wanted to I could take him. The minute we want to, my darling, and that's now, isn't it?

Paul, I wept, kissing the photograph, and Anna held my head and rested it on her slender shoulder.